Just

C000186012

Nina Kaye is a contemporary romance author who writes warm, witty and uplifting reads with a deeper edge. She lives in Edinburgh with her husband and much adored side-kick, James. In addition to writing, Nina enjoys swimming, gin and karaoke (preferably all enjoyed together in a sunny, seaside destination). Nina has previously published *The Gin Lover's Guide to Dating* and has also been a contender for the RNA Joan Hessayson Award.

Also by Nina Kaye

Take A Moment
One Night in Edinburgh
Just Like That

just like that

NINA KAYE

CANELO

First published in the United Kingdom in 2023 by

Canelo
Unit 9, 5th Floor
Cargo Works, 1–2 Hatfields
London SE1 9PG
United Kingdom

Copyright © Nina Kaye 2023

The moral right of Nina Kaye to be identified as the creator of this work has been asserted in accordance with the Copyright, Designs and Patents Act, 1988.

All rights reserved. No part of this publication may be reproduced or transmitted in any form or by any means, electronic or mechanical, including photocopy, recording, or any information storage and retrieval system, without permission in writing from the publisher.

A CIP catalogue record for this book is available from the British Library.

Print ISBN 978 1 80436 498 7
Ebook ISBN 978 1 80436 499 4

This book is a work of fiction. Names, characters, businesses, organizations, places and events are either the product of the author's imagination or are used fictitiously. Any resemblance to actual persons, living or dead, events or locales is entirely coincidental.

Cover design by Emily Courdelle

Cover images © Emily Courdelle

Look for more great books at www.canelo.co

Printed and bound in Great Britain by Clays Ltd, Elcograf S.p.A.

1

To Sandy, Fiona and Andie.

Chapter 1

'Jess, there you are,' a voice bellows from several feet away. 'I've been looking all over. Should have known I'd find you here.'

Excusing myself from the conversation I'm engaged in, I turn to see my manager, Craig, striding across the VIP tent towards me, his crisp dark tailored suit looking smooth but out of place in the laid-back surroundings.

'Is something wrong?' I ask him. 'Whatever it is, I'm on it.'

'Nothing's wrong,' he reassures me, perching his expensive gangster sunglasses on the top of his head, while being careful not to mess up his somewhat over-styled and thinning blond hair. 'Quite the opposite. Remember I told you we had someone important coming to check out the event today?'

I nod expectantly.

'Well, they came, they saw and they just verbally agreed a contract with us to run a similar event in Glasgow next year.'

'WHAT? That's amazing news!' I whoop. 'Was that the guy and the woman you introduced me to earlier?'

'That was them.' Craig puffs himself up smugly, the laughter lines around his eyes deepening as he smiles.

'You should have given me a signal or something so I could have been on my best behaviour. The way they were acting, I assumed they were old friends of yours.'

'Not as such. I've known Izzy a long time – a couple of decades it must be by now – but they're generally easy-going people, and I wanted them to meet Jess, not "Jessica".'

'Hey…' I cock my head quizzically. 'There's no "Jessica", what are you talking about?'

'I'm just kidding.' He nudges my shoulder with his own. 'All I mean is I wanted them to meet you in a more relaxed capacity. Izzy's full on but she also appreciates a bit of humour. Call it setting the backdrop.'

'Fair enough. Your plan clearly paid off if you got a verbal that quickly.'

'It wasn't that hard, really. I mean, look at this place. It's stowed out. A blazing triumph, and in the main, thanks to you.'

We wander out of the VIP tent together into the May sunshine, our senses immediately engulfed by buzzy laughter and excitement, delicious aromas and the sight of people milling around the scores of stalls, pop-up restaurants and outdoor bars – complete foodie heaven.

Gazing around the Meadows-based event, I sigh with satisfaction. 'I do love seeing a plan come together. We've been lucky with the weather – that's something I definitely didn't organise.'

'True, but it would have taken a complete washout to put a sizeable dent in today. This is by far the biggest and most impressively organised event of this kind the capital has seen. I'm thinking I'll have to give you a pay rise so I don't lose you to the competition.' He gives me a pointed look.

'Well, if you insist.' I try to hide my surprise that Craig is wise to Bree from the Cramond Event Company – our biggest competitor – sniffing around, making approaches on LinkedIn.

'I do. You're going nowhere, Jess. Let's talk on Monday, yeah? Now, I'd better get back to Izzy and Jon and show them a good time before they change their minds.'

Craig praises me with another 'well done', then sets off across the grass, weaving his way through the sea of people who are gathering for the on-stage entertainment we've organised with some of Scotland's hottest up-and-coming music acts. Food, drink and amazing live music – a winning combination without a doubt. I'm just thinking I should probably head back to the VIP tent to ensure all is still running smoothly when my phone buzzes in my pocket. Quickly checking if it's an SOS from one of my project team, I'm pleased to see that it's actually a WhatsApp voice message from my best friend, Amelia. Hitting play, I hold my phone up to my ear so I can hear it.

> 'Jess, milady. Hope you're killing it today. I ordered
> the sun for you, some unicorns too – let me know
> if they don't arrive. You're welcome. Hit me up
> soon or I'll have to come up there and dial for you.
> Laters!'

I chuckle, shaking my head at my friend's weird and wacky dialogue. On the face of it, you'd call us an unlikely pair. Me, the focused, rising professional – even in my part-time jobs while at university. Amelia, relaxed and alternative in every way. But all it took was our paths crossing during freshers' week, plus a sticky laminated cocktail menu, and we were smitten. Instant BFFs.

I record a very quick – and less off-the-wall – reply, promising I'll call her in the next few days, and as I turn to head back to the VIP tent, I almost collide with someone.

'Oh, sorry.' I look up at the tall, broad-shouldered male figure and my face breaks into a smile. 'Seth.'

'All right, Jess.' My brother grins at me, bright blue eyes shining as he runs a casual hand through his thick light brown hair. 'This is quite the party you've cooked up.'

'It sure is. I'm delighted. Didn't know you were coming today. If you'd said, I could have got you some VIP passes. Perks of the job and all.' I waggle my staff lanyard at him.

'I'm good roughing it, but thanks.'

'Are you here with your friends?'

'Just Thomas and Zain. I left them doing the craft beer tasting session while I came to find you.' Seth makes the universal 'boozing' gesture with his hand and I laugh. 'Wondered if you might be able to join us for a bite at some point? I know you're working, but surely you've got to eat?'

'I think I can manage that.' I check the time on my watch. 'You here for the evening?'

'Just a couple of hours then we're off to five-a-side.'

'So, you're going to fill up on beer and food and then go run around a pitch for an hour?' I raise a sceptical eyebrow at him.

'No different to any other Saturday.' He winks at me. 'Makes it more fun.'

'Whatever. It's your body to wreck, I guess.'

'It's all good, sis.' He squeezes my shoulder affectionately, before becoming distracted by two attractive women in their mid-twenties who are passing by, whispering and eyeing him up.

'Afternoon, ladies.' He flashes them a smile and I swear they almost go into cardiac arrest.

I roll my eyes. 'How is it that we look so similar – other than the whole gender thing – yet you attract the most sought-after beauties and get labelled a young Chris Hemsworth, while I seem to be flypaper for creeps and weirdos? We have similar facial features, I've got the baby blues, the lustrous hair, albeit it a bit longer—'

'Maybe what I have is not something you're born with.' Seth puts on a fake swagger and I biff him lightly with my handbag, then look around to check that Craig isn't watching.

'Maybe you're just full of shit. Go on, get out of here. I'll see you shortly.'

'See you in a bit.' He starts to walk away, then turns back to me. 'It's because most blokes have no taste, sis. That's all.'

'Aww, thank you.' I blow him a little kiss, well aware that he's just trying to cheer me up, but happy to lap up his words all the same.

Watching my brother disappear in the same direction as Craig, but with significantly more bounce to his step, I smile wistfully. I do wonder at times if Seth and I were adopted as part of a package deal. We're so alike, both physically and in our character: neither of us can sit still and we feed off

4

our interactions with others, though mine are more in a work context and his in social ones. Quite the contrast to our parents, who took off to Spain the minute they'd packed us both off to university, and who live like hermits in what seems like the smallest, sleepiest hillside village in the country. Perhaps if we *were* adopted, our parents didn't like what they got, so they went on the run soon as they were able to.

–

Craig makes good on his word by putting a meeting in my calendar for nine a.m. on Monday morning, which allows enough time over the rest of the weekend to give some thought to my side of the negotiation. It also apparently gives the competition a tiny window of opportunity to try and poach me from him.

At 8:45 a.m. that morning, I'm approaching our new office on Forrest Road – a converted shop space – nose in my social media on my phone, when a call from an Edinburgh number flashes up on my screen.

'Hello?' I quickly answer it, wondering who could be looking for me at this time on a Monday morning.

'Jess, good morning, it's Bree from the Cramond Event Company,' a glossy, purring voice greets me.

'Oh, hi.' I pull a surprised face at this direct approach, as all her previous interactions with me have been on LinkedIn.

'Congratulations on your successful event at the weekend. It was really quite special. I particularly enjoyed the Cava Cave.'

'You were there? I didn't see you, otherwise I would have said hello.'

'Well, I saw you, and I saw what you created, Jess. You're doing great things at Capital Events, but I know that won't satisfy you forever. I have big plans for the Cramond Event Company and I want you to be part of them when they kick off. Do you want to be working under the patriarchy for the rest of your days, or do you want to work for a strong female-led business that will give you opportunities well beyond the boundaries of Edinburgh, even the UK?'

While this chat-up from Bree sounds incredible, I'm used to her putting the hard sell on me online, and I haven't yet seen concrete evidence of the fruits she's dangling. Until I do, I'll be staying exactly where I am – but it's still good to keep her sweet.

'Thanks for getting in touch, Bree I'm really flattered, and I'm going to say not right now. I've got a few punchy projects in the pipeline, but you'll be my first port of call for a conversation when I decide the time is right.'

'OK, Jess. Can't blame a director for trying. Speak soon.'

I say goodbye and end the call, before heading straight to our office's sole meeting room to meet Craig.

'How are you today?' He deposits a flat white from the cafe across the road on the table in front of me as he enters the room.

'I'm great. What a weekend, eh? The local media coverage was outstanding.'

'It was indeed. And I hear there's already chatter among the sponsors about going bigger and better next year?'

'I might have been working on them in the VIP tent.' I sit back with a smile. 'Perfect time to introduce the idea: when they're tanked up on bubbly and canapés and soaking up the positive PR.'

'Well, it's working, so well done. I've already got three of them lined up for initial conversations next week – which leads me to why we're here. Jess, I don't want to do a dance with you. You're my most powerful asset in this place. Isla and Ravi are learning fast, thanks to your willingness to mentor them, but I'll be blunt, you're my cash cow, so what's it going to take to keep you?'

'Gosh, Craig, you'd be a rubbish poker player.' I chuckle. 'I've spoken to less desperate claims cold callers.'

'And you only get away with a comment like that because you're indispensable and you know it.' He taps his fingers on the table. 'So, come on, hit me with it.'

I pick up my coffee and take a long thoughtful slug, which is more about playing the game than reflecting, because I already know exactly what I want.

'Craig, you know I'm less about the monetary side and more about career growth and visibility on the high-profile projects...' I tail off for emphasis.

'I do.' He nods and waits for me to continue.

'But that doesn't mean a monetary gesture wouldn't be welcome. I've considered this carefully, and based on the value I bring to this place, I'm thinking—'

My thoughts are interrupted by my phone buzzing on the table, showing a call from an unknown number. Frowning at it, and assuming it's a spam call, I hit reject and return my attention to Craig, who gestures for me to continue.

'Sorry about that... so, yeah, as I was saying... by way of an uplift, I was thinking maybe ten per cent and perhaps a modest bonus for the events that exceed expectations – which by the way, are all of them.' I offer him a sparkling smile to punctuate this message.

Craig guffaws loudly. 'I should have known you'd come in here ready to play hardball. OK, yes and yes. What else? Because I'm well aware from your opener that you're by no means finished.'

'Correct. From a development point of view, I've been looking at professional qualifications and—'

I'm thrown off once again by my phone buzzing with another call from an unknown number.

'What the heck?' I jab at the reject button for a second time. 'Sorry, Craig. These spam calls are a pain in the backside.'

'Not a problem.' Craig doesn't seem fazed at all. 'Tell me about this qualification.'

'Oh yeah, so it's a professional accreditation in events leadership that would give me new skills and insight into how we can lift our offering to clients to a whole new level. I'm talking rivalling the best companies in London.'

'Well, that's an easy one to say yes to. Anything that takes the business forward and keeps our balance sheet looking healthy.'

'Thanks, it will be money well spent, I promise. And my final request is to be the lead on all high-profile events, including everything based in and around Holyrood Palace, the Scottish Parliament and the Glasgow deal you've just secured, as that's going to be mega.'

'Jess, you can be the lead on whatever you want,' says Craig. 'That's the easiest request of all to—'

This time it's Craig who's interrupted by my phone buzzing with yet another incoming call.

'Do you think maybe you should get that?' he suggests. 'Might not be a spam call after all.'

'Uh, yeah. Maybe.' I grab my phone, mouthing an apology as I answer it. 'Hello?'

'Oh, hello, is this Jess?' the caller asks.

'Speaking.' I offer a perplexed shrug to Craig.

'Jess, my name is Simone. I'm a nurse at the Edinburgh Royal Infirmary A&E. We found your name as an ICE contact in the wallet of a patient we have here.'

Thrown by this unexpected introduction, I rub my forehead in confusion. 'I'm sorry, what do you mean you found me under "ice"? And in whose wallet?'

'ICE means "in case of emergency",' the woman named Simone says. 'So, he's obviously someone you know well if you're his emergency contact. Unfortunately, we haven't yet been able to communicate with the patient, but there's a driving licence in the wallet that suggests his name is Seth McKenzie?'

As she says this, my stomach drops like a stone, then a chill runs through my spine alongside a rising nausea.

'Seth,' I murmur. 'He's my brother. What's happened? Why can't he talk to you?'

Chapter 2

Thirty minutes later, my taxi pulls up outside the Edinburgh Royal Infirmary. Hurriedly paying the driver, I sprint across to the accident and emergency department, not stopping until I reach the reception desk panting like a tired dog.

'Hi, my brother's been brought in and I got a call from one of the nurses,' I say to the receptionist before he even looks up. 'His name is Seth McKenzie.'

'No problem.' He smiles politely at me. 'Can I ask you to take a seat in the waiting area and I'll see what I can find out.'

'Um… OK…' I'm reluctant to do this when I don't know how long it will take, but a faint voice in my head tells me this person doesn't know anything and should be given the space to find out what's going on.

Retreating to a seat, I perch on the edge bolt upright, waiting anxiously for some news. I don't know whether it's the continuing nausea I'm feeling or the overpowering chemicals used to keep the hospital clean, but I find the smell of the place almost intolerable. That and the drab feel of the waiting area, being surrounded by so many sick and injured people. After what feels like an eternity, the man from reception approaches me and I stand up, expecting to be led somewhere.

'Your brother is having a CT scan just now,' he tells me. 'Someone will be over to see you soon.'

'Right…' I kind of know I need to accept this situation for now, but my desperation is overriding my ability to be placated. 'The nurse who called me said it was a suspected stroke. Do you have any other information? Any indication of how serious it is?'

'I'm sorry, I can't tell you any more than that.' The receptionist gives me an apologetic look. 'I'm sure it won't be long until there's some news.'

Frustrated, I sit back down, fidgeting uncontrollably, watching every move of the medical professionals who come and go. After a short while, my phone buzzes with a text from Craig asking if there's any news.

Our earlier conversation was obviously cut short after the nurse called me, and Craig was great. He called a cab and bundled me straight into it, telling me not to give work a second thought until I knew more.

I quickly respond to let him know where things are at, and as I hit send, I suddenly think of my parents. They need to know what's going on, but if I call them now, what can I tell them? What if it's not a stroke and just a false alarm? I wouldn't want to worry them for no reason. But regardless, something is clearly going on. The nurse told me that Seth couldn't even communicate with her – Mum and Dad should know that.

Keeping an eagle eye on the activity around me, I find my parents' number and put my phone to my ear. The elongated international ring tone sounds for a few moments and then someone answers.

'Jess, darling, how are you? Lovely to hear from you,' my mum's softly spoken yet upbeat voice greets me. 'I thought we were speaking at the weekend. To what do I owe this pleasure?'

I wince in anticipation of ruining her day – perhaps even her life, given I don't yet know how serious Seth's condition is.

'Mum, is Dad there too? I need to speak to you both together.'

'Of course, I'll just get him. You sound worried. Is something up?'

I refrain from answering her question and wait silently as I hear her calling my dad, who's clearly been outside from the noises and dialogue that follow.

'He's coming now,' commentates my mum.

Seconds later I hear my father clear his throat as he joins the call. 'Jess, love. Your mum thinks there's something wrong. You're all right, aren't you?'

'Yes, I'm fine. Well, actually I'm not... because Seth is not fine.'

'Sorry, honey, you're not making much sense,' says my mum. 'Are you saying something's wrong with Seth? He's not in trouble, is he? I've told him about getting too boisterous with those lads of his on his nights out, but he never listens.'

'It's not that, Mum. He's taken ill.' My voice cracks as I say this. 'They... they think it might be a stroke.'

There's a stunned silence. For a second I think maybe I've lost the connection and quickly check the reception on my phone.

'Are you still there?' I ask.

'We're here, Jess,' confirms my dad. 'It's just... a bit of a shock. Are you sure you've understood correctly? Seth is young and very fit. A stroke seems quite unlikely.'

'I know. That's what I thought, but I literally don't know anything else. He's having a scan right now and I've been told I'll be updated soon.'

'OK, sure. Well try not to worry, love. They always want to rule out the most serious conditions first. It's probably something far less sinister.'

'I would think so,' my mum pitches in with agreement.

Talking to my parents, even when they're so far away, acts as some comfort to me. We move on to some light chat about what they've been doing (very little from the sounds of it), which I know is their way of trying to calm me.

By the time I end the call, I feel more reassured. I've jumped to the worst conclusion and the chances are it's something way less concerning. Feeling slightly cheered, I scroll through my Instagram newsfeed until someone approaches me.

'Ms McKenzie?'

'Yes?' I look up and shove my phone back in my bag.

The woman is well dressed and confident-looking with kind eyes, which gives me an unjustified sense of reassurance.

'I'm Dr Rashi. Would you mind coming with me?'

'Of course.' I get up and follow her to a quiet seating area just beyond the reception area, where she sits down beside me.

'Ms McKenzie—'

'Oh, please call me Jess,' I jump in quickly.

'As you wish.' Dr Rashi politely nods acknowledgement of this. 'Jess, I head up the resuscitation area here in A&E and I have been overseeing your brother's care today.'

'That's good,' I say, without really knowing why. I just feel the need to say something.

'Seth was admitted at around nine a.m. this morning after taking unwell on a bus. He had not disembarked when the bus reached the end of its route and the driver became concerned. He checked on your brother and realised there was something wrong, so he called an ambulance.'

'Right...' While I'm keen to know how this all came about, I'm now willing Dr Rashi to get to the point.

'There is no easy way to say this, Jess. Your brother has had a stroke, the cause of which is unclear right now, but we should be able to get further information with an MRI scan, which we will do later.'

'It really is a stroke?' My mouth falls open as the false sense of security I'd been lulled into during my call with my parents disintegrates instantly. 'He's really had a stroke? But how is that possible? He's young, fit – fitter that most people I know. He drinks a bit, sure... he likes a night out, but would it really cause that?'

'As I say, we do not yet know the cause,' says Dr Rashi. 'Strokes are rare in young, generally healthy people, but they do happen.'

'Is... he going to die?' I feel my eyes well up as I ask this question, the swell of raw emotion almost taking over me.

'He is very poorly, but I believe that we got him here in time, and provided there are no secondary complications, he should make a meaningful recovery over time.'

'Oh, thank goodness. Wait... you said a "meaningful" recovery? What does that mean?'

Dr Rashi pauses briefly before answering my question. 'It means that we don't yet know the extent of the damage. We have stabilised his condition, but until we see more detailed images of his brain, we won't know if his neurological impairment is temporary or permanent. As soon as there is a bed available – which I am told will not be long – he will be moved to the intensive care unit where he will receive the very best care.'

I gulp as I take all this in. 'I've not had any personal experience with strokes... but I've seen things on TV. By "neurological impairment", do you mean walking, talking, being able to use his arms?'

'These are areas that can be affected, yes. But I would prefer that we do not speculate at this time. For now, all I can say for sure is that we know Seth's speech and mobility were initially affected, which is why he was unable to get off the bus or seek help. I will take you to see him now, but I must warn you, what you see will be unpleasant, and we currently have him in an induced coma to ensure he remains stable.'

'OK...' I swallow down the fear that's brimming; my sincere hope is that I can hold it together for my brother.

'Shall we?'

I get up from my seat. 'Yes. No matter what he looks like, I need to see him.'

Chapter 3

Dr Rashi leads me through to the resuscitation area and the first thing I become aware of is the sound of machines beeping and a flurry of activity as staff attend to another sick person on the other side of the room.

On reaching the trolley Seth is lying on, I gasp with shock as I take in all the wires and monitors, as well as how vulnerable he looks. It's as if my strong, lively big brother has been replaced by a paler, weaker doppelganger.

'Oh, Seth.' I rush forward, then stop, unsure what to do or if I might hurt him.

'Go ahead, please,' says Dr Rashi. 'He can't interact with you or hear you in the obvious sense, but there is research suggesting that coma patients fare better when their loved ones communicate with them.'

'OK...'

I take a faltering breath, then reach across and slip my hand into Seth's. It's limp and floppy, which gives me a bit of a fright at first, but it's also warm. I clasp it tightly. Leaning over him, I kiss his forehead and start to speak to him.

'Hey, big bro. What's all this then? I know you're not keen on your job, but this is taking things a bit far.' I let out an involuntary snorty sob at my ridiculous and inappropriate joke. 'I'm here for you, whatever you need. You've always looked after me, so now it's my turn to step up. I've let Mum and Dad know that you're poorly as well, so I expect they'll soon be on their way here to see you.'

I pause and look up at Dr Rashi, as if seeking her approval. She seems to sense this and nods.

'You are doing fine. I will leave you for now, but if you have any questions or concerns, please ask one of the nurses to contact me. We will make Seth more comfortable in a proper bed as soon as we can.'

'Thank you, doctor. Thank you for saving him.' My eyes well up with fat, prickly tears.

'Of course.' She nods again and then moves on to tend to her next patient.

I sit with Seth for about an hour, chatting rubbish to him, even reading him a chapter from an e-book I'm in the middle of. It's a surreal experience that I try not to think too much about, because I know if I do, I might very well lose my head. Eventually, I start to feel stiff and in need of something to eat and drink, so I venture along the seemingly never-ending corridor from the A&E department into the main hospital. It's so white and clinical, the smell of disinfectant haunting me as I go.

After buying a meal deal from the M&S Simply Food shop, I head outside into the hospital grounds in search of a bench and some fresh air, which I gulp down in large doses as my mind ticks over everything. I simply can't get my head around the fact that my thirty-two-year-old brother just almost died and that he may be left with permanent disability. I mean, how could it happen to someone like him? And why? It's completely senseless and almost too much to bear. But I know I have to deal with it, because falling apart will help no one. I need to focus on the practicalities, and the first of those is giving an update to Mum and Dad.

Quickly taking a few bites of my sandwich and some swigs of my mineral water, I then set my lunch aside, and pull my phone out of my bag to make the call. My mum answers on the third ring.

'Hello, darling, how are things going there? Have you managed to speak to Seth yet?'

'I've seen him, yes—'

'Ah, great. I'm glad everything is OK then.'

I hesitate, not relishing bursting my mum's bubble. She's clearly in denial, being so quick to jump to the assumption that Seth is fine.

'No, Mum. Everything is not OK. Is Dad there?'

'He's just coming inside now.'

I hear the door to my parents' veranda open and close and my dad approaching the phone once again.

'We're both here now, Jess,' says my mum. 'Go ahead.'

'Um... sure... so there's no easy way to say this... Seth has had a stroke. He's in an induced coma right now. It's unclear what state he'll be in when they bring him out of it, but... Mum, Dad, he... he nearly died.' My voice wobbles, then breaks, as I say these last words.

There's a pregnant pause while I wait patiently for my parents to digest this information. Eventually, my dad clears his throat.

'Jess, sweetheart, are you absolutely sure about this? You haven't misheard or gotten confused? Because I know that medical language can be difficult to follow, especially if you're in a state of stress or feeling anxious.'

I frown at this statement through my tears, unsure whether to feel offended at my dad's sweeping assumption that I've gotten this wrong.

'Yeah, I'm sure. I spoke to a doctor and I've been in to see Seth in the resuscitation room of A&E. He's unconscious, hooked up to all these machines. I haven't got this wrong.' I continue by filling them in on how Seth was found on the bus and what the doctor said about performing another scan to find out more about Seth's situation and prognosis. 'So, there you have it. I've understood perfectly well.'

'All right, darling. Just keep yourself nice and calm.' My mum tries to soothe me in a way that irks me. 'Your father was only trying to establish the facts, and this is a big shock for all of us.'

Gritting my teeth, I look up at the cloudless blue sky to stop myself from biting back. 'Well, now you have "the facts", it's more a question of what next? Do you think you can get a flight today?'

There's another silence and I hear something covering the receiver at my parents' end, along with some muffled conversation. This time I wait less patiently, wondering what they could possibly need to discuss right now. They should be getting straight online to book flights. I'll even do it for them myself if that's what's needed.

Eventually the line becomes clear again and there's yet more throat clearing from the other end.

'So?' I almost demand of them.

'We've had a chat.' My mum's voice seems somewhat strangled all of a sudden. 'And we've decided that dropping everything and flying to the UK right now – when Seth isn't even conscious – is probably not the right thing.'

'*What?*' I actually can't believe what I'm hearing.

'Jess, don't overreact to this, please.' My dad takes over from my mum. 'I know the automatic and emotional reaction you're expecting is for us to dash straight to the airport, but that doesn't make sense from a practical perspective. We can't actually do anything for Seth right now. He's in the best hands with the medics and you're there too. They probably wouldn't even allow three of us to sit around his bed at a time.'

'So, we'd do it in shifts,' I say this as if it's obvious, which it is.

'That's one way of looking at it. The other is that we'd be shelling out a lot of money for flights and accommodation when we don't know how long it will be until Seth is awake. We'd be better seeing him and providing support when he's conscious again.'

'I suppose there's some sense to that thinking,' I concede. 'Though they do say it's important to talk to him while he's in the coma.'

'And you will do a great job of that, I'm sure.'

'So, you'll come when he's awake then? Because whatever his prognosis, he's going to have a long recovery ahead of him and he'll need support.'

'That's something else we've just been discussing,' says my mum. 'We need to make sure that Seth gets the best care possible to support his recovery and we don't have a bottomless pit of money. Rather than us wasting it on flights back and forth and overpriced accommodation, we think it makes more sense to put that money into private rehabilitation services of some sort.'

Getting to my feet, I pace around the bench restlessly.

'You mean you're not coming over at all?' I'm shaking my head in denial of this possibility. 'Please tell me that *this* I've got wrong.'

'Not at all.' My dad placates me. 'We're only saying that we need to be smart about how we support Seth in his recovery. We'll pop across when they wake Seth up, of course we will.'

This statement is the hammer blow for me. I've always accepted my mum and dad's laissez-faire approach to parenting, because it's all I've really known. When they took off for Spain, I was able to see it how they did – as their turn in life to regain their sense of self after being Mum and Dad for all those years. My jokes about them running away from us because we're so different to them were just that: jokes. I'd always assumed they'd be there for us when we really needed them. But hit with this harsh reality of the worst having happened, I'm now left wondering if we were ever really anything but a burden to them. Perhaps having kids seemed like a good idea at the time, but in hindsight, given another chance, they probably wouldn't do it over.

Thinking of Seth lying on that trolley unconscious with machines tracking his vitals, I feel the blood in my own body start to pump aggressively. I begin to seethe, and before I know it, I've lost control.

'OK, great. You just "pop over" when it suits you then. You know, whenever you feel like showing some care and compassion for your son, who's pretty much at death's door—'

'Now, come on, Jess,' my dad interjects. 'I know you've had a shock and you're dealing with a lot. You're learning what it is to be an adult – and that's an important part of you becoming a resilient and independent woman. We won't be around forever, you know.'

'Oh, don't pull that nonsense with me,' I scoff. 'You're both in your late fifties. You'll be around for a while yet. You've clearly convinced yourself of "the greater good" here, but all I see is you throwing money at the problem, while dressing it up as the perfect "life challenge" for me—'

'Jess, please.' My mum's tone remains strained. 'You're in shock, as your father says, and we have the wisdom to act rationally and sensibly to this. Once you've had time to think about it, you'll realise it's the best solution—'

'No, I won't.' I kick at the ground in bare frustration. 'I really won't. But you just carry on thinking that way if it makes you feel better, and I'll go look after your son.'

I jab forcefully at my phone screen to end the call, and after a few more kicks at the ground I flop down on the bench, the fight having well and truly left me. How can they be so lax about their own son having a stroke? And how can they feel all right about putting the responsibility all on me? Perhaps they don't, but their precious life in Spain is just too important to them. Whatever their thoughts and motivations, one thing is clear: I'm on my own with this, and Seth cannot ever know how they reacted. His recovery is my number one priority – I will not have it hampered by the knowledge that his own mum and dad barely batted an eyelid when he was clinging on to life.

Feeling all this settling on me like a twenty-ton weight, a bubble of grief forms in my chest and within moments, big fat tears are rolling down my cheeks and onto my top. Swiping at my face while I dig in my bag for a tissue, I realise I have nothing to help stem the flow, and I cry even harder, until I'm a disgusting sobbing mess. In fact, I'm so lost in my grief that I don't even realise that someone is standing right in front of me.

'Are you all right?' a deep male voice filters down from above.

Looking up, I shield my eyes from the bright sunshine, and see a man hovering over me. He looks around thirty and is unshaven with dishevelled dark brown hair. He's also quite broad and muscular, and he's wearing overalls, suggesting he's a manual labourer of some kind. Even in my emotional state, I don't miss that he's quite attractive, in a rugged way. Making eye contact with him, I suddenly feel embarrassed by my behaviour.

'Oh... erm... yes, I'm... sorry... I didn't mean to disturb you.'

'You didn't disturb me. I was passing and I thought you might need some help.'

'No, I'm OK. Or at least I will be.'

'Have you had some bad news?' The man gazes down at me in a way that makes me feel small and vulnerable.

'Eh... yeah...' I give a long, loaded sigh. 'Something like that.'

'Do you have anyone you can call, maybe? You seem like you need some support.'

'Not really. They wouldn't be able to do anything anyway.'

'Right. Can I do anything?'

The man seems a bit uncomfortable, but he also shows no sign of leaving. I cross my arms over my body protectively. He's obviously trying to help, but it's clear he's no natural when it comes to comforting someone in distress. The best thing would be for him to leave me in peace, but for some reason, he doesn't seem to want to do that.

'I'm OK, really,' I reply. 'Thanks for your concern.'

Rather than taking the hint, the man lingers, looking thoughtful.

'How about I buy you a coffee?'

As he says this, the penny drops as to why he's still here. He's not a concerned citizen; he's hitting on me. That's why this interaction is so awkward: because his expressed motivations don't match his intentions. This realisation has me fizzing again, my fuse having remained short following my altercation with my parents.

'No, thanks.' I ensure my tone is firmer than before and avoid any further eye contact. 'I've got all I need here.'

He seems to accept this and turns away, then he hesitates and swivels back to me.

'Are you sure? I don't like leaving you on your own. Some company might help.'

Yeah, might help you get in my pants, or so you think, my inner voice spits. I'm now fuming at the audacity of this guy preying on someone in such a vulnerable state. Unfortunately, though, it's not unheard of. I've come across enough real-life stories to know I need to be well on my guard.

'*Look*, I don't need company or someone to share my woes with.' This time I fix him with a defiant stare. 'I'm not sure if this is something you've done many times or if you thought you'd try your luck today, but whatever it is, do me a favour and get lost.' I add some extra venom to this request, to make sure he gets the message.

The man's expression turns to one of surprise – most likely surprise that he's been caught out.

'Of course, I'll leave you in peace then.' He holds his hands up in a gesture of surrender and walks off.

Watching him go, I feel slightly guilty for being so direct, but as my mind trawls back over the interaction, that guilt disintegrates. He was at it. No question. But one thing's clear: he wasn't a pro. Forcing my focus back to what's important, I decide that I've spent long enough wallowing. It's time to get back to my brother and find out what we're facing together.

Chapter 4

Five weeks on from Seth's stroke, the doctors communicate that he's making enough progress to be discharged in the coming weeks and begin a dialogue with me over his care needs. They're confident that a home setting will be more comfortable and reassuring for him as he recovers.

Despite this progress, my brother is facing a long and difficult road back, with his consultant having confirmed he won't regain some of the function he has lost – principally the use of his left arm. This news devastated me, possibly more than it upset Seth when they told him. He all but took it in his stride – perhaps he was just glad to be alive. Thankfully, there was also good news: the cognitive impacts he has experienced are largely reversible. This means Seth's speech, which was almost incomprehensible at first, has the potential to improve significantly with intensive therapy, and he should be able to re-learn how to walk, but is unlikely to play football again.

With my parents having let him down so badly – though he doesn't know the half of it and I'm not about to tell him – my protectiveness over my brother has grown like a tumour. When they eventually did visit, I played ball and was civil while in Seth's presence, but I gave them none of my time or energy beyond that. As expected, they didn't try very hard to show me my judgement of them was wrong. Within two weeks, they were back in sunny Spain, living the life of riley, while I continued to put on a brave face and keep Seth's spirits up.

'How are you coping, sugar cream pie?' My bestie, Amelia, asks me one evening during a much-needed support call.

In the absence of my parents, Amelia's been my rock – actually, more like a huge sparkly gemstone, having helped me through the most difficult of times and kept me from falling into complete despair. The only place I've felt any real solace or sense of escape has been at work, where I plaster my best smile on my face each day and keep kicking ass in the events world, with Craig cheering me on (while he simultaneously tots up the earnings).

'I'm doing OK… I think.' I grimace at my phone, which is in my hand and on loudspeaker. 'Up and down, if I'm honest. I'm not getting enough sleep because I'm worried about Seth… about our future.'

'That's understandable.'

'I guess. I don't like it though. I was always so steady and unflappable before. Still am – most of the time – but every now and then my reactions are a bit… unpredictable.'

'How do you mean?' Amelia asks.

I shrug, even though I know she can't see me. 'It's not a big deal, but sometimes I find myself shying away from things I'd normally face head on. Then at other points I get pissed at stuff that wouldn't usually get to me.'

'Sounds like stress to me. You're on edge so you're operating in a different mode to usual, and your fight or flight instincts are kicking in. Give yourself a break, lovely. You have a lot going on and the process for having Seth coming to live with you sounds awfully complicated.'

'It is and it isn't.' I rub my forehead exhaustedly. 'The main thing is getting through the assessment. Thankfully, with my flat being on the ground floor and quite roomy, I've passed that part of it with flying colours. I just need to get a ramp fitted at the main door and some adjustments made to my bathroom. However, my job has been an area of concern, as he can't be left alone, but it's not like I can give it up – I need to bring in an income – nor would I want to.'

'Oh, I wish I lived closer. I was thinking… maybe I could look for something in Edinburgh, so I could be there to offer

23

you more help? I'm sure there are plenty of companies who need an ethically sourced, climate-friendly PR and social media warrior.'

'I have zero idea what that means, so I couldn't possibly comment.' I laugh weakly, my brain too scrambled to try and decipher Amelia's bizarre use of language. 'Thanks for the offer, but you stay where you are. The great city of London must need its warriors. Anyway, this is where my parents did come to some use. I put a major guilt trip on them and they couldn't agree fast enough to pay for a private carer. I'm about to start the process of hiring someone.'

'Good. At least the slippery toadstools are shelling out in that respect.'

'Yes, quite. I'm banking on being able to make it work, because I need my brother back, Meels. I'm lost without him.'

I pour truckloads of hope into that sentiment, however, after another couple of weeks of seeing Seth receiving compassionate but limited support and companionship in the hospital, while I'm at work for most of his waking day, I see the hope in my – normally upbeat and positive – brother's eyes begin to fade and his fight start to peter out. It's nothing short of soul destroying and as much as it pains me to have to take a financial and personal hit, I decide there's only one thing to do when I bring him home.

–

'Jess, how are you today?' Craig asks as he closes the meeting room door behind him and sits opposite me. 'I got some feedback from Izzy over the weekend that I thought you might be interested in.'

'Oh?' Despite this not being the reason for my meeting with Craig, my ears prick up with interest.

'She and Jon are really happy with the work you're doing on the Glasgow Food Lovers event. Particularly the fact that you've managed to secure Lewis Capaldi for the headline act.'

'That I am feeling a bit smug about.' I grin. 'I've always wanted to see him live.'

'Well now you'll have a "front row seat", so to speak. So, what did you want to talk to me about today?' He sits back in his seat casually, waiting for me to begin.

I clear my throat, unsure of my opener. 'Well, you know I've been back and forth to the hospital constantly over the last couple of months, visiting Seth.'

'I do.' He nods. 'How's the poor lad doing?'

I flinch a little at this description of my adult older brother.

'He's improving... slowly... and the doctors have agreed he's ready to be discharged.'

'That's good news.'

'It is. He'll still need to attend outpatient appointments and physiotherapy, that sort of thing, but they say he'll make more progress now at home.'

'Makes sense.' Craig shrugs in acceptance of this assumption. 'I'm guessing this isn't all you wanted to tell me though.'

I take a deep breath. 'Um... no... see, the thing is, Seth can't live alone. He's going to live with me.'

'Right. And how are you feeling about that? Big responsibility.'

'It is. Which is why I wanted to speak to you—'

'Ah, say no more.' He sits forward and drums his fingers on the table. 'You want to work from home more often, do more remote meetings with clients. Totally get it, not a problem. Long as the work gets done, I don't care where it's done from. That's the beauty of the digital age.'

Having not anticipated this response or even considered it as an option, I hesitate for a moment, weighing things up. It's appealing in so many ways – keeping my full-time income being the most obvious one – but it doesn't take long for me to see the issues it'll create, the main one being the impact it will have on Seth if I'm hardly around.

'Um... thanks for the offer, Craig,' I reply. 'But I'm afraid it's more complex than that. I'm going to be Seth's main carer

25

until he regains his independence. I've been told that could take a couple of years – if it happens at all. My parents live abroad and are bankrolling some of this, and there's some state-funded help we can get, but none of these things will give Seth what I feel he truly needs for his recovery.'

'Which is?' Craig's face has changed and he now looks concerned.

'Oh, don't worry, I'm not resigning or anything. I just think that Seth needs the kind of care that comes from someone close to him – as much as I can offer him, anyway. Craig, I'd like to reduce my hours to three days a week – Tuesday to Thursday – just for a year or so, to allow me to focus on my brother and give him the best chance I can at a future.'

I'm expecting Craig to look relieved that I'm not leaving the company, but little has changed in his expression, which unsettles me.

'I'll still bring in the money… manage all the same contracts.' I rush to reassure him. 'I'll work smarter and harder. You'll barely notice the difference, I assure you.'

'And what happens when a client wants a meeting on a Monday or a Friday?' he asks.

'I'm sure I can make myself available for the odd call or meeting, if that's needed. I can easily log on for video calls.'

He frowns in response to this. 'What if something urgent comes up that requires more of your time?'

'I can be reachable any time by phone?' I offer.

'Right. You see, Jess…' Craig sighs and raises his eyes to the ceiling, leaving me in no doubt that he sees my request as a massive inconvenience. 'I've been here before with staff members. I've had all the reassurances, been told that it won't get in the way. But the thing is, it has – every time.'

'But not with me. I can do this, Craig, I know I can.'

'You don't *know* you can, Jess. You don't have a crystal ball. You think you can and I'm telling you that you can't. It's just not possible to do the job of a full-time person in three days.'

'Then maybe we can hire me a part-time assistant with the money you'll save on my salary?'

Craig raises a sceptical eyebrow. 'Having an admin person pick up the slack is hardly a replacement for an experienced senior events manager.'

This use of language causes me to flinch for the second time during this meeting. Craig and I have always gotten on really well. He's heavily business driven – always with one eye on the balance sheet – but that's never been an issue, because I've always delivered what he wanted. It seems that our "bond" may have been more fragile than I realised.

'OK.' I wrack my brain for something that will re-establish the connection between us. 'I'll make myself fully available to them on my non-working days and that will still give me more than enough time with Seth.'

'It won't work.' Craig shakes his head.

'At least let me try. I'm basically offering to work for free here.'

'Jess, you know as well as I do, all it takes is for you to drop the ball one, twice max, and we've lost our clients to the competition. I'm going to lay this out for you, and I don't want any arguments or false promises. You can have your three-day week – I'm not a monster, I know how important it is for you to be there for your brother – but I'm taking you off the Glasgow contract and any others that I believe will be high risk to this company—'

'But you can't.' My eyes widen in desperation. 'I've built the relationships, I know exactly what they want. Who's going to take them on? Isla and Ravi aren't ready for that kind of responsibility. Surely that's the definition of high risk, right there.'

'It's all about calculated risk, Jess. Isla and Ravi are turning into top quality events managers, and they're hungry for the experience and opportunities, meaning they'll make damn sure they get things right. They won't take their eyes off the prize.'

'Like I have, you mean.' I feel a knot form in my stomach as I realise I'm being relegated to 'lack of commitment' status.

'That's not what I mean. Your priorities have changed, that's all. And you know that in this client-driven business, there's no room to hit the brakes. It's not personal, Jess.'

'No, I get that. You'd say the same thing to anyone.'

'I would.'

I swallow down a lump of raw emotion that's forming in my throat: a mixture of frustration, deep disappointment and a feeling of resentment towards my boss. While I can understand some of what he's saying, I still don't think it's that cut and dried. I'm really good at what I do and it feels like he's demoting me without even giving me a chance to prove myself. Feeling a strong inner tug, which I recognise as the instinct to abandon my plan to look after Seth and save my career, I look up at Craig. But as the words are forming on my lips, I know I can't let them escape. I'd be choosing myself over my brother, and that's not a decision I could ever forgive myself for. I need to suck this up, keep delivering the way I always do and show Craig that he's got this wrong.

'OK.' I lift my chin and my shoulders to bring myself back to being Jess the pro. 'If I'm giving up those contracts, what do you want me working on?'

Craig looks at me for a moment, as if trying to gauge whether I'm really on board. 'There are a couple of smaller gigs that are quite well advanced. They're much less demanding, and the clients are "one offs", so there's no real risk there.'

'Right… anything else?'

'A new client request has come in this morning. I was going to assign it to Isla, but I think this one will work well for you. You can make it your own and see it through from start to finish.'

'And *it* is…?'

'East Lothian Wildlife Park. They're a public attraction-slash-conservation business based near Haddington and they're struggling to make ends meet. The owner has been up front with me that if they don't find a new revenue source soon, they may have to close.'

I think for a second but come up empty handed. 'I've never heard of them.'

'Perhaps that's why they're failing,' says Craig.

'Do they not need a PR person then, rather than an events manager? Or the animal park equivalent of Robert Irvine from *Restaurant: Impossible*?'

'Perhaps. But they can't afford that. They think their best bet is a new revenue stream of "ticketed" events. They have six months to get their balance sheet looking more positive, otherwise they're effed. Sounds like an interesting one and something to sink your teeth into. We can talk to them about your availability up front…'

As Craig fills me in on the rest, I feel myself struggling to focus on what he's saying, which is not like me. It's also not like me to just roll over and take something like this, which for a moment almost fools me into thinking that maybe he's right to have removed me from my projects. But he's not. He's totally off the mark with this and he's dressing this new project up to try to sell it to me as something positive. Who is he kidding? This and those other poxy jobs will decimate my CV. From spearheading royal events and creating culinary magic on a massive scale in Scotland's capital city, to a rescue job for an unknown animal park in dire straits that's probably destined to fail anyway. I've just fallen from dizzy heights and it seems almost a certainty that there's no way back.

Chapter 5

The rest of my working week is made up of handing over my precious projects to my colleagues, and getting up to speed with the work I'm taking over from them. It's like the most painful game of 'swapsies' ever. I also spend my lunch breaks and evenings preparing for Seth coming home, which includes interviewing candidates to find a carer he can hopefully connect with. By the time the weekend comes, I'm both physically and emotionally drained. My damaged career weighs heavily on me. So much so, that I feel like a part of me has been chopped off, and by Saturday morning I have to have a serious word with myself as I drive to the hospital to collect my brother.

I can't afford for him to sense my wallowing negativity and feel like he's responsible for it. That will definitely hamper his recovery. So I give myself a mental boot up the backside and adopt the most joyous expression I can muster as I enter his shared room on the neurology ward.

'Hey, big bro.' I greet him, swooping in for a kiss. 'You ready to go?'

'Nearly,' says the nurse, who's packing up the last of Seth's things while he supervises her work. 'We're just waiting for the discharge letter and then you're free. Ah, here it is.' She takes an envelope from a colleague who briefly enters the room and passes it to her.

'Wonderful.' I smile at Seth. 'I'm excited that we're going to be roomies. I was so upset when you moved out and went to uni. Tried to convince Mum and Dad to let me leave school and go with you.'

'I... re... remem-ber.' Seth's speech is slow and faltering, though there has been some improvement since the first weeks after his stroke. 'Can... we... go... for... food?'

'Did you not have lunch? I thought they said I was to come at this time so you could eat first.'

'I... did. Had... an... ome-lette. Rubber.'

I glance guiltily at the nurse. 'You mean it was rubbish?'

'Yes... and... rubber.'

'Oh, like rubber.' I cringe.

'Don't worry.' The nurse pats my arm reassuringly. 'Seth has made no secret of what he thinks of the food here. It's pretty obvious he's a foodie, so this place would never measure up.'

'We're a family of foodies.' I confirm. 'About the only thing he and I have in common with our parents. Right, Seth?'

'Yup.' He nods agreement. 'So... food?'

'I'm glad to see you have your priorities straight, Seth,' says the nurse. 'I tell you, we're going to miss you around here. You've certainly brightened my days.'

'See...' Seth tries to wink at me, but it turns out a bit lopsided. 'I... am... a... bit... bro... bro-ken... but... I... can... still... pull.'

The nurse hoots with laughter, making it clear how much he does indeed brighten her days.

'All right, Casanova.' I shake my head at him. 'Let's get you home. Where do you want to get food on the way?'

'Bur... Bur-ger... King.'

'I should have known. My money's on a bacon double cheeseburger.'

'Yes. A... meal. Large.'

'Your wish is my command.'

The nurse helps Seth off the bed and into the waiting wheel-chair, and we say our goodbyes. There's actually quite a turnout to see him off, which brings a tear to my eye, as it reminds me of everything we've been through in the last eight weeks. I'm careful to hide this though, because if Seth gets wind of it, he'll give me a right slagging for being a soft arse.

It takes a bit of getting used to having Seth living with me in my flat on Montgomery Street. The biggest adjustment being that my first thought always has to be about him before myself, which is strange after enjoying an independent lifestyle for so long. It's also a bit disconcerting seeing how little he can do for himself and how much he depends on me. But we muddle on through and get on great, just as we always have. That's probably the one silver lining to all this. Seth is one laid-back guy, which works in his favour in this situation. He's patient and relaxed, and he's OK with the fact that his recovery is going to take time. The complete opposite to how I would be if things were the other way round.

It almost seems like he really is taking it all in his stride. Almost. When he doesn't think I'm looking, I see the odd moment of frustration – mostly when he doesn't manage to do something he's trying to do – or a hint of sadness in his eyes as he watches non-disabled young people on TV, but I don't let on. The last thing I want is to accidentally say something that he perceives to demean him – or worse, that makes him feel like a burden on me. In a nutshell: I don't ever want to break his spirit.

By the time Tuesday comes, I'm exhausted and in need of another weekend to recover from the one I've apparently just had. It's not just the running around after Seth. It's the learning curve I'm on. I'm learning how to be a carer, which is essentially like taking on a new job in an area I have literally no skills in. And I don't even have the luxury of going through training, I have to learn as I go. It's utterly draining, but the good thing in it all is that I can see how relieved Seth is to be out of the hospital with some normality and proper comfort around him again. The doctors were bang on: this is exactly where he needs to be.

Zooming along the A1 from Edinburgh to my first meeting with the management team at the East Lothian Wildlife Park, my mind is creating a list of things I need to pick up on my way home from work later. Having worked up a meals schedule at the weekend, and put in an online order to save me having to go out to the supermarket, I've since discovered that I'm missing about eight dry store items I assumed I either had or were in date. I've barely given any thought at all to my impending meeting because: 1) I don't expect this to go beyond a first meeting – they'll surely realise they need to call in the administrators rather than an events planner; and 2) on a personal level, I'm not remotely interested in this becoming my pet project (excuse the pun). My focus needs to be on helping Craig realise that he's made an enormous error taking me off the biggest contracts and putting Isla and Ravi on them instead.

After a short drive, I pull into the near-empty car park of the wildlife park, which is situated along a particularly beautiful and open stretch of country road between Haddington and the coastal towns and villages of East Lothian. The place itself is a bit inconspicuous. I'm pretty sure that if I hadn't plugged my route into Google Maps, I might have missed it and driven right past. The only thing that gives it away as a recreational destination is a large(ish) faded billboard sign that's partially covered by foliage from the surrounding bushes.

Climbing out of my car, I admire the tall pine trees flanking either side of the park while breathing in the fresh country air and enjoying the view. OK, this I can appreciate. The surroundings are stunning. The question is, what lies beyond the nondescript ticket booth and entry barrier? I'm about to approach and find out, when I remember yet another food item I've forgotten to buy (and start to wonder what I actually did remember to order), so I pull out my phone to add it and the other items to my notepad app. As I'm doing this, a stout, handsome woman in her late fifties or early sixties, with short wavy greying hair and a kind smile, appears in front of me.

'You're not Jess, are you?' she asks.

'I sure am.' I quickly stuff my phone back in my bag, switch into work mode and reach out my hand with a smile to the woman I assume is the owner. 'You must be Gwen.'

'Delighted to meet you,' she practically hollers at me, nearly breaking the bones in my hand as she clamps it with the strength of a bear. 'Come this way. The team are looking forward to meeting you.'

I follow Gwen through the now open barrier and into the park, which is more appealing than I would have first expected. It has a spacious, cobbled courtyard of sorts, which is framed by a gift shop, a cafe, customer toilets, another building that doesn't appear to be open to the public and a small entertainment arcade with the kind of games machines that are aimed at children. There's also a kiddie ride – a sort of merry-go-round, but with zoo-style animals – that takes pride of place right in the middle.

'This is cute.' I look around, pleasantly surprised.

'I'm glad you think so.' Gwen seems pleased by my comment. 'I always think it's important to create a good first impression. Show people what you have in store for them and help them have a positive experience right from the off.'

'I absolutely agree.' I decide now is not the time to mention that first impressions start from before people have even walked inside. 'What is it they say about job interviews… it only takes some hiring managers about ninety seconds to decide if they're willing to take you on.'

'That's the one. Do you mind if we make a quick detour so I can pass on a piece of kit to a colleague?'

'Not at all.'

I wander along beside Gwen, getting my first experience of the park's residents. The first thing I notice, as we move further away from the noise of the cafe and amusement arcade, is the sound of animals all around me, hooting and chirping, trumpeting and caterwauling. The place feels alive and exotic with what I'd describe as the noises of the jungle. It's a very different feeling to the one I got when I pulled into the nondescript car park with the faded sign. We pass a couple of giant anteaters, the otter enclosure, and some adorable mammals I don't recognise, but that look like a cross between a mouse and a kangaroo.

The combination of all this and the lovely fresh air makes me itchy to abandon the work aspect of this outing and go exploring – especially as I have no professional interest in this project.

Gwen makes her delivery then we almost double back on ourselves along another path that runs almost parallel, passing the meerkat enclosure as we go.

'Oh my goodness, look at these little guys,' I gush as I watch the furry little critters standing to attention, scanning the sky for predators.

'They've just had a brood,' says Gwen. 'Do you see their young over at the back there?'

Craning my neck, I gasp with delight as I spot four tiny fluff-balls tottering around, close to what I assume is their mother.

'They're adorable!'

'Our meerkats are one of our most popular residents. Thank-fully, they're also doing well in the wild, unlike many of the animals we have here. Did you know that habitat loss is the biggest threat for most species officially labelled as "threatened" or "endangered"?'

'I did not. Gosh, that's really sad.'

'It is.' Gwen nods, still watching the meercats. 'Which is why the work we do here is so important. We're a visitor attraction, yes, but we're primarily here to educate the public, so people understand how important the wildlife on this planet is and the perils it's facing – as well as how critical it is that we do everything we can to protect it. We're also involved in breeding programmes and conservation projects, partnering with charit-able organisations abroad. As a not-for-profit organisation, we'd normally be supporting them financially as well, but we've had to stop that since our finances got so tight. Essentially, we're doing our bit to make sure the world doesn't lose its most endangered wildlife.'

'Because of climate change?' I ask.

'That and other risk factors. Poachers are also a huge threat to wildlife. That's a real problem globally. You ready to meet the team?'

Having quickly become invested in the conversation, I have to bring myself back to the moment and remind myself why I'm here. It's certainly not for a fun day out looking at cute animals, nor a school trip-style educational experience. I'm here to talk events – and I'm rather hoping that conversation will turn into a *non*-event.

'Absolutely.' I ensure my tone is enthusiastic, despite my feelings on the matter. This may not be the type of gig I want on my CV, but I still very much want to show Capital Events in a good light and come across as both the professional and good person that I am.

We circle back to the courtyard and I follow Gwen into a building with a sign on the door that says 'Staff Only'. It appears to be the wildlife park's main office, probably where all the administrative processes take place. She leads me through an open-plan office area to the back where there are a couple of rooms with frosted glass windows. I can't see what's inside, but I can hear voices coming from the one Gwen is heading towards. She opens the door and walks inside, beckoning me to follow.

'Everyone, this is Jess,' she announces at a volume way too loud for the acoustics of the room, making me wince. 'Jess, come on in and take a seat. Let's get you a cuppa and then we can do proper introductions.'

Gwen makes her way across to a trolley laden with cups and saucers, a plate of biscuits and two large metal flasks with the labels 'tea' and 'coffee' on them. She then clearly realises she's forgotten to ask what I want, so I mouth 'coffee, please' at her with a smile, which she returns.

With my attention diverted to the refreshments, I haven't yet managed to say hello to anyone in the room, never mind take stock of who's there. Allowing my eyes to roam around the table, I nod a polite greeting to each of its occupiers, until my gaze reaches the other end and I stop short.

Sitting there, in overalls, is the man I accused of being a lech and barked at to get lost at the hospital the day Seth had his stroke. And he's looking less than impressed that I've just turned up in his office. So much for first impressions. Unless he's the work experience lad – which I sincerely doubt, given he looks about thirty – it seems I've just unwittingly walked into the lion's den.

Chapter 6

'Let's get some introductions done then,' booms Gwen. 'Everyone, this is Jess from Capital Events. As you're well aware, she's here to see if she can help with our financial situation.'

Her team appear to be used to her overenthusiastic ways, so I relax my shoulders and make an effort to get with the programme.

'Great to meet you all.' I spread my smile as wide as I can, and give another sweeping nod to the table's occupiers, being careful not to make eye contact with overalls man as I do.

'Thank you, Jess.' Gwen beams at me. 'I'm sure the feeling is mutual. Team, how about we each introduce ourselves, so Jess can start to put things together?'

Everyone round the table seems to be accommodating of this suggestion, except overalls man. He sits forward with a borderline sneer.

'How about we wait and see if she's going to be any use before we get overly familiar?'

I flinch at this and immediately try to hide my reaction.

Gwen cocks her head and surveys him appraisingly. 'Nick, I'm aware that you have some reservations about our rescue plan, but I'd appreciate it if you would at least respect the process – and our guest. You're not exactly making the best first impression here.' She throws me an apologetic look that's a clear reference to our earlier conversation.

'Sure, whatever.' The man apparently known as Nick gives a sarcastic shrug then leans back and casually puts his hands behind his head, his not unimpressive biceps flexing as he does this. 'I'm Nick. Head keeper here at the park. How are things since I last saw you?'

I blanch, having expected Nick to do as I was intending to do, and pretend we'd never met – for the time being at least.

'Things are… fine. Thanks for asking.'

'Not a problem.' He adopts a smarmy look. 'I thought it might be a step too far to ask, but I figured you wouldn't shout me down in front of this lot.'

Oh my God, did he just say that?

The faces round the table, which have been fairly neutral until this point, morph into expressions of curiosity as it becomes blatantly obvious that Nick and I have not only met, we have 'history'.

Gwen's eyes narrow in annoyance at Nick's disruptive behaviour, but it's obvious her interest is also piqued.

'I'm sensing that an introduction between the two of you isn't needed,' she says. 'Do you think we can keep this civil until we finish the meeting?'

I'm now fizzing mad and completely mortified. It was one thing for this Nick to hit on me at my most vulnerable, but to treat me as if I was the one in the wrong and pounce on me when I'm just trying to do my job is quite another. The problem is, I can't let this show, because right now I'm representing Capital Events. Craig will have my head on a stake if I damage the company's reputation. I take a deep calming breath and count to five.

'Of course, Gwen,' I reassure her. 'My sincere apologies. Nick and I have met briefly, but that's not a topic for today. Please continue.'

'Nick?' Gwen seeks the same confirmation from him through gritted teeth.

'Go ahead.' He waves her on. 'I'll keep schtum.'

'Good. Now before we go any further, has anyone else got anything they want to say or air, or can we get on with this meeting like the adults that we apparently are?' She looks around the table. 'No? That's a relief. There was me thinking the primates were outside.' She shoots daggers at Nick, who doesn't seem remotely fazed by this comment.

Gwen prompts the other members of the management team to introduce themselves and once that's done, she gives an overview of the situation at the park. The short version is very much what Craig told me: they're on extremely difficult terrain financially due to the rising costs of keeping the animals, a reduction in publicly-funded grants and visitor numbers not being as high as previous years – the latter having also had a knock-on effect on their animal sponsorship scheme. It's likely they'll close their doors by the end of the year if they can't figure things out.

'So, with all that going on,' says Gwen. 'We had a chat as a team and came up with a couple of options. We could look at bringing in a PR consultancy to help raise our profile and attract more visitors, or we could try to create another revenue stream, through putting on regular paid events of some kind.'

'And you decided on the latter,' I pitch in as a finisher.

'Exactly that. We feel it's our best chance and that hiring a PR company would cost more than we can afford to pay out at this stage. We can still do some work on our visibility and promotion, and we have Lauren here who can do all that as our marketing person.' Gwen signals to the petite young woman sitting opposite me. Lauren has curly red hair tied back in a ponytail, beautiful porcelain skin and she can't be older than about twenty-three – either that or her bright, girlish smile makes her seem younger than she is.

'Makes sense if you already have the skills in house.' I shrug easily.

It's dawning on me that Gwen and her team have thought this through carefully and what I thought would end in a 'thanks for the info, but we'll take another path' is looking like a foregone conclusion.

'And that leads me to your part in this, Jess.' Gwen leans forward in her chair, her gaze fixed on me. 'Having spoken with your boss, Craig, it sounds to me like you're going to be our guardian angel. He speaks very highly of you.'

At least that hasn't changed, I think to myself.

'He also mentioned that you'll only be available to work with us Tuesday to Thursday, but that's absolutely fine because I'm confident we can do the actual running of the events if you're able to help with the ideas, planning, logistics, that sort of thing.'

Thanks Craig. Now I look like a right slacker.

'Um… great.' I give an enthusiastic nod, despite feeling like I've had my wings clipped. 'Have you had any thoughts on what kind of events you'd like to put on?'

'We did a bit of brainstorming at last week's management meeting.' Lauren gets out of her chair and drags a flipchart noisily across the floor so I can see what's written on it.

'Something with school groups, question mark…' I read the green scrawl aloud. 'Summer BBQs like the ones we have after hours… something Christmassy… maybe a Halloween-themed event… OK… and what's on the next page?'

'Nothing,' says Lauren. 'That's as far as we got.'

'Right.'

I take a moment to weigh up how to respond, especially given that Lauren's supposed to be the resident marketing expert and these ideas are pretty scant. To be fair though, she introduced herself as the office manager and essentially seems to be an administrative jack of all trades.

'You have a starting point then.' I opt for a diplomatic response. 'Maybe our next step is to run another brainstorming session together to flesh out some of your existing thinking and see what else we can come up with?'

'That sounds great.' Gwen claps her hands enthusiastically. 'Doesn't it team?'

They all nod obediently, apart from Nick, who simply shakes his head and stares at the table in front of him.

'Let's get started then. Lauren, will you man the flipchart again?'

'Actually... how about we take a pause?' I look around the room at the slightly surprised faces, then focus my attention on Gwen. 'The most obvious and easiest way forward would be for us to continue where you left off, but I'm not sure that will get us the results you're looking for. I think the best way I can help you is to really understand what you do... what the park's all about.'

'You want to get those nice clean corporate hands dirty?' Nick gives a little snort and I notice a couple of his colleagues chuckling along, making it clear they think I'm one of these ivory towers-based consultants who does little more than play around on PowerPoint.

Well, that they have very wrong, and no matter how much I don't want to be here, I am not at all work-shy, nor do I have any aversion to getting involved in the thick of things. I've lugged crates of beer around, cleaned out mobile kitchen cabinets and donned a floor polisher on many an occasion.

'Yes, I do.' I look Nick straight in the eye to show him I'm not going to be intimidated by his cutting remarks. 'Gwen, if you don't mind, I'd like to use the next few days to shadow your staff here at the park and get to know the whole operation...' I tail off as Gwen looks slightly uncomfortable.

'How... eh... how much extra will that cost us?' she cringes as she asks this question, clearly uncomfortable with having to draw attention to the cash flow situation.

'If I have my way, nothing. I see it as an essential part of offering you the solutions you need. If you're in agreement, I'll call Craig and suggest that I spend the rest of today up until Thursday lunchtime on immersion activities – that's just getting to know and understand your operation, as I already mentioned. Then, on Thursday afternoon, I'd like to bring you all back together, if you can spare the time, for the brain-storming session. How does that sound?'

'It sounds wonderful, provided you can convince your boss.'

'I'm confident I can. I'll call him now, won't be long.' Holding up two fingers, I get up and leave the meeting room, and catch Nick rolling his eyes and sighing with impatience as I go.

A few minutes later, I return to the room with Craig's blessing, which I knew wouldn't be a problem. He may have tanked my career due to my life situation, but he still trusts my instincts and expertise.

'All sorted,' I say to Gwen.

'Wonderful.' She bangs the table with her fist delightedly. 'And while you were out of the room, we took the liberty of planning your familiarisation activities. Lauren and her team can give you a quick overview of the office activities; we'll also arrange a tour of the catering and retail operations, but the real "immersion" will be in the park itself. There's no one more knowledgeable and skilled with the animals than Nick, so you'll be spending the majority of the next couple of days with him. I hope the two of you will be able to get along.'

A feeling of deep dread washes over me. Gwen gives me a hopeful look and I involuntarily glance at Nick, who looks mighty pissed off that he's been volunteered for this. Well, that makes two of us, mate. But today I'm Jess, senior events manager, rather than Jess who is repulsed by lecherous men in overalls, so I'm just going to have to be my best professional self and suck it up.

'I'm sure we'll get along fine,' I reassure her, while digging my nails into my palm to keep me from giving myself away.

Chapter 7

Straight after the meeting, I'm able to put some much-needed distance between myself and Nick by persuading Gwen that I first need to experience the wildlife park through a customer's eyes. This is not actually a lie. If I'm going to help them bring more people through their gates at a premium price, I have to get a feel for what's on offer – and what might create that draw. Do I need to do it right now? That's debatable. But, given what I really want to do is stomp across to Nick and ball him out for his behaviour at the meeting, I figure I'd be best taking the time now to get myself back on an even keel and able to tolerate his miserable puss.

After changing into my running shoes in my car, and with the park map Lauren helpfully provided me with, I set off along one of the tarmacked pathways I walked along earlier with Gwen.

There are animal enclosures everywhere, which seem bigger than those at the zoos I've visited. There also appear to be more animals of different species sharing these 'habitats' than I've seen before (the ones that won't eat each other, I'm assuming). Information boards outside each one give me the name and an illustration of each of the occupying residents, as well as an overview of how they live in the wild. In most cases, the boards also share that these species are under threat, with declining numbers, and the conservation work that is taking place worldwide to protect them. It ignites a conflicted feeling in me: I really enjoy seeing the animals – their vibrant colours, fascinating behaviours, the wonderful sounds they emit – but knowing so many of them are here not just for educating the public, but because they're being squeezed out of their natural habitats or hunted by humans, is saddening.

I explore every part of the park, gasping in delight when I spot a tiny baby marmoset clinging to its mother's back, staring in awe (and a little terror) at the majestic male tiger as he stalks back and forth behind the glass panel of the enclosure, and giggling with fascination at the flamingos performing a dance-like walk in almost perfect synchronisation, their heads dipping and flicking from side to side, bright feathers pink as candyfloss.

After an hour or so, I make a pit stop at one of the cafes to grab a cup of tea to warm myself up. It's a cool day for late July, and having expected this to be a quick visit, I've not brought a jacket with me. Taking a seat at one of the tables, I sip at my drink while staring out of the window and quickly become distracted by the personal issues in my life: my effective demotion at work, the toll my caring responsibilities for Seth are taking on me (though I wouldn't have it any other way) and the infuriating absence of our parents in his rehabilitation, and our lives generally. While their financial contribution is welcome, money doesn't make up for a lack of presence and love. And even though he'd never say it out loud, I know that Seth is feeling abandoned by them. I sense it, and if it were me in his position, I'd feel it too. I'm deeply resentful of their laissez-faire attitude and their ability to leave me holding this responsibility alone.

I'm also exhausted, which acts as confirmation that I've done the right thing in reducing my hours at work. The idea of doing that just to 'be there' for Seth was a naïve one, because the reality is that I would never have been able to keep working full time with everything I need to do for him. Not that I begrudge him any of it, and I know he'd do the same for me. It's just hard, because my life has changed so drastically and my career ambitions have been put on hold. I still fully believe I could handle the bigger contracts and that Craig is treating me unfairly in that respect, though, and I'm determined to get at least a couple of them back.

As these thoughts swirl in my mind, they stir a familiar set of emotions in me: sadness, resentment and a feeling of having a huge weight on my shoulders. Deciding they're the last thing I need to be carrying around today, especially when I'm facing an afternoon in the company of noxious Nick, I get to my feet, scraping the legs of the chair loudly across the floor as I do, and stride out of the cafe.

Resuming my walkabout, I reach a fork in the path I'm following and take a left while making a mental note to circle back and see what's along the other one later. I pass an enclosure of some docile-looking mammals called capybaras, which are native to Central and South America, one housing a type of New World porcupine (what a surprise that was, discovering that some porcupines climb trees!), and some fascinating beasts called okapis that look like a cross between a giraffe and a zebra. Then I reach an enclosure where, at first, I can't see anything at all. It's not as big as some of the others, but it's full of logs and branches, large rocks, and plenty of areas for climbing. Peering inside, there's still no sign of life, so I look for the information board that will tell me who's inside and what I need to be looking for. There isn't one, so I shrug and move on, crossing to another enclosure that, according to the sign, is housing an animal called a red panda.

Craning my neck, I spot a flash of colour behind a tree, but the occupier seems either shy or not in the mood for being stared at. Well, I don't blame them really. I'm not sure I would be so obliging of nosey humans myself. I'm about to give up and move on again when the red panda pops out from behind the tree and climbs onto a branch, giving me a front row view of it in its full glory.

'Look at you!' I cry with delight. 'You're the cutest, fluffiest little thing.'

I watch as the animal scopes me out, then gets up on its hind legs like a tiny little person and has a good sniff at a piece of vegetation next to it.

'Oh, you are just *adorable*,' I coo at it in what can only be described as a babyish voice. 'I can't get over how adorable you are. Can I take you home?'

'We don't allow that,' comes a gruff voice from behind me and my head shoots round in surprise.

To my dismay it's Nick, and he has clearly heard every word. Heat creeps through my body; I'm partly embarrassed at being caught behaving so unprofessionally, and partly irritated that he just *had* to be there at that moment.

'Well, obviously,' I snipe at him. 'I didn't really mean I wanted to take him home. It's a figure of speech.'

'It's a her, actually.'

'What?'

'It's a her.' He points to the red panda. 'That one's a female.'

'Right. Whatever.' I fold my arms and stare ahead, hoping he'll take the hint and go away.

'Are you always like this?' Nick's tone is as cutting as it was earlier. 'All I'm doing is telling you the sex of the animal and it's like I've mortally offended you.'

'No. I'm just not into small talk with men who hit on vulnerable women at hospitals, or treat them like shit when they turn up at their work.'

'Taking the moral high ground, that's predictable. You were acidic at the hospital when I was only being polite, and you had no choice but to play ball in that room earlier, because your job depends on it. I'm more than aware of what you really wanted to say to me.'

'Yeah, well, that makes two of us,' I spit back without looking round. 'Your boss shut you up before you could air what was really on your mind.'

'Right, well, I'd like to say it's been a pleasure, but it's been the opposite. I only came to find you to give you some overalls to change into and ask you to meet me at the elephant enclosure at one p.m. so I can follow through on my orders.' He dumps a bag of clothing down beside me.

I turn and give Nick a scathing look. 'Not so keen once you realise you've met your match, are you?'

'Pardon?' He screws up his face in confusion.

'You heard me. You're just another one of those guys who preys on weak women, because you can't handle one who's got it worked out.'

Nick stands there for a moment and it appears I've left him speechless. He turns and starts to walk away, then stops and faces me once more.

'One: if you had it "worked out", you wouldn't need to speak to me like that. And two: sorry, but you're just not my type.'

He strides off, leaving me standing there open-mouthed and utterly astonished as the now forgotten red panda continues to watch on in the background.

–

Following my altercation with Nick, I consider calling Craig and telling him I'm sick and I need to go home. Never have I done this, never have I even thought about doing it, but the thought of spending the next couple of days in Nick's company is about as unappealing as a baboon's arse (I visited their enclosure earlier and, my goodness, that is one hell of a rear end). But tempting as it is to do a bunk, especially when I'm already dealing with enough in my personal life, I'm aware it will make my work situation worse and Craig will lose even more faith in my ability to keep on top of things.

Instead, I spend my lunch break in the park's main restaurant looking up online articles with titles such as 'How to deal with difficult people' and 'So your co-worker's an arsehole'. Nick may have mocked me for taking the moral high ground, but I know that's exactly what I need to do: rise above this nonsense and yank on my 'professional hat' so hard it's stuck fast. Irate, reactive Jess can't be allowed to resurface or I'm going to end up in deep shit.

Once I've eaten my surprisingly tasty lunch of chicken enchiladas, which was on the house thanks to Gwen, I get changed into the overalls I've been given in the toilets. Then I exit the bright, airy canteen-style restaurant into the huge open outdoor seating area, which is half-covered to cater for those well-known Scottish rainy days. Consulting my map, I identify the direction I need to head in to find the elephants and Nick. I'm a little early so I amble along the path leisurely, enjoying the sights of the animals I missed by cutting my tour short after my run-in with him. On my way, I pass some larger enclosures, which are more like fields. They're home to grazing animals such as zebras, gazelles, impalas and giraffes, some of which are sharing the same space quite harmoniously.

I stop and admire the giraffes for some time, these having always been favourites of mine. It's the combination of their majestic height, their curious features and the gentleness of their demeanour that gets me every time. The elders of the group stand regally, watching on as the younger giraffes cavort around in play. It's so mesmerising and calming, by the time I move on to meet my Nick-shaped fate, I'm in a far better mood.

Arriving at the elephant enclosure, I don't find Nick at first, nor do I see any elephants. However, there appears to be an indoor area connected to the outdoor enclosure, so I walk inside and the first thing I notice is the smell.

'Oh man, that's awful.' I cough and pinch my nose with my fingers, then focus my attention on the three elephants in front of me who are feeding on hay or grass or something from rope nets hanging from a height. 'You lot are truly charming, but gosh do you produce some smell.'

'So would you if you had to shit where you sleep.'

Ah, Nick, you know just how to wind me up. I turn and see him skulking behind me once again.

'Do you make a habit of sneaking up on people?' I ask.

'Not really.' He shrugs. 'Do you make a habit of talking to things that can't talk back to you?'

I inwardly curse at him and force a smile to trick my brain into thinking I'm fine.

'I like to think they can understand me.'

'Well, they can't.'

I purse my lips. 'How do you know? Have you ever been an elephant?'

'No, but I do have an understanding of science.'

I feel my hackles rise again and realise that we're already off down the same slippery slope I've only just climbed back up. This can't happen again. OK, what did I just read in those articles... deep breaths, count to ten, imagine him naked. No, wait, that's for when I'm nervous about something. Though I bet he doesn't look half bad naked. Dammit, this is not working.

'You all right there?' Nick raises an infuriating eyebrow and I'm sure I can detect a hint of a smile in his eyes, making me feel like he's just read my mind.

'I'm *fine*,' I say a little too firmly. 'Let's just get on with this, yeah?'

'OK then. Come with me.'

He leads me through a door into an area that's out of bounds to the public. It's filled with more nets of hay-like stuff, obviously ready to be put out when the current supply runs out, as well as cleaning equipment and other items I'm not familiar with.

'You said you were happy to get your hands dirty,' says Nick as he hands me a heavy implement that looks like a cross between a rake and a spade. 'So, I thought you could help me clear out the enclosure.'

I try and fail to hide my horror at this statement. 'You want me to go in there? Is it safe? I know elephants are meant to be quite tame, but I'm not sure I want to put that to the test.'

'We'll do one side of the enclosure at a time. They'll be quite far away from us and I expect they'll go outside soon too. They tend to do so after a feed.'

Nick unlocks a door leading into the enclosure and signals for me to go ahead of him.

'Right.' I peer through the doorway to check it is indeed safe before walking through it. 'And you want me to clear away the hay and branches on the ground?'

'No, that's food. I want you to scoop up the elephant poop.'

My eyes dart to Nick's face, looking for the amusement that should follow a quip like that, but there is none.

'You are joking.'

'Why would I be joking?' He actually seems perplexed by my reaction. 'We're working with animals here. They need their enclosures cleaned out. It's a big part of the job.'

'Surely there are other parts to the job that you could show me.' I place my hands on my hips in defiance.

'Yes, and we'll get to those. But this is the scheduled task for this afternoon and I'm a staff member down due to sickness, so this is where we start. I'll be doing it with you. There's a bucket over there that you drop it into.'

Resigned to my fate, I walk across to the first pile of elephant poo and look away as I try to scoop it up, but not having eyes on it is a mistake and a blob comes free as I try to manoeuvre it into the bucket.

'Arghh… it's on my foot,' I wail as I desperately shake it off and stare miserably at the brown mark remaining on my shoe.

I hear Nick stifle a laugh and my despair quickly turns into anger. This is all a little too convenient for my liking. Nick has it in for me, all because I wounded his ego a couple of months ago. This, quite literally, smells like putrid revenge. And I'm having none of it.

'You just couldn't help yourself, could you?' I finally lose my calm.

'I'm sorry?' Nick narrows his eyes at me. 'I didn't mean to laugh, but you are making a drama out of nothing.'

'Not that. I mean this whole thing. This isn't the scheduled task for the afternoon, this is you getting back at me. At least be man enough to admit it. I may be in a difficult position here because I'm representing my company, but I'm not going to allow you to make a mockery of me.'

'Jess, I'm not—'

'Save it, Nick, I'm not interested. I'm going to speak to Gwen.'

Throwing down the rake-slash-spade with a clatter, I march straight out of the enclosure.

Chapter 8

As I storm through the wildlife park in search of Gwen, every cell within me is fuming at Nick's audacity in using this situation to his advantage. Although I'm not entirely sure what I'm going to say when I find her, all I know is that I can't work with that man. He clearly has no moral compass, and while I haven't exactly behaved well myself, it's because he has continually pressed my buttons along the way. I'm well aware that as a professional, I should be able to rise above this and get on with my job, but sometimes it just comes down to the fact that some people are impossible work with.

Hurrying past what I recognise to be the red panda enclosure, I hear what I think is my name being called out. Stopping in my tracks, I lift my head and listen, then immediately regret doing so as Nick canters round the bend in the path behind me.

'Jess, wait.' He comes to a halt, looking a bit puffed and a lot stressed. 'Please don't go to Gwen with this.'

'Why not?' I attempt to stare him down. 'Worried you'll get sacked? Give me one good reason why I shouldn't tell her everything.'

'Because you're going to make a fool of yourself.'

'*Excuse me?* And how exactly am I going to do that?'

Nick runs a hand through his dishevelled dark brown hair, clearly perturbed. 'Because, God's honest truth, I didn't set that situation up. You jumped to the wrong conclusion, and all it will take is for Gwen to look at the staff roster and the cleaning schedule to realise that's what you've done.'

I continue to eyeball him, weighing up whether to believe his story. 'I could see in the meeting earlier that you're not exactly in Gwen's good books. How do I know you're not just saying this to avoid getting in deeper than you already are?'

'I guess you don't. I'm asking you to trust me.'

I snort with derision. 'Are you kidding me? I couldn't trust you as far as I could throw you with that bloody great dung rake you made me use. All you're doing is trying to cover your backside.'

I start to walk away again but Nick's words stop me.

'What is it that makes you so sure of that?' His tone is exasperated. 'Why do you have me pegged as this awful guy?'

'Because you've given me no reason to think anything—'

'Haven't I, Jess?' He walks right up to me so our faces are inches apart, and despite myself, I can't help noticing his dark espresso-coloured eyes and how his days-old stubble accentuates his already well-defined jawline. 'What happened in that hospital car park?'

'You hit on me.'

'No, what *really* happened? What are the facts?'

'Oh, I'm not doing this,' I scoff.

'Why not? Could it be because if you really think about it, you'll realise I did nothing wrong? That maybe you overreacted because you were already upset?'

'Do *not* pull the "hysterical woman" excuse with me.' I'm back to fizzing mad in an instant. 'I don't know what makes men like you think you can—'

'Jess, *stop*,' Nick assumes a commanding voice that shocks me into silence, then he softens his tone straight away. 'Please. You've got this all wrong. And not because you're a woman or you're emotional or anything like that. It's because you're human and things get lost in translation. And I haven't helped.'

'No arguments on that one,' I mutter, but I allow him to continue while staring into the empty enclosure I was curious about earlier.

'Thank you.' Nick acknowledges my climb down with evident relief. 'Look, at the hospital that day, I know how you think it went down. And on reflection, maybe offering to buy you a coffee did seem like I was hitting on you. But I assure you, I wasn't. When I walked past and saw you there, looking so broken, it reminded me of how my sister was the day our dad died of a heart attack...' He trails off and I look round at him, finally realising my error.

'Nick, shit, I'm... I don't—'

'It's OK.' He holds up a hand that's clearly intended as a gesture of peace. 'You don't need to say anything. You didn't know and I'm not looking for sympathy. It was a long time ago. I'm just trying to explain where I was coming from. When I saw you there, I guess the protective big brother came out in me and I wanted to help, but somehow, I got it wrong. I often get these things wrong.' He grimaces and seems to wrestle with himself internally for a second.

I glance back at the empty enclosure then turn to face him properly. 'So you weren't hitting on me? You really were just being a good citizen, and I balled you out?'

'Um... yeah. That's about the size of it.'

'And then when I walked into your workplace this morning – no surprises – you weren't exactly pleased to see me.'

'Correct again.' He gives an almost apologetic nod. 'All I saw was this judgemental woman who made a BS assumption about me. I guess I felt a bit emasculated, too. From being shouted down, and also because you've come to fix a problem we can't seem to fix on our own.'

On hearing this, the tension in my jaw subsides and my guard finally drops. 'When you put it like that, I guess I can see it from your side. Though this male pride thing...?'

'I know. You don't need to tell me. Not a good look.'

'You're right, it's not.' I fiddle with my watch awkwardly. 'And neither is ball-breaking a bloke who was only trying to help. I'm sorry for how I reacted at the hospital. Though I would suggest that you work on your approach if you want to play the shoulder to cry on.'

'I won't be doing that again, I assure you.' His expression tells me that he's dead certain about this.

'Oh no, I've broken you.' I put a guilty hand to my mouth.

'It's not you. I'm generally not a natural at that stuff. So, can we start again?'

I reach out my hand jovially in place of a verbal response, and as he smiles and shakes it, I feel a tingly sensation spread through my body. This is closely followed by an involuntary thought of what it would be like to kiss him, and I jolt with surprise.

'Are you OK?' Nick looks at me curiously as he lets go of my hand.

'Um… yes… yes, I'm good. Just relieved that I never followed through on going to Gwen. That would have been a career killer – she would have thought I was a paranoid lunatic.'

'I don't think so. She's a pussycat really. I just didn't want this to become a thing, because she might have become concerned enough to contact your boss. Not sure it would have done any major damage though.'

'Ha. You don't know the half of it.' I raise my eyes to the sky. 'I'm not exactly the shining star of my company right now.'

'Is that right? Well, maybe if you turn this place around, your glory will be restored.'

'I'd say that's wishful thinking. But I am going to find my way back, and however I do that, it definitely shouldn't involve creating a massive hoo-ha in this place.'

'Understood.' Nick's eyes crinkle with amusement. 'Well, how about we keep things on track and go and deal with that elephant poo?'

I wrinkle my nose in distaste. 'Sure… if we must. Oh, by the way, is there actually anything in there?' I point to the seemingly empty enclosure.

'Not at the moment. I've been getting the place ready. But there will be tomorrow. You'll be helping me, and I promise you – that part of the job, you're going to love.'

–

The afternoon passes quickly, despite me gagging and feeling like I'm going to throw up with every piece of elephant excrement I deposit in the bucket. The small mercy in the whole experience is that, after we've cleaned out the enclosure, Nick takes me to the outdoor area where the elephants are now hanging out, and we feed them apples over the wall as they use their trunks like arms to take them from us. I whoop with delight every time one of them reaches across and plucks one out of my grip, then plonks it into their mouth whole. Nick seems to have an amazing connection with the elephants and knows each of them individually by name.

'So that's Flora.' He points to them one by one. 'Then there's Zooey, Tomakin, Baboo and Elias.'

'It's amazing that you can tell them apart.' I squint at them, trying to clock some identifying features. 'They all look really similar to me.'

'They're actually quite different. It's about getting to know them: their personalities as well as their different physical characteristics. Tomakin's the head of the pack. He pushes the younger males around, keeps them in line, while Flora is like the matriarch. She's the only one who can give Tomakin a good rollocking if she thinks he's overplaying his hand. And Baboo's a bit of a wido. He's young and arrogant, will maybe take over the pack from Tomakin one day, but Tomakin won't let go easily and he really puts Baboo in his place.'

'Gosh, it's riveting.' I clasp my hands with intrigue. 'Like a daytime soap.'

Nick shrugs. 'We're not so different. Just animals ourselves really, only further evolved. Though I do wonder if we've come that far when I watch all the bad stuff on the news, like wars and terrorism and power plays by authoritarian governments.'

'Or women who go nuts at you when you're only trying to help.' I offer him an embarrassed smile.

'Yeah, that. Or guys who take the hump when their egos get wounded.' He gives me a side glance and I smile.

'Yeah, maybe we aren't that much more evolved than our chimp ancestors. That's who we descend from, right?'

He shakes his head. 'No, that's a common misunderstanding. But we do share a common ancestor with them from about ten million years ago.'

'Now that I did not know. This is like being on a school trip. Except I don't have a quarter bottle of vodka stashed in my bag.'

Nick laughs at this.

'So what do you think the downfall of humanity will be then?' I ask. 'Seeing as we're sort of on the subject.'

'Greed and narcissism. No question. The way the world is so connected these days, I think it's a really sad thing that we can't all work together to solve the big issues that we share – like climate change and protecting the world's biodiversity. Then these guys would have a chance in the wild.' He gestures to the elephants, who are still huddled together in front of us, swaying their trunks hopefully, despite us having run out of apples. 'It's all so self-serving and political.'

'It's depressing for sure.'

'You may judge this as a bit sad, but I much prefer spending time with animals over people if I'm honest. The thing I like least about humans is the disingenuity and the game playing. You never really know where you're at – unless it's someone you know and trust. These guys… they're way less complicated.'

Nick's face seems to cloud as he says this and for a moment I wonder if he's referring again to our misunderstanding, but there's something in his demeanour that makes me think it cuts way deeper than our surface-level feud. And interestingly, after spending the last several hours detesting and avoiding this man, I kind of want to know what it is.

Chapter 9

By the time I'm driving home that evening, I feel like I've been on work experience. After our stint with the elephants, Nick let me sit in on a vet's consultation with a sick (and very rare) tropical frog that the whole park team are desperately hoping will pull through. Then we joined one of Nick's team members while he oversaw the defining moment of the blue-crowned laughingthrush breeding programme through a thick paned window. This involved ensuring the exact right conditions were created to encourage the handpicked couple to 'get it on', and while I'd like to be mature and call it a moment of true beauty when they did, I couldn't help blushing and babbling through the main event like an awkward teenager watching a sex scene with her parents.

Whizzing back along the A1 and into the Edinburgh city limits, my brain pores over the thoughts that are continually taking up the biggest space in my mind: Seth's recovery and my work situation. The former, while it troubles me deeply, is largely out of my control. I desperately want my brother to fight his way back to the life he had before his stroke, but the reality is that will never happen. Though I'm not sure Seth has accepted that yet, and if it keeps him going, then I see no reason to insist on bursting his bubble. All I can do is give him what he needs to keep going – unconditional support, love and encouragement – while making sure he eats well and gets enough sleep and social stimulation. The rest is up to the experts and they seem to have everything covered.

My work situation, on the other hand, is less straightforward. While I had an enjoyable and somewhat 'escapist' day at the wildlife park – my unfortunate confrontation with Nick aside – it really isn't the type of work project that's going to set me alight. I can already see where their opportunities lie, and once I've done the brainstorming bit and sorted them out with some regular events to boost their revenue and take them out of the red, I'll be thirsty for my next challenge.

'Hey, Seth. How's your day been?' I greet my brother, who's glued to a reality TV series when I arrive home.

He barely acknowledges my arrival, so I see his new carer, Jackson, to the door.

'How's he been?' I ask. 'I was concerned about leaving him all day.'

'He's been in good form,' Jackson nods in acknowledgement of his own statement, his hazel eyes emitting a warmth that runs right through his character. 'Though I had to divert his attention once or twice when he asked if we could go out for a pint. Think we'll get on just fine.'

'That is so Seth.' I chuckle.

I know from the open and friendly conversation we had during his interview that Jackson is widowed with two 'adult children', as he put it: two daughters who are apparently close in age to Seth and I. He's in his mid-fifties, but he has the looks and energy of someone much younger. Not a grey hair in sight either. This I'm impressed by, given it sounds like he's had a lot to deal with in his life, and I'm already exhausted from just a few days of caring for my brother.

'If he's already inviting you out for a pint, it means he likes you,' I add. 'Sees you as one of his bros.'

'I got that. He's quite the character. Maybe one day we'll actually do that – even if it's alcohol free. I'm sure it would help him feel like he's living more of a "normal" life, but not until he's come on a bit further.'

'Well, I'm glad to hear that it looks like it will work out between the two of you. Thanks for everything, and see you tomorrow.'

I close the door behind Jackson and return to the living room for a second attempt at gaining my brother's attention.

'What do you fancy for dinner?' I ask him. 'You have the choice of spaghetti bolognese or chicken stroganoff.'

Seth continues to stare at the TV, mesmerised by the goings-on.

'Earth to Seth…' I wave in his line of vision.

'Huh…?' He finally snaps out of his semi-hypnosis and uses his working arm to fumble with the remote and pause the show he's watching. 'Oh… hi… sis.'

'Hi, nice to see you, Jess. How was your day?' I rib him sarcastically. 'I see nothing's changed with your TV habits anyway. You still have the full and rather irritating ability to completely block everyone out.'

'Aww… sis. I've… lost… so… much. Please… don't… try… to… take… that… from… me… too.'

'All right, cheeky.' I shake my head at him as he laughs at his own joke. 'Dinner. What's it to be?'

'Um… sp… spagh-ett-i.'

'So you did hear me after all?'

'No. I… was… bored… and… I… checked… what… was… in… the… fridge. Dinner… is… the… high… high-light… of… my… day… you… know.'

'I know.' I turn my face away to hide the pained smile that instinctively forms on it.

Seth is doing fine. Of course he is. He's Seth. He can cope with pretty much anything without it getting to him too much. But it pains me to see my strapping big brother more or less a prisoner in his own home – and his own body. His friendship group have been great. They visited him many times in hospital and a couple of them have already been round to my flat to see him, but the fact that he can't join them and has to spend three days a week hanging out with a carer kills me a little bit.

'What's… up?' Seth is looking at me curiously.

'With me? Nothing. Tough day is all. I'll leave you to your programme. Dinner will be in half an hour.'

Once I've prepared our food, I keep mine in the oven while I help Seth eat his. It's a slow process with his motor skills still being quite uncoordinated and the swallowing issues he's been left with. It also doesn't help that he seems more interested in hearing about my day now that his attention is away from the television.

'The… wil… wild-life… park… sounds… fun. Why… was… it… a… tough… day?'

I hesitate, cursing myself for sharing that. Seth knows nothing of my troubles at work and I'm determined to keep it that way. Much as he's laid-back about his own life, he would be upset to think that mine has been limited because of him. He'd insist on me going back to work full time and him having a carer five days a week and I simply couldn't allow that to happen.

'Oh, it was just something that happened there. Not important at all.'

'Tell… me.'

'Honestly, Seth. It's not that interesting.'

Seth's eyebrows knit together and he stops eating. 'Jess… are… you… going… to… do… this… for-ever?'

'Wh… what do you mean?' I stammer guiltily.

'Are… you… going… to… ba-by… me… be-cause… I'm… like… this?'

'I'm not babying you.'

'Yes… you… are.' Seth looks at me meaningfully. 'The… sister… I… know… tells… me… ev… ev-ery-thing. She… shares… the… good… and… the… bad.'

'I share stuff with you,' I protest.

'Yeah… insig-nifi-cant… stuff. You… would… always… chew… my… ear… off… about… things… at… work. Espe-cia-lly… when… you… didn't… get… a… project… you…

62

wanted... or... someone... ann-oyed... you. But... now... sudden-ly... this... stuff... does-n't... matter? I'm... recov-ering... from... an... illness... Jess... not... stupid... or... weak.'

This faltering tirade hits me square in the heart and guilt pools in parts of my body I didn't know I could feel it. By trying to protect my big brother from the things he shouldn't have to worry about, I've made him feel like he's a lesser being. This realisation leaves me conflicted, because he's right, I shouldn't treat him differently because of what happened to him and how he is now. But my instinct to protect him is so strong. As much as it pains me to be a bit disingenuous, I can only give so far on this one. I let out a loaded sigh.

'Seth, I'm sorry. You're right. I don't mean it to come across as me babying you, but I am protective of you. And you would be the same if it were the other way around, right?'

He considers this and shrugs. 'I... guess. But... I... am... telling... you... I... don't... want... it... this... way. If... I... can't... exp-eri-ence... the... ups... and... downs... of... real... life... myself, at... least... let... me... do... it... through... you.'

'That's fair. I'll tell you about my day then.'

He seems satisfied with this and starts eating again, which allows me time to quickly work out in my mind how I can share the frustrations of my day, without giving away what's really at the root of them.

'Go... on... then,' he prompts me eventually, clearly impa-tient to hear the 'juice'.

'OK... so, my boss, Craig—'

'The... guy... who... dresses... like... a... mafia... man.'

'Yes, that's him.' I giggle. 'He's put me on this project at the wildlife park that I really don't want to do. You know that I like to do the biggest, most high-profile events, right?'

'No... you've... never... men-tioned... that.'

'Hoi.' I swipe at him playfully and he grins back at me cheekily. 'Anyway, the wildlife park is failing and they want to find a new revenue stream…' I fill Seth in on the background of the park's plight.

'So… you… don't… want… this… project… because… it's… not… high… profile… enough?' he asks.

'Yes. It and the other small fry projects Craig's now giving me will look rubbish on my CV.'

'Then… don't… put… them… on… your… CV.'

'Well, it's not that simple…' I realise I'm about to stray into territory I don't want to enter. 'Never mind. The reason I had a tough day wasn't really about the project itself. It was more an interpersonal issue.'

'Did… you… kick… off… at… one… of… the… park… staff?'

'How did you guess?' I give a shamefaced smile.

'Be-cause… I've… noticed… you've… had… a… shorter… fuse… than… usual… rec-ently… and… it… might… affect… you… at… work.' He reaches out and nudges me with his better arm. 'Who… was… he… and… what… did… he… do?'

'How did you know it was a bloke?'

'It's… normally… a… bloke, and… you… cl… clear-ly… fancy… him.'

'What? No, I don't.' I feel my cheeks flame at this statement. 'He's so not my type, and I'm not his either. He even said so himself.'

'Guys… always… say… that… when… they… like… a… woman… and… she's… re-jec-ted… them. It's… pra…prac-ti-cally… bloke… 101. You've… re-jec-ted… him… right?'

'No, I haven't.' I think back to the hospital car park and flush deeply.

'Wow… you… have. This… is… better… drama… than… my… TV… show. Tell… me… the… whole… story.'

'OK, but let me grab my dinner first.' I get up, clearing Seth's now empty plate away, and head for the kitchen.

As I potter around, getting myself a drink and some cutlery, my mind defiantly ticks over what Seth's just said. I do not like

Nick in that way. I barely even know the guy, and he's not my type either. He might be quite attractive if you forget the fact that he's all gruff and antisocial and covered in animal faeces (at work anyway). My normal type couldn't be more different: well groomed, well dressed, the life and soul to match my extrovert personality. That's the kind of guy I'm drawn to.

No. Nick and I just need to get on, so that I can get through this contract without doing any further damage to my career. That's all. We'll be civil, maybe even friendly towards each other, but once the work is done and the park is back on track, I'm sure we'll be more than happy to go our separate ways: me back to the land of sophisticated events with VIP tents, and him to his beloved world of dung-filled animal pens.

Carrying my dinner through to join Seth again, this is solid and clear in my mind. I don't like Nick that way, nor do I have time for dating right now with everything that's going on. This project is nothing more than a temporary and unsolicited diversion for me.

Chapter 10

The next morning, after spending the late evening poring over employment law websites, I've come to the conclusion that not only is Craig being unfair, I think he might also be discriminating against me. Though it seems that's hard to prove – he'd essentially have to admit it, because he's using the excuse that the big contracts need someone full time on them otherwise it will be detrimental to the business. The only way for me to disprove that is to show that I can successfully manage those contracts in my part-time hours. And, of course, he won't allow me that opportunity. While I'm pretty pissed at him, I'm unwilling to kick that can to the point he decides I'm more hassle than I'm worth. Unfortunately, for now, it seems I have no options in that respect. I need to think of something else before Isla and Ravi get too comfortable running my projects.

Arriving at the wildlife park at nine a.m., I meet Lauren in the park office for an overview of her and her team's responsibilities. Though my priority is getting a feel for the customer-facing side of things, it will be useful to understand their skills and capabilities and how much I'll need to teach them – and the rest of the team – about running their own events. Her comprehensive tour of the office includes introducing me to each of her team members, all of whom seemed to regard me with some suspicion, as if I'm here to steal their jobs away, rather than help save them.

'And that's pretty much it,' Lauren concludes with a sweep of her arm.

'This has been so helpful, thank you.' I look around the room one more time, trying to commit everything she's told me to memory. 'You seem to be very well-versed in everything that goes on. How long have you worked here?'

I ask this because she seems very young for an office manager.

'Basically since the park opened,' she replies. 'I started working here part time doing admin when I was at school. Gwen is my mum.'

'You're kidding. I would never have guessed that.'

Though the position she's in now makes sense. She's had a head start with her skill set. I squint at her, trying to find any trace of a family resemblance, but with Lauren's slight frame, delicate facial structure and thick curly red hair there is none. Gwen is much sturdier looking, with harder features.

'I look more like my dad,' says Lauren, and I have to swallow down a laugh as my mind unhelpfully conjures up the image of a petite Little Red Riding Hood-like man being swept off his feet by Gwen.

'Right. And does your dad work here too?'

'No, he and mum are divorced.'

'I'm sorry, I didn't mean to pry.'

'Don't be.' She smiles at me kindly. 'It's way better that way. So, what's the deal with you and Nick?'

I was waiting for this. In fact, I'm surprised that Gwen hasn't yet hauled me aside and asked me the same question. Perhaps she's done so with Nick instead.

'Oh, nothing.' I keep my tone breezy. 'We met briefly by chance and had a bit of a misunderstanding. It's all sorted now. I don't really know him.'

'I see.' She nods reflectively, as if she doesn't quite believe me. 'We wondered if you were exes or something. It certainly seemed that way.'

'Who's we?' I raise a curious eyebrow.

'The rest of the management team. Excluding Nick and Gwen, of course.'

Great. We've managed to become the talk of the park, thanks to Nick's lack of self-control. Not the look I want when I'm trying to earn the trust and respect of the leaders here – and with Lauren being Gwen's daughter, it's unlikely that gossip will stay off her radar.

'I assure you, Lauren, there's nothing to be concerned about. Nick and I are on good terms now we've untangled our crossed wires, and I'm here purely in a professional capacity. I prefer to keep my work life and my dating life separate.'

To my surprise, Lauren leans in conspiratorially as one of her team members passes us, giving me the evil eye.

'We were actually sort of hoping there was something going on,' she says in a low voice. 'Nick's been on his own for too long. Hasn't been the same since his wife left him.'

'Oh… right.' I'm not sure how to react to this information. 'Well, as I say, I barely know him.'

'Maybe you should get to know him then.' She gives me a mischievous wink. 'He may be a bit grubby-looking from the work he does around the park, but I assure you, what's under those overalls is far more impressive.'

Dumbfounded by this comment, I emit a snort of laughter, which I quickly cover up with a cough when all eyes in the office land on me.

'Are you sure you and Nick aren't the ones with something going on?' I surmise.

'No, definitely not.' Lauren bats my question away. 'We spend a lot of time at this place, and on the few hot days we get in the summer, we normally have a barbeque after hours. I've seen Nick with his top off, that's all. And he's buff.' She reaches up and flexes her biceps.

Heat creeps up my neck as it did the evening before when Seth was questioning me about Nick – which in both cases has far more to do with the scrutiny on me, than my feelings towards him. No one likes to be verbally poked and prodded about a potential love interest, especially when other people are making a meal out of something that's not there.

Sidestepping the inappropriateness of Lauren's comments, I simply respond, 'Right, well, thanks for the tour.' I get up from the desk I'm perched on. 'I've got a tour of the catering facilities next, so I'd better get moving.'

'No probs.'

Lauren smiles brightly at me and I detect a glimmer of something mischievous and calculating in her eyes. This unnerves me slightly, because I know exactly what it's about. By mentioning that I keep work and dating separate, I've inadvertently let her know that I'm single, and the last thing I need when I'm trying to work is her and her merry band of fellow managers playing matchmaker.

-

My tour of the park's catering outfit is very useful, because it helps me understand the existing food and beverage options, as well as the potential for branching out and creating new menus if the events would benefit from these. Serge, the catering manager, is a jovial man with a (bad) joke for every occasion and I warm to him immediately. He's noisy and happy and affable – exactly the type of person I like to work with in my job.

After he's finished showing me round, Serge insists on feeding me lunch before I head off to spend the afternoon with Nick. Having had the enchiladas the day before, I opt for the park's signature burger, which is topped with bacon and halloumi and guaranteed to give me a dose of heartburn. It is, nonetheless, delicious.

'Do I, or do I not, make the best burger in East Lothian?' Serge demands of me.

Having never eaten a burger in East Lothian, this is an easy question for me to answer.

'Number one on my list. No question.' I supplement this feedback with the universal hand gesture for 'top notch'.

'And best in whole of Scotland?'

I bob my head from side while I contemplate this. 'OK, I'll give you it. I don't remember having anything significantly better.'

'*Yes!*' He punches the air with his fist and strides back to the kitchen, singing something upbeat in a language I don't recognise.

After I've eaten, I make my way to the same building the vet consultation with the rare tropical frog took place in yesterday – I sincerely hope it's recovering and that it hasn't croaked overnight (hmmm… perhaps my jokes aren't much better than Serge's). Pulling open the door to the animal hospital, as it's known here, I walk inside and make my presence known, as Nick could be in any of the four rooms.

'Hey, Nick, I'm here.'

Hearing a noisy rustling coming from room one, I'm about to open the door when he replies from elsewhere.

'In room three,' he hollers and I enter the room the frog was being treated in the day before.

He's bent over, looking intently into the tank.

'How's Violet doing?' I ask, biting my lip in anticipation of the answer in case it's bad news.

Violet is named after Violet Beauregarde from *Charlie and the Chocolate Factory* – the character who turned blue and inflated into a giant ball – because she's a bright blue poison dart frog and she's quite demanding in nature (so I'm told – I'm not really sure how a frog can be demanding).

'She's improving, thankfully,' he says. 'Starting to move around her tank again, but she's still a bit sluggish.'

'Oh, that's good news.' I join him by the tank and peer inside at Violet, who indeed is more active than the previous day. 'She does look more… froggish.'

'Froggish?' Nick gives me a funny look.

'I couldn't say "human", could I? I was looking for a similar turn of phrase.'

'Fair enough. How was your morning?'

'It was good, thanks.' My conversation with Lauren suddenly pops into my mind and I feel myself colour, so I turn away and pretend to be interested in the contents of the room. 'I got what I needed. Serge is fun.'

'He's certainly high energy.' Nick's still watching Violet's every move.

'Is that code for high maintenance?'

'No. If I think someone's high maintenance, I'll say they're high maintenance. Serge's a good guy, but I always feel exhausted and a little deafened in his company.'

I put a hand to my mouth to cover up a smirk. 'I guess I can understand that. Especially when you prefer the company of those who don't talk back, as you've mentioned. I didn't realise Lauren is Gwen's daughter. How does that dynamic play out here?'

Nick finally turns away from the tank and faces me. 'Someone's fishing this morning.'

'I'm not "fishing", I'm interested.'

'That's code for fishing.'

I'm about to protest my innocence, when Nick holds up a calming hand.

'Hey, I'm messing. Lauren's cool. There are no bad politics, if that's what you're wondering. Obviously, she got the job because of who she is, but she's good at it, if a little inexperienced.'

'That was all I wanted to know.' I give Nick my beady eye so he's clear I'm not a gossip. 'It's important that I get a feel for how you all work together as well as how the park operates.'

'Sure, whatever.' He shrugs in a way that leaves me wondering where he's at with my statement.

'So, what are we doing today?'

I'm keen to move the conversation on, not least because I'm feeling judged – and I don't know whether that's because I am being judged, or because Nick's demeanour brings out a level of insecurity in me.

71

'Today, we'll be working with the park's newest resident.'

'Which is?'

'You'll find out in a moment.'

He potters around, clearing away some bits and pieces, then beckons for me to follow him out of the room. I trail behind him into the corridor, where he stops and puts a finger to his lips. The rustling I heard when I first arrived is louder than before.

'Is that the new animal?'

'It is,' Nick confirms with a nod. 'I think you're going to like her.'

'Great, well, go on then.' I attempt to hurry him along.

'OK. One more thing before we go in. She's very timid, so you need to be calm and gentle around her.'

'Noted. Let's go.'

'Patient one, aren't you?' He gives me what appears to be a judgemental look, which I don't particularly appreciate.

'You don't get anywhere in life by being patient,' I snipe back at him. 'If I were patient, I'd lose every contract to my competitors, and I'd never produce the quality of events that have our clients returning to us year on year.'

'All right, it was just a joke.'

'Sorry, I missed that.' I smile sweetly at him. 'Maybe you need to work on your delivery.'

Nick shakes his head, clearly thinking that he never knows where he's at with me. Well, ditto, mate.

He holds a finger up to his lips and we creep inside the room. The rustling is louder for a moment, and then it stops completely. From behind Nick I can't see much at first, then he steps aside and looks to me for my reaction as I get my first sight of the park's newest resident.

She's a tiny little bear cub – probably not more than a few months old – with short dark brown fur and a caramel-coloured face and snout. She has oversized paws as young animals often do, with sharp-looking claws, and another caramel-coloured patch at the top of her chest that makes it look like she's wearing a collar. As she gazes up at us, her chocolate brown eyes wary of our approach, I feel my heart melt into a puddle.

'Oh my goodness, she's absolutely adorable,' I whisper. 'What kind of bear is she?'

'She's a sun bear,' says Nick. 'Her name is Rana.'

'I don't think I've ever seen anything so cute. Hello, Rana.' I adopt my talking-to-cute-animals-and-babies-voice, then I move a little closer to the cage she's in and crouch down. 'Aren't you just beautiful? Oh yes, you are.'

'I'm assuming you don't use that voice to get contracts either.'

'Wheesht, you.' I fire a look up at him. 'This little one looks like she needs a bit of love.'

'That's interesting. I thought I was the animal expert in the room.'

'Really?' I turn and this time he gets my full glare.

'I was only saying.'

'Well, don't. Tell me about her instead.'

Nick crouches down next to me, giving me a waft of his delicious eau de toilette as he does, and I have to remind myself that any bloke can make themselves smell good. A nice aroma may cover up the smell of animals, but it doesn't fix an annoying personality.

'She's come to us from a wildlife park down south that's just gone bankrupt. Her mother had a problem during delivery and died, along with Rana's only sibling, so she's an orphan unfortunately.'

'That's dreadful.' My hand goes to my mouth in horror. 'Poor little thing. I assume she can't ever be let into the wild?'

He shakes his head. 'No, she's been bred in captivity so she'll spend her life here, but we'll make it as fulfilling as possible for her. If she were in the wild, she'd face all sorts of threats, so she'll at least be safer with us.'

'You mean poachers and loss of habitat? Gwen mentioned that yesterday.'

'That's right.'

Nick goes on to explain that sun bears are severely endangered and that their numbers in the wild are estimated to have fallen by about a third in the last three decades due to threats such as deforestation, hunting and poaching. He tells me how, in some countries, the captured bears are kept in illegal bear farms, often in tiny cages and squalid conditions, and how their digestive fluid is harvested for traditional Asian medical practices. I'm left feeling shocked and outraged at this awful behaviour.

'I guess it's good she's at least safe then.' I find myself blinking back tears as I watch her cowering in her cage. 'Will she always be alone?'

'No, we'll look for a mate to introduce to her to when she's a bit older and we'll try to breed her to support conservation efforts.'

'So, she might end up having a family in years to come?'

'Yes. That is the plan. Though it's not quite the same as how humans do it.' The corners of Nick's mouth curl up in amusement.

'I know that.' I frown at him. 'It's just so sad. I want her to have a good future.'

Staring through the bars of the cage at little Rana, who's now having a sniff at us from the safety of the opposite side, a thought comes to me.

'What happens to Rana if this place ends up closing like the other park did?'

'We'll look to rehome her to. Don't worry, she won't be put down or anything, she'll be in high demand,' he reassures me. 'But some of our animals might not be so lucky.'

'Gosh, that must be a worry for you.'

'It is. That's why you're here. Anyway, you fancy a cuddle?'

'I can hold her?' My eyes light up.

Nick smiles at me. 'Probably not so much hold her as have her climb all over you. We can see if she'll come to you when we take her outside. That's our project for the afternoon, it's time to introduce Rana to her new enclosure.'

'Ah, the empty one along from the red pandas?'

'That's right. We'll get her into a smaller carry cage to move her. Are you ready?'

'Am I ever,' I declare with delight while thanking my lucky stars my afternoon will not be spent scooping up animal poo.

Chapter 11

Nick has to draft in one of his team members to help him get Rana into the carry cage, while I watch from the other side of the room. It's clear that the experience is stressing the bear cub and my instincts are to cry out at them to be gentle with her, but I keep my mouth shut, because they know what they're doing – and as Nick quite rightly (and a bit rudely) pointed out before, they're the experts, not me.

A short while later, I wait outside the enclosure while Nick and his colleague haul the cage inside and open the gate to allow Rana to leave it. I had expected her to make a quick bid for freedom, especially as the enclosure is far bigger and more interesting than where she was being kept before, but instead she cowers inside.

'Now it's a waiting game.' Nick appears beside me, gesturing to a bench that will allow us to keep an eye on Rana's progress in relative comfort.

'It must be scary for her, all this moving around.' I take a seat and he joins me.

'It's unsettling for her, which is why I was keen to get her out here as quickly as possible. This is where she'll grow her confidence before she's moved into a larger enclosure around November time, and then a full-sized one next summer.'

'Oh, so she'll move again?'

'She'll have to.' Nick gives an earnest nod. 'She'll eventually grow to about four to four and a half feet long and she'll need a lot more space.'

'There was me hoping she would stay all dinky and cute forever.' I sigh.

'Where do you get your knowledge of the natural world? Disney movies?'

I crease my brow at this unnecessary comment. 'No. Obviously I know she's going to grow bigger.'

'Not only that, she'll be able to rip you to pieces.'

'OK, thanks for that. Now you've really burst my bubble.'

'It's the reality of the situation, I'm afraid.' Nick sits back and crosses his arms. 'Sun bears are shy and reclusive animals, but be under no illusion, if they feel under threat, they'll inflict some damage with those claws. Too many people lack the respect you need to have for wild animals. Like those who keep big cats as pets and end up finding out the hard way.'

'Well, that is bonkers.' I shake my head. 'And also quite cruel. So, tell me then, when you suggested I have a "cuddle" with Rana, was that your way of getting revenge? Were you just pretending to settle things between us, while secretly planning to let a psycho bear cub loose on me?'

Though I'm just kidding, he looks at me with a deadly serious expression.

'I would *never* put anyone in danger. I take my responsibilities as head keeper very seriously, Jess.'

'Hey, I was only joking.'

Shocked by the strength of his reaction, I instinctively put my hand on his arm to reassure him, and as his troubled dark eyes land on mine, a sizzle of electricity passes between us. Taken aback by this unexpected chemistry, I quickly remove my hand and look away towards the enclosure, where I spot something moving around inside.

'Oh my gosh, look! Rana's out of her cage.' I'm on my feet in an instant.

'So she is.' Nick follows suit. 'Took her opportunity while we weren't watching. Clever one, she is.'

We approach the enclosure where Rana is tentatively snuffling around, checking out her new temporary home. As we get nearer, she starts and then stays stock still for a moment, watching our every move. Then, to my delight, she resumes her investigation, the urge to explore perhaps too strong to resist.

'I'm going in,' says Nick. 'You stay here. Let's see how she responds now she's got some space, and then we can make a call on whether you're getting that cuddle today.'

He disappears around the side of the enclosure towards the hidden entrance.

'You know, after what you just told me, I think I'm good,' I call after him.

He pops his head back around the side of the enclosure and fixes me with a sincere look. 'Jess, as I said, I would never put you in danger. It's perfectly safe with her being this young and I'll be there to keep an eye on things.'

'I know. It's just that... well, those claws may be small, but they look mighty sharp.'

'How about you don't make any decisions yet, and see how you feel once you've seen me working with her.'

'Sounds good.'

I watch as Nick enters the enclosure. At first Rana keeps her distance from him, but then he coaxes her with some food – a handful of berries – and she slopes warily across to him. When she starts to eat, I just about lose myself, not just because it's adorable, but because she has the longest tongue I've ever seen.

'*What is that?*' I all but shriek. 'Why is her tongue like that?'

Rana takes fright at my outburst and backs away.

'*Seriously?*' Nick growls, giving me a stern look, which reminds me that we're no more than reluctant co-workers. 'I'm trying to earn her trust here. This isn't a petting zoo.'

Hot faced and feeling stupid, I hover for a while longer, then excuse myself to the ladies. Nick seems almost relieved to be rid of me, so I make sure I take my time by buying a bottle of mineral water from the cafe, checking my work emails, and phoning home to see how Jackson and Seth are getting on. They're not long home from a walk-slash-wheel in

Montgomery Street Park across the road from my flat, which pleases me. I'm keen for Seth to get as much outdoor time as possible before the colder weather of autumn and winter is upon us.

After about half an hour, I make my way back to Rana's enclosure filled with dread. I feel like a naughty school child returning to class after behaving in a way that should leave me 'well and truly ashamed of myself'. I can't seem to figure Nick out. At times he seems warm and friendly, then things shift and I'm left in no doubt that he'd prefer I disappear. He's like a slightly toned-down version of Jekyll and Hyde. OK, massively toned down, but it's a similar principle.

Though I know I shouldn't make assumptions, I wonder if this behaviour had anything to do with why his wife left him. It would certainly be very tiring living with someone who would lovingly snuggle up to you one minute and criticise or reprimand you the next. That is, if he's ever the snuggling kind. I can't really see it at all.

'You took your time,' is how I'm greeted on my return.

My irrational mind instantly flits to how I'd quite like to launch my half empty bottle of water at his head, but then his next statement surprises me.

'Come in here. She's warming to me quickly, so I think she'll do the same with you – as long as you're quiet and gentle.'

I'm about to politely decline this request on the basis that I'm unfit for the job (as Nick himself pointed out), but when I reach their side of the enclosure, I swiftly change my mind. Little Rana, who appears to have been climbing on the branch next to Nick, reaches out and latches on to his shoulder, then leaps across and onto his back before tumbling off and doing the same thing all over again. It's like watching a toddler playfully tussling with their mum or dad, but with turbo-boosted energy and dexterity.

With Nick seemingly already over our spat, I decide I may as well join them. No point in missing out because I'm feeling wounded, and I'm not the kind to hold a grudge for something like this. On entering the enclosure, Rana doesn't spot me at first, and continues to play with Nick, but then I trip over a tree branch and that sends her scarpering to the opposite corner.

'Shit, I'm so sorry.' I keep my voice to almost a whisper.

I'm expecting another bollocking from Nick, but his focus seems to be on getting Rana to come back to him. He reaches into the container beside him and grabs another handful of berries. Sniffing at the air hungrily, she seems to smell them straight away and cautiously creeps back towards us.

'Stay perfectly still,' Nick whispers, and I instantly feel the urge to move, but I fight against it.

We remain like statues while Rana gingerly approaches, and as that insane tongue flicks out of her mouth, grabbing at the berries, scattering most of them onto the ground, I have to make a concerted effort not to get excited again. I watch, mesmerised, as she hoovers them up and then sniffs around for more.

'Here.' Nick holds out a handful to me. 'Take them and extend your hand out flat to her.'

As our eyes lock and he places the berries in the palm of my hand, I feel that same jolt of chemistry between us. This simultaneously makes my stomach flutter and my brain cry out in frustration, because it's so confused by reacting this way to someone who seems to tolerate me one minute, then wish I would spontaneously combust the next.

Shifting my focus to Rana, I reach out and offer her the fruity bounty. She seems nervous at first, but then she steps forward and delves into the feast with her tongue. It takes everything I've got not to freak out and cause another scene, but knowing how important this is to Nick, and how seriously he takes his work – and also that I'll get another dressing down if I do – I manage to keep my composure and enjoy the moment.

'There you go. Well done.' Nick acknowledges my success and I'm way more pleased by his praise than I should be. 'She'll warm to you quickly now.'

He's right. Within fifteen or twenty minutes of feeding Rana and gaining her trust, she's leaping from branch to branch, and occasionally attempting a climb of either Nick or myself, while I giggle with sheer unadulterated joy. It's probably one of the most incredible moments of my life.

I also can't help noticing that Nick's a natural with Rana. He has a real sense of her capabilities, pushing her to explore her natural behaviours while at the same time being well tuned into what she can and can't cope with. Watching him tussle with her, I'm left in no doubt that he has a soft and caring side, and before I can catch myself, I'm wondering what it would be like to be on the receiving end of it, and I'm feeling a little envious of the bear cub. Maybe I'd like those strong arms to be tossing me around, perhaps even pinning me down as he explores every part of me…

Or maybe that's a really, *really* bad idea.

Especially with our hot and cold working relationship and the fact that I have real stuff I need to focus on – like Seth and rescuing my career. Oh, and there's also the small issue of Nick having made it clear I wasn't his type. Seth may have called 'bullshit' on that one, but he hasn't met Nick. It's very possible the chemistry I'm feeling is completely one-sided, and attempting to tame this particular wild beast would only end in disaster and heartbreak.

Chapter 12

On Thursday morning, I bring the park's management team back together for a further discussion and brainstorm about the events they could put on. In a way, it's a moot exercise, because I've already come up with a number of ideas I think will boost their profits – none of which are on their existing sorry-looking list, apart from 'something Christmassy', which I can give far more meat to. But having learned the basic principles of managing change through a training course I once went on, I know that inflicting my proposals on them, and expecting them to just go along with them, is not the way forward. They'll see them as being imposed, which could lead to anything from unconscious sabotage to open resistance. I don't want to manip-ulate them either. That would be unethical. I therefore need to steer them in the right direction so they do genuinely come up with these ideas themselves, and perhaps even some better ones.

Rather than using the office meeting room, which is about as inspiring as a multi-storey car park, I arrange for us to have the session in the spacious partially covered outdoor seating area. That way, if it starts to rain, we can move under cover and continue working. It's a grey but humid day, warm enough to be outdoors, and my weather app is only showing a twenty-three per cent chance of rain, so I'm confident we'll be OK. Gwen has also taken the opportunity to arrange a barbeque for all the park staff afterwards, to keep spirits up, and hopefully build on the motivation to make this whole thing a success.

'Hi everyone, grab a seat,' I greet the management team as they wander into the space at 3:30 p.m., looking less than enthusiastic at the prospect of spending two hours with me. 'How has your day been so far?'

'Good, thanks.' Lauren is the only person to answer me, which is probably because she does similar work with the group with her HR hat on, and she knows how it feels to be ignored by people who don't want to be there.

There's a low-level murmuring as the rest of the group continue the conversations they were having on their way here, so I allow them to finish these off naturally before starting the session. To my disappointment, I note that Nick is looking particularly disinterested, but in a way, I can't blame him, given there's an adorable sun bear cub just yards away that he'd rather be attending to. However, I do have hope, now that we've got some level of rapport going, that he'll play ball and maybe even offer some support to rally the troops.

Eventually the chat peters out and the eight faces round the outdoor table turn towards me expectantly, so I take that as my cue to start.

'Hi… again.' I give them a little wave paired with a bright smile. 'Good to see you all again. Gwen, before we get started, I wondered if there's anything you want to say to your team?'

Gwen looks like she's been nudged out of a deep sleep. Her blank and somewhat bleary eyes meet mine and I nod encouragingly at her, while wondering if this is, in fact, a good idea. Perhaps I should have briefed her on the need to show her leadership and set some direction this afternoon, but I'm not her HR person. That's supposed to be Lauren's job.

'Um… right… yes.' Gwen gets to her feet and begins to pace back and forth slowly, head down while she attempts to come up with something on the spot.

It plays out as quite an awkward moment and there are several shared looks and smirks that she's completely oblivious to – which is probably for the best, because I need her unrattled and on point. Cringing on her behalf, I make a mental note to brief her next time we're bringing the group together to allow her to be better prepared. Eventually, she nods and seems to land in a place of agreement with herself, and we all wait with bated breath as she stops pacing and faces us.

'You all know the pressure we're under,' she all but bellows. 'You know the threat to the important educational and conservation work we pour our hearts and souls into every single day – to the park, our animals and livelihoods. Today I'm asking you to give this your all, to give Jess your full attention and effort, and to give me your commitment that you will fight for our survival. Because one chance is all we get at this, team, and I'm sure none of us wants to be lying in our beds six months from now, waiting for our Universal Credit payments, wishing we'd tried a bit harder. Am I right?'

Gwen's slightly shell-shocked audience stares mutely back at her.

'I said, am I right?' Gwen looks expectantly at her team and I feel pained and a little embarrassed for her, but I avoid joining in, knowing that this has to come from them.

'You're right,' says Lauren, adopting the role of rescuer once again. 'Come on, guys. What do you say?'

'You're right,' a couple of them mumble.

'Was that Mel Gibson's big speech from *Braveheart*?' I hear another team member whisper.

'OK, great, thanks Gwen,' I interject, unable to stomach any more of this. 'So you all know what's on the line here, right? I'm here to help you save this place and failure is not a word I understand, so let's step this up a gear. East Lothian Wildlife Park's future is in our hands and we're going to crack this – today.'

'Yes, we are!' chants Lauren, thinking I'm going for a speech similar in tone to Gwen's.

'OK, great.' I clap my hands together. 'Lauren's up for this. Let's get the blood pumping through the rest of you, before you go into hibernation mode on me. I'm going to set you a task: I want you to break into four pairs and go for a walk round the park.'

'How is going for a walk going to help us figure out what events to put on?' Nick asks.

'Good question, Nick.' I smile at him, assuming he's asked this question to show interest and offer me some moral support. 'While you're taking your walks, I'd like you to take on different personas and view the park through the eyes of four different customer groups: children and teenagers; twenty-somethings; middle-aged adults and parents; and retirees. Think about what's important to each of these groups. What will excite or please them? What would they pay extra for?'

'Could we not do that by sitting here and brainstorming those questions together?' Nick's forehead creases in a frown and my smile falters on realising he wasn't playing the role of ally after all.

'Well, yes. I guess we could, but where's the fun in that?'

'I'm not here to have fun, I'm here to solve a problem.'

I grit my teeth, irritation bubbling within me. 'I know that. It's not really for fun, it's about trying to get you think differently; about you seeing the park you're so used to through the eyes of your customers. It's an experiential exercise that will help you come up with fresh and exciting ideas. Your initial brainstorm hasn't been particularly successful, so I think it's worth trying something different.'

'OK. Why didn't you just say that then?' Nick shrugs compliantly, while a couple of the team stifle a snigger.

I want to walk across and cuff him across the back of the head for being such a pain in the arse.

'Glad you're on board.' I say instead, trying to hold back the sarcastic tone in my voice. 'Everyone clear on what's being asked?'

I look around the rest of the group hopefully and they seem to be accepting of the task, which is a relief.

'OK, great. I'll see you back here in half an hour.'

They get themselves into pairs and pick a scrap of paper out of the Tupperware I snaffled from the restaurant, which assigns them their consumer demographic. They then head off for their walkabout, while I silently stew and aim dung pitchforks at the back of Nick's head.

What is his problem? He's pleasant and accommodating one minute and the next he's hurling metaphorical grenades at me. It's bad enough him doing it in a one-on-one setting, but in front of the whole team? That's going to impact my credibility and potentially the success of this whole project. I decide I need to speak to him about it. It's that or go to Gwen, and I really don't want to have to play that card.

When the group returns from their half-an-hour-in-the-life-of exercise, I'm pleased to see the energy levels have picked up a bit.

'How was that?' I ask them, inviting them to take their seats once again.

'It was insightful,' says Lauren. 'A really interesting way to look at things.'

'Great. What else?' I cast my eyes round the rest of the group. 'Serge, what customer demographic did you and Monika talk about?'

'We were on the old-timers,' says Serge.

'The retirees.' I correct his labelling to encourage a more respectful discussion.

'Yes. We thought that they might have grandchildren they can bring here to give mum and dad a rest.'

'OK, perfect. What else?'

'They are maybe looking for things to pass time when on their own. Maybe also, for connection,' says Monika, the park's gift shop manager, in her lovely Eastern European accent. 'When I am in the shop, I am always having long conversations with our... more mature guests. I think, even if they have grandchildren, they are sometimes lonely.'

'Bingo.' I clap my hands together. 'Loneliness is an epidemic in our country – and it's not just older people who are affected by it. We also have an ageing population. Around one in five people in the UK are age sixty-five or over. That's a huge potential customer base to tap into.'

'Yes.' Monika looks thoughtful. 'And if we put on events for retired people – maybe weekly coffee mornings with park tours and special demonstrations – it would help them with connection, maybe even to build friendships.'

'Exactly. I love that idea. Thank you, Monika and Serge. OK, who's next?'

I work my way round the pairs, asking them to recount their conversations, which seem to have gone exactly as I intended. Not bad for an events person who only studied marketing briefly at university, if I may say so myself. From these conversations, we add the possibility of corporate events and a Christmas market running through December. The latter could be particularly lucrative as the park is the perfect canvas for creating a magical festive atmosphere.

Moving on to the final group of two, Nick and Hakeem, who's the head groundskeeper, I invite them to share their thoughts. I've intentionally left them till last to make sure Nick doesn't dive bomb the activity with one of his assault-style comments.

'We had the twenty-somethings,' says Hakeem with great discomfort, probably because he's in his fifties and feels a bit weird trying to get into the heads of the 'young 'uns'.

'OK, great.' I suppress a smile so as not to add to his unease.

For some reason, the idea of him and Nick lolloping round the park talking about what might excite young people is a source of great amusement for me. Nick may only be in his early thirties, but his position on the grumpiness scale makes him seem a lot older. I would have loved to have been able to listen in on their conversation, purely for entertainment value.

'So, what did you both come up with?' I ask them.

Hakeem looks at Nick, who blatantly ignores his plea to take over, then shifts in his seat and gives a little cough as he answers my question.

'I'm sorry, Hakeem. I didn't catch that.' I move closer to him, which seems to make him squirm even more.

'I… um… OK, this is only because my daughter is twenty-five, and she is mostly glued to one dating app or another…' Hakeem trails of and clears his throat awkwardly.

'Ah, I see.' My insides light up with enthusiasm as I realise Hakeem has stumbled upon exactly what I was hoping he would with the demographic group assigned to him. 'You're thinking we hold dating nights here?'

'Yes.'

'I think that's a brilliant idea. That group are likely to be our most difficult to get through the gates and the draw of possible romance as part of a quirky new dating experience might just be a winner. Thank you, Hakeem and Nick.'

My gaze lingers on Nick with some disapproval of him not supporting his teammate or engaging positively with the exercise, but he seems to be intentionally ignoring me. Scrawling this final idea down on the flipchart I've brought outside, I stand back to review the list.

'Gwen, I'm keen to know what you're thinking in a moment, but my initial thoughts are that we could focus on the Christmas market, as we have the gift of time on that one, and for me, it's a no-brainer. People love an outdoor festive experience. I'm also drawn to the event for retirees, because of the potential for it to be so lucrative – there's perhaps even an annual membership opportunity lurking there. And I'm also loving the dating nights idea.'

'I think they all sound wonderful.' Gwen looks elated by what her team have come up with.

'All right then,' I say to her. 'If you think your teams can cope with a little extra work, how about we set up three project teams and get the planning underway. With the right focus, we can get the dating and retiree events up and running quickly.'

Gwen looks round her management team, whose expressions range from looking ready to get going right this second to desperately seeking an escape route.

'With the visitor levels being what they are, most of us have capacity to get involved in this work,' she says to them. 'The only people I'll give a pass to on the planning are Nick and Hakeem, because their teams' work levels don't fluctuate as much based on footfall.'

Nick crosses his arms and adopts a self-satisfied smile, which makes me want to reprimand him for his lack of team spirit, while Hakeem looks deeply relieved.

'But,' Gwen continues. 'I expect both of you to support with any requests for help that relate to your areas of responsibility, or that will help to get the events up and running successfully. Understood?'

They both nod like sulky teenagers and I find myself wondering how all this is going to play out. Planning events is a tough and stressful business even when everyone is aligned and aiming for the same goal. But with the staff here being as unpredictable as the animals, it looks like I'll have more of a challenge on my hands than I first thought.

Chapter 13

At 5:30 p.m., we wrap up our brainstorming session, having agreed the key features of each event, and who will work on which project. While Nick and Hakeem were given a pass on being part of the project teams, I was pleased to see that Gwen stepped up and worked them hard during the remainder of our time together. This was helpful in that it kept things under control and it allowed us access to information we would otherwise have had to seek out later.

With the park having now closed for the day, the team members who have been keeping the place running trickle into the picnic area while Nick and Gwen fire up the barbeque. At the same time, Serge disappears then reappears with a pile of fresh produce from the main restaurant kitchen, and takes over from Gwen. I can't help eyeing the food and wondering how much it costs them each time they hold one of these barbeques, but then I remind myself that keeping the staff motivated is important – especially now with their jobs at risk. Plus, they're probably paying Capital Events a hell of a lot more.

The picnic area becomes busier and the employees, who obviously know each other well, start to mingle – sharing jokes and stories from their day. It's nice to watch and soak in the bouncy atmosphere, but it also makes me feel like a bit of a spare part, so I gravitate across to Nick and Serge at the barbeque.

'Can I help with something?'

'Yes, please.' Serge dumps a tray of bread rolls in front of me without hesitation. 'Please cut and butter each one.'

'Sure.' I grab a knife and the huge tub of margarine from a nearby table and begin my task. 'How did you both find the session?'

'It was good,' says Serge. 'Good to know that maybe we can save this park. I have been here just three years, but it already feels like home.' He places a hand on his chest and I can sense that he really means it.

'I love that you're so open and honest. That kind of passion is rare. What about you, Nick?'

'It was fine.' He shrugs with indifference and I laugh.

'See, that's exactly what I mean.' I cock my head comically.

'He is British, yes.' Serge gives a hearty chuckle. 'But he also needs the love of a good woman. That is what frees a man.'

Although Serge doesn't appear to have any ulterior motive with this comment (or at least I hope he doesn't), it catches me off guard and I struggle to find an appropriate way to respond. It also seems to have the same effect on Nick, who doubles down his focus on the burgers he's flipping.

'Do you have a husband at home?' Serge fills the silence by asking me and I feel myself redden, despite this being an innocent and reasonable enough question to ask when getting to know someone.

'Um… no…' I stammer. 'And I'm quite happy that way. I… uh… have a lot going on in my life and I want to do the career thing first.'

'Well don't wait too long.'

'Oh, why's that?' I'm expecting him to deliver the clichéd 'clock ticking' comment we women regularly hear in its various guises, and I'm poised to (light-heartedly) call him out on this, but he throws in a curveball.

'Because, Jess, if you leave it too long, all the best men will be taken and you will have to find your husband from the next generation down.'

Nick scoffs at this, clearly enjoying the suggestion of me having to find myself a toy boy. I shoot him a look, which he misses, his focus still on the burgers.

'Yes, well, maybe that wouldn't be so bad,' I muse. 'Men in my generation leave a lot to be desired.'

The smug look on Nick's face instantly evaporates, while Serge laughs heartily and excuses himself to the kitchen to pick up the condiments.

'What did you really think of the session?' I pause mid-buttering and turn to Nick.

He gives another shrug of indifference. 'It got you the outcome you wanted. What does it matter what I think?'

'It matters because, for this plan to work, it needs every single one of you on board – and the male pride you've admitted to having isn't going to save this park.'

A flash of annoyance crosses Nick's face, making it clear he regrets sharing that character flaw with me. Well, tough. It's not like it wasn't completely obvious anyway.

'Look, Nick...' I try to look him square in the face, but he's able to avoid eye contact by keeping his focus on the sizzling grill. 'Gwen needs you on board with this.'

'I am on board with it. I took part in the session, didn't I? What more do you want?'

'You could do it with a little enthusiasm.'

He sighs and rolls his eyes. 'So, basically the measure of whether I'm considered to be "on board" is whether I get all excited and join in when we have a group hug?'

'What? No. That's not what I mean at all.'

'Then what do you mean? Because as far as I can see, it sounds like you want me to have a personality transplant.' His voice raises in volume, causing some of the park workers to turn curiously in our direction.

'Nick, that's not it.' I lower my own voice in an attempt to defuse the situation. 'It's just that, when there are team members who lack enthusiasm, it can bring everyone down – and your team needs to really go for this or it's game over.'

'You think I don't know that?' He hisses at me with a defiant stare, then stalks off, thrusting the tongs into Serge's free hand as he returns from the kitchen with a box of condiments.

Serge watches Nick go then turns to me with a smile. 'Ignore him. He is always having these moods. I tell you, he needs a good woman.' He completes this observation with a pointed look.

'Well, don't get any ideas.' I wave my hands firmly in a cancelling gesture. 'Apart from not needing any further complications in my life, I hardly think I have a positive or calming influence on him.'

'We shall see.' He gives me a little wink. 'Perhaps he has met his match and you are exactly what he needs.'

Having heard enough, I finish off the last of the rolls then excuse myself, but not before Serge insists that I take a burger with me. Looking around, I don't see any groups I could easily join, and I'm not in the mood now anyway, following my fresh altercation with Nick, so I sit down at one of the picnic tables alone to eat my food.

'You OK there?' Lauren suddenly appears at my side.

'Yes, thanks.' I quickly chew and swallow a bite of burger. 'Just grabbing something to eat, then I'll get quick word with Gwen. Do you know where she is?'

'She nipped to the office but she should be back in a few minutes. I noticed you and Nick having a bit of a spat before. Lovers' tiff, was it?' She gives me a little nudge.

'Definitely not. I think he'd be quite happy if I buggered off back to where I came from.' I blanch as I realise what I've said. 'Sorry, that was unprofessional of me.'

'Don't apologise. He's not the easiest guy to deal with, though I bet that makes him great in bed. Oh, there's Gwen now.'

Lauren gives me a little wink and walks off, leaving me opened mouthed for the second time this week.

Gathering myself together, I approach Gwen, who's already engaged in a conversation with a staff member I don't recognise.

'Really sorry to interrupt. Could I have a quick word?' I ask her.

'Of course.' Gwen excuses herself and steps away with me to give us some privacy. 'Everything OK? You did a brilliant job today. Make sure you fill up on the food, it's well deserved.'

'Thanks, I appreciate the feedback, and I've had a burger. I wanted to grab you quickly to say I'm about to head off.'

'You're not staying? That's a shame.' She looks genuinely disappointed. 'They're fun, these staff barbeques. Would have been a chance to get to know people better.'

'I know, and I do apologise.' I'm not keen to elaborate on this lack of an excuse.

Gwen seems to read something in my face that I'm not even aware is on show. 'Say no more, sweetheart. Off you pop and we'll see you next week. We all have our homework so I'll make sure it's done by the time you're back.'

'Thank you. And, um…'

'Nick.' She purses her lips. 'It's none of my business how you two know each other, but how are you getting along?'

'We're up and down.' I cringe at having to admit this.

'That's par for the course with Nick. Don't read too much into it. He cares very deeply about this place and the people in it, but he doesn't know how to show it in a way that allows people to connect with him. Please don't give up on him.'

'I won't.' I say this more out of professionalism, my willingness to show him any compassion having checked out for the day. 'And even if he doesn't come around, it won't stop us moving this stuff forward. It would just be good to do it with him visibly supporting it as one of the leaders of the park.'

'I agree.' Gwen nods her understanding.

After saying a few goodbyes (though not to Nick, who's nowhere to be seen), I head for my car with Gwen's words circling in my mind and one repeating thought: how on earth am I going to get through the rest of this assignment without killing that man and sending my career into permanent freefall?

Chapter 14

Over the next couple of weeks, I find more of a rhythm with my caring responsibilities for Seth and start to feel like I'm getting on top of things. Jackson is a godsend. He's so accommodating and flexible, accepting that I won't always make it home by six o'clock. He's also amazing with Seth and I can see improvements in my brother already, even in such a short space of time. Seth also seems to be enjoying the time he and I spend together as much as I enjoy being with him and supporting his rehabilitation. His cheeky charmer nature is as strong as ever, which spurs me on, reminding me that I've done the right thing in reducing my hours at work.

I split my time between managing my boring and unfulfilling inherited projects and the wildlife park work, which at least provides a bit of variety and interest, even if it's for the wrong reasons. But the constant reminder of my 'demotion' when I'm around Isla and Ravi grates on me. Between having to listen to them chatting animatedly about the ins and outs of my former high-profile projects when I'm in the office, and the continuing tension with Nick at the wildlife park, my work – which had always been my 'happy place' – becomes a real stressor in my life.

One Tuesday morning in early August, I decide that I've had enough. Without having to put in any additional effort, I'm acing everything I'm doing and getting great feedback from all my clients, not one of whom have mentioned my working pattern and part-timeness. And I still have extra capacity to take on more. That must surely be enough to prove that, while I've reduced my hours, I'm more than capable of handling the high-profile projects – though I accept it wouldn't be as many as before. Feeling like this evidence should be more than enough to convince Craig to put me back where I rightly belong, I ask for some time with him.

'So, what did you want to discuss, Jess?' Craig takes a seat opposite me in the hipster cafe across the road from our office.

He's suggested we have our conversation here, which is a nice change, I suppose. It's certainly a more appealing environment, with its eclectic mismatched décor and the aroma of barista-brewed coffee, but it's not exactly somewhere I can become assertive if things don't go the way I'm hoping. This leaves me wondering if Craig's one step ahead of me, and having anticipated what's coming, he's created an obstacle to ensure this won't get intense or drag on.

I take a long sip from my cappuccino to compose myself.

'Craig, I want to talk to you about my work assignments.'

'Oh?' He seems taken aback. 'I thought you said you'd be able to manage the projects I've given you no problem.'

'That's the thing. I am, and I'm bored.' I sit forward and try to make meaningful eye contact with him. 'Other than the wildlife park – which is only semi-interesting because of the type of business it is – I feel like I've taken a step back in my career. I need more work. I need projects that will challenge me and give me a sense of fulfilment, like the ones I was managing before.'

'I see.' Craig stirs sugar into his coffee, then sips at it to check it's the right sweetness. 'I'm not sure what to tell you, Jess. You took a decision that altered your ability to deliver what's needed of you and I had to act accordingly.'

'Is that really what happened, Craig? The way I see it, you made a decision based on an assumption, with no evidence to back it up. Rather than allowing me the opportunity to show that I could make things work, you essentially demoted me.'

'I'm afraid it's not that simple, and if you did the job I do, you would understand that, Jess. I didn't jump to some wild conclusion. I made a calculated decision based on what I know about our clients' demands, as well as having dealt with a similar situation in the past.'

'Yeah, with someone else.' I point out. 'I'm not that person, whoever it was. And I understand your concerns about the clients, but I offered you a feasible solution: to be contactable on my non-working days and even attend important meetings in person where needed. Now I've gotten into a routine with Seth, I know exactly how I could manage that.'

'Being able to respond to things or attend the odd meeting is not the same as being at work.' A flicker of what looks like impatience passes across Craig's face. 'Let's not gloss over that important point. Then there's the issue that you need to be physically present at these high-profile events when they're happening, and they're often in the evenings or at weekends.'

I grit my teeth at this suggestion I don't know what's needed in my own job.

'I know that, but I can arrange care for Seth for event dates. Being at them is not a problem. All I'm asking is for you to give me a chance to prove I can do it. Craig, please. Put me back on the Glasgow project and I promise I'll blow you away. We wouldn't even need to tell the clients that I'm not working full time, because from their perspective, I would never be unavailable.'

As soon as this statement leaves my lips, I realise my error. I've killed it. Any chance that Craig was going to back down is extinguished in an instant. Craig's expression turns from one of defending his position to irritation.

'You're saying you want me to lie to our most important clients, so that you can have things your way?'

'No. No, that's not what I meant. I was only trying to show you that if you weren't to tell them, they wouldn't even know, because I'd be so on it. That's all.'

'That's not what you said.'

'No, it's not.' I stare out the window in frustrated resignation as I realise this conversation was never going to go the way I wanted. Craig was waiting for me to slip the whole time, and the moment I did, he jumped on it – to show me how I hadn't thought things through and couldn't justify my claims. He was never going to give me a chance.

'Jess, if I tell our highest paying clients I've assigned someone part time to their contract, what do you think they're going to think?' He pushes his coffee aside and fixes me with an appraising look. 'I'll tell you what: that we don't consider them to be important enough. Then they'll go elsewhere next time.'

It's clear he's not going to listen to me, but I can't help having one last try.

'Even if you tell them that part-time person is the best staff member you have?' I ask.

'Yes. Even if I tell them that.'

I'm so frustrated by his unwillingness to look beyond appearances and assumed perceptions, I even consider telling him I think he's discriminating against me, but I know it's a lost cause. All that will do is drive an even bigger and perhaps irreparable wedge between us. I can't risk doing that, because my one remaining hope is I will at some point be able to go back to full-time hours, if and when Seth gains back some independence. Based on Craig's reasoning and attitude, I'm pretty certain that if I do, he'll be more than happy to assign me the big gigs again.

'Well, I guess there's nothing more to say then.' I give a despondent sigh, drain my coffee and get to my feet. 'I'd better get myself across to the wildlife park. Thanks for your time.'

–

My head is full during my drive to East Lothian. Even putting on my favourite playlist at a ridiculous volume doesn't shift the deep feeling of resentment I have towards Craig. I keep thinking of all the things I could or should have said – and the thing I *did* say that gave him his opportunity to shut me down. It's all so unfair.

By the time I've parked my car and I'm heading through the entrance to the park office, I've worked myself into a right lather. This basically involves fuming and fantasising about marching into the office and telling Craig where he can stick his job. OK, so that's not at all realistic, though maybe approaching the competition is. I've been loyal up to this point, but I don't have any reason not to talk job opportunities with Bree from the Cramond Event Company now. She may well be more accommodating of my situation than—

'*Whoa*. Watch yourself there.' An irked voice cuts through my runaway thoughts as I narrowly avoid colliding with Nick, who's lugging a couple of sacks of what is probably animal feed.

'Oh, sorry.' I come back to the land of the *compos mentis* with a jolt. 'I didn't see you there.'

'No shit. You nearly took me out. Thought you're here to make us money, not injure our workers and waste our resources.' He nods at his cargo.

'I said I'm sorry.' I'm irritated by Nick's overreaction. I'm not up for his nonsense today.

'Hey, are you OK?' He peers at me and seems to take me in for the first time. 'You look… harassed.'

Like you care, Mr Hot and Cold.

'I'm fine.' I aim for a sweet smile but it comes across as borderline acidic.

This doesn't deter him.

'You sure? You don't seem yourself.'

'Oh, and you would know?'

Nick seems taken aback by this unexpected attack and to be honest, I don't blame him, but I'm also not in the mood to play nice.

'Well, I don't know you that well but—'

'Correction,' I cut him off. 'You don't know me at all. And you don't seem to want to. That's been pretty clear over the last few weeks. You tolerate me. You throw me the odd bone of companionable work chat, but I'm well aware from the rapidness with which you swing in the opposite direction that you'd rather I disappeared. So do me a favour and don't suddenly pretend you care about what's going in my life, yeah?'

Finishing my tirade, I stare accusingly at Nick, who I'm expecting to come back at me even harder. However, to my surprise, his expression turns almost regretful, then sympathetic.

'Sure,' he simply says, then he turns away and heads into the park, leaving me standing there, feeling ashamed and more confused than ever.

Chapter 15

Straight after my run-in with Nick, my head a jumble of negative emotions, I head to the park office meeting room, where I'm catching up with the events project leads. On entering the room, I can see that everyone is already there, so I make a beeline for the coffee trolly to allow myself a few extra moments to compose myself.

'Morning, how are you?' Lauren appears beside me, all bounce and high-energy, and picks up a mug. 'You seem a bit—'

'Please don't say harassed.' I stop her short.

'That wouldn't have been my choice of words. Is everything OK?'

I heave a sigh. 'I'm fine. It's just… Nick.'

'Ah yes, Nick. Cold, unfeeling, mildly infuriating?'

I scoff. 'All of the above?'

'Full marks. It does have the effect of "I wanna rip that shirt right off you" though, doesn't it?'

I give Lauren a side glance, thinking she's lucky she *is* the HR department for this park, otherwise she'd get herself in trouble with those remarks. 'Um… are you sure you don't have a thing for him?'

'Me? No. He's far too old and grumpy. He's a bit of eye candy to pass the time. A one-time lay at best. Anyway, I'm going to marry a guy from my uni course.' She assumes a dreamy expression.

This statement is a double dose of surprises.

'I didn't know you're at uni. And does this guy know this?'

'I'm doing a Masters course part time while I work here. And he doesn't know it, but he knows it… if you know what I mean.' She gives me a sly wink.

'I'm not sure I do.' I steal a curious glance at her, while adding milk to my coffee. 'But good luck with that.'

'Thanks. So, back to Nick, what did he do?'

'Nothing, honestly. I've had a bad morning and he was just there at the wrong time. Come on, let's get started.'

We take a seat at the table and start the meeting. The first thing I ask the group to do is share their updates, and I'm pleased to note that things are moving along nicely. As much as I thought Nick was shirking his responsibilities, it's actually easier to manage things without him and his undermining comments joining the party. Having taken the lead on the Christmas project, Serge shares that he's already in advanced talks with some suppliers, who can provide an authentic European Christmas market experience. Monika, who's leading on the retiree events, has canvased interest in the local villages and towns and has come up trumps. However, her research has signalled the need for the provision of transport, so we spend some time chewing over the figures from a selection of quotes she's received. Lastly, I invite Lauren, who jumped at the lead role for the dating nights, to give her update.

'I've got more than an update for you.' She gets out of her seat and goes to the flipchart, turning the page to reveal a perfectly mapped out plan scrawled in blue marker pen. 'I've got it all sorted.'

'Great stuff.' I clap my hands together with enthusiasm.

'Myself and my team have come up with the ultimate dating experience. Our daters will – wait for it – be matched based on their animal personality types.'

'Ooh, I like that. Tell us more.'

'OK, here it is.' Lauren flips over to the next page, revealing a similarly scrawled flowchart, and points to the first step. 'We obviously need to advertise our event in some way, maybe drum up some local media interest. When our daters sign up, they're asked to complete a self-assessment to find out their animal personality type.'

'I am thinking I would be big hairy gorilla,' Serge announces, then illustrates this point by pounding his chest King Kong-style, making us all laugh.

'Sounds about right.' Lauren gives him a once-over, and I swear there's a predatory glint in her eye. 'Anyway, as I was saying, they do a self-assessment and are assigned a personality type. We'll have them for animal groupings – primates, big cats, reptiles, etc – rather than individual animals.'

'Do you think people will be happy being labelled a "reptile"?' I wrinkle my nose as I say this. 'Especially as the first thing that comes to mind is that they're cold-blooded.'

'Yeah, maybe that's not so appealing.' Lauren shrugs, open to accepting this constructive criticism. 'At least they have a backbone though, right? Unlike the molluscs and the arthropods.' She giggles at her own joke and Serge gives a walrus-like guffaw.

'Yeah... I think you're getting a little carried away there.' I shake my head with a smile. 'Don't think any dater's confidence would be boosted by assuming the identity of a sea snail or an insect. It would become the shortest-lived dating service in history.'

'Fair enough,' says Lauren. 'But maybe the reptiles are looking a bit more appealing now?'

'We'll see. We may need to stick to more appealing animal groupings, or perhaps go with individual animal personalities, but I do like the premise so far. Carry on.'

'Cool. So, at the same time as they find out their animal personality, we review the assessments and put together the best matches.' Lauren moves her finger down the flowchart as she speaks. 'Then when they attend the event, we pair them off with three potential matches and they have three mini-dates doing different activities around the park – sharing a cocktail by the zebra enclosure, feeding the elephants, doing something arty like painting pictures of the penguins. At the end of the event, we bring them back together and they fill in a card to say which of the three people they dated they'd like to see again, and where there are matches, we put them in touch with each other. We could start with heterosexual matches, and if that goes well, we look at branching out. What do you think?'

'I think it sounds like a reality dating show and I'd love to see it play out on screen.' I grin at Lauren. 'Which means I'm sure people in that younger demographic will be interested.'

'Why just the young people?' asks Serge. 'We could offer it to the old timers as well.'

'I'm not sure the *retirees* would go for it.' I correct his use of language on this for the second time.

'I could find out,' says Monika. 'I have contacts I can tap into now. Dating among older age groups is on the increase, so you never know.'

'OK, sure.' I nod. 'Worth a shot, I suppose. But let's be open to tailoring things a bit differently for that group if needed. I can't imagine any of them wanting a Love Island-style experience.'

Monika gives me a short thumbs-up in acknowledgement of this while writing something in her notepad. Serge looks pleased that I've taken his suggestion on board.

'Lauren, this is a brilliant idea.' I join her at the flipchart and turn the page back to review the implementation plan. 'There are two things on my mind though. Firstly, how do we make sure the personality test has some level of credibility? It needs to be able to hold up against a basic level of scrutiny. And secondly, this implementation seems a little fast. I mean, you're talking about announcing it this week and having the first event in a fortnight. How are you going to get all this done in such a short period?'

'Perfectly segued. Thank you, Jess.' Lauren turns two pages on the flipchart this time. 'Not only do I have a plan and a process flow, I have a to-do list with the majority of the main tasks already ticked off.'

I'm almost floored with astonishment as I look down the list and see that Lauren has indeed done a lot of the development work already, including designing the self-assessment tool and building the online portal it will be hosted on. The remaining tasks, other than the advertising, are mainly logistical in nature, which I can offer my expertise on.

'Wow. Well done, you.' I give her an impressed look and she beams at me.

'I may have gotten a little carried away over this one, but it has been so much fun.' She picks up a pen and quickly corrects an error she spots on her list. 'And to answer your question, I'm studying behavioural science, which mixes well with my knowledge of the animal kingdom from working here. I'll ask one of my lecturers to have a look at the compatibility matrix I developed as well as the self-assessment content.'

'Great, that will help with the credibility aspect. Are you building the online portal yourself?'

'No, I've got one of my coursemates doing it. I also think I can fill our first few events through the university community, giving us time to get the word out more widely.'

My mouth drops open as she says this. Lauren isn't just the park's office manager because she's Gwen's daughter, she's highly capable.

'Lauren, I think you may just be the saviour this park needs. Your enthusiasm, ideas and drive are what will move this place forward. It makes me wonder though, why haven't you been able to use this talent before now?'

She shrugs. 'I don't know. I've been so bogged down in financial issues and staff issues and just trying to keep things afloat. I had to ask one of my team members to take on some additional responsibility to allow me to do this. First time I've been able to work on something interesting in ages.'

'Well, that needs to change, OK?' I give her an encouraging pat on the shoulder and she smiles in acknowledgement of this.

'It's a tight timeline, but if we throw everything at it, and if you can drum up the first customers, we can do this. We'll offer the first couple of events at a discounted rate, and make improvements as we go.'

'*Fantastic.* I'm so excited.' Lauren is evidently elated by my endorsement of her pet project. 'We'll make it work, Jess, I promise.'

'There's a hell of a lot to do, but seeing all this, I have no doubt you will. Just make sure your self-assessment isn't a turn-off.'

'Sure. I was actually only kidding about the molluscs and the arthropods, but I'll take another look at it.'

'Thanks. We'll also need to do a test run before the first event, so see if you can gather some people together for that.'

We finish up our meeting, and on stepping out into the fresh air, I realise how mentally and physically drained I am. All this business with Craig treating me so unfairly, being constantly on the go looking after Seth and my regular run-ins with Nick is really taking its toll. Deciding I need a short time-out, I head along one of the paths into the park, hoping that surrounding myself with its wonderful animals will give me the energy boost I need. I wander aimlessly for a bit, passing no more than a handful of visitors, which in itself makes it clear why things are so difficult financially for Gwen and her team. However, I keep this concern and other nagging thoughts at bay by enjoying the jungle-esque sights and sounds all around me. It's kind of a peaceful vibrancy, which perhaps makes little sense on paper, but it does give me a lift.

Before I realise what I'm doing, I've gravitated towards Rana's enclosure, where I find the sun bear cub snuffling around a piece of dead tree trunk, her long tongue probing the crevices, perhaps seeking out insects. She's so mesmerising, I settle down on the bench in front of her and just watch. Although she's already grown a bit in the couple of weeks since Nick brought her outside, she's still pretty tiny and I find myself desperate for a cuddle – though I know it would be less of a snuggle and more like the animal world's version of WWE.

Just as I'm starting to feel like I can face getting back to work, a noise behind me breaks through my musings. Shifting round on the spot, I see Nick walking in my direction carrying a bucket and a brush. *Great*. The last thing I need is to have to go into fighter mode when I'm already operating on my reserves. Sitting up stiffly, I brace myself for another conflict.

Chapter 16

My pulse quickens as Nick approaches – and not in a good way, but instead of continuing our earlier altercation, he just nods and greets me with a gruff 'all right?'. Then he passes me and heads straight for Rana's enclosure. Relieved that there's not going to be any immediate interaction with him, I relax a little and continue watching Rana lollop around. She seems quite content for a baby who's lost her mother, and while I don't necessarily want to acknowledge it right now, I know that has a lot to do with Nick. From what I hear, he's spent every available minute making sure that she's comfortable and coping with the change of environment.

Nick puts down the brush he's carrying before going into the enclosure, piquing Rana's interest. Her furry little head shoots up, then as he enters her space, she bounds across to inspect him and see what he's got for her. He has quite a job keeping her head out of the bucket he's carrying. It's entertaining to watch, but as we're not really on speaking terms, I try not to let my amusement show.

Nick feeds Rana some berries, which she gulps down with fervour, pawing at him and seeking more each time she's finished. Then once the food is gone, Rana appears to decide it's playtime and boisterously clambers over Nick, tussling with him as if he's a fellow bear. Having not seen the two of them in action together since that first day when he brought her out to the enclosure – though I have visited Rana several times alone since – I can see a real bond has developed between them. Nick has become Rana's surrogate parent and she's become fearless around him, which is as hilarious as it is adorable. She's like a battery-operated toy in turbo mode. A repetitive cycle emerges, which involves Nick assertively but gently picking her off him, playfully throwing her in a way that allows her to land expertly, then she immediately goes back for more. It's clear that it's a game to her and she can't get enough.

Watching the two of them is like a happiness drug. In the same way that Rana can't get enough of horsing around with Nick, I can't seem to get enough of watching them. I laugh and gasp at the more edgy interactions between them, feeling the previous tension in my shoulders dissipate. Then without thinking, I get up off the bench and move closer to the enclosure to get a better look.

'Do you want to come in?' Nick calls across, breaking my trance-like state.

'Oh... I, um...' I trail off, unsure how to respond to this, given the verbal bashing I gave him in the car park.

'She's a lot more confident now, as you can see. I can give you some gloves to protect your hands from her claws. She'd never do you any harm at this age, but she can get a little overexcited.'

Mulling this over, I decide that if Nick isn't holding a grudge over earlier, then perhaps I can let it go for now too. But with this repetitive pattern emerging between us, I'm going to have to do something to address this issue between us.

'OK, why not.'

He does a fine job of multitasking, continuing to manage Rana while reaching into his pocket and pulling out a pair of gloves, which he hands to me when I join him. Crouching down next to him, I smile and giggle nervously as Rana's focus shifts from Nick to me. I'm not worried she'll harm me, more that I won't be able to handle her version of play, which is very much rough and tumble. She pads across to me, a little tentatively at first, then she licks at my gloves with her long tongue, which I'm assuming is her way of getting a measure of me. Then, having obviously decided I'm no major threat, she tentatively clambers up my right side and onto my shoulders to scope the rest of me out.

'You're fine,' Nick says, as I continue to laugh nervously. 'She seems to like you.'

'Probably because I'm wearing your gloves. I'm like Nick Mark Two to her.'

'Perhaps. The scent might help.'

Rana continues to investigate me, snuffling away and licking at my clothes, then she takes a mini leap from me to Nick and sort of hangs off the side of him. He grabs her and gently chucks her to the ground and the game starts all over again – but this time with both of us. It takes a bit of getting used to, and just like the first interaction I had with Rana, Nick coaches me through it, encouraging me and making sure I'm comfortable with her. He even, at times, places a reassuring hand on my arm or guides my motions, showing me how to handle Rana in a confident and unthreatening way. This touch and the closeness of his face to mine, along with the subtle but alluring scent of his eau de toilette, stirs up something animalistic in me like it did previously. His behaviour is such a departure from our other interactions that I can't help wondering – once again – why he's so nice one minute, and then acts like a total dick the next. It's frustrating and confusing – especially because of how attractive I find him when he's like this.

After a short while, we leave Rana alone in her enclosure, but not before Nick's smeared honey on her log while I keep her distracted. Apparently, it's a technique used with young sun bears in captivity to help them learn how to forage for food with their tongues. I tell him that Rana must be learning well, because that's what I saw her doing when I first arrived and he seems pleased by this progress report.

Once outside, and without a cute bear cub to focus our attention on, things become more strained between us. While he's not mentioned it, he's obviously not forgotten about the incident in the car park either. We stand in silence for a few moments, then we both rush to speak at once.

'About earlier—'

'I didn't mean to—'

We both stop short and chuckle awkwardly.

'You go.' I gesture for him to continue.

He nods in appreciative acknowledgement of this. 'I was just going to say that I didn't mean to upset you earlier, Jess. That really wasn't my intention. It was meant to be a joke.'

'I know.' I aim my shamefaced expression at the ground. 'I'd had a bad morning and it wasn't fair of me to take it out on you. Though you should maybe work on your delivery of humour.' I look up at him with a wince, unsure how he'll take this.

'Not the first time I've heard that.' He seems a bit resigned. 'I won't be auditioning for a stand-up role any time soon. It could start a riot.'

I let out a cackle of a laugh. 'Now, see, that is funny.'

Instead of laughing with me, Nick looks a bit perplexed. 'That wasn't meant to be a joke.'

I straighten my face. 'Sorry. Anyway, as I was saying, it was a bad morning, so perhaps we could forget about it?'

'Unless you want to talk about it? I realise I'm at risk of getting balled out by asking that, so to be clear, I'm not hitting on you. Just wondering if maybe I can help?'

I look to the ground again, but this time it's to stifle a laugh. Nick really has a way about him; a way of saying all the wrong things at the wrong time. Sometimes it's infuriating, but in this case, when I can see he is well-intentioned, it's amusing and quite endearing. But do I really want to be sharing anything about my life with him? Certainly not anything too personal, like my situation with Seth. That said, I have an opportunity here to try and develop a positive working relationship with Nick, perhaps even a friendship.

'How about we get a coffee?' I suggest. 'And to be equally clear, I'm not hitting on you either. But if you're up for getting your ear chewed off about my career troubles, then who am I to deny you of that pleasure.'

He shrugs. 'I spend my day listening to all sorts of savage sounds, so one more won't hurt.'

My mouth twitches. 'That *was* a joke.'

'It was,' he confirms with a sly nod. 'I'm not completely socially inept. Only halfway there.'

Having finally buried the sizeable lump of animosity sandwiched between us, we amble along the path to the nearest cafe, which is a small outfit – more of a takeaway place with a handful of tables outside. I take a seat while Nick insists on buying the coffees.

Waiting for him to join me, I enjoy a bit of warmth from the sun, which is trying its damnedest to fight its way through the rolling, slightly ominous-looking grey clouds. Tuning into my surroundings, the distinctive call of the peacocks floats across from the other side of the park, along with the odd trumpet from the elephant enclosure, while closer by, I can hear a medley of cheeping and chirruping coming from the outdoor aviary. It really is a hypnotising environment. If it weren't for the fact that I'm desperate to regain all the things I love about my career, I could perhaps just live my days out in this park, immersed in the incredible sights and sounds, at one with the wonderful animals us humans have unfortunately made life so difficult for.

'I forgot to ask if you take sugar.' Nick appears at my side holding two coffees, jolting me back to reality.

'I usually do.' I reach up and take the one he offers me. 'But I shouldn't, so it's fine without. Thanks for this.'

'You're welcome.'

He takes a seat opposite me and for a moment neither of us seems to know what to say. It's a tongue-tied moment that likely stems from us never having been in each other's company without something else to focus on – whether that be playing with Rana, shovelling elephant shit or discussing the planned park events. Other than this morning, that is, and that didn't go so well.

I smile at Nick and he smiles back warmly. A simple, polite gesture is all it is, but it sends a tremor through me: a sense of a growing attraction on my part. That's all I need when I never know if I'm coming or going with him, and especially when he's made it painfully clear that I'm not his type. Not just because he said so, but because his 'type' seems to be cute and furry or enormous with grey leathery skin.

'So, what happened this morning then?' he asks eventually.

Having forgotten that we actually do have a topic of conversation to kick us off, I find myself regretting agreeing to have this chat. How can I tell him why my morning sucked without sharing the reason my career is in the gutter? Because I definitely don't want to unpack a whole load of personal stuff with a guy I barely know.

'Jess, you in there?' Nick prompts me.

'I had a conversation with my boss, Craig, and it didn't go so well.' I rotate my coffee cup with my fingers absently, while attempting to form my redacted explanation, unwilling to outright lie to him. 'The reason I'm here at the park is because he's taken me off the projects I was working on before.'

Nick frowns. 'Seriously? Why did he do that?'

'Because he's lost confidence in my ability to deliver, and if you don't mind, I don't want to go into the reasons why. It's nothing you or Gwen or anyone here needs to worry about. It's more personal than that.'

I look up at him, concerned at what I might see, but he simply nods his understanding.

'You don't have to share anything personal with me, Jess. I get it. But maybe I can ask you what's happened since?'

'You can.' I take a deep breath, attempting to quell the frustration I can already feel rising from just talking about this. 'I've tried to explain to him that he's jumped to conclusions and made the wrong judgement. That I'm perfectly capable of handling the challenging work I did before. I've also told him I don't have enough to do, I'm bored and I need more of a challenge.'

'And?'

113

'And he won't budge. Won't even give me the chance to prove myself. Part of me is thinking maybe it's time to jump ship – there's a woman from a rival company who's been trying to poach me – but I don't see why I should have to do that because he's being unreasonable.'

Nick smiles at me with what I initially read as sympathy, but as his gaze lingers a little too long, I can't help feeling like he's judging me and I prickle with defensiveness.

'What? I *don't*. I'm not the one in the wrong here.'

'Hey, I never said you were.' Nick adopts a soothing tone and takes a slug from his drink. 'I understand why you feel that way. So, that's the only reason you're here at the park then? Because of this situation? It makes sense in a way. When Gwen mentioned you were coming here, she was so pleased, because she'd looked you up on LinkedIn and saw that you'd led some impressive events.'

'And from her saying that, you assumed I'd be a jumped-up corporate pain in the arse.' I smirk.

'No. OK, maybe a bit. But you've turned out all right, other than being a bit over-confident and squeamish for my liking.'

'Well, thanks. I feel there's almost a compliment in there.'

'It's high praise coming from me, believe me.'

He grins at me across the table, his dark eyes crinkling sexily as he does, causing my insides to do that ice cream mixer flippy-floppy thing. It's the first time I've seen Nick properly come to life and show the good side of himself in human company. To say it's attractive is a massive understatement. It's like he's an industrial magnet, and I'm so drawn to him, I want to dive across the table and suck on his face in a manner not too dissimilar to the molluscs Lauren was talking about earlier.

'Erm… I'm sure it is,' I say instead, while trying to calm my overexcited hormones.

'What are you going to do then?'

'About what?' I'm still lost somewhere between my predicament and fantasising about snogging his face off.

'Your boss,' says Nick. 'It sounds like he's being an arse. Can you make a complaint or raise a grievance or something?'

I finally manage to drag my misbehaving brain back to the matter at hand.

'No, that's not an option. I mean, I know my rights as an employee and all, but he's the owner of the company. Set it up from scratch, and it's small. It would be the final nail for me if I were to make a big thing out of this.'

'I see. You're in a bit of a hole then it seems.' Nick sits back and looks thoughtful for a few moments. 'You said he won't listen to reason, nor will he give you an opportunity to prove yourself.'

'Yup. Lost cause, right?'

'Not necessarily. If he won't give you a chance to prove yourself, can you do it working with what you've got?'

'With two duller than dull corporate events I can manage in my sleep and this place?' I wave my arm in a dismissive gesture, then blanch as I realise what I've done. 'Sorry, that was out of order. I didn't really mean it.'

'Yes, you did.' Nick raises a judgemental eyebrow. 'But in a work sense. I get the impression you quite like this place.'

'Oh, I do. On a personal level, I love it. I wish more people knew about it, because it really has a therapeutic effect on me. In all honesty, it might be the only thing keeping me sane right now.'

'Then why not use it on a professional level too?'

'I'm not sure what you mean by that. I'm already doing everything that's been asked of me and there's no opportunity to show my capability on the same level as those other projects.'

'Are you sure about that? You're helping us set up a new revenue stream so we don't go under at the end of the year, but let's face it, we probably need a miracle to turn things around in the long run – not just a few events. You could be our miracle and you could save your career at the same time. Rather than just focusing on bailing us out of our immediate financial black hole—'

'I should focus on turning you into *the* go-to destination in Scotland with a headline grabbing, rags-to-riches success story that really sells the magic of this place.' It's as if I've suddenly woken up and smelled my opportunity.

'Yes.' Nick drains the last of his coffee. 'Though I'm not sure I would have put it like that.'

'You don't need to. I know exactly what you're getting at and you're spot on. I don't know why I didn't think of this myself.'

'Maybe because you were too busy wallowing in self-pity?'

My enthusiasm instantly neutralises and I glower at him. 'Why do you do that?'

'Do what? What did I do?' He seems completely oblivious to the impact his words have had.

With a sigh, I let my frustration dissipate. 'Let's just say I'm not the only one with blind spots. Anyway, forget that. What's important is that I'm going to get this place the publicity and funds it needs to turn it into an unmissable experience, so that you and Gwen and the whole team can look to the future with confidence. And I can have my job back. Thank you, Nick, you're a bloody genius.'

He grins at me, looking quite pleased with himself, and this time (even despite his clumsy remark), I want to kiss him for a very different reason.

Chapter 17

I spend the next week more motivated than I've been in my life. Nick's idea of using the park to show Craig exactly what he's missing is perfect, and right within my sphere of control. The only thing I don't like about it is that I didn't come up with it myself. Being so blinkered by the unfairness and the need for logic to prevail, I forgot that I have other tools in my arsenal.

Working with Lauren on the dating event is a dream. Not only is she 'on it', she's got this sparky energy that radiates and keeps me aiming for the sky and beyond.

Having consulted one of her lecturers about the dating event content – who endorsed her 'product' and awarded her a symbolic A+ for the exceptional level of research she'd undertaken – Lauren's coursemate who developed the online tool then makes the final adjustments, ensuring the right IT security and data protection protocols are in place. This incredible progress impresses me no end and also makes me incredibly grateful for the tech talent and drive of young people.

'Lauren, this online assessment is amazing.' I'm reviewing the questionnaire on my laptop at a desk in the park office. 'I know the park can't afford to pay your classmate, but I think we need to arrange a gift as a thank you.'

'Oh, it's fine.' Lauren, who's sitting at the desk next to me, casually waves away my comment. 'She's already made her demands and I've agreed to them.'

'Which are?'

'She gets to take part in the dating events for free.'

'Is that an indefinite arrangement?' My mind goes to the fact that we'd have one less paid place at each event.

'We agreed on five, then she has to pay after that.'

'Ah, perfect. You're a shrewd negotiator.'

'Another one of my many talents.' She strikes a pose, making me laugh.

'So, I think we're ready for our test run today.' I complete my review of the self-assessment and close the lid on my laptop. 'Your friends all know they need to complete the survey by midday, right?'

'They do. And I'll have them reviewed and matched before they arrive at four p.m. Although...' She tails off and looks at me tentatively.

'Although what?'

'A few of them have had to pull out last minute because today clashes with an assignment deadline. Bad timing, unfortunately.'

'Ah, that's a shame.' I grimace. 'How many have pulled out?'

'Five. But I think we can fill the spaces so we can still test the process with a full complement. I'll see if I can get some of the team to sign up.'

'To an impromptu dating event at their place of work? Really?' I give her a sceptical look.

She shrugs. 'It's not real though, is it? It's just testing the process.'

'OK, good luck with that. While you're sorting that side of things, I'll see to the logistics so we're ready to start bang on four p.m. Oh, by the way, I've been wondering about something... if all our daters have to come by car because of the location, it might limit the market we can tap into. It's also not very environmentally friendly and some of them might want a proper drink – you know, for courage.'

'I've actually been thinking about this too.' Lauren fiddles with the stapler on her desk. 'Keeping the alcohol levels down is probably a good thing, so our daters aren't judging their matches through prosecco goggles. But we also don't want to put people off – especially when there's a welcome drink, and cocktails and fizz are a feature of some of the mini-dates. We can look at chartering coaches, same as with the retiree events, and build that transport provision into the ticket price. It even helps with making the events catchier. How's this: we're launching our "Love on Safari" dating events where the animal instincts don't just play out at the park. Get it?'

'I do, and I think it's brilliant. This is great.'

'Yes. And if they prefer to drive, that's up to them. They get charged a cheaper price, but they miss out on all that extra love potential from not being "on tour".'

'*Boom*. Lauren, I think we might just be the ultimate events team. Put it there, partner.'

We share a slapping high five and grin at each other, before heading in separate directions to get this show well and truly on the road.

–

At three p.m., mine and Lauren's paths cross again while we're getting the final bits and pieces organised in the outdoor seating area across from the main restaurant. We've also set up indoors as a backup in case it starts to rain.

'OK, that's everything organised from my side,' I say to her. 'Serge has the welcome drinks and canapés ready, the mini-dates are prepped with team members allocated to turn them around after each couple, and Monika will be ferrying our guests here from the main gate so they don't get lost.'

'Perfect.' Lauren consults her own to-do list on the tablet she's holding. 'Think I've got everything done too. Oh, apart from, I have a favour to ask you.'

'Anything, shoot.'

'We're still one person down for the test run, so I was wondering if you would step in?' Her expression is one of pleading.

'*Me?*' I splutter in surprise. 'You want me to take part in the dating event?'

'Just to make up the numbers. It's not a real event, remember, and we said we needed to try it with a full complement. This is the only way to do that.'

'But surely you need me to oversee the event and support you with running it.'

'I'll manage fine, I'm sure.'

I look at her helplessly. 'Are you sure you can't find someone else to help out last minute?'

'Na-ah.' Lauren shakes her head. 'It's too late. They'd have to complete the self-assessment and I've already done the matches.'

'But surely then that means I don't have time to— *oh*.' I realise she's got me hook, line and sinker.

'I've got your completed version from when you were testing it out earlier.' She winces as she says this.

'Oh, you wee bugger.' I rub my hot face, feeling caught out. 'Did you plan this?'

'I didn't, I promise. I couldn't find someone to fill the final space and then when I was doing the matches, I saw your completed questionnaire from earlier. Please, Jess. *Please?* It's purely for the process. Everyone here tonight knows that it isn't about actual dating.'

'Well, that's a good thing, because with our pilot participants being a bunch of uni students, I'm hardly age appropriate for this event.'

'Oh don't worry, it's a part time Masters course. My class-mates are all studying and working like me. They're not a bunch of eighteen- and nineteen-year-olds, they're mainly around my age or a bit older.'

I ignore this comment. 'Plus, I wasn't actually paying much attention when I was answering the questions, so who knows what my personality type has come out as.'

'Actually, the best way to answer the questions is not to overthink them. Your first instinct is generally the right one…' She shrinks down in response to my glare.

Lauren continues to watch me hopefully. I really, *really* want to say no to this. Not only am I mortified at the thought of it getting around the park, it also feels quite inappropriate given my role here – even if it is just a test run. That said, my role *is* to turn the fortunes of the park around, and I did just agree with Nick that I need to do that with bells on to show Craig what he's missing. Experiencing the event first-hand will help me fine tune it to perfection, and that's surely more important than my pride.

I let out a resigned sigh. 'Fine. I'll do it. But you owe me big for this.'

'Absolutely. Thank you.' Lauren jumps up and unexpectedly hugs me. 'You're a star.'

Or a fool, I think to myself, as a feeling of utter dread washes over me.

–

An hour later, our pretend-daters are milling around the outdoor seating area, enjoying the canapés and drinks that Serge has put on for them. It seems that most of them know each other, which makes sense, given they're at uni together. There are also two members of the park staff, whom I recognise as being from Lauren and Nick's teams, as well as Monika, who have all been roped into taking part. Unlike me, they seem to be taking it in their stride and are making an effort to get involved in the chat.

'Why don't you go and join them?' Serge gives me a nudge and a wink. 'Your soulmate might be in that group. Go find him before someone else steals him away.'

'Ha ha, you're hilarious.' I shoot him a withering look, which makes him bellow with laughter.

'Serge, quit it,' Lauren commands. 'The more you do that, the more Jess is going to raise my debt to her for this.'

'Damn right,' I mutter.

She claps her hands together, ready for action. 'Shall we get this show on the road then?'

'If we must.'

Lauren doesn't miss a beat, and within about a minute, she has everyone seated and listening attentively. She then does a quick count and looks around her.

'Hmm... seems we're still waiting for one person... ah, there you are.'

I turn to see who she's talking to and my jaw drops as a glowering Nick skulks into the picnic area, triggering a few shared looks from the female daters, who clearly like what they see.

'Good to see you, Nick.' Lauren offers him a smile that's not returned. 'Thanks so much for helping us out.'

He slips into the seat next to mine, raising a judgemental eyebrow at me, which is hardly justified given he's here for the exact same reason I am.

'I was guilted into this,' I whisper, as Lauren kicks off her welcome to the group. 'What's your excuse?'

'Gwen promised me a new pressure washer for cleaning out the enclosures if I helped out. The one I'm using is faulty and cuts out half the time.'

'So, bribery then. Good morals your colleagues have.'

'I can work with bribery.' He shrugs. 'I use it on the animals all the time. It's sexual favours I draw the line at.'

I suppress a snort of laughter. 'With the animals or your colleagues?'

'Both, I guess.' He gives me a cheeky sideways glance.

'I can't believe Lauren had to get Gwen on your case. You must have put up quite the fight.'

'Does this look like something I would agree to without a significant sweetener?'

'Definitely not.'

He picks what looks like a tiny feather off his overalls and discards it on the ground. 'Well, at least we know there's no way we'll be matched up for the dates.'

'Why's that?' I ask, with one ear tuned into Lauren's explanation of the format for the evening.

'Because we've spent more time tearing strips off each other than getting on. We're more like scrapping siblings than lusting lovers.' He punctuates this statement with a sideways glance and what I interpret as a brotherly nudge, which causes me to wilt a little inside.

'That's true. A plus, for sure.' I force an affirmative nod.

It may be for the best that Nick doesn't find me remotely attractive. I need to focus on other things like Seth and saving my career, but there's something about being 'friend-zoned', no scratch that, 'family-zoned', by a man whose clothes you wouldn't mind ripping off, that really puts a dampener on things.

Once Lauren's finished with her introductory speech, she hands each of us a sealed envelope.

'What's this?' Nick turns his over and inspects it, then holds it up in the direction of the sun in an attempt to see through to the contents inside.

'You'll find out in a moment.' I tut at him. 'And you called me impatient.'

He simply frowns at me in return.

'OK, let me quickly explain how this works before you open them,' says Lauren. 'Inside the envelope is your own personal dater card. On the front it tells you which animal personality you are – based on the self-assessment – as well as a little about what that means. On the back, it tells you who your dating matches are for this evening.'

'How did you decide who's compatible with who?' one of the group asks.

'Great question, Abishek,' says Lauren. 'We used tried and tested principles to draw up a framework of compatibility, and we assigned scores to the different combinations of matches based on personality traits, values and beliefs. Then for this evening, we assigned you each a date with your three closest matches. There are four rounds of dating to allow for overlaps, so you'll each have one mini-date slot when you're free to wander round the park and see the animals – you can, of course, do that alone, or with the others who aren't on a date during that time, whatever you prefer. Does that sound OK?'

'Yeah, great.' Abishek seems satisfied with this answer.

I catch Lauren's eye, giving her a subtle thumbs-up to let her know she's nailing it. She seems pleased by this.

'Right, now you know how this works,' she says. 'Go ahead and open your envelopes.'

Nick and I share an eye roll in a mutual gesture of 'I can't believe we're doing this' and rip ours open. Pulling out the card inside, I scoff with amusement as I see my animal personality type.

'I'm a king penguin. Apparently, that means I'm sociable, committed, dependable and resilient – among other things. What animal did you get?'

'A shingleback lizard.' His brow creases. 'It says I'm smart and solitary in nature but also deeply affectionate and loyal towards those who I create a bond with. I'm not sure I would have put myself in that category.'

I lean across and read the explanation on his card. 'Oh, you are so a shingleback lizard. You're solitary in nature for sure. I don't actually know anything about you and you even admit you prefer animals to people.'

'I don't know anything about you either.' He eyes me moodily.

'Hey, we're not talking about me here. But good attempt to deflect the attention from yourself, Mr Solitude. I can't comment on whether you're affectionate and loyal to people you create a bond with, but you're certainly that way with the animals you look after.'

'Huh. Maybe it is more accurate than I first thought.'

Turning over my card to see who I've been assigned for my dates, I inhale sharply as I spot Nick's name in slot number three and quickly turn the card back over.

'What's up?' He glances at me and turns his own card over. 'Really? This can't be right. Is this right?'

Lauren overhears this and makes her way across to us.

'Is there a problem with your dater card, Nick?'

'Eh, not sure.' He scrutinises it as if the words might suddenly change in front of his eyes. 'It's matched me and Jess. That can't be right.'

Lauren consults her tablet. 'No, that's spot on. The two of you scored eighty-nine per cent on the compatibility matrix. Second best score here tonight.'

I feel my cheeks flame, while Nick shifts in his seat.

'Well, you know,' I stammer. 'I said I wasn't paying much attention when I filled it out.'

'Yeah, you keep telling yourself that.' Lauren gives me suggestive wink, causing my flush to deepen, then she trots off to help one of the other daters.

'Well, there you go.' Nick clears his throat awkwardly, his cheeks reddening in a way I haven't seen before, and it's obvious he's feeling as uncomfortable about this as I am. 'I guess we're going on a date.'

'Yup. I guess we are.' I chew on my lip while staring straight ahead, willing my beetroot face to cool down and stop giving me away.

Chapter 18

Shortly after the revelation that Nick and I are going on a date, Lauren sends us on our first pairings, which for me is a guy from Lauren's course called David. Like most of the men in the group – and contrary to Lauren's comments about their age – he appears to be at least four to five years younger than me, but he seems nice, if a bit wound up by the whole experience.

Our mini-date is activity based: we're going round the park's tree-top walk. The idea is that you get a better view of the animals living in the bigger safari-style enclosures and it does actually deliver on that promise. We've also been told that part of our activity together will be to take a zip line back down to the ground at the end of the walkway. This seems to have added to poor David's elevated cortisol levels, and I can only guess that he's not keen on heights or 'extreme sports' that involve heights.

'So where are you originally from?' I ask him in a bid to distract him.

His knuckles are white from clutching the handrail so tightly.

'Norwich,' he replies through a clenched jaw.

'Oh, Norwich is a lovely city. I visited it several years back. It's quite a trek from there to Edinburgh though. What brought you up here, rather than going to London, for example?'

'Um… well, the university has a great reputation, so… that was why I initially came here – for my undergrad.'

He pauses and peers over the edge of the wooden walkway at a small herd of animals similar to antelopes. This action seems to unbalance him and he flinches and pulls back sharply. I wince in a gesture of sympathy. This seems to be the worst possible activity for David and it's certainly not going to encourage him to recommend the dating events. I make a mental note to speak to Lauren about the sign-up form, so we don't traumatise any more of our customers with our activities.

'So you stayed on in Edinburgh once you graduated?' I prompt him, while coaxing him along so I can end his terror as soon as possible.

'Yes. I got a graduate job locally and my work are sponsoring me to do my Masters part-time.' He shuffles along the walkway while talking, and I subtly up the pace to keep him from stalling.

'That's great that you can do it that way. Means you can earn and gain your qualifications at the same time.'

I keep David talking all the way to the zip wire – which is even higher up and a good few hundred metres long – and when we reach the staff member who's ready to receive us, I quietly let them know that perhaps David should take the stairs back down. However, on hearing this, David objects and insists that he 'can do this'.

Unable to persuade him otherwise, the park team member simply shrugs, then hooks David up to the safety gear, and gets him ready to go. What follows is a truly painful experience, watching him grapple with himself and slam his feet down in a sudden braking motion every time he attempts to take off. But after what I count to be the forty-eighth try, he finally takes off. This appears to be due to him slipping rather than making the conscious decision to go, and I'm pretty sure the whole park can hear his screams as he zips down the line.

What's completely baffling is that when I join him at the bottom, he's looking much more casual, almost to the point of being smug.

'That was insane!' he declares. 'What an experience. I've really enjoyed your company, Jess, and I'd love to see you again.'

As he strides off ahead of me, chest puffed out, shoulders square, I have to try very *very* hard to suppress the fit of giggles that almost overwhelms me.

My second date, which is with a guy called Dae-Jung, is quite uneventful compared to my first, but only because anything would feel calm and composed in comparison to my experience with David. I do find myself thinking though that whoever ends up with Dae-Jung in the long term will be one very lucky woman. He's super polite, scarily intelligent and funny in an understated way. He's also very easy on the eye. If I were a few years younger is all I'll say – at the risk of sounding like a middle-aged lech.

After I've said a polite goodbye to Dae-Jung, who seems very happy to wave me on (I won't think too much about that one), I find myself having a mocktail at a patio table for two – with Nick. We're sat overlooking the flamingo enclosure on one side and a solitary giant tortoise on the other.

'So, this is weird.' I twiddle the stem of my martini glass.

'That's one word for it.' Nick looks so ill at ease he can barely make eye contact with me.

Seeing him that way, along with the pent-up discomfort I feel myself, resurrects the rush of mirth I had to suppress earlier with David. Despite my best efforts, I begin to lose my self-control.

'What's up with you?' Nick asks, without looking at me.

I wrestle with myself, trying desperately to remain composed, which makes it even harder for me to get hold of myself.

'Noth… nothing. Just, eh… ha… sorry… just something that happened earlier.' My hand jitters and I nearly knock over my drink.

'Maybe we should move that somewhere safe before one of us ends up with it in our lap.' He slides the glass in his direction with a hint of a smile. 'And as we've got half an hour to pass, how about you tell me a bit about yourself?'

'Is that how you always open your dates?' I let out an amused snort. 'If so, it's no surprise you're single.'

A spark of emotion flickers across Nick's face and I instantly regret my words, remembering what Lauren told me about him being divorced.

'Sorry, that was insensitive.'

'It's fine. But the answer to that question is "no", because I don't date. Period.'

'Why's that?'

I think I already know the answer to this, and why he doesn't seem to like humans very much – I suspect it's something to do with his ex-wife. But I can't help asking, because I'm coming to the realisation that, as much as he's a bit Jekyll and Hyde, I'm a little that way myself in response to him, too.

'I thought we were going to talk about you,' he replies, not giving me at all what I want.

'No, you decided you wanted to know more about me, and it seems I've decided I want to know more about you. So where does that leave us?'

'Shall we give the tortoise the deciding vote?' Nick asks, making me smile.

'OK, how about we take it in turns to ask questions? Then we both get our way and we might actually leave the park tonight knowing each other a little better.'

'Fine by me. What do you want to know?'

He takes a swig from his martini glass, which is an odd look on him, especially as he hasn't bothered changing out of his overalls for this event. He also has something brown smeared across his forehead, which I'm sincerely hoping is just mud.

'Where do you live?' I ask.

'Aberlady. You?'

'Edinburgh, near London Road. How long have you worked here at the park?'

'Nineteen years. I started as a general dogsbody after school, did my qualifications on the job and worked my way up.'

'Which makes you...?'

'Experienced?' Nick fixes me with a look of mind your own business. 'OK, thirty-six.'

I'm surprised by this. 'Right. I thought you were younger than that.'

'Is it a problem?'

I realise he's tuned into the age comparison I'm doing in my head – though hopefully not what I'm really thinking – and I feel myself blush. 'Why would it be a problem? It's of no odds to me what age you are.'

I realise this is actually true, because the part of me that wants to rip his clothes off doesn't give a crap about his age. Plus, he's not *that* much older than me, nor is he interested in me, so this whole thought process is moot.

'What's your favourite streaming show?' I rush to move things on.

'Hang on.' He narrows his eyes. 'You just had two questions in a row, so it's my turn.'

'I didn't realise we were playing to such strict rules.'

'I'd hardly call it a rule. It's more the premise of the activity which, by the way, you suggested – that we "take it in turns to ask questions".'

'And now you've squeezed all of the fun out of it by explaining that.' I sigh, then sit back and gaze across at the beautiful bright pink flamingos who are bunched together in a flock in their enclosure.

'Why do you have such an issue with me calling things as they are?' Nick's eyebrows knit together in a frown.

'I don't.'

His frown deepens.

'OK, maybe I do.' I pick at a bit of fluff on my top to avoid having to look at him. 'I guess it's because it always feels like you're trying to one up me and make me look stupid.'

'So, you think I'm a bad guy?'

'What? No.'

'That's what it sounds like. If I were doing what you've described, that would make me a bit of a tosser, don't you think?'

'I suppose.' I shrug. 'So I'm going to take a guess that you're not doing that? Because at other points you're quite nice.'

'Thanks. I think.' He gives a short chuckle.

'You're welcome. But it doesn't really help me understand what is going on. Why we keep butting heads like this.'

Nick rubs the days-old stubble on his chin. 'Have you ever considered that maybe I just don't see the world in the same way as you do? Maybe I focus on things that you don't, and if I think something to be relevant or important, I point it out.'

'It sounds simple and plausible enough, I suppose. It's just that it feels a bit crap in the moment.' I wrinkle my nose as I say this.

'Then how about you focus less on how it feels and more on trying to understand where I'm coming from?'

'Gosh.' I finally shift my gaze to Nick and to my surprise he holds it, obviously keen to get his point across. 'I guess that's me schooled.'

'I didn't intend for it to feel that way.' He seems genuinely disappointed by this. 'I was simply making a suggestion. Why don't you give me something back and then we're equal?'

'Ooh, don't tempt me.' I throw him a wicked grin.

'I'm serious. Give me something I can work with.'

'OK...' I sip at my drink thoughtfully, trying to put together the thing I most want to say to him in the most diplomatic way I can come up with. 'Don't take this the wrong way, but you come across as a bit of a grumpy grouch.'

'A grumpy grouch?' He repeats this back to me with his eyebrows raised.

Feeling like I've gone too far, I brace myself for what I consider to be an inevitable backlash, but it doesn't come.

'I guess I've heard different versions of that over the last few years,' he says, after chewing on my comment for several seconds. 'But yours is by far the most *Sesame Street* of them.'

'*Sesame Street*?' I snigger at this.

'Yes. Your description makes me think of Oscar the Grouch.'

'Oh yeah, I see how you got there.'

'I don't mean to be a "grumpy grouch" or a "honey badger" as Lauren has described me on occasion. Honey badgers have the reputation of being the world's most bad-tempered animal in case you didn't know.' He looks a bit pained by this label. 'I've had my fill of being let down by people in my life and I guess it's sucked the joy out of me or something. That's why I prefer to spend my time with the animals. They're way less complicated than people and they can't lie to you.'

I feel a pang of sympathy for Nick alongside a touch of sadness that he has so little faith in the human race. I can also understand where he's coming from to some extent, because I feel continually let down by my parents, but at least I have Seth. If Nick has a void and hasn't got anyone to fill it – and worse, the person who previously filled it hurt him – then that must be a very lonely place in life.

As I consider all this, an unpleasant thought creeps into my mind: if Seth hadn't made it through, or if he were to have another stroke and die, I would be alone. Sure, I have Amelia and other friends dotted around the country, but it would never be the same. That void would be a huge gaping chasm. I shudder at this thought.

'Are you all right?' Nick's face turns to one of concern. 'You look troubled.'

He reaches across the table and for a heart-stopping moment I think he's going to take my hand, but then his line of sight shifts. Instead, he picks up the napkin my drink was previously sitting on – I'm guessing to stop it blowing away in the breeze.

'I'm fine,' I reply, feeling disappointed and rejected even though I have no justifiable reason for this. 'Just had an unpleasant thought. Nothing to be concerned about.'

'OK, if you're sure. I'm always here if you need someone to talk to. Oscar the Grouch might not seem the most natural person to share your worries with, but he's a good listener.'

He points a finger to his chest and I melt a little at the sweetness of this gesture, which further adds to my disappointment that I misread his signals before.

'Seriously though, I mean it,' he continues. 'Though I don't really do people, the guys here – Gwen, Serge, Lauren, Monika, Hakeem – they're like family. While you're here, you'll be considered a foster member of that family, no matter how much you try and distance yourself from us.'

'I don't try to—'

'Yes, you do. Don't try and pull that one with me, Jess. You're like "Ms Career Woman of the Year", all professional and maintaining boundaries – apart from when we're sparring like brother and sister, that is.'

There is it again. Nick's clear signalling – whether conscious or not – that he doesn't see me as anything more than a slightly annoying but loveable sibling. Well, that's probably for the best, I tell the side of me that's continually disappointed by this. It wouldn't have been a good idea to get involved with one of my client's management team anyway.

Chapter 19

After my date-that-wasn't-a-date with Nick, I seek out Lauren and let her know I'm heading off. I've pre-agreed with her that I have to leave the event slightly early, which she's fine with. She's also absolutely buzzing at how well the pilot has gone.

'I can't believe how smoothly everything went.' She's practically jumping up and down on the spot. 'Jess, this has been a triumph.'

'It sure has.' I'm delighted to see her feeling so positive. 'You should feel very proud.'

'I do, but I'm also so grateful to you for this. For all your help and guidance and for coming up with this idea.'

'I didn't come up with this idea. Hakeem did – and then you brought it to life, which is the most important part.'

'Do you really think I'm that daft?' Lauren gives me a sly smile. 'Remember that I study behavioural science. You knew exactly what kind of events you wanted us to put on. You deliberately set us up with the right environment so we'd land on the ideas you wanted us to and think we'd come up with them ourselves.'

'No, that's not…' I start to deny Lauren's allegation, then spot the look on her face and hold my hands up in surrender. 'OK, you've got me. But I stand by my statement that you brought this event to life. I would never have thought of the whole "animal personality type" thing, nor would I have thought we'd have the capability to do it to such a professional standard.'

'Well, I guess I can take some credit then.'

'Most of the credit.' I emphasise these words as I say them.

'Aww, thanks.' She seems pleased by this. 'How did your date with Nick go, by the way?'

'It wasn't a date, remember? It was me doing you a favour to make up numbers.'

'Obviously.' Lauren has a twinkle in her eye. 'Anyway, how did it go?'

'Why aren't you asking me that about my other two "dates"?' I eye her suspiciously.

'Because neither of them were with the hot-but-growly head keeper of this place. Come on, give me some juice. You guys are off the scale compatibility wise.'

'So you said – which makes me question whether your personality assessment deserves an A+ after all.'

'You can't argue with the experts. I had a professor look over it.'

'Hmm...' I'm unconvinced by this. 'Then to answer your question, it was fine.'

'Just fine?' she asks with an impish grin.

'Yes. We used the opportunity to get to know each other better to improve our working relationship.'

'Yeah, whatever. But was there a spark? I can totally feel the chemistry between you when you're butting heads. You're like a couple of horny hyenas.'

'*Lauren.*' I warn her to lower her voice and she at least obliges.

'I'm just saying. There's something big between the two of you. The sooner you see that, the sooner you can start having amazing sex – and perhaps more.'

'OK, this conversation is over.' I scoff and start to walk away, but she grabs my hand to stop me.

'Jess, you do realise that I can see exactly what's going on. It's so obvious. It's killing me watching you lust over him and do precisely jack shit about it. Talk to me, please.'

Nick's words about me being overly professional and not letting my guard down ring in my mind and I give in.

'Fine. You're right, I'm attracted to him. Although I'm not totally sure if I like him, if that makes any sense. We get on well and then suddenly we don't. I think I might be starting to understand him a bit better, but it's still confusing and infuriating, and none of that actually matters, because he doesn't like me back.'

'Yeah, I'm calling bullshit on that one.' Lauren hoots with laughter. 'Where's your evidence?'

I reel off all the things that have happened and what Nick has said, and I see Lauren falter, but she recovers quickly.

'All circumstantial, my lord.' She waves away my concerns. 'You couldn't build a court case on that.'

'Nor would you throw yourself at someone with it in the mix.'

'Fair enough. But I'm still convinced I'm right. You'll see.'

'Whatever.' I sigh and pat her on the back. 'Now, I have to go because I'm really late.'

'Of course. See you next week. We can iron out the wrinkles before the official launch and maybe get Nick to help us with the logistics?' Lauren's voice is simultaneously loaded with smugness and laced with a touch of conspiracy as I walk away.

Refusing to entertain any more of her nonsense and not wanting to encourage her any more than I already have, I simply give her a wave over my shoulder.

Walking to my car, my mind involuntarily plays back the conversation with Lauren. She may be totally convinced there's something between Nick and I, but he couldn't have been clearer. That comment about me being part of the park family surely wasn't made without intent. Then there are the previous comments he's made about me not being his type, and how he told me he gives people like me a wide berth when we had our spat in the elephant enclosure. Even if I wanted Lauren's assertions to be true – purely to satiate the part of me driven by lust – it's clear that my feelings for Nick are not reciprocated. And as I've already told myself in consolation, that's very much for the best.

On reaching the car park, I unlock my car while still lost in thought, and it's only when I'm about to get into the driver's side that I hear someone calling my name. Looking up, I see Nick jogging towards me.

'Is everything OK?' My first reaction is one of concern. 'Has something gone wrong?'

He stops in front of me, trying to catch his breath, which tells me he's run all the way here.

'I've just been speaking to Lauren.'

'Oh shit, I knew I shouldn't have left early. What's happened? I'll come back with you.'

'No, it's not that.' He bends over, still puffed.

I stand there, perplexed. 'Either you're badly unfit or you've just attempted a four hundred metre sprint with no training.'

'The latter.' Nick coughs and then stands up.

'So what's going on? You have me on tenterhooks here.'

Having finally recovered, he looks me straight in the eye. '*This* is what's going on.'

Stepping forward confidently, he cups my face gently with his hands, then hesitates, looking suddenly uncertain. I give an instinctive nod and he follows through with the most delicious kiss I've experienced in a long time. It happens so fast, I barely have time to register what's going on, but as the feeling of his touch reaches every part of me, my heart quickens, my stomach leaps and my legs turn to mush. Allowing myself to melt into him, our bodies almost as one, all I know is that I don't want this to stop. His kiss and his touch match his brusque but caring demeanour: hungry and raw, but with a gentleness that oozes respect.

Eventually, we pull apart and start to laugh. It's that nervous 'what have we just done' type of laughter. Nick threads his fingers through mine, while I look at him coyly, almost unable to believe what's just happened.

'Well, that was a surprise. When you say you were speaking to Lauren, was that about this?' I gesture back and forth between our lips with my index finger.

'Might have been.' Nick looks shifty all of a sudden.

'She's such a little meddler.'

'Is that such a bad thing?'

'No, I guess not, given I was convinced you weren't interested.'

'I wonder how you got that impression.' He kicks at the gravel awkwardly.

As he says this, a thought comes to me. 'So you *were* hitting on me that day in the hospital car park. I was right.'

Nick looks appalled. 'Give me some credit, would you? Being totally honest, you were all red and blotchy that day, so I couldn't really see *who* you were.'

'An ugly crier from the sounds of it.'

Cringing at the thought of what a mess I must have looked, I finally realise how off the mark I was in accusing Nick of coming on to me.

'I genuinely didn't look at you from that perspective,' he continues. 'Then when you first arrived here – not all red and blotchy – I thought you were pretty, but a bit stuck-up.'

'Thanks.' I feel a bit stung by his lack of tact.

'Sorry. But I'd rather you know the truth than still suspect me to be a "lech".'

I shake my head in an attempt to digest all this. 'So when did you decide I was pretty *and* your type?'

'Not sure really.' He shrugs. 'You grew on me.'

'I "grew on you". What does that mean?'

'Well, you know…' He shifts uncomfortably under my scrutiny. 'Seeing you getting all gooey with Rana, it made you seem more human and… sort of cute.'

'"Cute", huh?' The corners of my mouth twitch as I continue to tease him with his own words. 'Well, maybe now's the moment to admit it was Rana that got me to see you in a different light as well. Big gruff man playing with tiny bear cub. What's not to like?'

Nick seems a bit embarrassed by this comment, so naturally I turn things up a notch.

'You might even go so far as to say Rana's secretly playing cupid—'

'OK, that's enough of that.' He cuts me off, his face flaming. 'Anyway, the point is… actually, I don't know what the point is.' He seems at a complete loss for words, making me laugh.

'I think *this* is the point.' I step forward and this time it's me who pulls him in for a lengthy, mind-blowing kiss, while I push how late I am to the back of my mind.

Chapter 20

Driving home to Edinburgh, I feel alive in a way I haven't felt in weeks. Basically, since Seth's stroke. Flitting memories dance through my mind: the feel of Nick's lips on mine, his firm but gentle touch, the way we moulded together so perfectly in those short moments – and I can't help but shiver with desire. I've never been the kind to need a man to complete me. I'm independent, ambitious, stubborn even. If I allow someone into my life it's because they fit with all that and add an additional positive element to my being. And boy, did Nick add the latter tonight. It was fireworks-meets-forty-piece-brass-band-playing-the-*Star-Wars*-theme-tune. He's definitely the right kind of distraction from the stresses I've been experiencing lately.

Turning up the music on the car stereo, I belt out the words to my favourite happy sunny day song, 'Mr Blue Sky', grinning to myself as I shoot back along the A1.

At home, my focus swiftly shifts back to reality and I'm full of apologies, especially as it's now after seven p.m.

'Jackson, I'm so sorry. I got… held up.' Hopefully he doesn't cotton on to the heat radiating from my face as I say this.

'Hey, Jess, no worries.' He greets me with a relaxed smile, easy-going as ever. 'I've told you before, I'm good for working later. Being straight, the extra pay helps.'

'OK, as long as you're sure?' I study his expression to make sure he's not just saying that to make me feel better.

'I'm sure. Serious. Any point you need me to work into the evening, on a weekend, whenever, you let me know.'

I squirrel this gem of an offer away. 'Thanks Jackson, I'll take you up on that, for sure.' Especially if it helps me with my career-saving endeavours, I think to myself. If Mum and Dad are going to continue to be in absentia, clearing their consciences with international bank transfers, then I may as well make use of that arrangement – so long as there's no detrimental impact on Seth.

I suddenly have an idea. 'Actually, seeing as I'm so late, I was going to pop over the road and get an Indian takeaway for dinner, if you fancy joining us? My treat, as a thank you.'

Jackson makes an exaggerated show of weighing up his options. 'Why not, eh? Saves me cooking.'

'Great. Why don't you head back through then and I'll grab a menu.'

I quickly get changed, then join the guys in the living room, handing the takeaway menu to Jackson so he can choose his food. I know that Seth and I will just end up having our usuals.

'Hi, Seth.' I plant a kiss on the top of my brother's head in my usual manner, but instead of receiving his usual laid-back – if now slightly lopsided – smile, he flicks me away with his better arm.

'Sis… you are… ruin-ing my… street cred.'

'What are you talking about? I always… oh.' I look to Jackson, who gives me a wink in return. 'Sorry, big bro. I'll try to remember not to do that when we have company. How was your day?'

'It was… great.'

'That's good. What did you get up to?'

'I met… a beau… beau-tiful woman.'

Seth's speech is coming along well through the therapy he's receiving. He's now able to put a couple of words together at a time, but the trickier sounds still pose him a challenge.

'Oh yeah? Tell me more about that.' I raise an eyebrow at Jackson and he waggles his own back at me in confirmation of this.

'Her name is… Alison. She was at the… phys… the phys-io's office.'

'I see. Is she a patient too?'

'No, she was… with her father. He had… a stroke, like me. She was… chatting me up.'

'Right.' I look to Jackson, who nods confirmation this time, and though I'm unsure why, I feel a little uneasy about this. 'So that must have been a nice ego boost.'

'It was. She asked me… if I'd… like to have coffee… in the park, one day.'

'She did?' My feeling of unease deepens. 'That's great. Shall we get our order in and you can tell me more over dinner?'

I submit an online order for collection to the takeaway restaurant and bustle around in the kitchen getting plates, cutlery and drinks ready. As I do, my brain ticks over what Seth has just told me. So a woman has shown interest in him. Why do I have an issue with that? It never bothered me before – but then, that was during a time when Seth was a big burly lad who could more than look after himself. Now he's… vulnerable. He can't walk – yet. He's coming through a major physical and emotional trauma, whether he admits the emotional side of it or not. He acts as if he's taking all this in his stride, but I know him well enough to pick up that he does struggle at times. He's just too proud to admit it. What if he started seeing this woman and—

'I know what's going on in your head.' Jackson enters the kitchen, interrupting my thoughts. 'It's perfectly natural to be protective of Seth. It doesn't make you a bad person, if that's what you're thinking.'

I wince at the accuracy of his observation and put down the glass I'm holding on the kitchen counter. 'I hadn't got to the guilt part yet, but it was coming.'

'You're doing a great job, Jess.'

'Am I? I mean, I hope I am, but I find it so hard to know. He seems happy but I see moments of frustration or sadness in his eyes.'

Jackson looks at me meaningfully. 'I'd be worried if you didn't, because that would mean he's in denial, and that doesn't help recovery. Seth's withholding all right; I can see that. But he's still in the early stages of accepting all this and getting used to his new reality, which, remember, is changing all the time. He's making steps forward and he'll only really know where he's at when those steps become smaller and smaller, until they eventually seem non-existent. That's when he'll know what he's really dealing with long term.'

'That's an interesting way of looking at it.' I reach for the glass, then retract my hand as more worrisome thoughts descend on me. 'How can I make sure I do right by him, Jackson? Our parents are a complete let-down, and while I want to throw my everything into this, I also still want to succeed in my career. Is that selfish – finding it a battle to put my needs second to Seth's all the time?'

'No. Absolutely not. If you don't look after you and your needs, you can't do the best for Seth. Also, if you do happen to end up with long-term caring responsibilities of any kind, a good career will help with the financial side – because I'm assuming your parents don't have a bottomless pit of cash.'

'You're right, they don't. I guess I need to double down and make sure I can provide for the two of us, just in case. Gosh, you know your stuff, Jackson.' I turn away for a second as the emotional weight of the conversation makes my eyes sting.

'I've been doing this for a long time.' He lifts the plates and cutlery I've prepared to set the table. 'Seen many situations, listened to a lot of worries, answered a lot of questions – most of them related to self-doubt and wanting to do the best for loved ones.'

'So how do I do that? My best, I mean.'

'Just keep doing what you're doing, give him some freedom to keep pushing forward and hold his hand along the way – metaphorically speaking, of course. You don't want to go damaging that precious "street cred" of his.'

I chuckle. 'No. That's particularly important to him. And the woman who's asked him out?' My face turns serious again.

'Honestly? I think you need to stay out of it. Seth's an adult. He's lost so much independence. Best leave him feeling like he has control over something in his life. You can't protect him from everything.'

'I guess you're right.' I wince at this thought, despite fully understanding where Jackson's coming from. 'Thanks for the perspective.'

'You're more than welcome.' He pats me kindly on the arm, then leaves the kitchen with the crockery.

Pausing for a moment to reflect on everything we've just talked about, I lean on the kitchen counter, my palms flat against the cool laminate. In a way, I feel lighter and freer, knowing that I'm doing the best job I can, and also knowing that my overprotectiveness is normal. It's something I can work on. However, one weight in my mind has just gotten heavier, and that's my need to get my career back on track. If I'm going to create a safety net for the future, I can't allow Craig and his prejudices to get in the way. That means it's time to start looking at other options on top of making the wildlife park becomes one of Scotland's top go-to destinations.

Then I catch another unpleasant thought circling in my mind, offering me a reality check I'm not sure I want right now: should I really be getting involved with Nick when my focus needs to be on Seth and my job?

Chapter 21

I chew on my Nick-shaped dilemma the whole weekend, in between looking after (and hanging out with) Seth, supporting him with his physical therapy 'homework', and doing the usual household tasks. It seems like a no-brainer at first: I have important, not quite life or death, but life-altering things going on that require my full attention. Getting involved with Nick means I will not be giving them my full attention – which means I should not get involved with Nick. Plus, he's a member of the management team I'm working with. While Lauren and Serge seem to be egging me on, and it's not expressly forbidden in my employment contract, it's also pretty much a no-no. My quandary is quite straightforward when laid out like that.

On the other hand, there's the argument that the more you try to stay away from something forbidden, the more you want it. Obviously, I can try not to give in to temptation, but let's face it, when you've kissed someone and you really want to kiss them again, and they want to kiss you – well, it's going to be hard to stop. Also, Jackson made it clear that I have to see to my own needs so that I have the energy and motivation to care for Seth. It's that argument of putting on your own lifejacket first. When I think about what that means in practice, it feels a little selfish, but I also know he's right. How can I step up and be the rock Seth needs me to be if I'm running on empty – physically, mentally and emotionally?

So, here's the deal: I'll see where this thing goes with Nick, but I'll make sure it doesn't interfere with my work at the park, nor with my arrangements for looking after Seth. In reality, what this means is that Nick and I will be able to spend lunch breaks together and not much more – unless Jackson's offer of doing some extra hours extends to enabling my love life. The good thing is that Seth seems to see Jackson as one of his bros, which means he'll be more than happy to spend more time with him.

I'll keep things light and casual with Nick, at least for now. I don't need the lines blurring and I don't want Nick to feel obliged to get involved with my situation; he's clearly been burned before in a past relationship, the last thing I want is to drag him into my own emotional mess, or to lead him into a relationship I can't fully deliver on myself. The easiest thing will be to leave Seth out of the equation altogether – though I realise keeping a secret that size may not be easy.

My heart pinches remembering what he said on our not-a-date, about animals not being able to lie to him. But this is different. It's for his own good – or at least that's what I'm telling myself.

-

By the time Tuesday rolls around, my stomach is filled with butterflies, making me feel part drunk on the anticipation of seeing Nick again, and part queasy with nerves for the very same reason. It's a bit weird having left things where they were with him on Thursday. We made no plans and didn't even swap numbers. We just kissed (a lot) then quickly wrapped things up because I had to leave. He had no idea why I was in such a rush and thankfully he didn't question it. I did, of course, look him up on Facebook and found a barely active account with a picture of him that looked about five years old. I then almost sent him a message through Messenger to get some chat going, but I backed off. Or wimped out, which might be a more honest way of putting it.

'Good morning, how was your weekend?' His wonderfully familiar gruff voice greets me as I'm getting out of my car at the wildlife park at 8:30 a.m.

'It was good, thanks.' I'm delighted by this unexpected welcome, my eyes flitting to the two takeaway coffees he's holding. 'Is that for me?'

'No, I have a meeting with Gwen in a moment.'

'Oh, that's awkward.' I feel my cheeks flush. 'I shouldn't have assumed, sorry.'

'Of course it's for you.' He grins at me in a boyish way I haven't seen on him before. 'I brought a couple of sugar sachets as I remember you said you normally take your coffee with it.'

'How thoughtful, thank you. I know it's bad for me but I can't quite kick the habit.'

'We all have our weaknesses.'

Nick's eyes linger on me, leaving me in no doubt that, at this moment in time, I'm his. This instantly reignites the animalistic feelings of desire that consumed me in this very spot five days before. My mind, replaying those charged moments on autopilot, quickly strays on to the next level fantasy.

'Have you got time to drink it here?' He gestures to a bench on the other side of my car, which is facing outwards across the fields and concentrated areas of woodland.

'Uh… yeah.' I drag my brain out of the gutter and force myself to put my lustful thoughts aside. 'I'm not meeting the guys until nine a.m., so I'm all yours for now.'

Despite my frisky inner dialogue, this is meant as an innocent comment, but the moment our eyes lock it becomes loaded with suggestion. Unsure what to do, we smile at each other shyly then make our way to the bench.

'What a lovely view.' I sit down and take my coffee from Nick.

'This is a great area generally.' He takes a seat beside me while I stir sugar into my drink. 'Do you know East Lothian well?'

'Not really.' I take a first sip and let out a satisfied sigh, which is as much about the company and the surroundings as the coffee itself. 'I grew up in Edinburgh, but other than the odd day trip to North Berwick, I've not spent much time here.'

'That's a shame. Though it does give me the opportunity to show you a few places. I mean, if you're interested, that is?' He seems to realise he's been presumptuous.

'That would be nice.' I automatically reassure him, while wondering when I might actually be able to do something like that.

Without being able to develop this conversation into a concrete arrangement, and with us not having spoken since our 'brief encounter' last week, we reach a dead end and sit in semi-uncomfortable silence for at least thirty seconds. During this time, it becomes obvious to me that we need to 'clear the air', so to speak.

'About last week—' we both suddenly say at the same time, then stop short and laugh.

'We seem to have a knack for that. Please, you go first,' I prompt him, keen to know where his head is at, although I already have an inkling from his actions this morning.

'OK, I… erm…' He clears his throat. 'I was going to say that I hope that you don't have any regrets about, you know… because I certainly don't.'

Though I suspected this was the case, I was still keen to hear him say it. I also find his awkwardness quite adorable.

'No regrets here either.' I place my hand on his in illustration of this and he looks more relieved than I would have expected. 'I actually nearly messaged you through social media at the weekend but then I chickened out.'

'Don't feel bad. I was exactly the same.'

'You were?'

'Yes. It made me feel like I was twelve years old again.' He screws up his nose ashamedly at this admission.

'Well, there was no sign of that twelve-year-old boy last Thursday.' I nudge him in the ribs cheekily.

'That is true.' He scoffs and his faces reddens slightly. 'Must have been the "now or never" chat Lauren gave me – which on reflection didn't have quite the urgency she made it out to have. Plus, I have an admission to make on that front.'

'Which is?'

'I may have knocked back some vodka before running after you out of the park.'

I erupt with laughter. 'So that's where the sudden boldness came from. There was me thinking it was some Hollywood-level gesture borne out of your overwhelming need to kiss me.'

This time Nick turns beetroot and tries to hide his discomfort by glugging at his coffee. Unfortunately, this results in him scalding his mouth and crying out in pain.

'*I'm sorry.*' My hand flies to my mouth and I reach out to him in concern. 'I was just teasing you.'

'It's fine. I'm fine.' He tries to wave the situation away, and in doing so, dislodges the lid on his coffee cup, causing the roasting hot contents to slop onto his thigh. This time he lets out a kind of manly yelp.

'Oh my goodness, Nick. Are you OK?' I hurriedly dig in my bag to find some clean tissues, then dab at his leg with them hopelessly.

'I'm fine, honestly. And there's no need for that. These overalls have been covered in a lot worse.'

'Of course.' I stop dabbing and look at him with big regretful eyes. 'I am sorry though.'

'For what? Making a joke?' He sets his now almost empty coffee cup aside on the bench. 'Am I such a "grumpy grouch" that you feel the need to apologise for lightening the mood?'

'No. I feel the need to apologise for you scalding yourself – twice – because of me trying to keep the mood light. We might need to complete a health and safety risk assessment if we're going to keep this up. Anyway, you were telling me about the vodka. Where did that come from?'

'I'll let you guess.'

'Lauren? No, Serge.'

'Spot on.' Nick nods. 'Much as I wanted to act on things, I was making my usual excuses to avoid having to put myself out there, and Serge overheard. He pulled out a hip flask and told me to "get it down me".'

'Which you did.'

'Yes, then I retched for a bit and thought I was going to be sick, before Lauren gave me some chewing gum to mask the taste and I eventually took off after you.'

'So romantic.' I giggle.

He shrugs and gives me a weak smile. 'I aim to please.'

'Well, the bit I experienced was romantic, and if you're OK with it, I'd like a rerun.'

'What, same again this Thursday? I guess I can do that, but don't be expecting it weekly. That would be taking the piss,' he quips.

'I was just referring to the kiss.' I bite my lip in anticipation, as Nick assumes a look of borderline panic – perhaps at the thought of making the first move on command and vodka free. 'OK, allow me.'

Having gravitated closer to each other during this exchange, all I have to do is put down my coffee and take Nick's from him – to avoid any further incidents – then I slip my arms around his neck and pull him into a deep kiss that's fizzing with longing. He responds hungrily, and before I realise what's happening, we're getting quite frisky and carried away, my whole body tingling with desire.

Suddenly, there's a loud thumping noise and we jolt apart. Following the sound, we turn and find to our horror that we have an audience. Lauren, the man who runs the park's ticket office and another female staff member I don't recognise are all glued to the window overlooking the car park, hammering on it, while laughing and making thumbs-up gestures at us.

'I think that means we've been caught,' says Nick, who doesn't seem at all bothered by this.

'I think you're right.' I gulp, as it becomes clear to me what this might mean. 'Suppose it would have been naïve of me to expect that Lauren and Serge would keep this on the down-low. You know how I said I want to rescue my career? Well, this could be what sinks it.'

'You think your boss will have an issue with it.' Nick says this as a statement of understanding rather than a question.

'At the very least, I think that's a distinct possibility. And to be fair, it wouldn't be wholly unreasonable of him to be concerned that it might damage the company's reputation.'

'Then in that case, let's go to Gwen – right now.'

I look at him in alarm. 'And say what? We don't even know what this is yet.'

'Doesn't matter.' Nick is already on his feet. 'It's something, and it's going to get round the place quickly, because that woman standing next to Lauren is essentially the source of all the park gossip.'

'Aww man, this is really not the start to my day I needed,' I grumble without thinking.

Nick's face falls and he looks really gutted. 'This is my fault, Jess. I apologise for putting you in this position.'

Realising the impact I've had on him, I regret my clumsy reaction and grab his hand tightly.

'Hey, you have *nothing* to apologise for. I'm a big girl. I could have declined your offer of having coffee here. It was also me that kissed you. I've made my bed and now I need to face the consequences, so you're right, let's go and speak to Gwen before it gets back to her another way.' I'm feeling way less confident than I'm making out, but there's no way I'm letting Nick carry that guilt. I reach up and kiss him tenderly on the lips. 'Let's see what the judge and executioner have to say, yeah?'

Chapter 22

Nick and I are immediately thwarted in our quest to speak to Gwen. Having forgotten in the heat of the moment that I have a project meeting to run, we quickly come up with a game plan for when we do speak to her, then I head straight to the meeting room, while Nick is left to find something else to focus on for the next hour until I'm free again. He looks a bit lost as I'm leaving him – despite what I've said, I know he still feels responsible for this mess I'm potentially in with Craig – so I give his hand another reassuring squeeze before I go.

In a way, it's funny how I'm the one dishing out the emotional support when I'm also the one with the most at stake, but having finally found Nick's vulnerable side, I feel this insane urge to protect him. Perhaps that's because I know he's been hurt in the past, or it could just be that I'm developing real feelings for him already. Whatever it is, it's at least a helpful distraction from what the nagging voice in my head is telling me that is, if Craig has a problem with Nick and I seeing each other, then I'll have no choice but to call it quits with Nick to save my career.

I sail through the project meeting agenda points at record speed, in the hope that I can maybe wrap things up a little early. Everything seems to be well on track, with Lauren ready to kick off the first paid events this week, and Serge having secured contracts with several suppliers for the park's Christmas market. Monika has made good progress with the retiree events, which will now have a chartered coach as part of the offering at an additional charge. She's also confirmed, much to our delight, that our group of retirees would in fact be interested in having some dating events of their own. That really brightens my morning, because it will provide a further revenue stream with minimal additional effort.

At the end of the meeting, which I manage to bring to a close twenty-five minutes early, I'm about to shoot out of the room when Lauren blocks my escape route with a telling glint in her eye. Thankfully, she waits for Serge and Monika to leave the room before saying anything, but it's clear she's after juice – and she'll be hard to put off.

'How are things with lover boy?' Her mouth spreads into a mischievous grin.

'I think you know how they are, given you secured yourself a front row seat at our morning coffee catch-up.' I raise a judgemental eyebrow.

'What? You think I was there on purpose? No, I was checking in with Gordon about…' She hesitates on seeing my sceptical expression. 'OK, I saw Nick getting coffees and heading for the gate and I was curious.'

'You mean nosey?'

'Oh, come on. I finally got the two of you together. You should be thanking me.'

'OK, thank you for giving me a giant pain in the arse of a problem.' I roll my eyes as I say this, but make sure to smile so she knows I'm joking. 'I'm now on my way to see Gwen with Nick to declare our "conflict of interest", which might or might not cost me my job and/or my career.'

'You'll be fine. Gwen's a pussycat. She'll probably thank you for taking him on.' She laughs loudly at her own joke.

'It's not so much Gwen I'm concerned about. Nick's certainly not. Though I'm not sure how she'll react if she thinks the contractor she's hired to save her business is putting more effort into getting it on with one of her management team.'

Lauren bobs her head as she weighs this up. 'I suppose if you look at it like that. Guess all you can do is have the conversation and find out. So, it's your boss you're really worried about then?'

Dammit. Why didn't I keep my trap shut? I've overshared and now all I want to do is hit the eject button. Floundering for a moment, I decide the best thing to do is avoid answering the question.

'Look, sorry Lauren, I need to go. Let's get a coffee at some point, yeah?' This isn't a wholly sincere suggestion, but I can't feel bad about that right now when there are more pressing matters to see to.

'Yes, let's.' She seems pleased by my invite that isn't really an invite, and I'm about to make my move when she looks me straight in the eye with an earnest expression. 'Jess, I get the impression you're dealing with a lot in your life, and I want you to know that I'm here for you. I can be discreet, I promise. Don't see me as your client's daughter, see me as a friend – someone you can trust.'

As she says this, something tugs at me inside, and I recognise this as a longing to share all the stuff I'm shouldering. While I do talk about things with Amelia on our calls, it's not the same as having someone physically there. A swell of emotion chokes my throat and I swallow it down before it can give me away.

'Thanks Lauren,' I simply say in response. 'I'll keep that in mind.'

–

After roaming round the park looking for Nick so we can speak to Gwen a little earlier, I eventually find him standing outside the main office waiting for me at five to ten.

'I think it's time we swapped numbers.' I throw my hands up in light-hearted frustration. 'I've been looking all over for you.'

'Is that maybe a bit premature?' He grimaces at me in an almost defeatist way. 'If this doesn't go the way we want, I'm all too aware it'll be over before it's even started.'

Unable to provide any meaningful reassurance, I mirror his expression. 'Well, the sooner we get in there, the sooner we can find out.'

'OK, but before we go inside…' He grabs my hand and pulls me into an embrace that makes me tingle from the top of my head to the tips of my toes, leaving me aching for more the moment he lets me go.

'Wow. You've conquered your shyness quickly.' I touch my lips gently.

'I guess when you think it might be your last, you have to make it count.' He looks genuinely sad and my heart melts.

'You know, I was thinking as I was walking around looking for you… if Craig has an issue with this, he can only really do so as long as I'm working with the park – which means we'd only have to behave ourselves until the contract ends or I can get myself moved back onto my previous projects.'

'Is that right?' Nick's face brightens and he reaches forward to tuck a flyaway section of hair behind my ear.

'Yes. So it wouldn't be over for good, it would be over for now. Though let's not underestimate how challenging it could be working side by side if that's the case.'

I flash him a suggestive grin and he visibly deflates at the thought of having to resist that ongoing temptation. This pleases me no end – I mean, who doesn't want to feel desirable? – and it seems like, right now, to Nick, I am currently the very definition of that.

'The really big issue here is my career at Capital Events, and how much more damage I've done to it.'

This time Nick takes my hand gently and places it on his chest protectively. 'Jess, whatever goes down here, I've got your back. Me, Lauren, Serge, the whole lot of us. We're going to save the park and save your career at the same time, I promise.'

'I wish I was as optimistic as you. Shall we?' I gesture to the door and with a final shared deep breath, we walk through it together.

Chapter 23

On entering the main open-plan office, I feel all the eyes of the room's inhabitants on us, projecting knowing looks accompanied by giggling whispers.

'Bloody hell,' I mutter under my breath. 'You weren't kidding when you said that woman was a major gossip. Everyone in here already knows and I can't imagine it was Lauren who told them.'

'Didn't I tell you?' Nick replies out the corner of his mouth. 'We may or may not have got to Gwen first.'

Reaching her office door, Nick knocks and enters with me trailing behind him like I'm walking to the stake. Gwen only momentarily glances up from the printed sheets of paper she's poring over.

'Ah, Nick, Jess. Come on in and have a seat.'

We sit down on the chairs in front of her desk and wait for her to finish what she's doing. When she eventually looks up at us properly, she takes off her glasses, her expression unreadable.

'I hear you two have something to tell me.'

I give Nick a sideways glance, unsure how to respond to this.

'Word has gotten round then, I assume.' He saves me the pain of having to do so.

'It has,' says Gwen. 'It's all that lot out there can talk about, and I'd prefer it if they would get on with some actual work.'

Hearing this, my stomach pools with a mix of guilt and shame, making me feel a little sick. I had hoped we could convince Gwen and Craig that Nick and I seeing each other wouldn't get in the way of our work, but what are the chances of that when it's already getting in the way of everyone else's? I realise I need to make this right – and fast.

'Gwen, I'm so sorry about this situation,' I rush to explain. 'I'm aware that it's completely unprofessional, and well… it just sort of happened off the back of the dating event rehearsal, but we will absolutely not go there again while I'm working here, I promise you that…'

I can feel Nick's incredulous eyes practically burning through me, and I know exactly what he's thinking: this is not at all how we agreed to manage this conversation. But the problem is, I'm in panic mode, and really, it's the only right thing to do.

'We didn't want you to hear it from the park grapevine,' I continue like a runaway train. 'We wanted to tell you ourselves and show you the respect you deserve, but I had my project meeting first thing and—'

'Jess, stop.' Gwen holds up a commanding hand and I cease my blabbering.

Daring a glance at Nick, I see him shake his head in disbelief at my manic outpouring, which makes me feel even worse, because now I'm worried that I've hurt him. The wait for Gwen to speak feels like an eternity. She appears to be gathering her thoughts in a similar way to when she prepared her impromptu speech for her management team the other week.

'Jess, Nick…' she addresses us eventually. 'I did hear this morning about how your working relationship has progressed to a romantic one.' I cringe as she says this. 'I've also heard that it is a very recent turn of events, so I imagine the two of you don't yet know what it means for you.'

I nod vehemently. 'Exactly, which means we can and absolutely will nip it in the bud.'

Nick shoots me a look that says '*Seriously?*' and I shrink back like a tortoise retreating into my shell.

'Perhaps you can let me speak, Jess?' says Gwen, and this time my nod is a sheepish one. 'All right, thank you. What I was going to say was that I apologise for the behaviour of that lot outside.' She jabs a forefinger in the direction of the main office floor behind us.

'They're nothing we can't handle. At least, that's what I thought before we walked in here and you did that.' Nick gives me a pointed look.

'What exactly did I do?' I snipe back at him, knowing exactly what I did but unable to own up to it right then and there under the weight of my mortification. Then, horrified by my actions, I turn to Gwen and apologise.

Nick however, doesn't seem remotely fazed by Gwen's presence. 'Do I really need to spell it out? You totally jumped the gun by—'

'All right,' Gwen interjects, silencing Nick. 'I can see that this situation is causing both of you some stress and I want to be up front, not least so I can put your mind at rest, Jess. I have no problem whatsoever with the two of you dating. In fact, it's been nice to see Nick with a bit of a spring in his step these last few days.'

A look of surprise appears on Nick's face.

She raises her eyebrows at him. 'You think I didn't notice? Son, you're my most treasured member of staff, because of your expertise and your commitment to the animals and the park. But I'm afraid to say, you've been a miserable bugger for the last three years.'

I have to stifle a giggle as Nick looks like he's been stripped to his underwear and paraded around the penguin enclosure.

'Right, well, thanks for the feedback,' he mumbles. 'I won't say it's timely, given it's three years late.'

'You were in no place to hear it three years ago, never mind three months ago, so don't give me that,' Gwen tuts at him. 'Anyway, as I was saying, I'm pleased that the two of you have… found a connection. I have no issue with this whatsoever, though that said – and I'm not sure I need to say this, because I trust you both implicitly – I would only ask that you don't let it interfere with your jobs.'

'It wouldn't interfere in any way, Gwen,' I assure her. 'There's no way I'd let that happen, and I really appreciate your vote of confidence in me, especially as you haven't known me long. It's just, well, for me, this isn't just about what you think, it's also about what my boss thinks when you tell him.'

'Why would I talk to him about this?' She picks up a pen from her desk and taps it thoughtfully against her left temple.

'Because it's a potential conflict of interest. Because Craig has placed me here to deliver a contract and I've blurred the lines between that and my personal life. He may think I've behaved unprofessionally and put this project, as well as the company's reputation, in jeopardy.'

Gwen puffs out her cheeks then exhales heavily. 'He will think that. Of course he will – which is precisely why I'm not going to tell him.'

'You're not?'

'No, Jess. Your boss, Craig, is… how do I put this nicely… no, sorry, there's no way to say it nicely. He's a twat in a suit.'

'I'm sorry?' I blink at Gwen in disbelief, then look to Nick, who simply shrugs.

She gets up from behind her desk and slowly paces back and forth, arms behind her back. 'I apologise if you find this unprofessional, Jess, but I'm the customer, I'm paying the bills, so I can say what I like. Would you agree with that?' She stops pacing and looks directly at me.

I chew my lip apprehensively. 'Eh… sure?'

'Good.' Gwen seems satisfied with my response and resumes wearing down the claggy office carpet, which I notice has a slightly shabbier looking patch right where she's pacing back and forth. 'You see, Craig's view of the world is very different to mine. Actually, let's test that theory. Would I be right in thinking he would want you to leave your personal problems at home? Would he perhaps be the type to lack empathy if you were dealing with something difficult in your life?'

An imaginary jackpot horn starts blaring inside my head. Gwen has no idea how close to the truth (and bone) she's landed. Squirming in my seat, I feel distinctly uncomfortable at the idea of being asked to confirm if my boss is indeed a twat in a suit.

'You don't have to answer that.' Gwen saves me from this discomfort, perhaps having never really expected me to give a response. 'I know I'm right. So, here's my way of management: you let people be people. You give them the tools, skills and direction they need to be their best, and you accept that you're hiring humans, not robots. This means that things will get messy from time to time. Life events will happen – good and bad – and your team members will, at times, fall in and out of love – or lust.'

My face blazes at this comment and I don't dare look at Nick, because I'm certain that together the two of us could toast marshmallows right now.

'A man like that doesn't really deserve to have you on his team, Jess,' Gwen continues. 'And if he won't respect you and treat you like a human being, he can't expect the same in return. As far as I'm concerned, this is your business and not his. OK? Dismissed.'

Nick and I share a confused look, unsure if we've heard right or whether we should get up and leave or not. Gwen guffaws and slides back into her seat.

'Sorry, forgive me. I've always wanted to do that. Listen you two: you have my full blessing to explore each other in any way you wish. So off you pop and have a good day.'

Gwen's unintended innuendo sends the heat in our faces spiralling into gas burner territory, and we can't get out of her office quick enough.

'What the hell was that?' I press my hands against my cheeks in disbelief once we're outside the office building and back in the fresh air, having shot past the nosey office staff as fast as we could.

'I should be saying the same thing to you.' Nick's tone is borderline accusatory, but knowing him better now, I can detect the (almost imperceptible) lightness within his statement. 'What happened to staying quiet till we got a sense of where Gwen was at?'

'Sorry, I caved. I'm not good in that kind of situation. Especially not recently,' I mumble as an afterthought.

'Not half. But it explains a bit about how your boss manages to keep you down.'

'Meaning?'

'If you don't stand your ground with him, he'll find it easy to discard you if he sees you as having lost your shine.'

'Thanks for that.' I flinch at this cutting statement.

'Hey, I didn't mean that in a bad way.' Nick lifts my chin with his finger and locks his eyes on mine. 'I was just stating a fact. This is crossed wires between us again. I want you to succeed, and to succeed you need to know your worth and fight for yourself. Don't hand the guy a reason to ditch you.'

'I guess you're right. I was trying to stand up for myself, but he seems to one up me every time. I always thought being good at what I do would be what set me apart from others, but it's the politics that really defines things. That and being able to fit the mould. Anyway, enough about that for now. What I want to know is: what was that in there?'

'That was Gwen in her full glory,' says Nick. 'She's quite the character.'

'I'll say. She's clearly been on her best behaviour with me before now.'

'I'd take it as a compliment. Means she's let you into the fold, and she doesn't do that with everyone. You are aware she's your boss's sister-in-law, right? Or was anyway.'

'What? No.' I gape at him. 'Are you serious?'

'Yes, I just assumed you knew. She and your boss's brother, John, are divorced, but it was an amicable split. John's still very much in the picture and Lauren and him are close.'

'Gosh, I had no idea.' I'm baffled by this revelation. 'It's a bit odd that Craig didn't tell me about it, but I guess he must have had his reasons. Her calling him "a twat in a suit" certainly makes sense now – she mustn't be that keen on him.'

Nick nods. 'They see life differently, that's for sure. John asked Craig to help out when the park hit problems and all Craig did was offer Gwen a twenty-five per cent discount on your company's services. She took it because it was better than she would get elsewhere, but I think it sticks in her throat a bit that he's stinking rich and so self-focused.'

Before I can respond, one of Lauren's team members comes out of the building, greeting us politely. She appears to be making a call, so we cross the courtyard and head into the park in search of some privacy to continue our debrief.

'Well, anyway,' I say, once we're out of earshot, 'the whole Craig thing aside, I knew Gwen was a bit quirky, but I didn't realise she was as straight to the point as that. That was…'

'Entertaining, uncomfortable, embarrassing?'

'Like I've never experienced before,' I scoff. 'Regardless of her relationship with him, I can't believe she called my boss that in front of me.'

'Is it an accurate description?' Nick asks.

'I never used to think so, but more recently I've come to that way of thinking. Even more so now after what you've just told me. And as much as it's great to have Gwen's support, Nick, I'm sorry, I'm still wondering if I need to tell him about us. Because that's who I am. Much as I wish I could be a bit more like Gwen, I'm not her.'

'I was afraid you were going to say that.' Nick stops and slips his arms round my waist, pulling me gently towards him. 'Any chance you can wait a couple more days? We're in safe territory now here, and I'd really like to explore a bit more of you before that "twat in a suit" has the opportunity to kibosh things.'

I smile up at him, some of the tension leaching from my shoulders. 'I think I can manage that. In fact, you have no idea how badly I want to kiss you right now.'

Nick looks around and clocks the nearest enclosure. 'I think Gwen would be OK with us having a post-discussion moment together. In here.'

He pulls open the door to the indoor viewing area and we bundle inside, pawing at each other in a way that's representative of the wild animals around us. Thankfully the enclosure is less 'aromatic' than some of the others in the park, so I'm able to put all my focus on Nick. I can still taste a hint of the coffee from earlier on his lips as he kisses me hungrily and I moan with pleasure at the sheer intensity of feeling such desire and being so desired.

'I can definitely wait a couple of days to tell Craig,' I murmur.

'Good,' Nick whispers in my ear. 'Because I'm going to need a supersized portion of you to keep me going until your contract ends.'

I snicker at his questionable attempt at erotically charged dialogue, which makes me feel like an upsell at McDonald's. It's not enough to throw me off though. Nick's so damn sexy, he's like nectar to me; I just can't get enough.

We're at the point where we're beginning to cross a line with hands being where they absolutely shouldn't be in a place of work, and items of clothing coming close to being removed, when the door to the enclosure swings open with a loud creak. We instantaneously jump apart and stand behind it as a group of primary school children trot into the space, chattering exciting, followed by what must be their teachers or parental chaperones. I balk at how close they came to catching us out and receiving an unsolicited sex ed lesson. Nick puts a finger to his lips and silently beckons for me to follow him out of the room, which I do on my tiptoes to avoid giving us away.

Once outside, we fall about laughing, wired by our close call. I straighten myself up and smooth down my hair as Nick watches me with a grin.

'What is it?' I demand with a smile.

'Nothing.' He shakes his head, still grinning. 'That was a bit close for comfort, but it was also...'

'Hot?'

'So hot. What are you doing tonight?'

'I'm… erm…' I hesitate, unsure how to play things. 'I have a prior commitment, I'm afraid.'

'No worries. How about tomorrow?'

I pull a face and Nick's grin dissolves. 'You're busy then, too.'

Seeing him looking so disappointed pains me no end. He must have – quite reasonably – thought that, with this being the beginning of something new, and us being that hot for each other, we'd both be going out of our way to free up our time. Which I ordinarily would – if it weren't for the fact that I'm a full-time carer outside of my job. But feeling so drawn to him, I know I need to find a way for us to spend some time together, especially if we only have a couple of days before I speak to Craig.

Taking both Nick's hands in mine, I seek out eye contact with him. 'Give me your number and leave it with me. I might be able to pull some strings.'

Chapter 24

Returning home later that day, I have to continually remind myself that having one night off for a date with Nick does not mean I'm a bad sister. I'm simply doing what Jackson said I must do: filling my own tank so I can be the best sister and carer I can for Seth. It's a hard sell, so I'm relieved that, when I broach the subject with Seth and Jackson, I receive a unanimous response that I must have my evening out. Jackson also reassures me (as he has already before) that he's more than happy to take the extra hours.

'Jess, I've got this, OK?' says Jackson.

'Yeah, sis,' Seth pitches in. 'We will be... fine. Jackson's cooking... is better than... yours.'

'Careful,' I warn him. 'This hand still has to feed you most other days, and it could add liver and bacon to our meal plan at any time.'

Seth looks repulsed. 'You... wouldn't.'

'Try me.'

'All right, I will... stop. Anyway... what are you... doing... tomo... tom-orrow night? Do you have... a date?'

'Maybe.' I bite my lip with embarrassment and look away.

'Oh, I'm right... who is he?' Seth's features illuminate with interest alongside a streak of mischief. 'Is he... rich, and... does he have... a six-pack?'

Jackson laughs loudly while I cock my head, perplexed.

'That's your first question?'

'It seems to be... what matters to... the people on the... reality shows I watch.'

'Jackson, I think Seth needs a different type of stimulation to support his recovery,' I joke. 'That crap will damage his brain even more.'

'You got me.' Jackson holds his hands up in a comically. 'We're actually glued to the reality channel all day.'

Seth snorts with amusement and I can't help smiling at him. I'm just so relieved that he's doing so well with all this. Having noticed that his friends haven't been round as much in the last few weeks, I was worried it would hit him hard, but he seems quite chilled as always.

'So, this guy,' Seth prompts me. 'You're not... dodging... this one. Who is he, and... will I approve?'

'All right. He's called Nick, and he's the head keeper at the wildlife park. He's a good guy, if a bit lacking in tact at times. Different to my usual type.'

I glance self-consciously at Jackson, feeling a bit weird about having this conversation in front of him, though I'm not sure why. He's like an extension to our miniature family unit these days and he hears and sees way worse than me chatting about a guy I like. He simply winks affectionately back at me, putting me at ease with that one tiny gesture.

'Nick.' Seth repeats the name, as if trying it out for a fit. 'And the... six-pack?'

'I'm not even going to answer that.'

'Spoil... sport. I had a... date today.'

'You did?' I look to Jackson to make sure Seth isn't just ribbing me, and he nods confirmation of this.

'Yup.' Seth puffs himself up in his seat, looking smug. 'With Alison.'

'Is this the woman you met in the waiting room?'

'It is. She's... bea... beau-tiful... and interesting, and... bea... beaut-iful.'

'You said that already.'

'Yes, but she's so bea... beaut-iful... it has to be... said twice. That's also... a word I'm... having problems with... in my speech therapy – so it's good to... keep practicing.'

'I see.'

I ignore the nagging feeling I get from this news, remembering my previous conversation about this woman with Jackson. Instead, I try to focus on the positive: that my brother seems to have found someone he connects with.

'Are you going to be seeing each other again?' I can't help asking.

'Yes. Thursday. We're meeting at… the Scottish… the, eh… Scottish… Na… National… Gallery… of… Modern Art.'

With his lingering memory issues as well as his speech limitations, Seth struggles to get this name out, but I'm pleased to see that he does manage. It's a real marker of his progress.

'And you're playing third wheel again.' I smile at Jackson, who shrugs easily.

'It's all good, Jess. It means I get to explore the gallery myself. I might even pop across the road and have a wander round Jupiter Artland too, if there's time. With the hours I work, there's never normally the opportunity for such luxuries.'

'You will… have time.' Seth grins at him. 'Alison can't get… enough of me.'

'So modest, eh?' I say to Jackson, jerking my head towards my brother. 'OK, great, well enjoy.'

'We will,' says Seth. 'Hey… if your… date goes well… maybe we can… go on a… double date.'

I chuckle. 'We'll see. Let's take things a step at a time for now.'

Nipping out of the room, I quickly type out a WhatsApp message to Nick.

> I'm good for tomorrow evening if you're still up for it? Xx

I can see that he reads the message straight away and starts typing, then a reply appears on the screen.

Sending him back a thumbs-up with a smiley face, I lock my phone and momentarily clutch it to my chest, feeling a rush of excited anticipation for the next day. Then, taking a deep breath to calm my teenage hormones, I return to the living room to take over from Jackson.

–

The next morning, I work from home – essentially avoiding Craig, so that when I do eventually talk to him about the situation with Nick, it will come across as my first natural opportunity to do so. Loaded with guilt about not being immediately up front, I have to remind myself that Craig has royally shafted me over the whole part-time hours thing. He hasn't treated me with the respect I deserve, instead making me feel like nothing more than a revenue-churning cog in his machine, so why should I run to him with my disclosure – especially when it's still such early days with Nick? I'm not even sure I could put a label on what we are if he asks.

I tick off my tasks for my other projects as quickly as possible so I can head to the wildlife park, which has kind of become my sanctuary – not because Nick is there, but because of the soothing effect the animals, Rana in particular, have on me. I drive to East Lothian under a dark and foreboding sky and pass a very productive afternoon with Lauren and Monika, who are both kicking off their first events this week. We make sure everything is lined up perfectly and I help them iron out any last-minute issues. Of course, there aren't many of these because – not meaning to be big-headed – I do know my stuff.

I'm expecting the events to be a breeze, given we've already done a test run with the dating, and the senior citizen coffee mornings are fairly straightforward. All we need is an endless supply of tea and coffee, some tasty baked goods (which Serge has all sorted for us), and a yoga instructor for those who would rather do something more physically challenging than wander round the park. The tickets are already nearly sold out for the first few weeks of both events, thanks to a brilliant effort by the wider team here (which to my delight, includes Nick), so we're ready to roll.

Having everything so well under control means I'm able to finish at 5:30 p.m., allowing me half an hour to get glammed up for my date with Nick. Once I'm satisfied that I look the part, I duck out of the empty staff changing rooms, sneak across the courtyard and head for Rana's enclosure, where I've arranged to meet him. The air is humid, the sky filled with huge, mushroomy dark clouds, which makes me wonder if we're finally in for a spectacular downpour.

On rounding the final bend, I see Nick sitting on the bench chatting away to Rana.

'What do you think, girl?' I hear him say. 'Do I scrub up all right? Long time since I've had a proper date.'

'Let's have a look at you then?' I call out jovially as I approach him.

Nick's head shoots round and he looks mortified. 'Oh, hi, I didn't expect you to be on time with everything you have on this week.'

'Clearly. By the way, in case that's a universal term of endearment for the women in your life, I'm not too keen on "girl" as a pet name.'

Nick gets up from the bench, giving me my first proper look at him, and I'm honestly rendered speechless. It's the first time I've seen him in normal clothes rather than those scruffy, stained overalls and it's almost like I'm looking at a different person. He's wearing slim-fit jeans and a stylish branded polo shirt that enhances his upper body in all the right places. He's also shaved and tidied up his hair just enough that it looks smarter, but also has a sexy just-out-of-bed appeal to it. He looks good. No, scratch that, he looks smoking hot. Like, sizzling on a grill territory – in my eyes anyway. All of a sudden, I feel a bit insecure, as if my subconscious has made a fresh judgement on him and decided he's out of my league.

'You all right?' Nick steps forward to greet me properly.

'I'm… yeah, I'm fine.' I lean in to receive his kiss, which is slow and lingering.

'You look incredible,' he murmurs in my ear and my moment of insecurity passes as I remember I've spruced myself up, so I might just pass for someone who's not completely punching.

'So, where are we off to this evening?' I ask. 'I'm looking forward to a proper introduction to East Lothian.'

'I have quite the plan actually.'

Nick gestures towards the bench and I sit down, saying hello to Rana as I do. She's investigating (or rather, hanging from) a new ledge that Nick has added to her enclosure, so she doesn't even seem to notice I'm there.

'I thought we'd take the scenic route.' Nick flops down next to me, putting his arm around me, and I instinctively cuddle into him. 'I'd like to show you a few of the coastal villages in the area – Gullane, Longniddry and the like – then I thought we could have a walk on the beach before dinner. I've booked an Italian restaurant in North Berwick, so if it's not too late after, maybe we can have a wander round the harbour there too…'

While Nick is sharing his plan, it dawns on me how long it's been since I've had a night out. It was something I always took for granted, being young with no ties. Seth's social group, who took me under their wing when I returned to Edinburgh, provided me with ample opportunity for nights out. They were more about hitting the bars of George Street hard than the romance that I expect tonight will bring, but they were symbolic of my freedom. Or mine and Seth's freedom – which I'm unsure if we'll ever get back.

'Hey, where did you go?' Nick cocks his head to interrupt my line of sight. 'Do you not like the sound of what I have planned?'

Realising that my mind has wandered at the most inopportune time, my attention snaps back to the present. 'Oh, sorry, no, it sounds great. Really great.'

He looks at me uncertainly, so I pull him into another kiss – and ensure it's a particularly steamy one – to make sure there's no doubt in his mind whatsoever that I'm all in.

Chapter 25

Following a magical mystery tour of the vast East Lothian countryside and the nearby coastal villages in Nick's four-by-four, we arrive in yet another pretty little village call Dirleton. Nick gives me a quick tour of the place, which is essentially just pointing out the village green and a majestic castle ruin, before turning off the main street and driving along a narrow country road until we reach a small car park. Thankfully, despite the sky having threatened to pour buckets on us all day, it has held off. The sun is even peeking through every now and then to offer us some warm evening rays on our faces.

'Where are we now?' I ask.

'This is Yellowcraig beach.' Nick opens his car door to get out and I follow suit. 'It's one of the best beaches in the area. Have you really never been?'

'No, I've only ever been to North Berwick beach, but I'm excited to discover something new. This is such a beautiful area. I don't know why I haven't spent more time here.'

'I guess when you live in the "big smoke" you forget there's a world outside of it,' he teases me.

'It is a bit like that, I guess.'

We cross the car park and take a pathway, which I'm assuming will lead us to the beach, chatting lightly about Rana's developmental progress as we go. Nick's pleased with how she's coming along, and it's so lovely seeing him like a proud dad. He really is a big softy at heart, it seems.

It feels warm and companionable being with him, and at the same time exciting. I can feel my senses are on high alert, to the point I just want to grab him and kiss him and never stop. Or better yet, sneak into the overgrowth and devour every little bit of him, right there. I realise that could result in anything from tick bites and Lyme disease to my underwear (and other bits of me) feeling like sandpaper, but it's almost worth the risk. Almost.

As we climb over the dunes on to the beach, Nick slips his hand into mine and it feels so good, I decide that I can settle for this over an alfresco romp for now. Stealing a glance at him, my heart skips as he smiles back at me, and gives my hand a little squeeze.

'Oh, wow, this is lovely.' I come to a sudden halt, drinking in the panoramic view of the seascape in front of me.

There are lashings of powdery sand, a rocky area off to the left and frothy waves crashing onto the beach from the Firth of Forth, right where it meets the cold expanse of the North Sea. A tiny island with an old white lighthouse perched on it is visible in front of us, surrounded by the rippling azure body of water, while sand dunes, grassland and forest frame the beach inland from where we've walked.

'It's nice, huh?' says Nick. 'And see, there's North Berwick Law off to the right.'

I follow his line of light. 'Ah, so it is. So, with growing up in Aberlady, you must have spent a lot of time here.'

'I did, yes. Many summers building sandcastles and exploring the rock pools hoping to find sea creatures.'

'And freezing your butt off in that water? It looks cold.'

'You get used to it. We can have a paddle if you like?'

'Really?' I screw up my nose, not at all sure that's a good idea.

'Why not? I'm not sure I've ever been here without at least getting my feet in the water.'

I continue to waver, erring on the side of 'thank but no thanks', which prompts Nick to cajole me further.

'Come on. What's the worst that could happen? You've scooped up elephant poo. Surely everything from then onwards should be a breeze.'

'You'd think, eh?' I throw him a beady-eyed look, then do a quick memory check to make sure I'm not about to reveal an unsightly set of toenails or something worse. 'OK, you're on.'

Nick seems delighted that I've risen to the challenge, and – after continually losing my balance – holds me steady while I remove my socks and running shoes, which I put on for this part of the date on his advice. Then I roll up my ankle-high skinny jeans as far as they'll go, while he expertly takes off his own his own shoes and socks without so much as a wobble.

While I know it's a bit shallow, I can't help sneaking a look at his feet to make sure they're feet I could see myself lying next to in bed. My squeamishness is something that extends beyond the likes of animal excrement, and I'm ashamed to admit that I've previously ended a promising relationship solely because the guy had the worst case of toenail fungus ever to have existed in the history of humanity. To my relief, Nick has very normal-looking feet, and while I'll never be volunteering to suck his toes, I'm sure I'll be all right cosying up beside them, as long as they stay at the end of the bed where they belong.

'Ready?' he asks.

'Let's do it – before I change my mind.'

We pad across the sand towards the water's edge in our bare feet, avoiding stepping on the bits of broken shell and seaweed – which gives me the willies, but I put on a brave face – as we go. Nick strides straight into the water without a care in the world, while I stop dead the moment my feet feel wet and cold.

'Come on, you can do it.' He beckons me to join him.

'I've changed my mind,' I call out to him. 'I'll stay here and work up to going in next time.'

'Nonsense. Get yourself over here. It's great for your circulation.'

'My circulation's just fine, thank you very much. I'm not an old lady.'

'You clearly have no real understanding of what causes circulation issues,' Nick scoffs.

'Maybe, but I don't need a lesson on it either.'

Nick frowns at me and shakes his head. 'OK, you leave me with little choice here.'

He wades back out of the water towards me.

'You don't need to come out because of me. I'm happy to… arrgh!' I let out a yelp as Nick expertly scoops me up and walks straight back into the water.

'What are you doing?' I kick my legs helplessly, trying to release myself.

'Keep that up and you'll end up going in head first,' he says to me and I stop struggling. 'This is the best way to face your fear, because it won't be nearly as bad as you think. Now, keep still and I'm going to lower your feet in gently.'

'OK.' I close my eyes tightly and hold my breath. My whole body seizes up in anticipation as Nick puts me into a standing position in the water. 'Ahh, it's freezing!'

I hop up and down as the icy water licks at my calves.

'Stop thinking about it and just walk around a bit,' he instructs me. 'Focus on the view.'

Doing as he says, I find myself quickly acclimatising to the water, and before I know it, it feels wonderful and cool and therapeutic and I can't imagine ever wanting to get out again.

'This is amazing. Why haven't I done this before?'

'Because you let your brain convince you of awful things that are not really that awful. Now you know that, maybe you can look at shovelling animal poo in a different way.'

'I'll *never* be able to look at that in a different way.' I give a resolute shake of my head. 'And don't even think about telling me it contains skin-rejuvenating properties or some bollocks like that.'

'Actually, elite Japanese women have used nightingale faeces in face masks for centuries…' Nick tails off with a sheepish smile as I shoot him a look.

'Let's just enjoy the moment, shall we?' I reach up, snaking my arms around his neck, then kiss him softly on the lips, mainly to distract him and discourage any other moment-killing comments.

We wade our way along the shoreline, chatting and sporadically kissing until we run out of beach, and then we make our way back again. It's a magical feeling being there with him, with the waves crashing around us, washing away the stresses and strains I've been feeling recently. By the time we're heading back up the beach, shoes in hand while our feet dry off, I almost miss the water already.

'That was incredible.' I swing my arms dreamily. 'Can we do that again at some point?'

'Anytime you like.' Nick catches my hand and gets a firm grip on it in a way that makes me feel wanted, almost… loved.

'Cool. I wonder if it's too far to come on my lunch break.'

'Not if you're happy to make it a quick dip. Maybe we could arrange to have a long lunch one day and bring a picnic?' He looks at me hopefully.

'That sounds awesome.'

I'm genuinely elated at this suggestion, especially as it doesn't involve me asking for Jackson to provide cover. I work more than enough extra hours through longer days to justify a long lunch.

'And now you're used to the water, we can also come back one weekend and go in properly.'

'What do you mean by "properly"?' My eyes widen with alarm.

'You know, the open water, wild swimming. You'll love it.'

I'm about to embark on a long-winded defence to make it clear to Nick all the reasons that this is a bad idea, when there's a sudden crack of thunder. Within seconds, huge fat drops of rain are pelting the sand around us like missiles, getting heavier by the second.

'Oh shit, we're about to get soaked,' says Nick. 'We're going to have to make a run for it.'

I don't need to be told twice. Still clutching our shoes, we take off along the path at speed as the rain comes down in sheets, quickly becoming torrential and creating mini-rivers around our feet. The visibility is so bad, it becomes almost impossible to see where we're going or what we're running on, and before I realise what's happening, I've tripped and gone down hard, yowling in pain as my face makes impact with the soaking wet ground.

Chapter 26

'Are you sure you don't need to see a doctor?' Nick asks me for the fifth time since we got back to his four-by-four.

He gently dabs at the scrapes on my face with antiseptic-soaked cotton wool from the first aid pack in his boot, while I do my best not to wince in pain.

'Once again, I'm sure.' My fingers seek out the swelling in my cheek self-consciously.

'I feel like this is my fault.'

'I know you do. But you didn't conjure up the downpour or embed that bloody great rock in the path, did you? For a logical guy, you're being very illogical right now.'

'I know.' He grimaces as he inspects my wounds. 'I just don't like seeing you in pain, and if we hadn't come here and I hadn't pushed you into—'

'Hey. Enough of that.' I place my hand on his leg in a gesture of reassurance. 'You didn't push me into anything.'

He assumes a sceptical expression.

'OK, you did dunk me in the sea against my will, but I could have objected more strongly if I was really unhappy about it. You just gave me one of the best experiences I've had in quite a while.'

'Only one of the best?'

'Actually, no. *The* best. Life has been a bit tough recently and tonight has been the ray of sunshine I needed to remind me what living is.'

Nick smiles on hearing this, but still appears somewhat troubled.

'I'm just sorry we'll have to call it a night sooner than planned.'

'Why would we do that?' I give him a quizzical look.

He looks at me as if my fall has made me delusional. 'Because you're hurt and bleeding. You should probably take it easy. I'm not even sure you should be driving home alone.'

'Hey, I'm fine. A few scratches and bruises aren't going to send me home to bed.'

'Are you sure?' His expression is a mix of hope and concern.

'I'm sure. Let's go back to the park and change so we don't turn up to the restaurant soaked and manky. I have my work clothes there and you must have a clean set of overalls at least.'

'I have better than that. I keep a few changes of clothes there for when I'm doing overnighters.'

'You do overnighters?' I'm surprised by this piece of inform-ation that's been casually dropped in.

'Only when we have orphan animals that need regular feeding. If they're not able to come home with me for one reason or another.'

'Oh, wow. I had no idea.'

'Why would you? Anyway, clean clothes aren't necessarily my only concern…' He hesitates and looks awkward.

'You're worried people will think you did this to me.' I touch the gashes on my bruised, swollen face and he nods almost imperceptibly. 'OK, you don't need to worry about that at all. I'll be sure to share my war story – and the fact that it's our first date – very publicly.'

–

We arrive at the restaurant half an hour late for our booking, with Nick having phoned ahead to apologise and explain about my accident. They're very understanding and even have a bag of ice wrapped in a towel ready to help with the swelling. I make a point of talking and laughing about our adventure at Yellowcraig beach with the with staff member who takes us to our table, as I promised Nick I would. And it's just as well I do, because all eyes are on my injured face as we take our seats at our table.

We chat about everything and nothing while we order our food and eat our respective and delicious starters of seared scallops wrapped in pancetta and burrata with sticky roasted tomatoes. I may have a face like Shrek that's throbbing and burning, but I feel better and more alive than I've felt in ages. Nick is interested and attentive and everything I could hope for in a date. And that's before factoring in the chemistry that's crackling away between us.

Every time our fingers touch, I feel an insane level of desire coursing through me. Part of me wants to recklessly abandon the meal and tell Nick to take me to his place, but I've made a conscious decision not to succumb too quickly. Call it my professional conscience or whatever, but I do feel a moral obligation to resist a bit longer – just so I'm 110 per cent sure this is going somewhere before I sleep with my client's head keeper. It almost sounds sordid when I put it that way, but I know that if I do things in what I consider to be the right way, I'll have nothing to be ashamed of. It'll also make me feel better if I can look Craig in the face when I tell him about us, knowing I haven't yet done the nasty with Nick.

'Can I ask you something?' I sip at my alcohol-free beer while we wait for our mains to be served.

'You can ask me anything,' says Nick.

'It's kind of personal.'

'Ah. Well, I have no secrets, so shoot. I think I might know what this is about anyway.'

'You do?'

He pauses before answering as we're served two dishes of steaming hot pasta that smell absolutely divine.

'You want to know what happened with my wife.'

I feel the uninjured side of my face colour. 'It was that obvious?'

He bobs his head in a non-committal way. 'Let's say I know what my workmates are like. There was no way you wouldn't have heard something through the park jungle drums. And then, of course, Gwen made that comment the other day about me being... what was it she called me?'

'A miserable bugger.' I giggle at the put-upon look of resignation on Nick's face, but beneath it, I can see the same slightly wounded expression he had that day.

'Aww, don't take it personally.' I reach across and take his hand in mine. 'I don't think you're a miserable bugger.'

'Not anymore. But you did, didn't you?'

'Only for a really short period. Maybe a month or so.'

'So, most of the time you've known me. Great.' He picks up his fork and spears a piece of tortelloni glumly.

'I think the most important thing to keep in mind is that this has clearly been a temporary state for you. Somewhat elongated, perhaps, but temporary nonetheless. It's not who you really are.'

'That is true. Please know that that's true.' He puts his fork down suddenly and holds my gaze.

'I can tell.' I give an earnest nod to show I'm being genuine. 'You don't need to worry. What happened, Nick? What did she do that broke you so badly?'

'She cheated.'

'Oh.' I almost roll my eyes at the sad predictability of this. 'Not very original, but enough to break a person's spirit. Did you know the guy? How long was it going on?'

'It wasn't an affair. She was on multiple dating apps and she was using them for hook-ups. She basically cheated on me with about thirty different guys – and that's just an estimate, because she had no idea of the true number.'

'You're kidding.' I'm so shocked, I drop my fork and it clatters on my plate, attracting more unwanted attention from our fellow diners. 'How could she... why would she... I don't even have any words.'

'That was pretty much my reaction when I found out.' He chuckles gravely. 'I should have seen the signs. She was elusive and secretive with her phone, but I loved her so much at the time, I just didn't want to see it.'

'Nick, oh my gosh, that's unbelievable. She didn't just stamp on your heart, she... put you at risk.'

'I know.' He looks very uncomfortable all of a sudden. 'And in case you're wondering – because you have every right to – I've had all the tests done. Immediately and then repeated after a period of time. I'm clean.'

My faith in humanity sags a little as I see him looking so ashamed when he did nothing wrong.

'That wasn't what was on my mind, Nick. But thank you for being so up front about it. What was in my head is how she could be so devoid of a conscience. If she wanted to have that freedom, she should have left you first and allowed you to find your own way. Such selfish behaviour.'

'Yes, she should.'

He hangs his head and I can see that this is still painful for him, probably now for reasons of pride and self-esteem rather than having lost the love of his live. He couldn't really love someone he clearly didn't know.

I rush to change the subject. 'I'm sorry, I didn't mean to open old wounds and perhaps I should have waited a bit longer to ask.'

'Not at all. I'm glad it's out in the open now. Since that shitshow, I've sworn to myself that I won't get involved in anything complicated. No baggage, thank you very much, I want a simple life from now on.'

On hearing this, I try to ignore the uncomfortable swirling that kicks off in my gut. With my situation, I'm a far cry from what Nick has communicated he wants. Unwilling to face this unpleasant thought, I banish it to the back of my mind.

'I had actually sworn off women and pledged myself to protecting animals and conservation until you burrowed your way into my head,' he continues.

'Lovely image.' I wrinkle my nose at this description. 'You make me sound like a tapeworm.'

'Not intentionally.' He finally pops the piece of pasta in his mouth and chews reflectively. 'So, tell me a bit more about you. Have you had your heart smashed into oblivion? And what about family, friends… who's in your life, Jess?'

'Ooh, that's a lot to unpack. Let's start with the relationship stuff. I've never reached oblivion, but I've had a couple of what you might call longer-term relationships that just fizzled out. I was hurt, probably more from feeling like I wasn't that desirable to them, but thankfully, there were no dramatics involved. Not great matches, I suppose. Guess I've never met someone who really sets me alight.'

Locking eyes with Nick, I realise I'm lying. I hadn't met anyone like that – until now. The chemistry crackles between us, our unsaid thoughts and feelings swirling around us like fireflies in a night sky. It feels clear to me that we're both in the same place: we're aware that something very special is growing between us, but at the same time we don't want to jump in too fast and risk ruining everything.

He seems to sense my muddled thoughts and gestures for me to continue.

'Um, sorry.' I clear my throat. 'And family-wise, it's just me and my brother here in Edinburgh. My parents live abroad.'

I tell him a bit about how I went to uni and became an adopted member of Seth's friendship group when I returned, my childhood friends having moved on to other places.

'It's good that you get on so well with your brother,' says Nick, after I've explained all this. 'I'm an only child, and I was always envious of people with brothers and sisters. Felt I missed out. But I've come across a few toxic sibling relationships through friends and acquaintances, so I've realised it's not always the dream scenario I imagine it to be.'

'Oh, for sure. I consider myself really lucky that Seth and I are so close, which is why I was so—'

Alarm bells suddenly clang in my head, bringing me to a halt. I was about to casually mention Seth's stroke and everything we've been through in recent months. The level of ease with which Nick and I seem to connect – particularly given what he's shared about his ex-wife – makes me feel like I could open up to him about it. However, it's not a story of war wounds from the past, it's very much my here and now, and it's both 'complicated' and 'baggage'. Not that I see Seth as baggage obviously, more that I have responsibilities that have me heavier laden than a cart horse, and they won't mix well with a fresh and frisky, tearing-each-other's-clothes-off-at-every-opportunity early-stage relationship. It's something that rules my whole world right now. Something emotional and very complicated – exactly what Nick has just indicated he doesn't want or need in his life. And I can absolutely understand that after all he's been through.

I don't want to risk this amazing evening together by lumbering him with the revelation that I'm a carer for my brother, who might or might not regain his independence. Because it means I probably can't have the kind of relationship Nick's looking for – not right now, or perhaps ever. I don't even want to think about it, because the potential ramifications are too much for my wearied brain to take.

'Jess, where have you gone?' Nick reaches across and gives my hand a gentle squeeze.

His wonderful touch brings me back to the here and now. 'Oh, sorry.'

'You seem to do that a lot. Is everything OK?'

'Yes, fine. I obviously get distracted easily. What was I saying? Ah, yes, Seth. I was so grateful to Seth and his friends for absorbing me into their group the way they have. It's been great to join them whenever I need a good night out or to let off some steam.'

'That is good.' Nick's eyes linger on mine, and for a second, I think I can read something in them, as if he's not entirely convinced by my story.

'So, yeah, that's me.' I wind up that part of the conversation quickly and shift my concentration to my pasta al limone, which is getting colder by the minute, but is still exquisite. 'How about the park? Are things looking up now there's some money coming in for the first events? Gwen and I don't tend to talk financials on that level.'

'She's cautiously optimistic, I think. Maybe it will take a while for her to feel like things are more secure. Let's call it a hopeful start.'

'That seems like the right word for it. I'm "hopeful" that it'll also help turn my ailing career around.'

'Want to talk about it? I know you told me your boss had lost confidence in your ability to deliver, but you never said why.' He shrugs in a way that tells me he's not putting any pressure on me, but he could be a listening ear.

I hesitate again, desperate to share everything with Nick, but still holding back because that will open Pandora's box. With all that's been said this evening, I'm not sure our fledgling relationship can handle it – and suddenly, I want that relationship more than anything.

'To be honest, there's not that much to it,' I say, after landing on a response I'm comfortable enough with sharing. 'I knew Craig was commercially minded, but I never had him down as ruthless. Turns out he's that and more. I was his cash cow until I asked to reduce my hours and he realised his company wasn't the single most important thing in my life. Now I'm as good as dead in his eyes.'

'What a dick.' Nick shakes his head, though he seems pleased that I've shared this with him. 'It's sad when people can't see past money and success.'

'It is. Which is why I prefer people who can.' I smile at him and he smiles back, our eyes continuing to communicate unsaid messages, and, if I'm not mistaken, rather primal thoughts and urges. With such a charged atmosphere between us, I'm starting to wonder if I'll to be able to hold back on getting it on with him until I've spoken to Craig – or even much beyond the doors of this restaurant. Did Nick not say he lived nearby? If not, that's a pretty roomy-looking four-by-four.

Chapter 27

Despite our animalistic urges, Nick and I just about manage to contain ourselves. Instead of getting steamy in the back of his car after dinner, we share a moonlit walk around the charming North Berwick seafront, with its sandstone harbour walls, tethered sail boats bobbing in the water and sandy beaches stretching out on either side. Then we drive back to the wildlife park where he drops me off at my own car around ten p.m. Driving home with my music blaring, replaying the highlights of the evening in my head over and over, I feel completely invigorated.

Needing someone to share in my euphoria, I hit the button on the steering wheel to activate the in-car speech recognition system, and command it to 'call Amelia'. It's getting late, but I've never known my best friend to hit the sack before midnight – tonight being no exception.

'Hi, sugar mouse, I was just thinking about you,' she greets me after three rings. 'What's new?'

'Does something have to be "new"?' I smile to myself, knowing full well I'm about to share something not just new, but also juicy, and Amelia's going to love it.

'Uh, yahuh, with you it does.'

'Oh, I'm sorry, Meels.' My smugness is immediately replaced by guilt. 'I'm really crap at keeping in touch, even more so now. I've just had so much—'

'Nooo, no no no,' she cuts me off. 'I'm sorry, that came out all pixilated. I feel like I've been put through a sieve today. What

I mean is I want to hear your juice, because I know there's juice. It's a guy, isn't it?'

'Might be.' I'm suddenly all coy.

'OK, I'm comfortable. Dish it, vixen.'

I quickly fill Amelia in on the Nick situation, including a blow-by-blow account of our date, which she laps up with relish. I'm on such a high chatting away to her, it doesn't even occur to me to share Nick's previous situation with his wife and what he said about not wanting anything complicated in his life in the future.

'He sounds like a right peach cobbler. Delicious or what?!'

'I certainly think so.' I'm grinning from ear to ear. 'So that's me, how are things with you? Anyone exciting on the go?'

'Ah, you know me. I like to explore, try out new things.'

'By "things" you mean people?'

'Yah, though I have heard that VR dating is going to be big in the future. For me, that's like hot chocolate with cream *and* marshmallows.'

I grimace. 'I think it sounds like pure hell, but I know you're not one for tradition – or boundaries of any sort really.'

'No.' She pauses. 'But I'll make an exception for your wedding if you want me as bridesmaid. As long as I can have two "plus ones" if circumstances create a need for that.'

'You can have as many "plus ones" as you want. Though I think you're getting a little carried away. It's only been one date.'

'We'll see.' Amelia's voice adopts a sing-song tone. 'I can sense things, you know.'

After we hang up, I spend the rest of the journey playing back my date with Nick, and by the time I reach my flat, I've gotten ridiculously carried away and already imagined him proposing to me. In my silly little fantasy, he does it in Rana's enclosure, with the adorable little bundle of fur using me as a climbing frame and me being shocked to discover the ring box hanging round her neck. This, of course, is complete head-in-the-clouds idiotic claptrap, which I hold Amelia fully responsible for, after the nonsense she was spouting about her 'senses' during our call.

Obviously, I need to get hold of myself. It's far too soon (and quite possibly bonkers) to be thinking that way, and if we were to ever get to that point, Rana would be a fully grown bundle of wild bear who could rip my face off with a single swipe. Not so romantic after all.

Planting my feet firmly back in reality, tonight has shown me two things. The first being that Nick is a completely different person to who I first thought he was and I really want this to go somewhere; the second is that, because of my situation, 'going somewhere' is going to be tricky. Nick has been clear that he's looking for something far less complicated than his previous marriage, which means it's unlikely he'll want a woman who has to focus the majority of her time on another man, even if it is her brother. He also deserves to have someone who can be as devoted to him as he will be to them as that's what he missed out on before.

What that means is that I can't tell him about Seth. Not yet anyway. It's too early to show him the sacrifice he'd have to make as the partner of a carer, plus I'm not sure I'm ready to show him that side of my life yet. It's just too fragile and vulnerable. Besides, within a few months, I'll have a better sense of how independent Seth is or isn't going to become. If I can keep things light between Nick and I for a while, it means that when I do share my situation with him, I may be in a freer place, and able to show him how things will continue to improve. What that means for now, however, is that I need to resist my primal urges, because once that line is crossed, we're moving into overnighters territory, which is definitely not an option in the immediate future.

-

The next morning, I'm back at the wildlife park, and with the majority of the preparations done for the dating and retirement events kicking off today, I spend an hour with Serge on the Christmas market planning, before taking a stroll to see where Nick is. Of course, I should have guessed: I find him playing a game of wrestling with Rana in her enclosure, which she simply cannot get enough of. She's so high energy and the snuffling noise she makes as she battles with him is just too adorable. It's obviously not 'playing' as such, he's encouraging her natural instincts, but it does always look such fun. She climbs all over him, and every time he successfully fights her off, she rebounds straight back over to him like a cute, fluffy bouncy ball.

'You seem to be having to put in more effort these days now she's getting bigger,' I say by way of a greeting.

He looks up and grins, and I can see the sweat beading on his forehead even from where I'm standing.

'I'm exhausted, but she's developing brilliantly, so it's worth it. A couple more months and she'll need be moved to her next temporary enclosure, which is bigger. And I'll need to start being more careful around her as she matures.'

I feel a little tug in my heart as he says this. 'Does it not make you sad? That after having such a close relationship with her, you'll soon have to remain at a distance?'

'It does and it doesn't.' He shrugs and continues to play-wrestle with Rana as he chats away to me. 'I've been doing this a long time, so I've seen a lot of animals off into their adulthood. Of course, I'll miss that side of things. There's nothing quite like the feeling of interacting with a young animal like Rana, but at the same time, her reaching that milestone means she's healthy, I've done my job right and we're keeping our conservation commitments.'

'That's a good way of looking at it.'

'It is.' He nods, then seems to lose his focus for a second, which is enough to throw off the balance in their 'game'. '*Ouch*... dammit, she's nicked me with her claw.'

'Shit, Nick, are you OK?' I rush to the enclosure entrance while he distracts Rana with some food and makes his way out to me. 'I'm so sorry,' I babble. 'That was my fault. I was distracting you. How bad is it? Have you had a tetanus jab, or whatever it is you need, recently? I can call for help.'

'Hey, chill.' Nick grasps me gently by the shoulders to calm me. 'This stuff happens all the time. Painful in the moment, but nothing to worry about. It's just a scratch, see?'

He holds out his arm, which is red raw and bleeding just above the glove line. It looks like more than a scratch to me, but I don't want to make a song and dance about something he's clearly not concerned about.

'OK, sure. But, for the record, I am sorry.'

'When you fell last night and I thought it was my fault, did you not tell me I was being daft?' He fixes me with an appraising look.

'Uh-huh.' I look up at him with guilty eyes.

'Well then, enough said.'

He smiles tenderly at me then draws me into a reassuring embrace, which includes a rather delicious but salty kiss. I try not to think about that part too much. If I'm going to be in a relationship with a head keeper, I'll have to learn to deal with a lot more than a sweaty upper lip.

–

Later in the morning, the very first of Monika's senior citizens' coffee mornings kicks off. Within minutes, the place turns from peacefully quiet into a raucous rammy, as around sixty retirees descend on the place, looking hungrier than the park's African painted dogs. We attempt to shepherd them straight through to the main picnic area; however, we've overlooked one small but significant detail: the gift shop is in their line of sight, and they're making a beeline for it in droves.

As much as the extra spend would be welcome and we should capitalise on that opportunity later, right now it's an unscheduled diversion we don't have time for. I quickly assign Lauren the role of gatekeeper, telling them we have time built in later and that the event is about to start.

Once we have everyone perched at the picnic tables in the covered area – because unfortunately a light shower has come on – Lauren takes the lead (this being Monika's preference as she's quite shy) and gives the group a big hearty welcome.

'Good morning, everyone.' She beams at them. 'Welcome to East Lothian Wildlife Park. I hope you're all well?'

'We're well. Shame we can't say the same for the weather,' one woman grumbles, and a muttering of agreement sweeps through the group.

'Not to worry,' says Lauren. 'We have waterproof ponchos at the ready for anyone who needs to borrow one for the guided tour.'

'Are you telling us that if we don't want to do yoga, our only other option is to get soaked through?' one particularly plummy-sounding woman asks with a tut.

'Ach, it's not heavy. And it's supposed to dry up soon. Anyway, us Scots have never been put off by bit of rain, have we? If we did, we'd get nothing done.' Lauren lets out a belly laugh, hoping to appeal to a shared sense of humour, but her joke falls flat.

There's another ripple of dissatisfaction – louder this time – and she shoots an uncertain glance in my direction. It's not the whole group, but it's enough of them to ruin the morning for everyone. This is one of the reasons I'm here. I've had to gee up many disgruntled event attendees in my time; those who have the potential to turn a fantastically organised event into a miserable experience. Giving Lauren a signal to stall for two minutes, I scan the area, seeking inspiration, and as I do, I spot Nick hovering nearby. I flash him a quick smile, which he returns more tentatively, having clearly picked up on the atmosphere. Then an idea hits me and I dart across to him.

'How do you fancy helping to rescue this situation?' I clasp my hands together in a begging gesture.

'What do you need?' he asks. 'Anything, just tell me.'

'Thank you. What I need is to make it worthwhile getting a bit wet, and also...' I lower my voice and relay my proposal to him.

Two minutes later, I re-join Lauren in front of an increasingly restless crowd. Her face is flushed with exasperation.

'I don't know what you're about to do, but thank you in advance,' she murmurs out the corner of her mouth. 'Who'd have thought people in this country would have such an issue with a few drops of rain? Why did they even sign up if they hate the thought of getting a bit damp?'

'People will never cease to surprise you.' I smile at her sympathetically and turn to the group.

'Hi, everyone. My name is Jess and I'm here with Lauren this morning to make sure you have a great experience. Now, it's clear that some of you aren't keen on our well-known friend, the Scottish drizzle, and that's fine, because we've got something else a little bit special lined up for you. Something that wasn't mentioned on the programme, but that will be an ongoing feature of these events.'

I glance across at Nick to check he's not ready to murder me for saying this last part, which we haven't actually agreed, and he nods that it's fine.

'Our head keeper, Nick, is going to take those of you who prefer warmer climes for an exclusive and unparalleled experience. This will be held in our magical tropical house where you'll get a VIP tour and a front row view of feeding time, which is always a great time for photos. Perfect to share with your grandchildren, don't you think?'

There are a few 'oohs' in response to this, which is a good sign.

'Now, we can only do that for fifteen of you today,' I continue. 'So, if you're happy to brave the weather, we suggest you join the outdoor tour. But if Nick's special experience is something you'd like to do another time, we can get you booked on to another coffee morning today at a twenty-five per cent discount, and we'll reserve a place for you on Nick's tour then.'

This time, a more positive murmur reverberates through the group and I breathe a sigh of relief. It's worked. They're coming around.

'So, is everyone all right?' I ask, and receive a collective 'Yes'. 'Great, then, Nick, why don't you come over and say hello.'

Nick wanders across, giving a wave and a 'hi, there', and I notice some of the women most put out at the idea of getting rained on sit up attentively.

'Put me down for the tropical house, I'm all for getting hot and bothered with Nick,' one of them cackles and there's a collective snicker among those who I'm now labelling the 'troublemakers' of the group.

'Oh, my God, what have you gotten me into?' Nick looks mildly terrified.

'You don't fancy adding in a strip show, do you?' I giggle. 'That'll gain you one hell of a regular clientele.'

'When I said I was happy to do anything, that wasn't quite what I meant.'

'Yeah, sorry about that. They'll probably be quite tame once they're up close and personal. I've seen this type before, you'll be fine.' I give him a little wink and address the group once again. 'OK, everyone who's doing yoga, can I ask you to head to the staged area just over on the right there. And if you want to join Nick's session today, pop your hand up now.'

I'm relieved to see about the right number of hands, but Nick's terror intensifies as he clocks that he's about to spend the next hour with the women who were lusting over him only moments ago.

'Good luck,' I mouth to him with a cringe, and then send our guests off in their respective directions.

—

When the yoga session is over and the other two groups have returned from their park activities, Serge and his catering team are ready and waiting. Industrial-sized tea and coffee urns line the buffet tables alongside enormous platters of scones and various cakes and traybakes. It's a delicious-looking spread, and to my relief, our guests seem delighted with the offerings.

They settle in clusters at tables both indoors and out, their boisterous chatting and laughing echoing in the high ceilings of the park restaurant and carried by the breeze outside. The scene reminds me more of a school trip than a pensioners' coffee morning. Their energy is infectious and I find myself feeling invigorated by the experience.

Looking around, I spot Nick attempting to sneak off, so I dart across the restaurant and exit it at the other side to cut him off.

'Not so fast.' I place my hands on my hips. 'I want to hear about your experience with our clientele. How did it go, Mr Studmuffin?'

'How do you think it went?' He looks highly uncomfortable.

'Oh, Nick, was it really that bad?' I soften my stance and my expression turns serious. 'They were a bit frisky but I thought they'd actually behave themselves when they were with you. If they did anything that made you feel—'

'*Gotcha*.' His face breaks into an impish grin.

'Seriously?!' My hands return to my hips, but this time in mild outrage. 'I thought you were about to tell me you'd been... violated.'

'Sorry, I couldn't resist. They were fine, just as you said they would be.'

'You cheeky sod,' I scoff.

'Cheeky, but apparently also a "studmuffin", right?' He reaches out and takes my hand, then yanks me around the side of the restaurant and kisses me intently.

'Nick, we can't do this here.' I reluctantly pull away from him. 'The event I'm running is right there. What if someone sees us?'

'They won't see us, and you need a break. Let Lauren and Serge take the reins for now.'

'Well, I guess I have been working *really* hard.' I melt back into him, while manoeuvring further out of sight.

Moments later, we're shocked back to reality by a harassed-looking Gwen stomping past on the path muttering to herself. Nick puts a finger to his lips, but keeps his other arm firmly wrapped around my waist. Standing stock still, I pray that she won't see us, because this definitely isn't delivering on her request of our 'thing' not to impact our work. My heart thudding in my chest, I watch her with panicked eyes, willing her to keep moving. Then, just as it's starting to look like we're out of the danger zone, Gwen must sense our presence, because she shoots around suddenly and clocks us, causing me to leap away from Nick guiltily.

'Nick, Jess, come with me.' Gwen looks like a woman not to be messed with.

'*Shi-i-t*,' I give a low groan.

Even Nick looks concerned by Gwen's expression and tone. He reaches out and grasps my hand to let me know we're in this together, but I shake my head and pull it away.

This is bad. Gwen specifically asked us not to let our relationship interfere with our jobs, and now she's caught us skiving off like two naughty teenagers hiding behind the bike shed. To make things worse, from the way she was stomping around, it seems like she was looking for us – which means someone must have seen us together and complained to her.

Chapter 28

Nick and I trail silently behind Gwen all the way to the court-yard and into her office, where she gestures for us to take a seat. Unable to bear the tension any longer, I launch straight into an apology.

'Gwen, I'm so sorry. That was so unprofessional of us. You trusted us to keep our relationship separate from our jobs and we abused that trust. I realise it's simply unacceptable and we deserve whatever action you feel is appropriate under the circumstances.'

Stealing a glance at Nick, I'm expecting – no, almost hoping – to see the same flabbergasted reaction to my previous panicked outpouring, but his face is ashen.

'Are you done?' Gwen asks me with one hell of a poker face.

'Erm… yes. Sorry.' I shrink into my seat and chew on my lip anxiously.

'OK, great. Because you two having a snog round the side of the restaurant is the least of my worries right now.'

'It is?'

I sit forward and Nick does the same.

'If it's not that then what's going on, Gwen?' he asks. 'I've never seen you looking so… serious.'

Before Gwen can answer, Lauren bursts into the office.

'Sorry, Mum, I didn't realise you were looking for me.' She scoots past Nick and I, taking the remaining free seat in the room. 'What's up? I'm not getting good vibes here.'

Gwen gets up from her desk chair and begins pacing. '"What's up" is that the bank has declined the additional business loan I was assured I would get.'

'*What?*' Nick looks shocked. 'We were relying on that loan to keep the park open until Christmas. Your business relationship manager knew that.'

'He did, but apparently someone at the bank has had a change of heart. They think we're too big a financial risk, and even if we get out of the hole we're in, we'll hit a bigger one further down the road.'

'I can't believe this.' Nick rubs his jaw in dismay.

'Me neither.' Lauren's face has drained of colour. 'I know our options are limited, but is there nowhere else you can get the money from?'

'No.' Gwen continues her pacing. 'I've tried several avenues. All dead ends.'

'How long till we close?'

'About two months.'

Lauren shakes her head vigorously in denial, while Nick puts his head in his hands and lets out an anguished cry. I instinctively put my arm around him, then glance uncertainly at Gwen, who waves a hand telling me to go ahead.

'We have to do something,' says Nick. 'This cannot be the end. Those animals need us; the job we do is too important. Do the bank not get that?'

'They do.' Gwen nods. 'Believe me, I've tried all the arguments. I gave them quite the speech.'

I cringe as a rogue thought passes through my mind that, from what I've seen, Gwen's speeches aren't the most compelling. Batting it aside, I focus on her, Nick and Lauren and their visible pain at the idea of losing the place they love most in the world. It just can't happen. It's clear that Nick lives for the park, and I'd put money on it being exactly the same for Gwen, perhaps even for Lauren.

There must be something we can do to save it – something that will bring in an injection of cash to plug the gap. Something like…

'I know what we need to do.' I suddenly stand up.

'You do?' Nick, Gwen and Lauren ask in unison.

'Yes. We're going to hold a fundraiser event. A huge one. There's nothing that's a bigger threat to our world right now than climate change. People love animals and they want a future for their kids. We're going to show them how important this park is, and we're going to appeal to their community spirit.'

'Surely something like that will take a couple of months to plan,' says Gwen. 'We don't have the luxury of time. Our fortunes need to turn around in a few weeks if we're to have a chance at saving this place.'

'It doesn't need to take a couple of months.' I shake my head determinedly. 'We just need to be smart about it. Use what we already have at our disposal and get some charitable donations.'

'I don't know.' Gwen sits back down, looking unsure. 'It feels like too big an undertaking, and I can't afford to pay Craig for the additional support we'd—'

'You won't need any. And actually, as he's still essentially your brother-in-law, the stingy bastard should be helping you for free.' I blanch at my own behaviour. 'Sorry, that should not have come out of my mouth.'

'You think I care?' Gwen guffaws, temporarily distracted from her woes. 'You already know that to me he's just a twat in a suit.'

'Yes, I suppose I do.' I let out an almost maniacal laugh. 'OK, so let's focus here… I can manage all the activities and logistics.'

'And I'll help,' says Nick.

'Me too.' Lauren's face is already regaining its healthy glow.

'Great, so Nick, Lauren and I will handle that. We'll make the most of the park and use some of the ideas that we've put into the other events. We can get Serge on to his supplier contacts to see if they can help with donations on the food and drink side of things, and we can do an appeal for prizes for a prize draw. Then all we need is some really good PR to get the word out, and I know just the person who can help us…'

By the time, we leave Gwen's office, I'm firing on so many cylinders, I'm in danger of taking off. I didn't realise how much I cared until I heard Gwen's awful news. The potential implications for the animals, and the broader staff and management team, many of whom I now see more as colleagues than clients, is too much to stomach. I've moved on from seeing it as a blight on my CV, and as much as I'm still desperate to revive my career, I also need to make sure the park has a future. For Nick, for Gwen, for everyone here. Plus, if I can help them save this place under near impossible circumstances, then there's no way Craig can continue to keep me down. I'll have more than proved myself.

'Are you really confident we can pull this off?' Nick asks me, as we leave Gwen and Lauren talking in the office and head back towards the retirees' event to check everything's still going smoothly.

'As confident as I can be.' I feel slightly nauseous as my mind tries to comprehend what I've just signed up to, but I refuse to let my monkey brain hijack me and distract me from this challenge. 'If we don't try, then it's game over. I don't know about you, but there's no way I'm letting this place go down without a serious fight.'

Chapter 29

Having neglected to think through the consequences of leading a fundraiser of the size I was suggesting in Gwen's office, I had to seek Seth and Jackson's blessing to take on the project. As part of that, I also had to be completely sure that everyone was happy with the arrangement and no one was feeling taken advantage of or left high and dry. The arrangement being that, for the period running up to the event, Jackson would move in and take over as a Seth's full-time carer, while I would stay at a small family-run hotel in the charming little village of Dirleton for easy access to the park.

Thankfully, the hotel owners were willing to give me a very generous discount on one of their four self-catering studio apartments, as I was booking such a long stay with them. And the best thing about it all was that I made sure mine and Seth's pathetic excuse for a parental unit would foot the bill for the extra care. Of course, they were happy to shell out, because it eased their woefully tiny consciences that little bit more.

The next three weeks are a whirlwind. Between overseeing the scheduled dating events and coffee mornings – which thankfully, the park team are largely on top of – and planning the fundraising-event-to-end-all-fundraising-events to save the place, I barely have a spare moment in my waking life to think about anything else. Though I do make sure my other projects are ticking over to keep Craig at bay.

I work round the clock with Nick, Lauren and some enthusiastic volunteers (who are also desperate to keep their jobs), leaving the hotel at seven a.m. each morning and not returning until ten p.m. As well as planning the event itself, we put a plan into action to spruce up the park, because every person who comes to the fundraiser is a potential future customer and/or word-of-mouth recommendation. I also enlist the help of Amelia, who's more than happy to lend us some remote support, and within a couple of days she gets us up and running with some killer social media content to promote the event. This includes designing us some eye-catching e-flyers with the tag line: 'Help save the best conservation project you've never heard of', which we're also able to print off and hand out in the local towns and villages, and in and around Edinburgh, appealing to the good nature of the small businesses – cafes, restaurants, hairdressers and the like.

'Won't that strapline make us look bad?' Nick had asked, when Amelia unveiled her stroke of genius via video call at one of our project meetings. 'If we're admitting people have never heard of us, then aren't we admitting to being a failure?'

'Nah-ah.' Amelia had firmly rejected this statement, shaking her head so violently her huge hoop earrings bashed her in the face. 'It adds a layer of intrigue. People will want to know what they've been missing out on, so they'll check you out. It'll work, I promise.'

So, after twenty-two days of living on espressos and very little sleep, we find ourselves jittery with nerves at our last project meeting on the eve of the event.

'Do you think it will work?' asks Hayley, who's a member of Lauren's team, and looking very anxious indeed.

'Honestly? I don't know.' I shrug, unable to give her the decisive response she's seeking. 'It depends on whether the local community connect with our message and turn up on the day, but I certainly hope so.'

'You'll get your turnout,' says Amelia's confident face from the wall-mounted TV screen. 'I know my stuff, soldiers. You've got them by the tear ducts.'

I watch Hayley's face brighten along with several others in the room and I feel the need to dampen down the expectations a bit. I don't want everyone's hopes getting sky high and then plummeting in an earth-shattering way if we don't pull this off. Even if we do get the turnout, our fundraising goal – a.k.a. the sum we need to stay open beyond the next five weeks or so – is pretty huge. It really is a gamble whether we'll make it.

'OK, everyone, I'm sorry to be the misery guts here, but I want you to stay realistic.' I flatten my palms on the table and look round its occupants. 'It might work out or it might not. Let's just focus on putting everything into tomorrow, yeah? We've got huge numbers showing interest in the event online, which is brilliant, but we need those people to actually turn up and pay entry. And we need to make a lot more money through our activities, food sales and by boosting the animal sponsorship scheme. So, make sure you come with your A-game tomorrow and be ready to sell your hearts out.'

'*Yeah! Wooooo!*' hoots Amelia from the TV screen, so close up that we get a view of her tonsils. 'Wish I could be there. Go and smash it.'

'We will.' I laugh, as Amelia gets up from her seat and does a premature victory dance, much to the amusement of the project team – especially as all we can see now are her boobs jiggling around while she does it.

Stealing a glance at Nick, to see what he thinks of my bonkers best friend, he simply shakes his head with bewilderment. But I'll take that. He obviously doesn't find her offensive like some (boring and unimaginative) people do.

Suddenly aware that it must be getting late, I look at my watch and see it's gone eight p.m.

'OK, everyone. Let's call it a night. You need some proper sleep before this thing, so shall we meet at eight a.m. tomorrow?'

There are a couple of groans round the table.

'I know, I know. It's early for a Saturday. But this is it. One last push.'

'You can have a lie-in tomorrow, or a lie-in every day when we close for good.' Nick aims some pointed looks around the table and the groaners quickly buck up their attitudes.

'That was a bit harsh… but true, I guess,' I say to him once Lauren and the rest of the project team have filed out of the office.

'They needed to hear it.' He makes no apology for his words, then wanders around the table and takes me by the waist, kissing me tenderly.

Closing my eyes, I let the loveliness of the moment wash over me, feeling lighter all of a sudden. However, this lightness is quickly replaced by the desire I've been struggling to resist since Nick and I got together, and we start to get a bit carried away.

'Um… I'm still here, you two,' Amelia's voice unexpectedly interrupts us and we pull apart, colouring with embarrassment.

'Shit, sorry, Meels.' I make my way over to the screen. 'I totally forgot we were catching up after the meeting.'

'That's OK, sugar mouse.' Her lips curl up angelically. 'I mean I'm game for a threesome, especially with this sexy big cat – *raaar*, by the way, Nick – but I feel I'll be at a disadvantage here.'

'*Amelia*,' I scold her and pirouette round to see Nick's reaction.

'Ahem… maybe I should head on.' He quickly heads for the door.

'OK, but wait for me before you leave for the night?' I call after him. 'I'll only be a few minutes.'

Giving me an awkward over the shoulder thumbs-up, he then disappears out the office so fast you'd think his arse was on fire. I turn back to Amelia.

'*Really?*' I cock my head to the side in judgement. 'You couldn't have waited a little bit longer before introducing him to that side of you?'

'Girl, chill.' She giggles away to herself silently, making me think for a moment that we've lost sound. 'He's going to have to get used to me at some point, isn't he?'

I realise this is not a rhetorical question.

'I hope so.' I rub my forehead exhaustedly. 'It's still early days. We haven't even... you know.'

'What, why? You've been staying at a hotel for three weeks. It's pretty much the law that you have to "do it" in a hotel room.'

'It's a studio apartment, not a hotel room.'

'That's irrelevant. Is it you or him that's dodging the deed, because that could mean—'

'It's nothing that needs to be analysed,' I interrupt her runaway train diatribe. 'We've barely had time to sleep or eat in the last three weeks, never mind get down and dirty.'

'That sounds like complete tree bark.' Amelia's face turns suspicious. 'What are you not telling me, Jess?'

'Nothing... seriously... let's just leave it and chat through these final couple of points about tomorrow.'

'Eh, no way. Out with it, you sneaky swordfish.'

I sigh with resignation. 'All right. I'm keeping that side of things out of our relationship for now, because once we start having sex, he'll expect us to stay over at each other's places.'

'And?' Amelia looks understandably confused.

'And I can't have him stay over at mine, because he doesn't know about the situation with Seth.'

'WHAT??'

'I know, I know.' I quickly explain what Nick said on our first date and how I'm hoping Seth will recover enough to allow me a more straightforward relationship with Nick – so we actually have a chance at a future together.

'Jess, I love you like a pixie sister, but this is atomic insanity. That incredible man has been through the ringer with his ex-wife because she was a lying, cheating scumbitch, and you're—'

'It's not the same,' I protest. 'I'm not lying. I just haven't shown him all of me, and for good reason. He was clear that night about what he wants – nothing "complicated" and "no baggage". Plus, he deserves to have someone who's totally devoted to him. I can't offer him that right now. But I'm really hoping to be able to, and I want to paint it as a real possibility when the time is right. Seth's improving every day.'

Amelia closes her eyes for a second while she digests this, then opens them again. 'Yeah, well, I hope you've got your cards laid out right. I also hope you're not gambling on Seth making a near full recovery, because you know that's not guaranteed.'

'I do and I'm not, OK? Now let's move on.'

I quickly change the subject and Amelia briefly gives me some tips on how to maximise our online visibility the next day while the event is happening. On her advice, we've also set up a page on a fundraising platform called FundedCauses to boost our income and increase our reach.

Once I've said goodnight to her, I make my way outside and find Nick sitting on a bench, messing about on his phone.

'Sorry about that.' I ruffle his hair affectionately. 'Amelia is a bit… alternative. She takes a bit of getting used to.'

'Will I have the opportunity to get used to her?' Nick looks up at me with a searching expression.

'Wh… what do you mean by that?' I'm caught off guard by this question, which is a departure from the light and easy-going interactions we've been enjoying since getting together.

'I mean…' He puffs out his cheeks contemplatively. 'I guess I'm wondering where this is going, Jess. I really like you, but since our date, we've only seen each here at the park. As much as I enjoy that side of things, I was hoping for a bit more than that.'

My immediate reaction is one of panic, having not picked up on any sign of Nick's unease with our situation. I knew I couldn't continue as we were indefinitely, but I had hoped I could keep things ticking along a little longer.

'I'm sorry, Nick, I didn't know you were feeling that way. It's been a crazy time though, we've been surviving on caffeine and adrenaline. It's not really been the right point to throw dating into the mix.'

'But that ends tomorrow, right? Regardless of the outcome. So will things change then?'

It takes all of three seconds for it to dawn on me that Amelia was right. This situation is unsustainable, and my answer to his question will shape everything that happens between us going forward.

'Yes.' I give a resolute nod, then lean over and kiss him firmly on the lips to show I mean it. 'I'm still at the hotel tomorrow night – thought it would be unwise to check out on the day of the event – so why don't you join me for "dinner, bed and breakfast"?'

Nick's face immediately brightens. 'I would love that.'

'Then it's a date.'

Pulling him to his feet, he slips his fingers through mine and we walk to our cars together.

'You know, I was starting to wonder if maybe you weren't in the same place as me,' he says.

'Really?' I feel saddened to hear this. 'Why would you think that?'

'Maybe because you seemed happy to keep things casual. But I can see now that I was wrong. It was just the work stuff.' Nick stops and fixes his gaze on mine. 'Jess, I really want this to go somewhere. You're so amazing and beautiful and… uncomplicated. I hope that from now on, whatever happens with the park, that we can spend a lot more time together.'

Gazing back at him, I hear myself say: 'Me too.' Then I spend the rest of the walk to my car wondering how on earth I can possibly follow through on that assertion, and feeling a bit sick that one of the three things Nick said he likes about me is that I'm 'uncomplicated'.

Chapter 30

The next morning, my phone alarm wakes me at 5:30 a.m. and within an hour I'm coasting along the country roads to the wildlife park trying not to think about that word Nick used the evening before. Pulling into the car park, I see that Nick is already there with Hakeem, the head groundskeeper, and Gwen. They're hanging one of the new signs Amelia told us we needed after I gave her a tour of the park by video link. It was the one financial investment we agreed to make for the event, because, according to her, 'first impressions will make you soar or splat'. And we most certainly did not want to splat.

'That looks amazing,' I call across to them while retrieving my handbag and locking my car.

'Doesn't it just?' Gwen takes a few steps back to admire the huge billboard that Nick and Hakeem are still nailing to the wooden structure behind it. 'We also have a few smaller ones for the road to catch people's attention as they pass.'

'Perfect. Well, I'll leave you to it and get on with the preparations inside.'

Lauren, Serge and Monika arrive not long after me, followed by the other project team members who steadily stream into the park between 7:30 and 8 a.m. Once everyone's arrived and we've had our final meeting, the place becomes a hive of activity. We're buzzing from a mix of determination and apprehension, and it feels like the park's residents are picking up on this. The honking and hooting, screeching and chirruping, particularly from the primates and the birds, seems to be several decibels louder than usual.

'Do you think they know what's going on?' I ask Nick, while wishing I hadn't, because I sound completely ridiculous. But he doesn't make me feel stupid at all.

'Animals are very perceptive,' he replies from under the stall he's trying to fix the leg of so it doesn't collapse. 'Obviously they can't understand the circumstances or the complexities, but they can pick up on a change in atmosphere and behaviours. Early mornings are normally quiet here, so they will likely sense that something is different.'

'That's so cool. By the way, I've decided I'm going to be a gold sponsor for Rana. I know it sounds a bit weird, but I feel like she's a family member or something and I want to make sure she's well taken care of.'

'It's not weird at all,' Nick grins up at me adoringly. 'If she were able to understand what you're doing, I'm sure she'd be one very happy sun bear.'

We continue to get the place set up, then at ten a.m. on the dot, we (metaphorically) open the gates to our big event and wait in the courtyard with bated breath for the arrival of our first customers. It's a painful few minutes, which turns into a painful hour as we watch little more than a handful of people trickle into the park. By 11:15 a.m., Gwen is pacing back and forth, hands on her head, muttering to herself about all the things she'll need to do to make sure the park's closure is done right. Casting a glance at Nick and Lauren, I expect to see some fighting spirit they can use to bring Gwen out of this state, but they look as defeated as she is. Unable to bear it anymore, I move across and gently take her by the arm.

'How about we go work on your speech for later?' I suggest.

'Why?' She looks at me with wide, traumatised eyes. 'There's no one here. Our plan has failed. I'm better off spending the time working out the closure plan.'

'Not yet. We still have more than five hours until this thing is over – and two hours till your speech. You can still make a difference with it, regardless of how many people are here.'

What I don't want to say out loud is that we definitely don't want a repeat of her monologue a la Mel Gibson from the team brainstorming session some weeks back. Today we really need her to kill it, so by taking her for some coaching, I can hopefully see off that problem. It will also save her the agony of the fundraiser equivalent of watching paint dry.

After quite a bit of coaxing, she grudgingly gives in and I escort her into the park office where we run through her speech, and I give her some pointers. These include standing on a fixed spot to avoid giving our visitors motion sickness, and keeping her plea both focused and impassioned (and unre-miniscent of *Braveheart*). It takes several attempts to even begin to make some progress, but it's progress nonetheless. Just as I've gotten her to the stage of swaying like a sunflower in the wind rather than prowling back and forth in the manner of her beloved big cats, Lauren bursts into the office out of breath, looking completely wired.

'Is something wrong?' I jump to my feet, alarmed.

'No. The opposite. Something's… *right*,' she declares, still trying to get her puff back.

Gwen and I share a confused look.

'Come and see.' Lauren grabs her mum's hand and hauls her back out of the office with me in hot pursuit.

Emerging into the courtyard, we gasp with astonishment as we're faced with a solid stream of people pouring into the park. Scores and scores of them, chatting and laughing excitedly. Families, groups of younger people, retirees.

'They came,' I say in almost a whisper. 'Thank goodness they came.'

'Jess, this is a triumph.' Gwen slings an arm around my shoulders. 'I should never have doubted you. I mean I didn't really doubt you, I perhaps doubted that the community spirit was there, or the understanding of the importance of conserva-tion and education. It's actually possibly more—'

'Mum, please stop.' Lauren clamps a hand across her mother's mouth to silence her.

'Listen to your daughter.' I chuckle, as Gwen attempts to pry Lauren's hand away. 'She's trying to tell you exactly the same as I was when I was coaching you on your speech. She's just doing it in a less eloquent way. Fewer words make a bigger impact.' I signal to Lauren to let go of Gwen and she does.

'All right.' Gwen sniffs, a little put out at having been manhandled like that, but then she refocuses on the flow of supporters coming into the park, and she can't help but beam at us. 'I won't let you down.'

'Good.' I put my arm around her shoulders and give her a squeeze. 'Because we're not out of the woods with this yet. We need them to spend generously while they're here. Come on, let's get across to the picnic area to help out.'

–

An hour and a half later, I'm bursting with pride watching Gwen deliver a powerful and emotive speech in front of hundreds of people, who from the looks of it, are having a great day out. She only starts pacing once and thankfully catches herself, then sort of moonwalks back to her spot, making me wince on her behalf. But aside from a few odd looks and giggles from some of the children, she pulls it off without causing too much of a distraction. She takes a couple of slight detours with her narrative but they're actually quite amusing and seem to keep her audience entertained.

As she's wrapping things up, Nick and Lauren appear at my side.

'Have you seen the camera crew?' Lauren points to the other side of the stage I wangled free hire of from a supplier I have a long-term relationship with.

'Oh wow. Are they from TV? It would be great to get some coverage on the local news.'

'It's an online news outlet. I've looked them up. They have half a million followers.'

'Fantastic. That's exactly what we need.'

There's a loud burst of applause in response to Gwen's final thank you and she steps down off the stage.

'Erm… Lauren, are you seeing what I'm seeing?' I ask her, as the camera crew make their way over to Gwen.

'Yup. Looks like they want an interview.' She grimaces, aware that an unscripted Gwen might not be such a good thing. 'Don't worry, I'll oversee this, Jess. Always fancied being an internet sensation, and I reckon a mother-daughter "zoo crew" will do it.'

'Break a leg,' I call after her, then turn to Nick. 'How are the animal demonstrations going?'

'Great. The visitors are loving getting a closer look at our park residents. Rana has, of course, stolen the show. I'm half expecting her to become an online celebrity by the time the day is out.'

'Perhaps her and her keeper?' I raise a suggestive eyebrow.

'I sincerely hope not.' He looks appalled at the idea. 'She's the star. I'm just the—'

'Support act?'

'I was actually going to say "staff".'

'Well, you're a lot more than that to me.'

'Now that is something I like to hear.' He leans in, giving me a kiss that's fleeting but loaded with meaning. 'I can't wait for tonight.'

'Me neither.' I bite my lip coyly.

Despite my concerns about taking our relationship to the next level, while at the same time continuing to meet Nick's criteria of being 'uncomplicated', I'm more than ready to feel every part of him against my bare skin. A rush of longing courses through me at this thought, and I turn away to stave off a flush I can feel coming on. As I do this, my eyes sweep across the crowd and land on a familiar face looking straight back at me.

'*Shit*,' I mutter under my breath. 'Nick, that's my boss, and he's coming this way. I think he just saw us kiss.'

Chapter 31

Nick stiffens beside me, which I know is not just in anticipation of what might be about to go down, but also at what might spell the end of our relationship (for now). Because I never did get round to telling Craig about us. With all our time being sucked up by the planning and preparations for today, I didn't have the bandwidth or the appetite for such a conversation. I had to stay 100 per cent focused.

'Hi, Craig,' I greet him, swallowing down a gulp. 'I wasn't expecting to see you here today.'

'Everyone else seems to be here, so why not me as well?' He doesn't even look at me, his focus fully on Nick. 'I gather you're the head keeper here.'

'That's right, I'm Nick. Good to meet you.' Nick shakes his hand with what I can't help thinking is a stronger grip than he might ordinarily exert.

'Jess, can I have a quick word?' Craig finally shifts his attention to me.

'Of course.' I glance at Nick, who excuses himself and heads for the barbeque where Serge and his team have a seamless production line in operation, preparing burgers, hot dogs and pulled pork sandwiches to order.

Craig and I step away to the side where it's quieter. I can feel my body jittering with nerves and I so badly want this to be over.

'I gather you and Nick are… involved,' says Craig.

'Yes.' My eyes instinctively fall to the ground in shame, then I look up at him. 'Craig, I'm so sorry you had to find out that way. I was going to talk to you about it, and then things just turned crazy with organising this event, and—'

'Jess, it's fine.'

'It is?' I blanch with surprise.

He nods. 'You're not the first to get involved with a client – or in this case, a client's employee – and you most certainly won't be the last. What's most important to me is that the company reputation stays intact and the work gets delivered. I know you won't allow this to get in the way of your integrity and sense of professionalism, will you?' He gives me a look that feels like more of a warning than a question, making me think he'd prefer situations like this didn't arise, but he grudgingly accepts they're a fact of life.

'Of course not.' I wipe away the tiny beads of sweat that had pooled on my forehead. 'That you can be certain of, and I hope that today is evidence of it.'

Craig turns and surveys the sight before us: people everywhere, eating food at picnic tables, perusing the stalls, enjoying drinks at the outdoor bar while listening to the music from the local band who have occupied the stage following Gwen's speech (with strict instructions not to play too loud, so they don't upset the animals). There are even some people up dancing. The place is alive, buzzing like it should be all the time.

'I'm impressed, Jess. When you and Gwen proposed this event, I genuinely didn't think you could pull it off in the time that you had available. But you did it, so you must get kudos for that. It's fantastic, and I'm looking forward to hearing the final tally with the fundraising. I know Tonya will be thrilled if the park is saved. She's very fond of Gwen – as am I.'

I don't know Craig's wife well enough to judge if this statement is sincere, but I can't help thinking the last part of it is not. Surely if Craig were that fond of Gwen, he would have done more than give her a measly discount on his services; this is a man who has some of the biggest contacts in his little black book.

'Let's keep everything crossed then, eh?' I say. 'Are you sticking around for a bit?'

'No, unfortunately. We're out with some friends tonight, so we'll need to get the house in order before the babysitter arrives.'

'Of course. Have a lovely evening then. I'll see you on Tuesday.'

See you for a conversation about getting one or two of my high-profile projects back, I think to myself.

Craig heads off to gather up his wife and kids, and as I watch him go, I feel a spark of excitement in my gut. With the help of the amazing team here at the park, I've pulled off one hell of an event, over and above the work I was sent here to do. I've also shown how I can be flexible and put in extra hours where they're needed. Provided the numbers go the way I'm hoping they will, there's no way he can fob me off with his previous excuses.

I wander across the busy outdoor space looking for Nick to tell him the good news, but I can't see him anywhere. Wondering if he's gone to Rana's enclosure because it's become a meeting point of sorts for us, I turn back on myself and head in that direction. Just as I'm passing the same place where Gwen busted Nick and I having a snog three weeks before, an arm reaches out and grabs me, pulling me round the side of the building. Giving a startled yelp, I see it's Nick, who's obviously been waiting for me to pass.

'How did it go?' He seems tortured by the wait. 'Are you OK? Did he give you shit? Please don't tell me tonight is cancelled, because I've been able to think of nothing else all day.'

For a split second, I consider playing a prank on him, but when I look into his eyes, which are brimming with equal measures of concern and hope, I just can't do that to him.

'We're fine.' I spread my arms in a gesture of complete bafflement. 'He was fine. I can barely believe it.'

'Sort of fine or completely fine?'

'More or less completely fine. It's so weird. Everything about who Craig is at work told me he wouldn't be all right with this, but he is – though I suspect it's grudgingly. I can't quite get my head around it.'

'This is great news.' Nick grins and draws me in close, planting an affectionate kiss on my nose. 'We can be a proper couple now.'

'Exactly that.' I beam back at him, while wondering how the hell I'm going to make that work, when tomorrow I'm returning home to Seth, and he's the top priority in my life.

A few minutes later – following some delectable tongue action – Nick and I emerge from behind the wall, timed thirty seconds apart so as not to attract any unwanted attention or send the park grapevine into overdrive. He goes first, striding back in the direction of the main festivities, then I follow suit, noting that the band now have half the place up dancing. Nodding at Serge and his team members as I pass the food stands, I then swing by the animal sponsorship stall, where I'm pleased to find the monthly pledges are stacking up nicely. Rana, of course, has the highest number of people sponsoring her, followed closely by the giraffes and the elephants. Putting the clipboard back on the table and thanking the park team member who's currently manning the stall, I'm about to go and check in with the bar to make sure they're still well enough stocked, when I spot yet more familiar faces in the crowd – this time it's my brother and Jackson.

'Oh, bloody hell.' I mutter to myself, feeling a renewed sense of rising panic. 'Everyone really has turned out today.'

Chapter 32

I stand stock still, caught in the horrible dilemma of whether to walk in the opposite direction and plead ignorance later, or whether to approach them and risk the possible fallout if Nick spots us. Deliberating this for a moment too long, the decision is then taken out of my hands.

'Jess. Hey, Jess. There she is.' Jackson strides towards me, grinning from ear to ear.

'Oh, hi.' I plaster on a reaction of surprise. 'What are you doing here? I didn't know you were coming today.'

My eyes roam past him to Seth, whose wheelchair is being pushed by a smiling woman I've never seen before. She's very attractive, with the most incredible mane of wavy raven-coloured hair, and her makeup looks like a professional applied it.

'We didn't plan to,' says Jackson. 'Seth suggested it. Said he would often come to the events you organised before, so it felt like a natural step forward in his recovery to have him start doing that again.'

'Right, great.' I look around nervously, my radar trying to pinpoint Nick's position, but I can't see him, which means he could appear out of nowhere at any time.

'Who's this then? A friend of yours, Jackson?' I gesture towards the woman, while mouthing 'hi' to Seth.

'No, this is Alison.' He emphasises the name and for a moment I'm blank, before it clicks.

'Ah, Alison. I see.'

Before I have the opportunity to say, do or think anything further, Alison parks Seth's wheelchair, then bounds across to me like a playful pug. She grabs my hand and sort of holds and shakes it at the same time.

'Jess, it's so lovely to finally meet you,' she gushes in an Irish accent, her huge emerald green eyes fixed on mine.

I can see the attraction from Seth's perspective straight away. She's quite stunning, and that accent is definitely a winner. But there's something about this whole Seth having a girlfriend thing that puts me on edge.

'It's good to meet you too,' is all I can manage, while I battle an overwhelming rush of feelings I can't catch or even begin to make sense of.

An awkward silence follows, and we stand there smiling at each other mutely, while I continue surreptitiously scanning the vicinity.

'Alison was excited... to see the park,' says Seth.

'Yes, that's right.' Alison jumps in as if this was a pre-rehearsed cue. 'Seth told me about Rana the sun bear cub. She sounds so cute.'

'Yeah, she's pretty special.' I try and fail to maintain eye contact with Alison, while keeping a lookout for Nick. 'I think the sessions with her are finished for the day though.'

'Oh, that's a shame. They sounded like great fun.'

'Who fancies... an ice cream?' Seth suddenly announces. 'Jackson, let's go... get some.'

'Eh, sure.' Jackson glances at me uncertainly, reading my less than positive reaction to Seth's unsubtle attempt to get Alison and I chatting.

'None for me, thanks,' I reply. 'I'm on the clock.'

As Jackson wheels Seth towards the ice cream stall, I give Alison a tight smile, unsure what to say to her.

'You've done a great job here today, Jess.' She takes the lead on attempting to break the awkwardness between us. 'I hope you reach your fundraising target.'

'Thanks, so do I.' I continue to look around me uncomfortably.

There's another silence, which Alison fills for a second time.

'Seth's doing really well. I'm so impressed by his positivity and determination. Not sure I'd be able to do the same in his situation.'

I'm not sure why, but I bristle at this comment. Perhaps because I feel it not to be Alison's place to be making those observations.

'He's certainly done well so far, but it's a long-term battle, so he needs to stay focused and not allow himself to become distracted. I wouldn't want anything to get in the way of his recovery.' This time I look her square in the face, making it clear that if she's in any way going to mess my brother around, she'll have me to deal with.

'Of course.' She looks mildly terrified, and I feel satisfied that I've got my message across.

'Here we are.' Jackson and Seth return with three ice creams, handing one to Alison, who plasters a happy smile back on her face.

'I hope you two… are getting along.' Seth grins at us. 'We can still… go and see Rana… can't we, Jess? Even though the… sessions are finished.'

'Yes, of course.' I brighten at the idea of them moving on. 'I'd come with you but I have to stay and oversee things here. If you take that path over there past the restaurant, then take a left when it forks, you'll find her enclosure a minute or so further along.'

'Great. Will your… boyfriend be there? I'd like to… meet him.'

'Who, Nick?' I look at Seth in alarm. 'Would we say he's my boyfriend? I'm not sure. We've not been together long and I don't know him that well. Might be a bit soon to introduce you. Anyway, I'm sure he's run off his feet.'

'OK.' Seth shrugs, looking a bit disappointed. 'Maybe another… time then.'

'Yes, absolutely. If and when things do reach that stage between us.'

'Well, you've obviously got a lot going on.' Jackson clasps his hands together. 'So we'll get out of your way and let you get back to managing things here.'

A wave of relief washes over me, followed swiftly by an unpleasant soaking of guilt as I watch them set off in the direction of Rana's enclosure.

'Who was that?' Nick appears suddenly behind me, causing me to jump with fright.

'Gosh, you're like a stealth missile,' I tut at him, partly in a bid to distract him. 'Think I just lost a few minutes of my life.'

'Sorry.' He gives me an apologetic-slash-mischievous look. 'Are they friends of yours?'

'Um… they were keen to see Rana, so I gave them directions.' I opt for saying as little as possible to avoid having to lie.

'Shame that they've missed the sessions. I guess I could always—'

'Rana's had a lot of excitement today.' I shut him down quickly. 'She's probably needing a bit of peace to forage and stuff.'

'I guess you're probably right.'

Exhaling heavily, I'm relieved at having escaped a potentially tricky situation, but at the same time I feel wretched about manipulating things the way I did. That's not at all who I am, but I can't risk bringing the men in my life together. Not yet. Things are already a little shaky with Nick thinking I'm not that into us as a couple. The last thing our fledgling relationship needs is him finding out I can't commit to him in the way he's hoping. I just need a bit more time to see if that scenario will change – then I'll face into things and accept the outcome, whatever that may be.

–

The event comes to a close at 4:30 p.m., though many of our supporters have left of their own accord quite a bit before that. This seems to include Seth, Jackson and Alison, whom I thankfully haven't bumped into again. With things well under control, Gwen, Nick, Lauren and I are able to disappear into the office to tot up the make-or-break calculations, while the rest of the park team members see people out and begin the clear up.

'OK…' Gwen pores over the figures on the spreadsheet in front of her. 'With the event admission sales, food and drink revenue and paid activities we're nearly halfway to our target. Lauren, what did we make through the sponsorship scheme?'

Lauren finishes tapping at the calculator she's holding and holds it up to Gwen. 'That's the total for the initial pledges, paid today. It includes some one-off donations that some people preferred to make instead of setting up a monthly direct debit.'

'OK, thanks. Jess, how have we done on the FundedCauses page?'

'It's gone really well through being shared on social media, though the donations have slowed up a lot in the last couple of hours.' I bring up the page on my phone and hold my screen out to Gwen so she can jot the number down on the notepad she's using.

'Thanks. I doubt we'll get much more from that now the event is over, so let's call that a final figure and see where it leaves us.' Gwen plugs the numbers into her spreadsheet and sits back with a loaded sigh.

'What is it, Mum?' Lauren peers over her shoulder. 'Is that a good sigh or a bad sigh?'

Nick and I share a nervous look.

'It's a bit of both,' says Gwen. 'Factoring in the cost of the new signage for the park, we're about a thousand shy of the sum we need to plug the gap until the revenue from our events and the boosted animal sponsorship scheme becomes steady – provided that happens.'

'We can find a thousand quid between us, surely,' I say. 'I'll donate two hundred straight off the bat.'

'Me too,' Nick and Lauren say in unison.

'There you are.' I watch Gwen in earnest. 'That leaves a hole of only four hundred pounds. We'll make that. We might even get it through the FundedCauses page.'

'That's very generous of you.' Gwen offers each of us a melancholic smile in turn. 'And of course, I will do the same. But where this leaves us is not much of an improvement on limping from one month to the next. Even with the events you've set us up with, Jess. I had already accepted this reality but I guess I'd hoped that, from all the publicity in the run-up to today, there might be one or two very generous donors in the mix.'

Nick and I share another look, and it's clear we're thinking the same thing: the odds of that happening were so slim. Seeing Gwen looking so defeated makes my insides twist.

'Gwen, what are you saying?' Nick sits forward apprehensively.

'I don't know...' Gwen gets up out of her seat, then sits back down as she realises she's about to start pacing, glancing at me guiltily.

'I only suggested you don't do that during your speeches. Knock yourself out.' I gesture for her to continue.

'Thanks. It helps me think, you see.'

We watch Gwen silently pacing back and forth thoughtfully, head down, focused but troubled. The room feels tense while we respect her need for mental space and wait for her to reach a conclusion.

'Yes, all right,' she says to herself out loud after her period of deliberation.

Nick, Lauren and I almost suck the air out of the room through a collective intake of breath. Seeing Nick's face, I reach under the table and take his hand, and to my surprise he squeezes it tight, letting me know how vulnerable he feels right now.

'What have you decided, Gwen?' I ask.

She sits back down and regards us solemnly. 'I'm afraid I've decided it's for the best that we close the park – and that we do it now. We can use the funds raised to make sure the animals that we are able to rehome are well looked after in their transition period.'

'You're saying there are some animals that won't be rehomed…' I balk, suddenly feeling a bit sick.

'Yes, unfortunately. My hope is that it will only be the ones that are at the end of their natural lives though.'

I don't feel any better hearing this.

'Are you sure about this, Gwen?' Nick shakes his head, denial already setting in.

'I'm sorry, Nick.' Her eyes glisten on meeting his. 'I'm just exhausted by this constant fight for survival. It's not fair on any of you, and it's not fair on the animals.'

'It's also not fair on you,' I say.

'No, I guess not.' Gwen's now glassy eyes meet mine, then Lauren's and Nick's. 'I'm sorry I couldn't make this work.'

Lauren throws back her chair and leaps on her mum with an enormous protective bear hug. 'It's not your fault. You did everything you could.'

'You did.' Nick now looks like he might even cry, which sets me off.

We both pile on top of Lauren and Gwen and hug it out, all too aware that there's a payroll full of wonderful dedicated staff who, after throwing everything into today, are about to lose their jobs and their beloved animals.

Chapter 33

My 'dinner, bed and breakfast' arrangement with Nick goes a bit differently to how I expected following Gwen's heart-breaking decision – especially as she decided to tell the park staff right after making her decision, rather than stringing things out. They were all there for the fundraiser, so it was an easy way for her to make the announcement to everyone together at once. Seeing their hopeful faces crumple after all that hard work was just too painful. Nick's team took it especially hard, which made it all the worse for him. The only saving grace for them was that the fundraiser hadn't been a complete waste of time.

I make it clear to Nick that we can have our evening together another time (though I don't have any idea of when that might be), but he's adamant that we continue with our plans in an attempt to lift our spirits. The mood is obviously not one of jubilation, so instead of ripping each other's clothes off and enjoying a saucy pre-dinner aperitif, we opt for a more customary drink in the hotel bar.

'How are you feeling now?' I ask Nick, who's sitting opposite me, looking utterly deflated. 'I notice you're on round four hundred and twelve of rotating your whisky glass.'

He stops turning his tumbler and rubs his unshaven chin instead. The stress and turmoil he's feeling is evident, but he tries to put on a brave face.

'I'm fine.'

'You don't need to pretend you're OK for my sake,' I continue. 'You've just found out you're losing your job. Anyone would be worried about that.'

It would appear that this statement is all that's needed to get Nick to open up. He looks at me with mournful eyes.

'It's not just a job though, is it? It's my life. Those folk are like family, I've told you that before.'

'You have.' I nod, just relieved that he's finally talking.

'They mean the world to me, and so do the animals.'

'I can imagine it's like losing a much-loved family pet, only magnified times a thousand.'

'I suppose you could say that.' He almost smiles at this, but it swiftly turns into a grimace. 'I don't think of the animals as pets though. It's a different relationship, even with Rana, despite the fact she sees me as her play buddy. I have a respect for them that's difficult to describe. They're all magnificent; wonderous creatures of nature that have evolved over millions of years to survive in some of the most unfriendly or dangerous habitats in the world. They're so much more than pets. They're miracles. I mean, in our whole universe, this is the only planet we know to be inhabitable, and on top of that, able to support the diversity of life that we have here. That's so special. Those animals should be cherished and protected at all costs, and what does the human race do? It lets them die, brutalises them to the point of extinction, because of our own selfish and materialistic pursuits.'

'You know I've never thought about it like that before.' I feel the weight of his words settle on me like an iron blanket. 'You're right, they are miracles. Every single one of them. They absolutely should be cherished.'

Nick disappears back into his whisky glass reflectively, so I excuse myself to the ladies, my mind relentlessly ticking over his words. This is so wrong. The park is too important to let go, but what's the answer? I'm no expert on rescuing a failing business. Feeling hopeless, I unlock my phone and quickly draft an Instagram post with my favourite picture of Rana and Nick. I lay bare my sorrow over the fate of the park and then add some relevant hashtags, before posting it. It's my way of channelling my feelings so I can stay strong for Nick and the others.

Returning to the bar, my eyes land on a despondent Nick, and I realise I need to do something to distract him from the misery he's feeling.

'Hey, you.' I slip into the seat beside him, draping my arm around his neck. 'Can I kiss it better?'

'Kiss what better?' He gives me a puzzled look.

'I don't know. I was going for a figure of speech, but I'm not sure that was the right one.'

I wrinkle my nose, feeling a little daft, but at least I've succeeded in creating a temporary distraction.

'Well, a kiss from you is going to make anything feel better.' He slips his arm around my waist and kisses me deeply, sending tingles to every extremity of my body.

'Is that right?' I nibble seductively on his bottom lip, pinning him with my best sultry look. 'Then how about we push our dinner reservation back an hour and go upstairs?'

The suggestive nature of my question seems to finally shake Nick out of his funk. His eyes flicker with lust and I know he's feeling everything I'm feeling right now. The unquenched sexual chemistry that's been building between us finally reaches boiling point, and we hot foot it out of the bar so fast, we almost forget to sign for our drinks.

–

Having finally taken that all-important step across the threshold to becoming lovers, Nick and I seem to take things up a level emotionally as well. We enjoy a romantic meal together in the hotel restaurant, playing footsie under the table, while talking in earnest about things we'd like to do together in the future. We're so lost in each other, it's a wonder we manage to order and eat a meal. Being with him in that way, our bodies moving together as one, was way better than I ever imagined – a good portion of which was probably down to the fact that we'd waited so long and had developed a strong connection. It was so much more than sex, and at the same time it was the best sex I've ever had.

Nick manages to put the stresses of the park to the back of his mind for the evening – likely helped by the copious amounts of wine we drink with our meal and the fact that we return to my room straight after dinner for round two, three then four. It's about four a.m. by the time we finally give in to exhaustion and fall asleep, wrapped in each other's arms.

When I wake up several hours later, my head pounding, stomach rumbling, despite the huge meal we consumed, I wonder if we might have slept in and missed breakfast. Plucking my phone from the bedside table to check the time, I'm pleased to see that there's still fifty minutes of breakfast service to go. Provided I can get Nick out of bed sharpish, my hangover will be well tended too with a full Scottish breakfast.

Deciding to give him another ten minutes, I lie back and check my notifications. There are a few WhatsApp messages, including one from Jackson telling me there's no need to rush home, as well as some Facebook and Instagram alerts.

Remembering my Instagram post from the evening before, I open up the app and see that my post has had a bit of engagement.

'Gosh, one hundred and twelve likes and twenty-two comments.' I raise my eyebrows. 'That's a personal best by a long shot.'

'Do you always talk to yourself?' Nick murmurs from beside me.

'Only when I have strange men in my bed.'

He gives a sleepy chuckle.

'Morning, sexy man.' I lay my phone back on the night stand and snuggle into him.

'Morning. Have we missed breakfast?'

'Not if we get up now.'

'Excellent. I assume you'll need to shower first?'

'You're obviously well trained.' I untangle myself from him and head for the bathroom.

Once I'm showered and changed, and Nick is in the bathroom, I settle back down on the bed, keen to have a look at the comments on my Instagram post. Reading them one by one, I smile wistfully at the messages of support, tapping on the 'like' button as I go. Then, partway down, I see a message that's different to the others, it says: 'When did you last check your fundraising page? Looks like your situation might have changed.' Puzzled by this, I navigate to the FundedCauses page and my jaw drops in astonishment.

'*Oh my word*... NICK!' I leap off the bed and hammer on the bathroom door, my heart pounding in my ribcage, adrenaline coursing through my body.

Chapter 34

Quickly packing up my stuff, we race to the wildlife park, and after abandoning Nick's car in the middle of the car park, we all but fall through the door to Gwen's office, sweating and out of breath.

'What the—' Her head jolts up from the paperwork she's poring over. 'What's going on? Is everything all right?'

Panting heavily, I'm unable to form a proper sentence. 'Sorry... yes... fine. Donation on... FundedCauses... page. *Look.*' I thrust my phone in Gwen's face, and she takes it out of my hand so she can actually read what's on the screen.

'"What an amazing event you put on yesterday,"' she reads aloud, quoting the words on the screen. '"Your park and everything it stands for is too important to be left to shut down." That's nice. And they're given us a three hundred and fifty pound donation. It's generous, though was it worth half killing yourselves to show me this?'

'Look again,' Nick instructs her.

Gwen narrows her eyes at us curiously then squints at the phone.

'Three hundred and fifty *grand*?' She rubs her forehead in complete bafflement. 'Is this a joke? Did you amend this somehow?'

'Of course we didn't.' Nick shakes his head at her.

'Then... it's real? We've had more than a quarter of a million-pound donation?'

'Uh-huh.' My face spreads into a wide grin. 'The park is saved, Gwen. You don't need to close. This is exactly what you had hoped for.'

Gwen seems utterly bewildered. She just sits there, staring at my phone screen, shaking her head in wonder, while Nick and I share a look.

'Um… Gwen? Are you OK?' I probe.

'Who's it from?' Her dumbfounded gaze meets mine. 'All it says is the donation came from "anonymous" and that it was made late last night. I mean, who gives away three hundred and fifty grand just like that?'

'Not many people.' Nick slips into one of the chairs in front of Gwen's desk and I follow suit. 'But there are good folk in the world who play the philanthropist role. It won't be the first time it's happened, that's for sure.'

'But to do it anonymously? That's quite novel, is it not? And if they were at the event yesterday, it must mean it's someone local.'

I shrug. 'Perhaps, but not necessarily. We promoted the event on social media, so in theory, they could have travelled from anywhere.'

'I think we need to forget about who it's from,' says Nick. 'If they wanted us to know who they were, they would have come forward and spoken to us yesterday. I think we have to take this as the kind gesture it's intended to be, and focus our efforts on making sure the park has a stable future, don't you?'

This last statement seems to bring Gwen out of her discombobulated state.

'You're right. That's exactly what we need to do.' She gets out of her seat and starts pacing at a rate I've never seen. 'With that size of donation, the park isn't just saved, we can make some changes that will set us up for long-term success. We'll need to have a management meeting, think things through, tell the staff—'

'Gwen?' Nick interjects before she takes off.

'Yes?' She stops dead.

'How about you let this sink in for a moment first?'

'Good idea.' She takes a couple of deep breaths, then looks at Nick and I, her eyes overflowing with emotion. 'I'm stupefied by this. It's unbelievable. No, it's bloody marvellous! After everything we've put into this place, we get to stay open. We're really getting to stay open…'

Having redirected her energy to digesting the incredible news, Gwen resumes her pacing, before bounding round the side of the desk and hugging us so tightly, she inadvertently puts us both in a head lock. She then loses her balance and topples into Nick's lap, which results in two red faces (them) and me losing control of myself due to the hilarity of it. To say she's thrilled is like saying a Euromillions winner is quite pleased with their win, and at one point the sounds coming out of her mouth are somewhere between crowing cockerel and howling bloodhound, making it difficult to work out if she's celebrating or crying – it turns out to be a bit of both.

Once Gwen's calmed down enough to think and act rationally, she swears Nick and I to secrecy, then triggers the emergency call tree process to ask everyone on her payroll to come to the park for an announcement at midday. From what we hear back from the management team, there are no grumbles from anyone, as they are all aware of the seriousness of the situation. We also contact the FundedCauses people, just to be sure there are no issues with the donation, which thankfully there aren't. Then, having missed breakfast, the three of us head to the park restaurant to enjoy a celebratory brunch on the sly.

–

At midday, Gwen, Nick and I arrive at the picnic area outside the main restaurant, where the park employees are milling around, looking miserable. I really feel for them, particularly knowing that there's no reason for them to be carrying that burden anymore, but at least I know their anguish will soon turn into relief and jubilation.

'Are you ready?' I say to Gwen, who's quivering like a pneumatic drill, still as pumped on adrenaline as she was earlier.

'Am I ever.' She puffs herself up, her fists clenched as if she's going into battle.

'Then off you go.' I give her shoulder an encouraging pat. 'Oh, and remember, don't pace.'

'Gotcha.' She gives me a theatrical wink and, in this moment, I'd bet the whole three hundred and fifty grand she won't be able to stand on one spot while she makes this announcement.

Nick and I discreetly link fingers and watch as Gwen climbs on to the stage that's still erect from yesterday's event.

'Morning everyone.' She smiles soberly at the glum faces staring back at her. 'Oh, it's afternoon now, isn't it?' She checks her watch, then starts fiddling with the cuff on her top, which appears to have gotten caught in the strap.

There's a low ripple of amusement as she becomes distracted, wrestling with the fabric, which fortunately lifts the mood slightly.

'You good?' someone shouts from the crowd, bringing Gwen back to the moment.

'Yes, eh... all good.' She nods at her team members while giving her cuff a good tug, releasing it and probably damaging her top in the process. 'Sorry.'

'She must be finding this so tough,' someone close by says to their co-worker.

I steal a glance at Nick and he waggles his eyebrows in response.

'Right, so, a big thank you to you all for giving up part of your Sunday to be here,' Gwen finally continues. 'Yesterday was a huge success. I couldn't have been prouder of you all for what you achieved in such a short space of time. Your commitment to this place has been remarkable and I want you to know that you all have a special place in my heart.'

She pauses briefly and takes a deep breath.

'Which is why it was so damn tough for me yesterday to make the decision to close the park. This place is like home. It's like a family – a really big one – and that's because of you…' Gwen's right leg begins to twitch as she says this.

'Oh, here we go,' I say out loud without thinking, earning myself a dirty look from a nearby worker, who doesn't know what's about to come and understandably thinks I'm being rude.

Nick, having seen this, squeezes my hand in reassurance while I pull a cringing face, then return my attention to Gwen, who's still telling everyone how fabulous they are.

'…and it's this commitment from you all, that makes me so honoured and, quite frankly, ecstatic to be standing up before you today with not bad, but good news…' Gwen begins pacing, as predicted, as she builds up to her crescendo.

The sea of expressions turns from crestfallen and dejected to curious and hopeful.

'This morning, our very own Jess – yes, I consider you one of our own—' Gwen gives me a meaningful look as she clocks the pleasantly surprised expression on my face '—our Jess, who pulled out all the stops to get our amazing fundraiser over the line yesterday, woke up to an anonymous donation on our FundedCauses page.'

'How much was the donation for?' calls out a worker who's clearly getting impatient with Gwen's elongated announcement.

'That's just what I was about to tell you, Byron.' Gwen stops pacing and kind of semi-crouches down, making her look like she's having an alfresco pee.

This unfortunately attracts a few stifled sniggers, which thankfully she doesn't notice.

Gwen reads out the message on the FundedCauses page first, then does the big reveal. 'We've received – wait for it – three hundred and fifty thousand pounds!' She jumps up and throws her hands in the air to add impact to this revelation.

The crowd of workers is stunned into silence for about half a second, then the place erupts into cheers and cries of disbelief. The atmosphere is electric, with colleagues hugging each other and jumping up and down with excitement, while I make a mental note to strongly advise Gwen never to squat like that in front of an audience again.

Chapter 35

After an hour or so of chatting with an endless stream of park workers, all wanting to thank me for saving their jobs, Nick walks me to my car and we say a cosy goodbye.

'Thanks for everything, Jess.' He nuzzles my neck in a manner that makes me want to jump straight into the bushes with him. 'You really did pull out all the stops for us. We're so grateful to you.'

I shrug. 'I was just doing my job.'

'Come on, it was a lot more than that. If you hadn't led the way on the fundraiser, there would have been no event and no FundedCauses page for anyone to donate through.'

'OK, fair enough, but this place is so important to you all, and now it's important to me too.'

Nick looks thoughtful. 'Your career is also important to you. Is there anything Gwen or I can do to help you get that back on track? Surely your boss can't question your capability now. You've done way more than was ever asked of you.'

'Oh, don't worry.' I grin at him. 'There's no way Craig can ignore this success story. I've got a one-to-one with him on Tuesday morning, and I fully intend to make the most of that time.'

We chat for a few moments longer, then say our good-byes and I get on the road. As the greenery of East Lothian, dampened by a squally shower that's recently come on, whizzes past me, I realise I need to make a call.

'Call Amelia,' I instruct the in-car speech recognition system.

It rings just twice before she answers.

'Jess, mate, how did yesterday go?' Amelia's bubbly voice comes through the car speakers. 'I've been peeing my pants waiting to hear.'

'There was no need to soil yourself over it,' I quip. 'Anyway, since when do you call people "mate"?'

'Since I'm trying out a new "look".'

'Right.' I navigate my way across a roundabout. 'So what colour is your hair now?'

'About five different shades of pink.'

'Sounds very My Little Pony.'

'Nah, mate, it's retro. Think pink pick-and-mix. Anyway, less about that, give me the juice.'

I shake my head at my friend's fabulous outrageousness and quickly fill her in on the events of the last thirty-six hours.

'You are shitting me,' she cries out when I tell her the final piece about the obscene anonymous donation, and she falls about laughing (I think) when I throw in a mention of Gwen's unfortunate squat.

'That's an image I'll never get out of my head,' I snigger, enjoying this chat with my bestie. 'So, there you are. That's you caught up. Pretty cool stuff, eh?'

'I'll say.'

'Oh, and I need to thank you for all the social media marketing advice you gave me. Without it, we would never have managed any of this.'

'All I did was give you the know-how – which really you could have researched yourself online. It was you who put it into practice. Your win, 'kay?'

'OK.' I smile, while manoeuvring my way on to the slip road for the A1. 'Thanks, Amelia. For everything. I miss you.'

'I miss you too. We'll see each other soon though. Was thinking I could come up for a visit just before Christmas? I'll stay in a hotel, obviously, as I know you have a full house.'

'Ah, brilliant, definitely. It might involve spending quite a lot of time in my flat though, with Seth being, you know...' I wince, hoping this won't be an issue.

'Obviously,' Amelia replies, to my relief. 'We'll give Seth a Christmas season to remember. And I'm looking forward to seeing that hot man of yours in a Santa suit.'

'Um… he's not actually Santa, nor does he work at a seasonal grotto, so I'm not sure how that's going to happen,' I scoff, before saying goodbye and ending the call.

Forty minutes later, I'm back home with Seth, having sent Jackson off for a well-earned rest – but not before giving him a summarised version of the weekend's events, at his insistence. Both he and Seth were riveted by the story, which made me realise that this is one I'll be telling for years to come.

'So how have you been?' I hand Seth a cup of lukewarm tea, which is how he has it to avoid any unnecessary accidents. 'I feel bad for being away so long.'

'Don't feel bad. You had to… do that… and look what you… achieved,' he says. 'You saved a… an important… cons… con-ser-vation project.'

'Yeah, I guess I did. Though not single-handedly. The team down there are so dedicated. It was impossible not to get sucked into their cause.'

'I wish I… could have met… them yesterday. Espec-ially Nick. I need to… scope out my… future brother-in-law.' Seth gives me a wicked grin.

'Steady.' I shake my head with amusement. 'We've only been seeing each other a few weeks.'

'Well… whatever… it would have been… nice to meet him.'

'Yeah, sorry about that.' I try to ignore the similarly sized wedges of guilt and shame competing for space in my gut, as I'm reminded of how I deliberately kept Nick and Seth apart. 'It was such a hectic day. Another time?'

'Sure, but…' Seth's face clears and he appears to be struggling with something.

'What is it, big bro?'

'You're not… embarr-assed by me… are you?'

This time it's a ten-ton truck of shame that flattens me in one go.

'What? *No.* Never. Please don't ever think that, Seth.' I swoop in on him with a ginormous, reassuring hug. 'I could never be embarrassed by you. I'm so proud to call you my brother. Always have been, always will be.'

'Sure.' He looks only partially convinced.

'Seriously.' I grab him by the shoulders and look him straight in the eye. 'This situation does not change a thing in terms of how I view you. You're my amazing, talented, caring, hilarious, good-looking big brother.'

'OK.' He seems to cheer up a bit. 'It's just... I have my... consultant appointment... on Tuesday, and... I'll get an update... on how well I'm progressing, as well as... what that might mean... for my long-term recovery.'

'Of course. I forgot about that. Shall I take the afternoon off to go with you?'

This is actually the last thing I want to be doing while pleading my case for being reinstated on my big projects on Tuesday morning, but my brother's health and wellbeing come first.

'No, Jackson is... taking me,' says Seth. 'We've talked about it... and he knows what... questions to ask... because of his... exp-erience working with... people like me.'

'People in long-term rehabilitation, like you,' I correct him. 'You are not defined by this.'

'Yes. That's what... I meant. Also, I'm having... coffee with Alison after. Her dad will be... in for a physio appoint-ment... and Jackson said... it would allow him to... nip to the... super-market, while I'm with her.'

'No problem.' I force my expression to remain neutral at the mention of Alison, because hard as I try, I just can't get comfortable with the idea of her dating my brother while he's in such a vulnerable position. 'If you change your mind, let me know and I'll speak to Craig about taking a few hours off.'

'Anyway, back to me... meeting your hunky... boyfriend,' Seth sips at his tea while I'm poised and ready to assist if he has any difficulties. 'Why don't you… invite him round… at the weekend? Or we could go… to the wildlife park… and meet him there?'

'I'm sure we can sort something out.'

I'm careful to keep my tone casual and Seth seems satisfied with this. However, on the inside, I'm starting to panic, because I've no idea how to handle this situation. I knew it would be tricky trying to navigate things with Nick when he doesn't know the full picture, but I didn't expect Seth to be on my case to meet Nick this quickly. How exactly am I going to get out of this one without Seth feeling like I'm hiding him away – which I am, but for a different reason than what he thought? Even if I can successfully deter Seth, how can I keep my relationship with Nick going smoothly when he now expects more from me, and I can't commit much of my time to him?

Chapter 36

On Tuesday morning, my eyes ping open the moment my alarm goes off, and my internal battle cry is perfectly tuned before the soles of my feet hit the laminate floor. Today I get my job back. I know I never lost it in the traditional sense, but it certainly feels that way. There's something about watching your junior colleagues take over your work that's basically the career equivalent to being emasculated. So today, I'm in full assault mode. I won't be rude or aggressive, but I will put my arguments across more firmly than before, and I will make sure Craig understands that his assertions have been wrong.

That's the plan, but the reality plays out quite differently. My first mistake is getting a takeaway coffee from the cafe opposite our office on my way in. Shortly after drinking it, my whole body is jangling from a combination of pre-meeting adrenaline and the nuclear hit of caffeine it provides. Probably not the wisest move to be completely wired going into this conversation. My second mistake (which is actually my first, if we go by when I first made the assumption) is thinking that Craig will analyse the logic I present to him in the way that I expect him to.

'Jess, we've been here before.' The tone of Craig's voice is bordering on frustration. 'Did you pull off a blinder with the wildlife park? Absolutely. You've set them up with a brilliant new revenue stream, and you went the extra mile with that superb fundraiser. Does that change the facts at hand? No. You're still working part time, which means your reduced availability could still cause issues with high-profile clients – and we can't afford to lose *any* of those clients.'

I can feel my blood reaching the point of becoming hot broth.

'Craig, with respect, have I not just spent three weeks working round the clock to deliver that "superb fundraiser"? Does that not show how "available" I can be?'

'Do you have the money to stay in a hotel and pay a live-in carer every time there's a need to do that?'

'Well, no, but that was an extreme set of circumstances. On any other project I'd have more planning time to make sure everything is lined up perfectly.'

I continue to argue my case, once again having to explain my job to Craig – a man who hasn't been 'on the ground' in years – and once again feeling resentment rising at having to do so.

'Doesn't matter.' Craig shakes his head in rejection of my logic. 'The point is, you don't know what might come up, and without the ability to respond immediately to any issues that arise, you're a risk to the company. This isn't personal, Jess.'

I stare at him in disbelief. 'That is actually true, isn't it? It's not personal, because we're all expendable to you.'

'Jess, that's not at all… um, really not…' Craig is so stunned by my boldness, he struggles to form a response, so I keep going.

'You see us as commodities… resources, and not much more. You decided I'd outlived my usefulness because I'd chosen to care for a family member rather than let him rot in a home.'

'This is ridiculous.' He finally finds his voice, but he's flapping and I know I've got it spot on. 'Utter drivel, with no real basis whatsover.'

'OK, if it's "drivel", then let me have my projects back and I'll show you how wrong you are about me being "a risk to the company".'

'Jess, you are jumping up and down on razor thin ice here.' Craig adopts an undertone of menace, which shocks me into calming down my accusatory stance. I may think he's corporate scum at this precise moment, but I need to keep my job.

'Sorry,' I mutter. Closing my eyes for a moment, I attempt to ground myself.

'I understand you're upset.' Craig reins in his tone as well. 'But you can't go around making accusations like that. This situation, as much as you don't like it, is permanent unless you resume full-time hours. You're going to have to find a way to deal with that, or I suggest you start looking for a new job.'

I'm filled with fury at his snakiness, and the fact I have no choice but to let this go. All I want to do is flip the table between us in a heated rage and storm out. But that will obviously cost me my job – and quite possibly my clean record as a citizen – so instead, I mumble that I understand and I'd better get back to work.

As I'm getting up from my seat to leave the room, a new realisation hijacks my consciousness: I need to find a new job and jump before I'm pushed – or I'm pushed over the edge.

Chapter 37

I spend the rest of the morning stewing at my desk, pretending to be busy and productive, but the minute the clock on the wall hits twelve p.m., I roll back my desk chair and head out for lunch. I badge it this way because I've never really been one to take lunch breaks when in the office. I'd usually keep working at my desk, forking something healthy from a Tupperware, barely noticing the day passing by. That same Tupperware is currently nestled at the bottom of my bag, and today it will only see the light of day once I've made an important call.

Making my way along the street, I cross at the three-way junction between the university and the Quartermile and take the path to the Meadows. Once I've found an empty bench away from the main tree-lined thoroughfare, I sit down, and for a few minutes I just watch the people around me in the vast open green space, chatting, laughing, some of them speed walking, doing yoga or playing sports. It's exactly the vibrant but calming environment I need right now. Then, once I feel ready, I look up the number I want and put my phone to my ear.

'Jess, fabulous to hear from you,' says a syrupy voice in my ear moments after I've spoken to the receptionist. 'I thought Riley had gotten mixed up when he told me he had you on the line. How are you?'

Sitting up straight, I try to convince my wearied body and brain to play along. 'I'm good thanks, Bree. Firing on all cylinders, as usual.'

'I bet you are. I saw in the local press you almost single-handedly saved East Lothian Wildlife Park from closure. Well done, you. I'd never heard of the place. That bit of clever PR will do them wonders.'

'I certainly hope so.'

'Not a doubt in my mind. Lovely little side-gig for you on top of all the biggie events you lead.'

I purse my lips. This is not how I wanted to kick off this call – with Bree calling my biggest success of late a 'side-gig'. However, I try not to let this distract me from my goal.

'So, tell me…' she continues, saving me from having to respond '…to what do I owe the pleasure of this call today? Not looking for a favour from the competition, I hope.' She gives a tinkling laugh.

No time like the present. I take a deep breath to bolster some confidence, which oddly, I'm finding it hard to muster right now.

'No, nothing like that.' I chuckle, mirroring her tone. 'I'm actually interested in chatting about that job offer you said would remain on the table.'

'Really? Well, this day just got a whole lot more interesting. Though if you don't mind me asking, why are you looking for a move? Capital Events has some meaty contracts – ones you know I'd love to steal away from them—'

'And I could help you do that,' I jump in quickly. 'Once the restrictive covenant in my contract times out.'

I'm trying to divert Bree away from the question she's asked, so I can make myself a no-brainer choice for her, before I tackle my reason for leaving.

'This all sounds wonderful,' says Bree. 'Though I'm still keen to hear why you're looking to move on.'

Dammit. There's no way to gloss over this. She wants the hard facts, and because I'm planning to ask for part-time hours, there's no point in skipping over that detail at this stage. She'll find out anyway. Bree is exactly the type to go digging. Anyway,

I'm banking on her looking past my situation to the finely tuned talent being offered to her on a plate, so I may as well get all my cards on the table.

'I need to be honest,' I say. 'It's a little uncomfortable for me to share.'

'Try me.'

'OK, well, Craig has essentially demoted me. He's removed me from the high-profile projects because of a personal situation, and despite me more than proving my capability, he won't let me take the lead on them again.'

'I see.' She pauses briefly. 'We all have personal situations that come up from time to time, so that seems a bit harsh, given your track record.'

'That's what I think.' I nod vigorously, despite the fact Bree can't see me.

'If you don't mind me asking, what is this "situation" you've been dealing with?'

Raising pleading eyes to the sky, I give Bree a quick summary of the events of the last few months: Seth's stroke, my decision to care for him as well as how I'm optimistic that it will be a temporary situation, and how Craig responded.

'Jess, I am truly sorry to hear about your brother,' says Bree, once I've shared all of this. 'It sounds like a nightmare, especially with your parents not being around, and such a terrible fright for you. I expect anyone with an ounce of humanity would have done the same as you if they had the choice to do so. I also expect you couldn't have lived with yourself if you'd allowed your brother to go into full-time care.'

'Exactly that.' I'm so relieved that Bree not only understands, but also supports my decision.

'So, are you saying that you'd be looking for the same three-day week arrangement with me?'

'Yes. And I know I could do it. I've more than proven myself to be capable and I'm just as effective working those hours. I'd just need to handle a slightly smaller workload.'

There's a short silence then Bree clears her throat. 'Jess, you know how highly I rate you...'

This is all a need to hear to know this conversation is not going in the direction I thought it would. My hopes are immediately smashed to pieces and all I want to do is cut the call, but I have no choice but to stay on the line and endure the long-winded excuses that are about to follow.

'I would be delighted to have your expertise and offer you a role on our team, however I'm afraid I can't offer you a position as a senior events manager. That role has to be done on a full-time basis, with additional hours as needed on weekends.'

Though I can tell it's a lost cause, it's not in my instincts to roll over the moment I'm told 'no'.

'I can easily do the additional weekend hours because I can plan those in and arrange cover. And I can make myself available to take important calls on Mondays and—'

'Jess.' Bree brings me to a halt by simply saying my name. 'Look, this isn't personal, it's business.'

'That's what Craig said.'

'And he's right. The fact is: I need my most senior people ready to respond to our clients' needs pretty much round the clock, and right now, you can't do that. It's not a criticism, it's just how things are. I'm not going to demean you by offering you a more junior role, because I don't think that would be the right thing for either of us, but what I will say is, once your situation is more stable, if you want to go back to full-time hours, the role you're looking for will be waiting right here for you if you want it.'

After a few pleasantries, which include Bree assuring me she won't share our conversation with anyone, we say our goodbyes. This is a relief, as the last thing I need right now – especially when I have zero options or leverage – is Craig finding out I've been shopping around for a new job.

Leaning back on the bench, I pick at my lunch while mulling over the conversation I've just had. Bree took the same line as

Craig, which on the face of it, makes it seem like that's just how things are and that their responses are reasonable. But the resentful feeling in my gut tells me they're not; that they're just using the full-time hours thing as an excuse and what's really behind it is that they're not supportive of flexible working arrangements. To them, it's a sign of reduced commitment. Whatever it is, it's clear to me that I'm stuck where I am for now, and that's not a great position to be in. In fact, it's so bloody infuriating, I want to return to the office and dump the contents of my Tupperware over Craig's head.

While I'm ruminating over all this, I feel my phone buzz in my bag. Pulling it out, the home screen alerts me to a WhatsApp message from Nick.

> Are you coming to the park today? I miss your beautiful face. X

I smile ruefully. All I want to do right now is snuggle into him and tell him all about the wicked witch and wizard of the events world, but I can't do that. He knows so little of my situation, and the last thing I need is to accidentally out myself while in full frustrated conversational flow. I have to get the timing right (i.e. once Seth is more independent) and manage things really sensitively, or else I'll be mourning the loss of Nick as well as my career.

No, I can't go to the park today. I'm too fragile and, at odds with my usual extrovert self, I need some time alone. I quickly message him back and say I'll be there first thing tomorrow for a project meeting, then I get up and drag myself back to the office.

Chapter 38

When I get home that evening, having trudged dejectedly from the office, I'm mentally and emotionally exhausted. It takes a huge amount of energy being miserable at work, especially when time seems to go at about half the normal speed. On opening the door to my flat, I'm met in the hallway by Jackson, which is no strange thing in itself, only today the wide grin I'm used to seeing is replaced with a grim, serious-looking face.

'Can we talk somewhere privately?' he asks me.

'Of course.' I usher him through the hallway and into my room, closing the door quietly behind us. 'What's going on? Was it the appointment? Did he get bad news? I knew I should have been there.'

'Why don't you sit down?' Jackson gestures to the bed and I sink onto it, while he does the same beside me. 'Seth did have some bad news today. Not awful, but they said they would have expected more progress with his fine motor skills and physical mobility by now.'

'Oh, no. This is bad.' I put my head in my hands, feeling gutted for my brother.

'It's not what we were hoping for, but as I said, it's not awful. He could still make the level of recovery they were initially aiming for, but the chances of that are a bit slimmer now. They're very happy with his speech though, which we know is coming on really well.'

'So what happens now?'

'Much the same. The physical therapy will continue – they'll adjust his programme slightly – and then we'll have to wait and see how things progress.'

'How is he?' I grimace. 'He's always so positive but this must be a blow to him.'

'He's disappointed obviously, but he's taking it better than most would, I'd say. However, that's not the only issue.'

I blanch. 'There's more? Please tell me it's not something that will make his life harder. I've been worried about the potential for another stroke.'

'It's nothing to do with Seth's health. Not in a direct sense anyway.' Jackson looks like he's struggling to find the right words.

'Just tell me, Jackson.' I rub my palms against my thighs, bracing myself. 'Whatever it is, I can take it.'

'OK. I'm really sorry to be the messenger here, Jess.' He winces. 'After Seth's appointment he met Alison for a coffee as planned, and she called things off with him. He's devastated.'

Frenzied anger rushes through me like lava. 'I *bloody* knew it. I *knew* she'd break his heart. Didn't I say? It was too weird, her striking up a relationship with Seth. It's like she was projecting, or whatever you call it… you know, because of her dad. I mean, they say women marry their father, but that was—'

'Jess, please.' Jackson touches my forearm gently, which has the instant effect of winding me down. 'It's not what you think. Alison finished with Seth – because of you.'

'*Me?* What the hell have I got to do with it? That just sounds like an excuse.'

'It's not an excuse. She felt intimidated by you at the wildlife park on Saturday. She picked up on your judgement of her—'

'I wasn't judging her.'

'Really?' Jackson raises an eyebrow, challenging me to rethink that statement.

'OK, I was. But all I did was make it clear to her that Seth needs to stay focused on his recovery and not be messed around.'

'Surely you must have known the impact your behaviour towards her would have, Jess. You're a smart woman. So why drive her away?'

Jackson's scrutiny makes me feel like a tiny organism under a microscope.

'Because Seth doesn't need any more problems in his life.' I clock another look from him and deflate. 'OK, I didn't want her around and I didn't trust her motives.'

'Do you have any good reason for that other than the fact she's beautiful and non-disabled and you're wondering how she could possibly be interested in Seth as he is now?'

This question smacks me with the force of a bird hitting a window. I'm completely stunned by the answer I realise I have to give, and the connotations of it. I've been prejudiced. Not intentionally, nor even consciously. I thought I was being protective of Seth, and I probably was, but without realising it, I was also seeing him as someone who couldn't possibly be loved by a woman like Alison. And what's worse, I've been judging my boss for behaviour that I've been unknowingly exhibiting myself – only in a different way.

'Jackson, what have I done?' I look at him with wide, shameful eyes. 'All I wanted to do was protect Seth and now I've ruined his life.'

He gently takes my hand in a show of compassion I don't feel I deserve.

'You haven't ruined his life, but you have really hurt him. He tried to convince Alison that he would speak to you and sort it out, but she told him, no matter what happened, she would always feel that judgement was there. She couldn't face being in a situation where she would never truly be trusted or accepted.'

'I need to speak to him.' I get up from the bed. 'Will you come with me?'

'Of course.'

We go through to the living room together, where Seth is sitting on the sofa staring at the TV blankly. I sit down beside him, while Jackson takes a seat on the armchair at the other side of the room, giving us some space.

'Seth, Jackson told me what happened with Alison,' I say to him. 'I'm so sorry.'

'You're sorry she's... gone, or you're sorry... I'm hurt?' Seth's voice is thick with accusation.

I glance nervously at Jackson then focus my full attention on my brother. 'Being honest, probably the latter, because you're my priority, but I realise now that I haven't been fair. And I shouldn't have spoken to her the way I did.'

'She was... amazing, Jess.' He finally turns to face me, his words teeming with emotion. 'She saw me for... who I am. And you... treated her like shit.'

'I didn't—' I glance at Jackson again and he shakes his head, discouraging me, as trying to defend myself will only fuel the fire. 'Sorry, you're right. But Seth, I can fix this—'

'No, you can't. Alison has made... herself clear, and... she's asked me to... respect her decision. You've done enough... damage, Jess. Just leave... things alone now. In fact, please... leave me alone. I don't want to... be around you... right now.'

'OK, sure, if that's what you want.' My eyes sting unbearably at this rejection from the most important person in my life.

Seth says nothing further and fixes his gaze back on the TV, so I get up and leave the room, wiping tears from my cheeks as I go.

Jackson follows me out of the room into the hallway, where we speak in hushed tones.

'He's never going to forgive me.'

'He will.' Jackson hands me a tissue from the box in the hallway. 'Just give him some space for a day or so, as he's requested.'

'In any normal situation, that wouldn't be a problem, but I have to feed him, wash him, help him to the toilet... I can't just disappear for the night...' I tail off and look at him helplessly.

'How about I stay over so you can do just that?' he suggests. 'Then you can see how things are tomorrow after work?'

'Really? You'd do that?'

'Of course.'

'I think it's the only way that I can do what Seth is asking – and I owe him this.' I dab at my face, the tears now coming thick and fast. 'Thanks, Jackson. You have no idea how much I appreciate your support. I'll pay you extra for this, because of the inconvenience.'

'Do you have a spare unused toothbrush?'

'Uh… yeah.'

'Then there's no inconvenience. Why don't you go and pack a bag? I'm sure your man will be more than happy to have you to himself for the night.'

Jackson obviously intends to cheer me up with this comment, but as I head for my room, all it does is make me feel completely alone. I can't go to Nick, because I don't trust myself not to break down and tell him everything. The last thing I want to do is introduce him to the complexities of my life while I'm in full crisis mode – especially when he's told me one of the things he likes about me is that I'm 'uncomplicated'. My only option is to check into a hotel for the night, and hope that Seth will be willing to tolerate me after he's slept on this – not that I feel I even deserve that.

Chapter 39

Having checked myself into a cheap hotel on York Place, I lie on the bed in my room for a while, staring absently at the news on the TV. I'm past the crying stage and now I'm just numb from the cumulative impact of the day's events: my hopeless meeting with Craig, my even more hopeless call to Bree, which left me with the grim realisation that I'm stuck where I am with my career indefinitely, and then worst of all, the discovery that I'd broken my big brother's heart. Me. Not Alison. I left her little choice and she did what anyone would surely do in that situation. How can I blame her for that?

Eventually emerging from my emptiness, I'm twitchy and anxious, my bog-standard hotel room feeling more like a prison cell. I try to settle myself but it's fruitless, and when I reach the point where I'm pacing the room like Gwen on amphetamines, I decide it's time for a change of scenery. Grabbing my handbag, I take the lift down to the hotel bar.

It's smallish and kind of cosy, with modern furniture and mood lighting. I don't want to be alone with my thoughts, and the idea of sitting in a high-backed booth by myself is almost as suffocating as being stuck in my room. So I head for the bar, and climb up onto one of the bar stools.

Looking around from my elevated position, I can see that I'm the only customer in the place. In fact, I'm the only person here full stop, because there's no one behind the bar either.

For a moment, I wonder if it's closed, then a voice comes from behind me.

'Sorry, love.' A man with a stocky frame and a well-manicured salt and pepper beard scoots round behind the bar, giving me a broad smile. 'What can I get you?'

I frown; I haven't thought about this, and I'm not in the frame of mind for making even the simplest of decisions.

'I… eh… I'm not sure.' I scan the vast collection of bottles behind the bar, seeking inspiration, but I come up empty-handed.

'Maybe a long drink? G&T? Vodka lemonade?' he suggests and I shake my head. 'Or do you like cocktails?'

'Yes. Let's go for a cocktail. What's the strongest one on your menu?'

The man narrows his eyes slightly, as if trying to get a measure of me, and I realise it's probably not the best thing to walk into a bar and essentially ask for 'rocket fuel'.

'I've had a bad day.' I shrug unapologetically. 'Need something to take the edge off. It'll be my first – and probably only – drink.'

'Fair enough.' His smile this time is sympathetic with a dash of concern. 'Here's the menu. Why don't you tell me what you fancy?'

I'm mildly disappointed that he's not just going to point something out for me, but he obviously doesn't want to be a co-conspirator in whatever mess he suspects I may end up in. Scanning the menu, my eyes zoom in on the word 'tequila'. Yup, that'll do it.

'I'll have a Mexican Martini.'

I hand him the menu back and pull my phone out of my bag to see if Seth's been in touch, but he hasn't and I know he won't be. Unable to bear the distance between us when things are such a mess, I tap out a quick text to Jackson and he answers in less than a minute to say that everything is fine and under control.

'*Et voilà.*' The barman places the thinly stemmed martini glass in front of me on a paper coaster. 'Enjoy.'

'Thanks.' I flash him a grateful look.

Taking a long sip of my drink, the zinginess and alcoholic heat seem to instantly reach all the parts of me aching for an escape from the horrible situation I've found myself in.

'Is it good?' The barman asks.

'So good.' I exhale heavily. 'Just what I needed.'

'Glad you like it. It's certainly got the strength you're looking for. Are you a resident here?'

'Yes, just for the night.'

'Has you being here got anything to do with your bad day?'

'Nosey one, you are.' I crinkle my nose so he knows I'm making light of this.

'Comes with the job.' This time it's him who shrugs unapologetically. 'I've helped out many a toiling guest in my time. Barman-slash-counsellor, I am. Even considered doing a qualification, but it cost too much.'

'That's a shame. Certainly sounds like you would have put it to good use.'

'Ah, what can you do, eh? I'm Eamon, by the way.'

'Jess,' I introduce myself in return.

'So, what is it then? Men troubles? Women troubles?' He potters around, cutting fruit and polishing glasses while he talks to me.

'Not as such. Though I've probably cocked up that side of things too.'

Aware that I've nothing to lose by sharing with him, and I'll never see him again after tonight, I fill Eamon in on my predicament, giving him the full ugly picture. It's surprisingly therapeutic. He listens quietly, only breaking full concentration occasionally to serve drinks ordered through room service or for the restaurant.

'Sounds like you've been through the ringer,' he says, once I'm finished.

'That's one way of putting it. Maybe I'd feel sorry for myself if I hadn't kicked my brother square in the teeth while he's already down.' I hang my head shamefully.

'Are you maybe being a bit hard on yourself? I'm sure he'll forgive you.'

'I'm sure he will too – eventually. That's the worst part. He's such an amazing guy, he doesn't judge anyone. He would never have done the same to me.'

'Give it time. Sure, you messed up, but it's what you do when you realise it that counts, and time heals all wounds.'

'I guess. Do me another?' I gently nudge the base of my glass in his direction.

'You sure?'

'Yes. Two cocktails are hardly going to be the end of me.'

'Just checking.' He gives me a little salute.

We chat some more while I sip away at my second drink, then a man enters the bar and hops up onto a bar stool. Catching this newbie stealing glances in my direction, I sneak a look at him and give a little 'wow' under my breath. He's around my age with a broad frame, sun-kissed blond hair and deeply tanned skin, which I decide can only mean one thing.

'You a surfer?' I ask him, my inhibitions lost somewhere in my drink.

'Sure am,' he replies in his sexy Australian accent. 'You look down. Want some company?'

I weigh this up for all of one second. 'Why not.'

He shifts himself along to the bar stool next to me. 'I'm Shane. And you are…?'

'Jess.'

'Course you are.' He gives me a little wink, and I have no idea what he means by this, but he's just the distraction I need right now, so I don't really care.

'Another of the same for my new friend here,' he says to Eamon, who raises his eyebrows at me.

I go out of my way to pretend I didn't see him, so he has no choice but to honour the request.

While Shane and I chat away animatedly, Eamon melts into the background, and is eventually is replaced by another staff member. It's obvious Shane is trying to flirt with me, meaning I have to continuously rebuff his efforts, but at the same time I'm enjoying this stress-free evening after the day I've had. The last thing I want when I've badly (but unintentionally) hurt the person I love most in the world, is to be alone with my thoughts in my hotel room. And that's before even considering my failing career, which is weighing on me so heavily. So instead, I lose myself – and my inhibitions – in Shane's good-natured company and more drinks.

After two rounds of tequila slammers, in follow up to my third cocktail, Shane suggests heading out somewhere where there's more going on.

'I thought you'd never ask,' is my giggly, intoxicated reply, before we drunkenly charge our way out the hotel and into the night.

–

I'm standing outside the assembly hall of my high school, waiting with my schoolmates to enter our final sixth-year exam. We can almost taste the freedom, only a few short hours away. While we mingle, half excited, half terrified, I feel a cool breeze whipping around my waist, which I find odd. Then I hear someone say 'Geography is my favourite subject. I'm so glad it's the final exam.'

'What?' I turn in their direction anxiously. 'I thought this was modern studies.'

'Modern studies was yesterday,' says another voice from behind me.

I quickly shift back round but I'm unable to identify the owner of the voice. 'No, that can't be right. I can't have missed it.'

'Did you miss it like you missed getting dressed today?' A third voice is accompanied by echoing laughter and I look around wildly, seeing people but not really recognising anyone.

Then I look down in horror to discover I'm not wearing anything on my bottom half.

'*Stop laughing! Stop laughing!*' I cry out.

'Stop laughing.' I bolt up into a sitting position in my bed, sweating, breathless. Then a razor-sharp pain rips through my head and I immediately lie back down and wait for death to take me.

Obviously, it doesn't. So I lie there, trying to orient myself through the thick porridge that is my hungover brain. I'm in my hotel room – the room I booked because I screwed over my own brother. I went to the bar, chatted to the barman, talked to some Australian bloke, went out drinking with that Australian bloke – Shane, I think his name was – and—

Oh, bloody hell. I shoot up again, my head clanging like a Sunday bell, scanning the bed and the room around me. At least there's no one here. That's a promising start. But I have no memory of anything that happened after we went out. I really hope I didn't do anything I'd regret.

Reaching for my phone, seeking answers – my camera roll and social media being the best bets for finding compromising evidence – the screen illuminates and my eyes zone in on multiple missed call notifications from Craig, Gwen and Nick. My focus then shifts to the clock.

Sh-i-i-te. It's Wednesday, it's eleven a.m., and I'm not at work.

What have I done? The shock is too much on top of already feeling like I've drunk my body weight in tequila. Throwing back the covers, I rush to the toilet, where I heave up my guts over and over, before returning to the bed to get myself together.

That's when I see it.

On the floor is a hotel key card holder. At first I assume it's mine, then my gaze moves across to my bedside table, where there's another one sitting next to my phone – which must be my own. Reaching down to pick it up, another wave of nausea washes over me on seeing a room number that's not mine. It's

Shane's. No doubt about it. I remember the barman asking him for his room number to charge the drinks to. Looking around for further signs that he's been in here, I then spot the half-drunk glass of water sitting on the bedside table, on the opposite side from where I slept. I know it's not mine, because my water glass is sitting – almost accusingly – right beside my key card. It's at this point that I also note with dismay that I'm only wearing my knickers and that's not how I usually sleep.

Taking all this in, my head spins violently as it hits me that, not only have I just compromised my job by going AWOL, I've also cheated on Nick.

This final revelation is too much, and I begin sobbing loudly. I cry and cry until I've nothing left in me. Then, once I'm calmer, knowing I have to address the biggest problem of all first, I put my phone to my ear and call Craig.

Chapter 40

I consider telling Craig I'm unwell and that I slept in because I'd been up most of the night (not actually a lie, but not particularly honest either), but I decide this is dangerous territory to cross into. Anyone could have seen me out last night, and having already withheld my relationship with Nick from him, I can't allow myself even one more step onto that slippery slope. Instead, I confess that I'm having some personal issues, and tell him I'll sort myself out pronto. As much as I hate him for how he's treated me, today is a mess of my own making, and I have disrespected him as my employer. I can't lose my job; that would hurl Seth and I into a financial black hole that even my waste of space parents wouldn't be able to bail us out of. They're not *that* well off.

Craig's patience with me, it seems, does have its limits after all. He gives me an informal verbal warning and a very clear message that if it had been one of his 'real' clients I'd been supporting, I would have been facing formal disciplinary procedures. He tells me to take the day off to 'sort myself out' and that he expects me to go down to the park the following day to apologise to Gwen. Of course, I had been planning to do this anyway.

After speaking with Craig, I then call Jackson and confess my sins (although I leave out the bits I'm most ashamed of). He also tells me to take some time – Seth is nowhere near ready to have me around him yet anyway and me being hungover would possibly only fuel the fire. On his advice, I call reception and add another two nights to my stay, then meet him briefly outside my flat so he can pass me some additional clothes. I make sure to message Nick to let him know I'm OK, but that I 'have some stuff going on' and I'll see him tomorrow.

I spend the rest of the day and evening sleeping off my hangover, self-reflecting, ruminating and berating myself, because I've let things get out of hand and basically hit the self-destruct button on my life.

When Seth had his stroke, I decided that my career had to take a back seat and my brother had to come first. However, I never really allowed that to happen in practice. I should have accepted Craig's decision to remove me from the meaty projects, rather than fighting it so hard. Even taking into account what Jackson said about being able to secure Seth's and my financial future, I can't hand on heart say that's why I went into battle with Craig. As well as being concerned about my future career prospects, my pride was hurt, I now realise. It was humiliating being succeeded by my junior colleagues, so I refused to let things go.

Then, of course, my eye came off the ball even more when I got involved with Nick. The chancer pick-up guy from the hospital car park who started off as a grumpy co-worker and became the man I wanted a future with. Past tense. Because after everything that's happened, a future for us is impossible. I've misled him into thinking we can build something magical together when we can't. I can't offer him the uncomplic-ated, baggage-free life he wants, and he knows nothing of my responsibilities in relation to my brother. I had thought I could tell him when those responsibilities lessened, but with Seth's recent news, the chances of me ever having that level of freedom have diminished. On top of all that, I've betrayed him in a manner that only makes me less of a shit than his wife in divisible terms. These realisations make me feel sick and heartbroken in equal measures.

It's over. From now on, my full focus will be on Seth. I'll earn back his trust and put everything into caring for him and getting him as well rehabilitated as possible. I'll go through the motions at work, keeping my head down and ensuring my pay check is safe. That hopefully won't be too hard, because since I've had the grim realisation that I've been nothing more than a money-spinning cog in Craig's greedy wheel, the shine of my former high-profile career has worn off a bit. And love will have to go on the back burner for the foreseeable future. That's the only way from here which, while deeply painful, isn't so difficult given I've destroyed any chance I had with Nick by cheating on him anyway.

-

As agreed with Craig, I drive down the wildlife park the next morning to apologise to Gwen. And while I'm there, I'll have to staple on my big girl pants and give the bad news to Nick. This is, without doubt, the part I'm dreading the most.

At nine a.m. on the dot, I knock on Gwen's office door and she calls for me to enter. Once inside, she gestures for me to take a seat, while she finishes up what she's doing on her computer.

'Gwen, I'm so sorry about yesterday.' I rush in with my apology the moment she focuses her attention on me. 'I was completely out of order. I've never done anything like that before and I'm so ashamed of my behaviour. I'll understand completely if you no longer want me working with you here at the park.'

I bow my head, fighting back the tears as I await her response. She seems to be reflecting in the way she does, making it the longest ten seconds of my life.

'Jess, do you think you know me well enough by now to gauge how I might react to this?' she asks me eventually.

'Um… not sure.' I don't know where she's going with this, so I err on the side of caution.

'You're really not sure? How about you hazard a guess?'

I look up at her, puzzled, while she leans forward, hands clasped with her index fingers pointing to the ceiling. Her gaze is fixed on me.

'Now I'm not sure I want to in case I get it wrong.' I wince at my own cowardice.

'All right, how about I frame the question differently? What kind of person do you think I am?'

'Well, that's an easy one. You're super committed to the park and your people. You're fair, you're caring and you treat your employees like family.'

'See, that wasn't so difficult. Now, how about answering my first question again?'

'Eh… OK…' I give this some thought. 'Maybe you would be forgiving, understand that people are human and that they make mistakes?'

'Spot on.' She bangs the desk with her palm, making me jump. 'Even people like you make mistakes, Jess. And everyone has a breaking point. What I'm more concerned about is: what's going so wrong in your life that you've lost your way? And how can I help?'

It's such a big and human question that I start to cry, and then it all pours out – every last bit.

–

Over an hour later, I emerge from Gwen's office with red eyes and a blotchy face. Keeping my head down to avoid making eye contact with anyone, I leave the office and head across the courtyard.

'Jess, wait.'

Lauren has followed me outside. She catches up with me and places a sympathetic hand on my arm.

'Are you all right? My mum hasn't upset you, has she? It wouldn't be like her to be unforgiving.'

262

'It's not like her at all.' I smile weakly through my glassy eyes, thinking back to Gwen's earlier questions. 'I've just got some stuff I'm working through. I'm OK, honestly.'

'Well, I'm here if you ever need anything. We all are.'

'I know that. Thank you. You're an amazing bunch.'

I give her another flimsy smile, then scuttle across to the ladies toilets block to tidy myself up before anyone else sees me.

Once I've applied enough concealer to hide the redness and reapplied my eye makeup, I go looking for Nick, keen to get this hell over with. Gwen didn't judge me at all, but she did suggest that, once I'd spoken to Nick, I go back to my office to let things settle. With the events planning and management being well progressed, I'm not needed on-site as much anymore anyway. Gwen also swore that she wouldn't share a word of what I told her – which didn't include the fact I'd cheated on Nick, that would have been a step too far.

I look around for several minutes, making a pit stop at Rana's enclosure.

'Hey, girl.' I settle down on the bench momentarily, watching the bear cub climb a tree trunk then tumble ineloquently onto the man-made ledge at the highest point in her enclosure. 'Gosh, you're getting good at that. You'll be a pro in no time.'

Rana sniffs at the air, as if acknowledging my presence, then resumes her adventure, making me laugh in adoration as she snuffles and pokes her long tongue into the crevices along the ledge.

'Ah, you know how to cheer me up, little bear. Maybe I'll swing by again later. Think I might need you after what I'm about to do.'

Feeling slightly less suffocated by my impending task, I call Nick to find out where he is and join him by the big cat enclosures. He and his team are doing routine checks to make sure there are no weaknesses that could potentially allow one of the magnificent, but highly dangerous, animals to escape.

'Hi, gorgeous. Am I pleased to see you.' He greets me with a heart stopping grin.

This fills me with sadness and an almost irresistible urge to melt into his arms instead of breaking his heart.

'Hi.' I turn my cheek into his kiss and he falters, clearly picking up on this. 'Is there somewhere we can talk?'

'Yeah, sure.' He looks perplexed. 'These guys are all over this. Is everything OK?'

'Let's just find somewhere quiet.'

We make our way across to the building where Nick had first introduced me to Rana and grab a couple of chairs once we're inside.

'So, what's going on?' he asks. 'Why do I get the feeling that I'm about to be dumped?'

I wince for the second time this morning, his use of language making it sound so callous.

'I *am* about to be dumped.' Nick's expression turns to one of disbelief.

Although he'd sensed something wasn't right, he was obviously hoping he was wrong.

'Please don't use that word.' I'm barely able to look at him.

'What word would you prefer?'

'I don't know. None, I guess. Nick… I… can't do this. You and me, it's not going to work.'

'I get that.' His mood is creeping into something darker. 'Any chance you're going to give me a reason? A proper one, I mean?'

He deserves the truth, I know this, but it's all too much. I can't face the look of bewilderment and hurt that would inevitably follow when he realises I've hidden who I really am; that I'm just another person in his life who's let him down. Nor could I face the raw (and justified) anger that would come from him knowing I'd slept with someone else – and so carelessly, on a drunken night out. Best case: if I were to share my situation with Seth, and Nick happened to be understanding of this, it doesn't change the fact that I cheated on him. He would never forgive that, so why go through the pain – for both of us – of explaining any of it?

Unable to give him a real reason, my brain automatically leaps to the one thing I know I shouldn't do or say.

'I think you saw this thing between us as more than it is.'

Nick inhales sharply in response to this. I can almost see the thoughts in his brain lining up as he tries to make sense of it. Then he nods, as if coming to some sort of conclusion.

'I was just someone to pass the time with. A bit of a fun distraction while your career was off track.'

I desperately want to tell him how wrong he is, but I can't. Not without making things a whole lot more complicated. Because once one truth comes out, it will all inevitably come out.

'Yes,' I say through gritted teeth. 'I never intended for it to be anything more. I'm sorry if I led you on.'

'Right...' His eyes fill with a deep anguish that I so badly want to take away from him, but I have to leave things alone and let him deal with this his own way.

He gets up and just stands there for a few moments, then he walks out of the door in silence, closing it softly behind him.

I sit quietly for a moment, taking long, deep, shaky breaths, knowing I need to hold it together in case I pass him on my way out. Then to my surprise, he re-enters the room.

'You know, I was going to let this go quietly.' His voice quavers with emotion. 'I was going to keep my cool, because at least then I'd have got through this with my dignity intact. But I'm sorry, fuck that. You did lead me on. I didn't dream this to be something more. You let me think it was. Is that what all you women do? Because that "type" is all I seem to come across. Does it make you feel powerful or attractive or something?'

'Nick, no, it doesn't—'

'Please don't talk. You've said your piece. It's my turn.'

I say nothing further and simply hold my hands up in a gesture of surrender.

'Thank you. I'm now going to tell you how this feels.' He stares me straight in the face, and I have to look away. 'I want you to know, so that maybe next time you think twice before shitting on a guy's heart. You let me fall for you; I mean properly fall for you. I couldn't trust anyone after my wife, then I met you and I thought you were different. Like, really special. But all you were was another version of her...'

I flinch, because he's closer to the truth than he realises, and I hate that I've hurt him so completely.

Nick tails off and looks out the window, wiping a rogue tear from the corner of his eye. I don't dare move or say a word, because it's clear he's not finished.

'See, this...' he turns back to me, his eyes glistening with hurt '...this is why I prefer animals over humans. They won't lie, they won't cheat, they won't stamp all over you when you're at your most vulnerable. I let myself be fooled into thinking I was wrong to shut myself off like that. Well, one thing's for sure, I won't be making that mistake again.'

With those final words, Nick exits the room again, this time letting the door slam behind him.

Chapter 41

On my way out of the park, I stop by Rana's enclosure again, as I suspected I might feel the need to. Even though I'll still be making trips out here fairly regularly for the foreseeable future, this feels like a kind of goodbye. I won't be able to join Nick for play time with her anymore, nor will I feel comfortable having a wander around. Craig has assigned me a couple of new – depressingly unchallenging – projects, so my attention and focus will be diverted elsewhere. My visits here will be more in-and-out-in-an-hour, perhaps sometimes even virtual. There will be no real need to be here in person for things like the weekly project meetings.

'Hi again, Rana,' I greet her with a soft voice on approaching the exterior of her enclosure. 'You still giving this place a good hoovering?'

On recognising my voice, Rana stops snuffling at the tree bark she's inspecting and lollops across to me. Getting up on her hind legs, she then sniffs at the air, which I guess must be her way of checking me out. Crouching down to be at her level, the additional fencing keeping us at a slight distance, I chat away to her, without really thinking about the fact that she doesn't understand a word I say. It's weird, but she almost feels like a friend. She has her own little personality, all the animals do, so I can understand why Nick feels the way he does about them.

'I won't be seeing as much of you anymore unfortunately.' My voice breaks as I say this and I rub my jaw, the weight of this moment pressing down on me. 'I've got other work I have to do – not that I want to – and, well, I've royally messed things up.

Anyway, you take care of Nick for me, yeah? He's one incredible guy who I will very much regret leaving behind.'

Rana, of course, doesn't answer me. She's also lost interest – probably because I've got nothing for her to eat – and is now using her huge long tongue to investigate a crevice in a tree trunk. Letting out a quiet sob, I say goodbye to her and then head for my car, wiping tears from my face and blowing my nose as I go.

–

By the time I finish work for the day, I'm beyond exhausted and all I want to do is curl up into a ball and go to sleep. This is what I have every intention of doing, so I don't have to face the horrendous feelings of loss that are coming from every angle: Seth, Nick, the park, a job that means something to me and gives me a sense of achievement. The only saving grace in it all is that, with Seth not speaking to me, I can just shut the world out for the night.

On entering the hotel, I pass reception, nodding hello to the staff members as I go, and hit the button for the lift. A few seconds later, there's a ding, and as the doors spring open, I move aside to let the occupiers out, one of whom happens to be Shane from the other night.

'Oh hey, Jess.' He flashes me a row of almost perfect white teeth, the slightly crooked bottom row making his grin seem a tad lopsided. 'How you doing? You game for another night out?'

'Um, no, thanks.' I redden, wondering two things: how he can be so casual after what happened between us; and how long he hung around after we did the deed. Did we agree to part ways, or did he sneak out while I was comatose?

'How about a drink in the bar then?'

'I'm not feeling too well, actually,' I say to get the message across.

'Ah, two-day hangover, is it?' His eyes crinkle with amusement. 'No surprise, given the state of you. I'm not sure you'd have made it back to the hotel, never mind your room, if I hadn't been with you.'

The receptionist glances across at us curiously and I haul Shane out of earshot.

'Firstly, I wouldn't have been in that state if it weren't for you. You were the one who suggested going out, remember?'

He shrugs in acceptance of this, so I continue.

'And secondly, do you make a habit of taking insanely drunk women back to their rooms and sleeping with them, because I'm pretty sure that's—'

'Whoa, slow down, would you?' He seems completely blindsided. 'I didn't touch you, other than to help you get back and into bed. You spent the whole night going on about some bloke called Nick and another called Seth. I mean, I like a bit of adventure, but I'm not into that polyamorous stuff.'

'Seth is my brother, you dolt.' I play-thwack him on the arm. 'So, wait, are you telling me nothing happened between us? Like, absolutely nothing?'

'That's exactly what I'm telling you. You'd left your key card in your room, so the night porter let us in and hung around at the door – don't think he trusted me, given the mess you were in. I got you some water, then I put you to bed – fully clothed – and went back to my room. If you woke up naked or something, that's not on me.'

'For real?' I pin him with a look that says 'don't bullshit me'. 'You're telling me the God's honest truth?'

'Yeah, serious. We can ask to speak to the night porter if you want proof. You were in no fit state for anything.'

'Oh, thank goodness.' I clasp my hands together and raise my eyes to the ceiling. 'Sorry, no offence.'

'None taken. So, about that drink?'

'Definitely not.'

'Was worth a try.' He pulls a cheeky face. 'Your man Nick's a lucky bloke.'

'He would be if we were still together.' I look away from him, suddenly feeling overwhelmed with emotion.

'Ah shit, I'm sorry Jess.' Shane pats my shoulder sympathetically and wanders off.

Hitting the lift button again, his words reverberate round my head like a pinball, a jumble of feelings, thoughts and excuses all bouncing around, making it impossible for me to get a sense of anything. Then suddenly I jolt with clarity. Shunning the open doors of the lift for a second time, I turn around and march straight back out of the hotel to try to fix what I've broken.

Chapter 42

The next day after work, I head back to my flat via the hotel, who kindly stored my luggage for me, saving me the embarrassment of taking it to the office and facing questions from my colleagues. Jackson hasn't exactly given the all clear, but he can't hold the fort any longer due to personal commitments, and I can't reasonably expect him to either. It's time to face into things with Seth. Plus, I have an ace up my sleeve I'm hoping will tip the balance in my favour.

'I'll leave you both to it.' Jackson mouths 'good luck' to me as he heads out of the living room for the front door.

Sitting down on the sofa next to Seth, I can still feel the hurt and resentment radiating off of him, which is not a great sign.

'Hi, big bro.' I smile gingerly and take his hand in mine.

'Hi.' He doesn't pull it away, but he also doesn't look at me.

'I know you're still angry at me and I completely understand why. I did a bad thing. I was seeing you in a way that wasn't right – partly out of feeling so protective towards you, but that's not really an excuse. You're still the same person you were before, and you absolutely deserve to have the love of a hot woman in your life.'

The corners of Seth's mouth twitch at this, igniting a tiny spark of hope within me.

'I was focusing on the wrong things, thinking I was doing what was best for you. I was also hiding the fact I was struggling with my job, because I didn't want you to have to shoulder any more than you already were.'

On hearing this, he looks at me for the first time. 'What's been... going on with... your job?'

His slow and deliberate pronunciation of each word fuels my reluctance to voice my own problems. There are so many constant reminders of his vulnerability. But if I want my close relationship with my brother back, I know I need to bury my protective instincts and show him that I see him as an equal. Which I absolutely do – I've just gotten a bit lost along the way.

I fill him in on what's been going on, including the situation with Nick. I also make sure Seth knows he'll be my only priority from now on. He listens attentively, not once interrupting my flow. Then, when I've told him every last thing, he cocks his head in an appraising way.

'OK, first thing... Craig's a dick. He's always been a dick... but at least... you were getting something... out of working with him. You need a new job... I will help you with that. I have way too much... time on my hands... so I will do some... online research for you. I'll find some companies... who support flexible working... that you can reach out to. I'll also help you... with your app-lications.'

The unbearable load of feeling like I've lost the most important person in my world begins to shed as Seth talks. Now I'm the one staying quiet, allowing him to take the lead and reassume his role as my biggest supporter – as I am for him.

'Second, you know there's... no way I'm going... to let you sacrifice... everything for me. That's not how... this is going to work... and if you try to... you'll do my bloody head in.'

I chuckle guiltily at this, fully aware of what he means.

'You need to tell... all this to Nick,' Seth continues. 'I've not met the guy, but from... what you've just told me, I'm not sure he's... going to react... to all this in the way... you think he will. It sounds to me... like his definition of... "uncomplicated"... might be a bit... different to yours.'

'Oh, I'm not sure about that one, Seth.' I'm unable to stay quiet on hearing this. 'Even if you are right, I've kept things from him. He understandably has trust issues, so that on top of everything that's just gone down is going to be a major red flag.'

'Well, you won't know… until you speak to him, will you? Where's the… go-getter sister I know?'

I shrug pathetically. 'She's realised she can only be a go-getter if her circumstances suit others.'

'There may be some… truth in that. We're both at a… disadvantage now, but we can… keep fighting on. We'll do it… together, yeah?' He nudges me affectionately with his good arm.

'OK, yeah.' Seth's rallying spirit is starting to rub off on me. 'I really am so sorry about Alison and how I've got things so wrong, Seth.'

'Look, it is… what it is. I know you meant… well, and I had no… idea you were struggl-ing… in the way you were. I forgive you. Now can you… forgive yourself?'

He pierces me with a look that reaches my soul, and I know in my heart that I can. Because with my wonderful brother being prepared to forgive me, dwelling on things would be illogical and self-indulgent, and it would risk further damaging our relationship.

'Thank you, Seth.' I wrap my arms around him and squeeze tight. 'By the way, how are you feeling about the consultant's judgement of your progress? I know how big a blow that must have been.'

'It was.' He nods. 'But Jackson and I have… been chatting and we've… come to the conclu-sion that… he can do one.'

'Sorry, what?' I let out a confused giggle.

'No one gets to… decide how well I'm… going to recover but me. And I've decided… I'm going to prove… him wrong. I've been doing some… intensive exer-cises… over the last few days… and I'm sure I've made… some progress already.'

'That's amazing. Go you!' We share a crooked high five. 'How about we go for a walk in the park then, and you can show me your moves?'

'Sounds good to me.'

'OK, perfect. Just give me a moment to send a quick message and we'll head off.'

Ten minutes later, I push Seth's wheelchair across the road to Montgomery Street Park. It's a lovely evening, which despite it being the wrong side of mid-September, feels more like July or early August.

We're not the only ones who have decided to make the most of this unexpected warm spell. A group of young lads are playing football on one side of the park, while children shriek with joy in the small play area. There are also plenty of people dotted across the grass, either reading alone or laughing and chatting with friends.

'How nice is this?' I angle my face towards the sun and enjoy soaking up its rays.

'It's pretty sweet,' says Seth. 'Park me up... will you? I want to try walking.'

'Walking?' I'm alarmed by this request. 'Are you sure that's a good idea?'

'I do it in my... physical therapy sessions... so I'd like to try it... here, in a more natural setting.'

'I thought you used bars or something to hold on to.'

'I do, but I've been... managing some steps... without them. Don't worry, I'm not... going to try and walk... round the park or anything. I just want to... feel free and independent... for a few moments.'

'Seth, if you hit the deck, I might not be able to get you up again,' I warn him.

'I'm willing to take... a chance on that.' He's already trying to get out of his chair. 'I really think... I can do it.'

'All right then, but only if you take my arm.' I glance to the left where I see someone approaching us. 'Actually, to be safe, let's have you take both our arms.'

'What do you mean... by—' Seth's gaze follows mine and he stops short. 'Alison?'

Alison, who has come to a nervous halt, gives a stunning, doe-eyed smile, then takes a few tentative steps towards him.

'Can I...?'

'Can you ever.' Seth's face lights up like the Hogmanay fireworks. 'What are you... doing here? Were you just passing?' His expression makes it clear he sincerely hopes not.

Alison looks to me and I nod. This is her story to tell.

'Yesterday evening I got quite the surprise,' she says in her lovely soft Irish accent. 'Jess reached out to me via Messenger and invited me for a drink.'

'I think you mean I begged.' I pull an exaggerated grimace.

'Well, yes, but I wasn't going to mention that.' She beams at me and Seth is so stunned, he doesn't know which of us to look at.

I giggle, delighted to see my brother all plucky again.

'She told me how sorry she was,' Alison continues. 'And that the person I'd met was not the sister you know and love. We talked for some time, and as much as I was sceptical at first, I realised that Jess was being genuine. She couldn't bear that she'd come between us, so here I am – if you'll have me, of course.'

'Of course, I'll bloody... have you,' Seth declares. 'And I mean that... in both a relation-ship... and a naughty sense. Get over here.'

'If I may be excused...' I cringe and head off for a walk round the park to give them some space.

I want to spare myself the inevitable gag reflex that would come from witnessing my brother getting all slushy (and perhaps slightly frisky) with the woman he's head over heels for. There's also the fact that, right now, while my own heart feels shredded from losing Nick, I really don't need a reminder of what I've lost. I'm doing my best not to focus on it and put all my energy into Seth, but it's like this constant almost unbearable ache in my chest and my mind.

By the time I've done a lap, they're more than reacquainted and Seth's bursting with curiosity.

'How did you know... where to find Alison?' he asks me. 'I don't think I... told you much about her.'

'Probably more that I didn't invite you to.' I wrinkle my nose remorsefully and Alison waves this away, helping me feel more at ease. 'I basically put Jackson through a hard-line interrogation – in the nicest possible way. Got every piece of information he knew about her and the rest I pieced together online.'

'Is that where he... went when he... "nipped out for some milk"... last night?'

'Yes, I called him from the street. Asked him to make that excuse and meet me outside the flat. I didn't want you overhearing a phone conversation in case things didn't pan out or you got mad at me for interfering. I'd even brought the milk for him.'

'Ha, that's brilliant.' Seth is thoroughly chuffed and entertained by the secret squirrel operation that went down to get his girlfriend back. 'Sis, you have... more than redeemed... yourself. Thank you. Our next focus will be... on getting you a... kick-ass new job.'

'Works for me.' I grin at him and Alison, who, now I can look at them together in a positive light, make quite the cute couple. 'Now, how about you try that walk you were talking about? We can flank you on either side.'

Alison and I help Seth out of his wheelchair and let go, leaving him in a wavering standing position. All my instincts are screaming at me to reach back out and steady him, but I fight them hard. It's very clear that Seth wants to do this alone.

He tentatively puts one foot in front of the other, deep concentration etched on his face. It's an action that most people take for granted. They don't even need to think about it. But for Seth, who's re-learning these most basic movements and actions, it's an exhausting fight to achieve even the simplest of tasks.

'Ah, you're doing it!' I practically squeal with excitement as he manages several more slow and unsteady steps, Alison and I staying close the whole time. 'This is amazing, Seth.'

'Jess, with the... greatest respect... will you shut up?' he says through gritted teeth from the sheer effort of trying to remain upright. 'You're... putting me off.'

'Sorry.' I wince at being told off and Alison giggles at us.

'I think I'm going to enjoy the dynamics between you two,' she says. 'Seems like great craic.'

'We're like ninety per cent... best buds, ten per cent... squabbl-ing toddlers.' Seth rolls his eyes and Alison laughs harder.

'Hey, how come she's allowed to distract you?' I complain.

'You really want me... to answer that?'

'Um, no.' After his earlier suggestive comment, I most definitely don't need to hear any more.

Seth takes a few more steps, then stops, panting hard from the effort. Alison and I step forward to hold him steady, and he seems happy enough to take this support while he's resting.

'You OK?' Alison asks him after a couple more goes. 'You seem like you're getting tired.'

'I'm fine.' Seth tries to continue unaided, but he's becoming more unsteady by the second and it's obvious he's run out of steam.

She reaches out and gently touches his arm. 'Hey, sexy man. You have nothing to prove to me and you know how I feel about you. How about you call it for today?'

This is all it takes for Seth to stop and accept that he's done, and from the way he looks at Alison and how she looks back at him, I can tell they've both found their soulmate. This fills my heart to bursting point, because all I could ever want is for Seth to find his happy ever after. However, watching this wonderful exchange between them also reignites the agony of losing the man who might just have been my own soulmate, and in an instant, my decision is made.

'Alison, Seth, would you be OK if I headed off for a bit?' I ask as we help Seth back into his wheelchair. 'There's somewhere I need to be.'

'Of course,' says Alison. 'We'll head back to the flat together.'

I look at Seth to check his reaction, despite the fact that at this particular moment, he's probably never needed me less.

He grins at me. 'Go get him, tiger.'

Chapter 43

Hurrying through the gates of the wildlife park, a jangling ball of nerves suddenly rises up within me. So much so that I almost miss one of the park team greeting me with a wave from across the courtyard. All I can think about is how much I need to talk to Nick right now, and how terrified I am that he's going to tell me where to go. And I wouldn't blame him. I let him down big time and I expect he won't know if he can trust me not to do the same again. Whatever happens, I have to accept the outcome – whether I like it or not.

I visit all of Nick's most regular haunts, but he's nowhere to be seen. This feeds my feelings of anxiety and vulnerability to the point that I start to feel shaky and like my legs might give way. I can also, to my displeasure, feel stress-induced beads of sweat dripping down my back. Finding the nearest bench, I settle down on it and try to get myself together, rubbing my temples while taking long slow deep breaths.

'Jess?' A voice seems to come out of nowhere and I look up.

'Nick.' I attempt a smile but it falls flat. 'I've been looking for you.'

'Well, here I am.' He shrugs, his expression unreadable. 'Do you need something?'

I get to my feet and walk nervously towards him. 'Yeah, I do. I need to apologise, and I need to explain myself.'

'OK.' He eyes my fidgety stance. 'Shall we take a seat for this? Maybe you'd be more comfortable that way.'

Still possessing the dexterity of a newborn giraffe, I don't need to be asked twice. I return to the bench, while Nick follows and takes a seat beside me, leaving a distance between us that practically screams 'we're not a couple anymore'. Flinching at this, I inhale shakily before starting to speak.

'Nick, my brother, Seth, had a stroke a few months ago.'

'The day I first met you at the hospital.' Nick grimaces as he takes this disclosure in.

'Yes.' I chew my lip guiltily. 'I'm so sorry I didn't tell you. I was holding off for good reason though.'

'Holding off? It seems you didn't want me to find out at all.' His tone is cutting, his hurt evident.

'Not in the way that you think.' I look up at him to convey that I'm genuine. 'I didn't want to end things with you, please believe me.'

There's a short silence between us while I wait for Nick to respond.

'I know you didn't,' he says eventually.

'You do?'

'You're not the only one who paid Rana a visit after you broke up with me.'

'You overheard me talking to her.' I colour at this realisation.

'Yes.' He nods, kicking at a stone on the ground. 'But I kept out of sight, because I was confused and I didn't know what to do with that information. One thing that seems obvious, though, is that you didn't break things off because all you wanted was a meaningless fling.'

'No, I didn't.'

'Then why did you break up with me?'

My insides squirm under Nick's scrutiny. 'Because I'd kept things from you. My brother being the main one. You made it clear that, after what you went through with your ex-wife, you wanted a simple life with no baggage. That was the last thing I could offer you. You might not remember but you even said one of the things you liked about me was that I was "uncomplicated". I thought if Seth improved and became more independent, I'd have more time to spend with you. My head is such a mess at the moment with everything going on with Seth and work, and I hoped once everything had sorted itself out and I could properly focus on you, maybe we'd have a chance...' I tail off, unsure where to go next.

Nick rubs the back of his neck, looking baffled as he takes all this in.

'Jess, when I said I wanted a simple life with no baggage, I meant in terms of my next partner and how they would treat me. I wanted someone who would...' He hesitates and suddenly looks like he doesn't want to complete his sentence.

'Tell me,' I urge him. 'I won't judge you.'

He leans forward, elbows on his thighs, puffing out his cheeks. 'I find it difficult to say this stuff out loud. I guess what I'm trying to say is... I just wanted someone who would only want to be with me. Who would... adore me the way I would adore them. I didn't mean I needed their attention on me 100 per cent of the time, or that they couldn't have anything else going on in their life.'

'Even if that might cause tension in a relationship? Like if I couldn't spend enough time with you? You were already getting frustrated before. You said it yourself.'

'That was because there didn't seem to be any logical reason why we weren't seeing each other outside of work. Now it all makes sense.'

'And?' I wet my lips with apprehension.

'Well, if I'd known about your situation, it wouldn't have changed anything for me. I would have been more than happy to take a back seat to your brother, or better than that, I would have wanted to be a part of both your lives. Offer some support, rather than being regarded as a separate unit.'

'You really would have wanted that?'

I feel a swell of longing. All I want to do is dive into his arms and kiss him, but I'm acutely aware that what Nick has just shared is based on a parallel reality – one where I didn't hold all this back from him.

'Of course, I would have.' He looks pained by the suggestion that he might have seen things otherwise. 'It was you I fell for, not your circumstances. They just happened to be part of the package. As I said, I just want to be with someone who wants me – and who won't lie to me and won't stray. After the experience I went though, it's all that really matters to me.'

I'm about to try and convince Nick that, despite what I've done, I can be all that and more. Then his words trigger a flash of memory, and I remember I have something else to come clean about. Something that might change the way he sees me.

'Nick, I haven't told you everything. There's another reason why I broke things off.'

'Right…?' His expression understandably turns cautious.

'The other night, I went on a bender. My boss had refused to listen to me over my job, and Seth was furious with me because I'd driven his girlfriend away. It's a long story and all sorted now, but the point is, I had to check into a hotel and I got drunk in the hotel bar, which led to me going to a club with a bloke I met there.'

'Ah, shit.' Nick looks away and shakes his head, making me panic.

'No, no, it's not what you think.' My words tumble over themselves in my attempt to put his mind at rest. 'Nothing happened, and I never wanted it to, but the morning after, I did worry I might have done something stupid. I had no memory of the night after we left the hotel, then I found something belonging to the guy in my room. I jumped to the wrong conclusion and thought I'd betrayed you. That told me that I couldn't be the woman you were looking for.'

'So, what really happened?' Nick appears relieved, but it's obvious he – quite rightly – needs to hear the rest of the story.

'Apparently, I spent the whole night yapping on about you and Seth – to the point he thought I was in a throuple. Oh, and I got so hammered, he and the night porter had to take me back to my room and put me to bed.'

Nick lets out a bellow of a laugh. 'You're something else.'

'I know.' I give a wry grin, relieved that the mood between us has lightened a little. 'Not my finest hour by any stretch. But it obviously means I'm the faithful kind, because he was one of these smokin' hot surfer guys... who aren't my type at all,' I rush to add at the end.

'Listen, I would have no issue with you being able to appreciate a good-looking guy. It's just that monogamy is what I want.'

'Me too.' I sigh, taking in his rugged, man-about-wildlife-park features that I find so damn attractive. 'So the big question is: can you forgive me? And also... do you think you can trust me?'

Nick's expression turns serious again. 'Honestly? I'm struggling with that a bit. You haven't exactly been forthcoming with me.'

'I know.' I feel my eyes well up at the real possibility that he's about to tell me 'no'. 'But if you give me another chance, I'll never give you reason to doubt me, I promise. It's not who I am, Nick. I've just lost my way these last months with everything that's been going on.'

There's a short and almost unbearable silence while he appears to be weighing up what I've said.

'I suppose it's understandable,' he says eventually. 'You were clearly having a difficult time and I guess that means you lost perspective. So... if you really didn't sleep with that guy—'

'I didn't. I swear,' I jump in quickly.

'And you won't hide anything like this from me again—'

'I won't so much as go for a pee without you knowing about it.'

Nick scoffs. 'That might be taking things a bit far.'

'Call it the lengths I'm willing to go to?' My eyes are like saucers, fixed on his while I nervously fiddle with the bracelet I'm wearing.

'All right, I hear you.' He reaches out and gently takes my hand, eyes soft and resolutely on mine. 'Shall we give it another shot then? Any new relationship is always a risk, even without the kind of drama you and I have just gone through, and I'm willing to take that risk with you.'

'Yes, please.' All the tension and worry I've been feeling finally drains from me like a plug being pulled.

I tentatively lean in towards him and he meets me halfway for a spine-tingling, toe-curling kiss, as a hooting applause breaks out not far from us. It appears we've attracted some attention from a gaggle of park employees who are hanging around nearby. Breaking apart, we laugh and give them an embarrassed wave.

'Oh, man, everyone's looking at us now.' I put my hand to my mouth self-consciously.

'Let them. I couldn't be prouder to be seen with you.' Nick pulls me into him and we kiss again, while my body aches with desire.

When we finally come up for air, I snuggle into him.

'Nick, I'm so happy we're back together, and also that I can be open about everything now.'

'Me too.' He tweaks my nose affectionately. 'So, what happened with your boss? Tell me how that went down.'

'I will.' I nod. 'But how about we go and tell Gwen and the others our good news before that lot beat us to it?'

Chapter 44

On Seth's request, I arrange for him, Alison, Nick and I to spend Saturday at the wildlife park together, so they can meet and get to know each other. Nick sets up a VIP behind-the-scenes tour for Seth and Alison, who didn't get to see as much as they'd hoped at the fundraiser – in particular, of Rana. And boy does he deliver on that. We're treated to various feeding experiences – the one with the giraffes being my personal favourite – the special rainforest tour he puts on for the retirees, playtime with the seals, and then, of course, with Rana, who steals the show as ever. Thankfully Nick stops short of getting us to pick up the elephant poo, but he does relish the opportunity of recounting my first days at the park and all that went on.

'Oh, my gosh, that's so funny.' Alison is almost doubled over as Nick delivers what I would call an 'overexaggerated' version of my tantrum in the elephant enclosure. 'I have to say, I don't really blame you, Jess. The smell in that place was enough to turn my stomach.'

'See?' I put my hands on my hips and aim daggers at Nick, who's enjoying all this a little too much. 'Then he has the audacity to talk about how animal shit is used as part of a beauty regime by rich people in Japan. I mean, come on, read the room.'

'Stop it, you're killing me.' Alison laughs even harder.

'I quite like that... you put my sister... in her place,' Seth says to Nick. 'She's had ideas... above her station... for far too long.'

'Hey, don't you dare start siding with him just because he's your new buddy.' I shoot my brother a warning look.

It's light-hearted because the truth is I'm both relieved and delighted that he and Nick are getting on so well. They seemed to click instantly, and given that Seth's friendship group have all but left him behind, I'm so pleased that he's got a new blokey pal to meet those needs in his life. In fact, the four of us seem to make the perfect little group. Alison, while I'm a little intimidated by her looking like an angel sent down by the special man upstairs, is the most kind and gentle person. I also have a feeling there's a wicked sense of humour in her, that I fully intend to tease out over time.

Seeing how she looks at Seth, there's no mistaking how she feels about him. They're completely besotted with each other, which makes my heart do a skip and a jump, because this is all I could ever want for my brother. Finding love could have been a lot harder in his situation. This, of course, makes me feel even more awful for having judged Alison the way I did and driven them apart, but I know I have to accept I'm not perfect and make my peace with that.

'Hi, you lot.' We're interrupted by Gwen.

'Oh, hi.' I'm delighted she's made an appearance. 'Come and meet my brother and his girlfriend.'

I do the introductions and we chat pleasantly for a few minutes.

'I was actually wondering if I could have a word with you, Jess,' says Gwen, when there's a natural lull in the conversation. 'Nick, can you come too?'

Puzzled by this request, I try to catch Nick's attention, but unless I'm mistaken, he seems to be avoiding eye contact with me. 'Sure…' I say, feeling anything but.

We let Seth and Alison know we'll be back shortly and follow Gwen to the nearest cafe, which is the one that only has tables outside. Taking our seats, there's a nervous churning in my stomach; a feeling that something's going on. I cross my fingers that the huge donation the park received wasn't stolen or some other type of illegal money.

'Is something wrong?' I can't help but rush to ask.

'You could say that.' Gwen shoots an involuntary side glance in Nick's direction, confirming my growing suspicion that he already knows what this is about.

'Oh, no.' My stomach sinks like a dead weight. 'Are you having to close after all? This can't be happening. After everything, and then thinking the place was saved—'

'Jess, stop talking.' Nick silences me. 'And Gwen, I know you like to build up to your big speeches, but for the sake of my girlfriend's sanity, please can you cut to the chase, just this once?'

Temporarily distracted – and elated – by Nick calling me his girlfriend, I initially miss that Gwen is speaking to me. Gathering myself together, I sit up straight and give her my full attention.

'...actually no, you haven't just done a wonderful job kick-starting the events programme here,' she continues talking, unaware that I've only just tuned in. 'You've been an all-rounder. You've rolled your sleeves up and gotten into anything that's needed—'

'Except the elephant poo,' Nick can't help throwing in.

'Anyway...' Gwen casts him a bemused look, causing me to snicker and shake my head, '...to keep this conversation focused as Nick has asked, Jess, I've been thinking about your predicament at work. Nick also came to me this morning with a proposal, and after a good discussion, we're both in agreement.'

'Agreement about what?' I raise a curious eyebrow, while ping-ponging back and forth between them.

'I'd like to offer you the role of senior events manager here at the park.'

'*What?*' I'm stupefied by this statement, it being the last thing I would have expected to come out of Gwen's mouth. 'Can you afford that?'

'We've crunched the numbers and we believe that a permanent events role will more than pay for itself over time. We actually need one if we want to turn our park events into a serious revenue stream. In fact, if things go well and the events take off, we could see you having your own team rather than borrowing resource from the other teams.'

'You're serious?'

'Of course I'm serious.' Gwen leans forward in her chair and smiles at me. 'Now the only thing is, I probably can't pay you what you get at that twat in a suit's jumped-up company—'

I let out a snort of amusement, then put my hand to my mouth ashamedly. 'Do you honestly think I'm on good money? With Craig as the director? I was never there for that. It was always about the high-profile events, the stretch and the development opportunities.'

'Well, I guess that solves that problem then. Though the question is: would a role like this be enough for you?'

'In comparison to the new projects I've been assigned, it's like a dream come true. Anyway, I've learned a bit about what's really important and what's not in the last few days, and it turns out feeling valued and doing something worthwhile trumps chasing the biggest projects – not that I'd have a chance at them now anyway.'

I pause and take a reflective breath, my mind in overdrive. 'Gwen, I'm blown away by this offer, I really am, but as you know, I'm caring for my brother and I can only work three days a week. I realise you would probably prefer to have someone full time.'

Now it's Gwen's turn to snort. 'Jess, just because the bloody Craigs and Brees of this world can't see what a gem they have in front of them, doesn't mean I can't either. You deliver as much as, if not more than, many people who work full-time hours. I was expecting you to want to work the same hours – it's actually partly why the role is affordable for us – and here's my salary offer to you, pro-rated for your three-day week, of course.'

She scrawls a figure on a piece of paper, turns it face down and pushes it across the table with two fingers, the way actors do in movies. It makes me think she's always wanted to do that, and I have to swallow down a giggle.

Picking up and reading her salary offer, my brain kicks back into high gear.

Over the last few months, it's felt like my life has been thrown up in the air and all the respective parts have landed in the wrong places. Except now I'm realising that they haven't. They've fallen in exactly the right places. They've shown me a life and a future that's so much more meaningful than what I had before; what I could have even imagined.

Would I still turn back time if it were to mean Seth never had a stroke? Of course I would – in a heartbeat. But that's not how life works. I've accepted Seth's position and the challenge we're facing together, but I don't need to accept how everything else has turned out. What Gwen's saying right now is that she wants me to be a permanent member of the park family. That doesn't just feel like the right place for me, it feels like home: somewhere I can do amazing and important work with my wonderful new adopted family.

As this realisation settles over me like a cosy blanket, my mouth breaks into a wide smile.

'Gwen, you've got yourself a deal.' I reach out to shake her hand.

The moment I do this, I'm startled by a sudden ruckus around me. Lauren, Serge, Natalie and a few other park colleagues I've gotten to know come bursting out from behind the cafe, cheering and whooping. Lauren sweeps in, hugging me tightly as I struggle to take it all in.

'How did you lot find out about this?' Gwen demands jovially, once everyone's settled down. She looks accusingly at Nick.

'I didn't say a word.' He gives a baffled shrug. 'You know nothing stays a secret in this place though.'

'Jess, welcome to the family.' Gwen reaches across and squeezes my hand. 'We are honoured to have you join the park team.'

'And I'm honoured to be invited into the fold.' I beam at my new colleagues, then take Nick's hand under the table and mouth a heartfelt 'thank you' to him.

Chapter 45

Nine months later

On reaching the vast outdoor seating area of the wildlife park, Alison and Seth gasp with delight, and I'm not the least bit surprised by this. Though I've been overseeing this event, even I'm in awe of the sight before us – particularly as I'm viewing it for the first time through the eyes of a visitor, and with the anticipation of an enjoyable evening ahead.

The whole place has been given a beach party theme. The ground is covered with lashings of fine white sand, an imitation boardwalk has been erected on top of it (mainly for accessibility, but it looks great) and freestanding tiki torches enhance the relaxed vibe. The picnic tables have been accessorised with shells and sea life related props, while rows of stripy deck chairs are lined up in front of a DJ box and a huge screen showing a montage of tropical beach videos. There are even beach umbrellas, beach balls and scuba gear, which have been strategically positioned to complete the effect, as well as a surfboard wedged upright into the ground sporting a welcome message for our paying guests. And, of course, there's food and drink to fit the occasion. Enticing aromas waft across from the stalls offering a range of barbequed dishes, summery salads, cocktails and mocktails.

Rotating delightedly on the spot, enjoying the warmth of the balmy evening, while bobbing to the chilled summery anthem that's filtering through the air (at a volume that won't negatively impact the park's residents), I can't help but feel a sense of immense pride. With a contented grin, I reflect on how everything has changed so much – and for the better – in recent months.

Seth has continued to improve, though he's not quite at the stage of being able to walk any distance without his wheelchair. We remain hopeful though. And not only have Alison and Nick been welcome additions to Seth's and my cosy unit, they've transformed our quality of life. They've rallied around us, making sure we're both cared for in ways that have made the pressure and uncertainty of our situation far easier to manage. This, of course, was music to my parents' selfish ears, because it meant we could cut back on how much we needed Jackson around (though he's very much become a friend as well as an employee). That's their loss though, because for the first time since they emigrated, Seth and I decided not to join them at Christmas or for our usual summer get-together – and we'll possibly never do so again. Not because of Seth's accessibility issues, but because our family is right here in Edinburgh and East Lothian.

'Hey, gorgeous.' Nick joins us, slipping his arms around my waist and pecking me on the lips. 'How ace is this, us getting to be the customers for once?'

Despite me offering to be here in my capacity as the event lead each evening, Gwen insisted I leave some of the responsibility to her and the management team, who I made sure were well-versed on all potential issues that might arise and how to solve them.

'It's awesome.' I snuggle into him, breathing in his manly scent. 'How did Rana's move to her new enclosure go?'

'Fine, generally. She wasn't keen to get in the crate, which caused a delay, but she's settling in OK. Lots for her to explore.'

'Oh, that's good news. It's a great space for her, especially now she's so big. I must admit though, I still miss playtime with her. She was such a cutie when she was little.'

'Yeah, she was. Guess we'll just have to play with each other instead then, eh?' He waggles his eyebrows at me suggestively, making me laugh.

'Jess, there you are,' a voice calls out, and Amelia charges across to me, dragging a woman I've never seen before behind her. 'It's so good to see you.'

She lets go of the woman's hand and throws her arms around me in a long overdue hug.

'It's great to see you too,' I reply into her now bright blue hair. 'Been far too long. Who's this you have with you?'

Amelia steps back, grabbing the hand of the woman with her once more. 'Jess, this is Luna. Isn't she all bubblegum and lollipops?'

'She means she's delicious,' I translate for Nick.

'Oh.' He nods as he takes in Amelia's slightly odd description.

'It's lovely to meet you, Luna.' I step forward, giving her a friendly hug. 'It seems you've made quite an impression on my bestie.'

'I hope so.' She squeezes me back.

As Luna gets acquainted with Nick, Seth and Alison, Amelia pulls me aside.

'She's the one, Jess.'

'You mean she's the one for now?' I reply in a low voice. 'Until you decide you like a six-foot rugby-playing bloke call Terrence.'

'No, I really mean it. This is it. She's the salt to my pepper.'

I pull an astonished face. 'Oh my gosh, you're serious. Does that mean you'll only need one plus one at my non-existent wedding?'

'It means exactly that.' Amelia is radiating contentedness in a way I've never seen before.

'Meels, I'm so happy for you.'

We hug again, clutching at each other like best friends who haven't seen each other in an age do. Especially when so much – both good and bad – has happened in that time.

'So, here we are,' I say, when Amelia and I eventually break apart. 'A perfect group of six. Shall we get something to drink?'

We head to the outdoor bar, where Nick and I get the drinks in, while the others become acquainted. It's a perfect summer scene. As perfect as you can get for what's about to come.

Returning with the drinks on a tray, we hand them out and commandeer one of the picnic tables, while 'oohing' and 'ahhing' over the tantalising flavours.

'How's your job going here, Jess?' Luna asks me. 'Amelia told me you'd had a hard time where you were before.'

'I did.' I nod, taking a sip of my Halekulani, a cocktail I've never tried before, and it's so delicious I'm wondering why. 'But that's all in the past now, thankfully. Things are so much better here. We've got a full schedule of events underway – we've already done January detox days, Valentine's nights and Easter treasure hunts, we have these beach party nights, and there's plenty more to come. We're even making the events as sustainable as possible by running them on renewable energy from the solar panels we've recently had donated to us.'

'It sounds like the park is doing well then?'

'Things are looking a lot healthier, yes. We're hoping the boost in revenue will allow us to resume our financial support to international conservation efforts, and we're also putting in place a proper schools education programme, which will kick off next year.'

'Aww, that's great. I'm pleased that things have worked out for you. It's a fab place and the location is great too. The air is so fresh here.' Luna breathes in deeply as if to illustrate her point.

'You should both come up again and see it in the winter,' I suggest. 'It's so pretty with all the lights and the festive decorations. We did a Christmas market at the end of last year and it was a sell-out. Amelia had hoped to come up for a visit and see it, but she caught a bad flu and had to cancel.'

'I'm sure we can manage that.'

'Maybe we could do it all together?' I look round the rest of our group at Nick, Seth and Alison. 'Another get-together here at Christmas?'

'Oh, yes, please,' says Alison. 'I can't get enough of our family and friends discount.'

My gaze shifts to Seth, who hasn't said anything, and he gives me the nod I've been waiting for. I know why he's not engaged in this conversation. He has bigger things on his mind. Getting up from my seat, I hold his wheelchair steady while he pulls himself into a standing position.

As soon as Seth's steady on his feet, I step far enough away to give him the space he needs for this moment, but stay close enough to follow through on my obligations. He turns to Alison, who appears confused.

'Alison, you bounded into my life… at a time when I most needed to be… surrounded by positivity,' he says, his speech now far improved, but laced with nerves. 'And within hours of meeting you, I knew you were… someone really special. You saw me, not someone who'd had a stroke. You saw a man who… just wanted to be loved and be in love, without judgement or question.'

Alison's face is a perfect picture of surprise and emotion as Seth nods at me again, and I step forward to help him get down on one knee. It's not the easiest manoeuvre, but we've practiced it and seen it through with only minor wobbles. Seth then pulls a ring box out of his pocket and expertly opens it with his good hand.

'I know we've only been together for a short time,' he continues, 'but I've come to appreciate that life can change in an instant… and that I should grab opportunities when they arise, rather than wait. I also know some would think it too fast, but for me… when you find someone as incredible as you, you make sure you never let them go. Will you make me the happiest guy in the world… by agreeing to marry me?'

We all hold our breath while we wait for Alison to answer. She, in the meantime, is trying – and failing – to hold back the big fat tears that are escaping down her cheeks.

'Oh Seth, of course I'll marry you.' She lets out an enormous sob-cum-laugh and drops to her knees, allowing Seth to slip the sparkling diamond ring on her finger. She then kisses him so hard she almost knocks him over.

Nick, Amelia, Luna and I (and the people around us, who have obviously been watching this go down) burst into rapturous applause, then someone toasts 'the happy couple' and everyone follows suit.

'So, you were in on this, you sneaky one.' Nick slips his arm around me once we all sit back down, after lots of hugs and congratulations for Seth and Alison.

'Yup.' I puff myself up proudly. 'He asked me to help him pick out the ring.'

'Are you a little envious?'

I narrow my eyes with a sly smile. 'Testing the water, are you?'

'I can neither confirm nor deny. But let's just say, after the experience I had marrying the wrong person first time round, I share your brother's logic in not letting the right one get away.'

He leans in for a kiss and I melt into him, thrilled by what I've just heard, but also pleased that Seth got his moment first. After everything he's been through, he more than deserves it. And I know that, for Nick and I right now, this park, the people we have in our lives and the wonderful animals – Rana especially – are more than enough.

Acknowledgments

With this being the fourth novel I've had published, what I'm discovering is that there are only so many ways to thank the same people. Feeling somewhat daunted by the task at hand, I did consider a straight copy and paste job, but then that would be cheating. And believe me, I'm not complaining. It really is a nice problem to have.

Just Like That holds real meaning for me in a similar way to *Take A Moment*. While it's not a story inspired by my real-life experiences, it does give a generous nod to disability/health related issues and inequality in society, both of which I have first-hand experience of. I'm a big believer in valuing people for who they are and what they can bring in a workplace setting when offered a fair opportunity to do so, and it saddens me how many people are on the receiving end of unfounded judgements and unfair treatment based on a 'label'. *Just Like That* also continues a theme I've threaded through my other published novels, which is that everyone deserves to have love in their lives.

As always, there is quite a line-up of people to acknowledge who have played an important role in providing guidance and direction and/or moral support. As ever, a massive thank you to my incredible husband, James, for continuing to cheer me on, as well as helping me work through my thinking when I have a mental block (which unfortunately happens fairly regularly with my health situation). A big thank you also goes to my mum and dad and the rest of my wonderful family, who are without doubt my biggest supporters. I'd also like to thank Sandy Barker and my sister-in-law, Geraldine, who were both early readers of *Just Like That*.

To my agent, Kate Nash, and my editor at Canelo, Emily Bedford, thank you yet again for all your guidance, support and brilliant ideas/suggestions. You really do make me a better writer and I continue to learn from you all the time. I'd also like to express my sincere thanks to the whole team at Canelo for their hard work in getting *Just Like That* out in the world (with THE most stunning cover, if I may say so myself). Getting a book to publication really is a team effort and your contributions are so appreciated.

To my author besties: Sandy Barker, Fiona Leitch and Andie Newton. What can I say? You're the best thing since the invention of the online thesaurus. Though to be clear, you have a lot more to offer than a different way of saying 'significant'. I can't tell you how much I appreciate your friendship, support and awesome humour. I often feel like I don't do enough to thank you, so I hope that dedicating this book to you all might go some way towards that.

I'd also like to express my thanks to my all my brilliant friends and colleagues. It's so wonderful to have your continued support. And to all my readers, thank you once again for buying, reading and reviewing my books. I find it hard to put into words how much it lifts me and spurs me on when I read your positive reviews or receive your lovely feedback.

Finally – and I realise this is perhaps a little unorthodox – I'd to acknowledge the wonderful city of Edinburgh and the beautiful region of East Lothian for providing such a rich and inspiring canvas upon which to craft my story. I am so lucky to have you on my doorstep.